SECOND HEAVEN

Also by Judith Guest

ORDINARY PEOPLE

JUDITH GUEST

SECOND HEAVEN

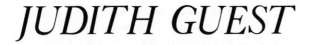

THE VIKING PRESS / NEW YORK

A condensed version of this book appeared originally in
Family Circle magazine.

LIBRARY OF CONGRESS CATALOGING IN PUBLICATION DATA
Guest, Judith.
  Second heaven.
  I. Title.
PS3557.U345S4   813'.54   82-70124
ISBN 0-670-62830-1   AACR2

Printed in the United States of America
Set in CRT Janson

for Judith Goren,
who was there
at the beginning,
and for my parents,
who are always there

I wish to thank my editor,
Pat Irving Frederick, for
her help and her friendship,
and for all that she has
taught me about letting go

The sun shall be turned
into darkness, and the moon
into blood.
                    —*Old Testament*, Joel 2:31

It seemed to be heaven, for there was
afterwards a heavenly brightness.
I can indeed have my thoughts about this
but as yet I dare not be too confident
because it concerns something that
is to happen.
                    —Swedenborg's *Journal of Dreams*

SECOND HEAVEN

MICHAEL

❧

1

*I*t was after five o'clock when he left the courthouse. Pushing open the glass doors, he felt the wall of heat push back at him, the sun pouring more heat down on his head. Unseasonable weather for May in Michigan; in the nineties for the last two weeks, and no rain in sight. How long had it been since they'd had any? Those farmers around the state with vineyards and cherry orchards would know. A bad summer ahead if this did not end soon.

He walked toward the parking lot, feeling the sweat break out on his forehead. Underneath his suitcoat his shirt was sticking to his back. Hotter now at five o'clock than it had been at noon; the air so thick you could make a fist and squeeze it through your fingers.

While he waited for the air conditioning to take over, he drove with the windows down; turned the vents so that the cooled air would spill upward into his face. Ahead of him a green Ford sedan with a Shriner's fez in the rear window made as if to complete the turn onto Telegraph Road, then halted in the middle of the intersection. *Damnit, move.* He laid on the horn, and the car shot through the turn. An old man driving it, hands high on the wheel, jerking around to see what was the matter. *Nothing. It's hot. I'm sorry.*

This weather tempted people, charged everything with a dangerous energy. Tiny explosions in the air wherever you looked.

Lighting a cigarette, he stroked his jaw with the heel of his hand. His tooth was really starting to hurt. At lunch, when he had felt the pain snap cleanly through bone to flood his cheek, he had worried that there was no time for this; the calendar was jammed from now to the end of June; the work was piling up. Each night he was more tired than before; he had barely enough energy left for the sports page and a shower. He would fall into bed at eleven o'clock.

This afternoon, when Bill saw him leaving the office, he had asked, "You're going back out there today?"

"I said I would."

"Listen, partner. There is nothing for us out at Juvenile. This is how we get in over our heads, taking on these shit cases for nothing."

"It's a favor, Bill."

"No kidding. I hope she appreciates it."

"Anyway, it's not for nothing. I got her this very nice settlement last year that she's been trying to give away ever since."

"Fine. See that you let her."

Passing the Pontiac Mall he noted the billboard, faded and peeling in the sun, that announced in big red letters: RODEO! APRIL 10–16! REAL LIVE HORSES! COWBOYS! Set out in an open field. He had never noticed it before. Had such an event actually occurred? If so he had missed it. He wondered if it had been a success. Nothing along this stretch of road ever struck him as having much potential for that; driving it always reminded him of the riots, burned-out skeletons of buildings, vacant lots with *For Sale* signs planted amid the greasy weeds. The businesses that survived—rent-all stations, chicken shacks, and Donut shops, everything jazzy and hyphenated—all had a prefab look about them, as if they could disappear overnight. Most of them did. The only building of permanence, the old Pontiac Laundry, stood abandoned on its narrow triangle of land: the graceful, arched windows boarded up, the brick walls festooned in orange and blue graffiti. Sad. Somebody ought to buy it, fix it up, make it into an artists' co-op, or maybe a good restaurant. They could use one around here.

The highway widened as he crossed Orchard Lake Road, smoothing out to accommodate the businesses of Bloomfield Hills—realty companies, furniture showrooms, and decorator shops; groups of low modern buildings housing architects, photographers, doctors, lawyers. He passed their own offices, saw that Bill's car was gone. He and Gretchen were going sailing tonight. Bill had invited him too—a nice, lazy evening on Lake St. Clair; dinner at Bayview. He had declined. Too hot, even for that; plus, he couldn't stand the thought of the drive downtown through rush-hour traffic. No, what he wanted to do most was sleep. He would go home to his apartment, relax, try to forget about the heat.

Glancing down at the gas gauge, he saw the needle wavering on red and swung into the Mobil station above Long Lake Road. With the motor off, he waited while the attendant, an old man, bare-shouldered, in gray coveralls, worked on the car in front of him. The old man looked up and smiled. "Be just a few minutes here."

He nodded and leaned back in the seat, stretching his arms over his head. The air shimmered outside the car. This was the first smile he had seen today. Out at Juvenile the clerk had looked as though she was harassed beyond endurance.

"I'm telling you, sir, we have no one listed under that name. When did you say she was brought in here?"

"It's a 'he.' Spelled G-A-L-E."

"Well, it doesn't say anything on the admission sheet about his having an attorney."

"He's about to get one. If I can get in to see him."

"We can't allow visitors in the locked facility after four-thirty, sir."

"Look. It's four-thirty-five. How about if you make an exception?"

"I'm sorry."

"Then would you call Steve Bray for me in Youth Assistance? Extension 234?"

She had done it, but the look she gave him conveyed her contempt. Slick lawyer type. Looking for a way around the rules.

The old man appeared at his elbow. "Sorry to keep you waiting," he said. "Awful hot day."

"No problem."

"Fill it up for you?"

"Please."

A smooth humming noise as he lifted the hose from the pump. The smell of gasoline heavy in the air. The old man worked on the windshield, spraying it, wiping it off with a square of rose-pink paper.

"People gotta get serviced under their hoods," he said.

"Pardon me?"

"Lady ahead of you. Trouble with her thermostat. People let those things go; before you know it, you got big trouble. Got to get serviced under your hood regular."

He nodded and grinned, felt his spirits lift suddenly. He would have to tell that one to Bill.

He opened the door to his apartment, welcomed inside by an ocean of cool, washed air. He, the grateful swimmer, stripped off his coat and tie, made his way out to the kitchen. Taking a glass down from the cupboard, he filled it with ice, poured tea over it from the pitcher on the counter. He drank carefully, keeping his tongue anchored over the sore tooth.

He stood at the kitchen window, looking out at the parking lot and the man-made hill beyond it, built to shield the complex from the traffic noise of Hunter Boulevard. The hill was covered in lilacs, a waterfall of lavender pouring over green grass. Of the seasons he had witnessed from this window, he liked spring the best: its lilacs and forsythia and flowering crabapple trees, the tulips and daffodils growing alongside the low fences. He had chosen the place mainly for its location, had not counted on the beauty of it. It was within easy walking distance of downtown Birmingham, good for the kids. He didn't want them to feel stranded, far away from their old friends, when they came to visit.

He refilled his glass and went into the bedroom, turning on the TV, hanging up his coat and tie in the closet. Loosening his shirt, he lay down on the bed. He would have to call Cat soon. She would want to know what had happened out there this afternoon.

He looked around the room, admiring the decorating job he had done: navy, green, and white–striped wallpaper, bright-green carpeting, navy bedspread with matching drapes. After eight months he was not yet tired of the combination. He thought that was a good sign. He liked bright colors, wanted to be surrounded by them the moment he opened his eyes in the morning. None of your bland, Holiday Inn decor; he didn't want people wondering whether anybody lived here or not.

The carpeting in the living room might have been a mistake, though. He liked the name: Blackberry Wine. With the pale walls, beige leather couch and chairs, beige curtains, he thought he had hit upon something spectacular. Bill had told him to get a waterbed and a lava light and he would be in business.

The spare bedroom had just been finished last week; he was proud of that, too. A single bed, desk, and dresser, all of darkly polished wood; across one wall, an arrangement of shelves designed to hold all manner of items—books and magazines, assorted trophies, pictures, records, tapes. Anything the kids brought along with them and needed to store. Too bad he hadn't had it ready at Christmastime, when Natalie was here. She had had to make do with a rollaway cot and a couple of makeshift shelves he had put together out of bricks and boards. She hadn't minded, though, being more interested in the social life than in the accommodations. She had even made friends with two ten-year-olds in the building who asked the other day if she was coming back this summer.

He prayed that Daniel's visit would go as well. They were such different types, his son and his daughter. Natalie made friends as easily as breathing. Daniel's relationships were more serious and long-term, based always on choice and not need. It was not likely that he would meet any fourteen-year-old apartment dwellers that he would want to pal around with all summer. No doubt he would be spending all of his time in the old neighborhood. Well, that was all right. This move had been hardest on him. He needed to get back here, if only to see that things were not always as you remembered them.

He stared at the framed picture on the dresser of the two of them—Daniel looking down at the ground, scowling, hands in the pockets of his jeans—he hated posing for pictures; Natalie in her bathing suit, dripping wet, having just come out of the lake. Taken last summer, just before the move. One dark-haired, one blond. Natalie's smile sweet and solemn.

He glanced at the clock: six-ten. What the hell, he would call tonight. It had been a couple of weeks since he had talked to them; Daniel, organized and efficient like his mother, would want to know about the plans. The plane reservations were made. He had left Daniel's ticket open-ended, not being exactly sure when he would want to book his return: late in August, probably; just in time to get ready for school. His own ticket for Friday, the fifth of June, round-trip from Detroit to Washington, lay on the dresser. He was anxious to see them in their new surroundings, so he could picture them there when he called; it would make them seem less far away.

He drained his glass, setting it back on the nightstand. Reaching for the phone, he dialed the Washington number.

"Hello?"

"Hello, Joy."

"Michael! How *are* you?"

"Fine. How're you?"

"Fine, fine. Well . . . this job's got me crazy, but otherwise I guess I'm all right." She laughed. Self-conscious, as always, about revealing things to him. He didn't know if this was true, or if he merely read it into things. It seemed that he knew less about her now than he had when they had first met; harder and harder for him to imagine that they had once been married. Eleven years of his life bound up with hers. Now they had trouble finding enough words to get them safely through a telephone conversation.

"I wasn't expecting you," she said. "I almost didn't recognize your voice."

"The kids around?"

"Sure. We just finished dinner. I'll get them."

She put the phone down, and he leaned back against the pillows. Lighting a cigarette, he took a deep drag, put it in the ashtray beside him. Not recognizing his voice, that would be a first. What would that feel like? Of course it was an unfair test; he was the one who always called; he knew whom to expect on the other end. When his kids failed to recognize it, that would be a bad sign. A sign of further estrangement.

"Hullo, Dad."

"Hello, Daniel, how's it goin'?"

"Okay. Pretty good."

"What're you doing?"

"Nothin' much. Talkin' on the phone."

Old family joke. They both laughed. The voice sounded deeper to him since the last time, faintly Southern; not a drawl, exactly, but close.

"How about you, Dad?"

"Well, I went to see the Tigers play last Saturday."

"Yeah? How'd they do?"

"They lost."

"Same old guys, huh?"

"No. Different guys. Same old team, though. Say, I was thinking of signing you up for baseball. You'll be around for the whole season, won't you?"

A pause. "That's Babe Ruth, isn't it? You have to try out."

"You can do it when you get here. I checked it out. They've got a couple of tryout dates in June."

"That's a tough league, though. You gotta know what you're doing. You could get wounded." Another silence. "I guess I'd really rather not, Dad. If it's okay with you."

"I ran into Tim Hughes the other day. Jesus, has he gotten tall. He told me he made the freshman basketball team at Seaholm."

"Great. Hey, listen, did you get the new stereo?"

"I did. It's terrific. I mean, it looks terrific. I don't know how it sounds."

"You kidding me?"

"No time. I've been too busy to hook it up. It's the best one around, though, the salesman tells me."

"I can't believe you haven't even made any tapes!"

"I'm waiting for you."

"It's simple, Dad. You just have to set a couple of dials."

But he hadn't bought the equipment for himself. He couldn't stand the thought of Daniel sitting, moody and restless, around the apartment while he waited for his father to come home from work. At least there would be a good stereo system. At least there would be the telephone. Cokes in the refrigerator, and anything else he wanted, just name it. Let this work out, he thought. Let it be the pattern for all of their summers together.

"Natalie wants to talk to you," Daniel said. "Just a second."

And then his daughter's voice came on the line, high-pitched, heavy on the italics. No change there. He was glad.

"Daddy, hi, I'm pretty *mad* at you! It's been two weeks, and you promised you'd call last *Thursday!*"

"Baby, I'm sorry. I was in court all that day."

"And all night, too?"

He laughed. "Hey. You can always call me, you know."

"You're never *home!* I called you once and you weren't even home."

"Well, I'm home now."

"I wanted to tell you I got the part in *Sleeping Beauty.* We're doing almost the whole thing. And some people might come down from New York to see it. Do you think you might be able to come, Daddy? It's in October."

"I don't see why not."

He could picture her, his golden daughter with her back arched, up on her toes. Her pale hair swept up off her neck, fastened with a silver barrette. Her big violet eyes with heavy blond lashes, and that slender little girl's body that was never still. Ballet was her whole life, she had told him at Christmas. Her life would be full of romance, he knew. Capital R. It couldn't happen to a nicer kid.

"What do you want for your birthday?" he asked her.

"Don't laugh," she said. "A horse."

"Since when?"

"Since I just got finished taking riding lessons."

"Jesus, I can't keep up with you."

"What time will you be coming?" she asked.

"My flight gets in at five-thirty."

"And we'll go out to dinner together."

"Sure. Big celebration. You pick the spot."

"We'll have fun, Daddy. There's lots to do here. The FBI and the Space Museum, all kinds of stuff. Last week Ed took us to see the Senate."

"How was that?"

"Pretty boring," she confessed. "But the Capitol was fun. There was a guy standing on the steps telling everybody how the world was going to end in two weeks. I wanted to go up and talk to him, but Mom wouldn't let me."

"Smart Mom."

"Ed says people are always doing that, talking about stuff on the Capitol steps. He says you have to get a permit from the police, but after that you can do anything, because it's freedom of speech."

Smart Ed. He took another drag on his cigarette; looked at it; put it out. Smoking too much these days, letting the habit take him over again.

"You know, I wish I wasn't going to camp this summer. I could come to Detroit with you and Daniel."

"We'll work something out. Your mother told me you might have a free weekend near the end. Hey, listen, baby, put Daniel back on for a second, will you?"

A pause. "He left, Daddy. Did you want me to tell him something?"

"No. That's all right. It wasn't anything important. Tell him I'll see him soon. You, too."

"Okay. 'Bye."

" 'Bye."

He hung up; sat for a moment, staring at the television screen. Then he leaned back against the pillow, letting the gray and white figures take over inside his head. More craziness in Italy. Another political kidnapping. Five bodyguards killed, a man dragged from his car and taken away, a high-speed chase, the city of Milan in turmoil. Hell, why go to Italy? Enough craziness right here; go down on Twelfth Street, or Piquette and Brush. No help for it; things were out of control. He felt his mood sinking again, and he pressed a hand to his cheek. Pain filled the left side of his jaw with discomforting heat. He would have to do something about the tooth. Tomorrow, for sure.

The telephone rang shrilly in his ear; he reached over, lifting the receiver without opening his eyes.

"Michael, you're home, thank God. I was getting worried."

"Sorry. I meant to call, I fell asleep." He swung his legs over the side of the bed. "What time is it? Is it late?"

"Seven o'clock. I'm sorry if I woke you up."

"No, that's okay."

"Did you see him? Is he all right?"

"I saw him. He's okay. And there's a preliminary hearing tomorrow morning at nine o'clock. At the courthouse. You should be there."

"What happened when you went out there? Did they tell you what it was all about?"

"His father filed a petition with Juvenile Court. I don't know what's in it. I couldn't get a copy. It was too late in the day."

She was silent a moment. "But what has he done? He hasn't done anything that I can see. It doesn't seem right that they can just walk into a public building like that and arrest someone."

"He hasn't been arrested, just taken into custody."

"What's the difference?"

He stayed away from that one. No lectures on Juvenile Law: she would not be in the mood.

"Dave said they took him out in handcuffs," she said.

"Who's Dave?"

"His counselor at school. Dave Cornelius. He was the one who called. He's upset about how the whole thing was handled, Michael. He said to tell you he'll be glad to help in any way he can. With information on his school attendance and his grades and things."

"Fine."

"I feel awful about this. I still can't believe it's happening."

He could believe it, knowing what he knew. The few times he had seen Gale at her house, his own friendly overtures had been met with a cool and private arrogance that he knew was designed to provoke him. A difficult kid, he thought. Secretive and suspicious. Nothing that he saw today had changed his opinion.

"So should I just meet you there at nine tomorrow?"

"Right," he said. "In the lobby."

She took a deep breath. "You're a good friend, Michael. Thank you again."

"Forget it."

He rang off, reached down to untie his shoelaces, easing off his shoes. A mistake for her to have gotten involved here. No good would come of it.

Ever since the day she had first come to his office and sat across the desk from him, with her gloved hands folded demurely in her lap—the Good Little Girl, waiting for him to tell her what to do—he had felt a strong sense of connection with her. Her fair hair was pulled back from her face; the pink lipstick contrasting sharply with her deep tan. Christmas in Florida or the Bahamas, he had guessed, and been right. She and her husband had taken a final trip together to see if things could be worked out. They could not, in her husband's opinion. So here she was.

He had typed her easily that day: attractive, slightly-spoiled-but-pleasant first wife of prominent physician, about to be let go. He listened while she recited the facts of their separation, making it sound like the troubles of some distant relative or the plot of a novel she had read. Throughout the narrative were various opinions expressed by The Doctor: "Alex says it shouldn't be too much of a problem, working out the financial details of the settlement." "He thinks I should keep the house and live in it for a while, not try to sell it until the market improves." "He wants me to see a therapist. He says the headaches are emotional." This last in her calmest, most controlled voice, so achingly intent upon revealing nothing that she revealed all.

Did she want the divorce, also? She seemed surprised by the question; said that was hardly the point. He asked where she had gotten his name, assuming it was some friend of hers whose divorce he had handled in the past. From the Yellow Pages, she told him; she always went right to the A's for everything—plumbers, repairmen of all kinds. That funny, spaced-out smile appearing then for the first time. They had both laughed.

Since then he had advised her on a number of things—investments, contracts, her future plans. She had taken his advice about half the time. Not a bad average.

Last winter she had been working at an art gallery in Birmingham while she assembled her portfolio, nerving herself to start looking for a position in fashion illustrating.

"If I get the job I want," she said, "I'll be able to live off that salary. It will be much better money than what I'm making now. Along with the sale of the house, I'll be in good shape."

"That's great."

"So. What I'd like to do is give the money back."

"What money?"

"You know. The settlement. I don't want Alex thinking he has to take care of me. I can take care of myself. I don't want him doling out money to me for the rest of my life."

"He's not doling out money; you earned it. You worked twenty years keeping house, raising your daughter, seeing to other people's needs."

"They were my needs, too," she said. "Anyway, not the child support, I don't mean that. It belongs to Chris. And whatever Alex wants to do for her is fine with me. I just don't want him carting me around on his back like some cross he has to bear forever."

"It's not forever, it's seven years. Let's keep it straight."

"I just don't want it. You don't understand. I'm the one who wants to be free of it."

"Fine, you don't want it, then give it away. To the church of your choice, or your favorite political party. How about the Cuban Relief Fund?"

"You won't help me?"

"Not me, I'm strictly Domestic Relations. I don't administer charities. Listen, your problem is that you've got no imagination. Go out and buy a motorcycle; ride around for a couple of years and learn about America. Better yet, increase my fee, support your local Lawyer's Pension Plan. Give me a minute, I'll help you think of some dandy ways to get rid of it."

"All right. I see it was a dumb idea, bringing this to you."

"I swear to you, Cat, you're a hell of a lot freer with it than you'll be without it."

She had taken his word on that one, at least. Still, if he had any real power over her, he would like to use it now. This was dangerous stuff she was fooling with, and it didn't seem to him that she had thought enough about the consequences. What did she really know about this kid? She had let him move in with her in January almost by accident, it appeared to him. At least she had only the vaguest notion of how it had come about. When she called this afternoon to ask for his help, it was as if there was no need to explain her sense of urgency. Gale was in trouble. Therefore, she was the one to help him. Period.

He picked up his glass, heading for the kitchen. Maybe he should have asked her out for dinner, and they could have discussed it. No, forget it: by the time he showered and changed and got to her house—he wasn't hungry, anyway, and his tooth hurt like hell.

So what was he doing, going through the refrigerator? A carton of leftover chop suey from Pearl's Restaurant. How long had that been in there? He tossed the contents into the sink, along with an open can of peaches that looked suspiciously dark about the edges. What remained was a half pound of butter and two bottles of tonic water. Jesus but people got weird when they lived alone. Exactly what Bill had warned him against. He was getting more moody, less social, his steps slower, his skin looser. Old Man Atwood, the guy who lives upstairs.

He shook his head. Come on, things can't be that bad, not yet. Here were a couple of steaks in the freezer, along with some french fries from McDonald's—proof that in fact he did plan ahead. As for his social life, he had had two dates in the past week. Admittedly, one was a lunch date with his secretary on the occasion of her thirtieth birthday. But the other had been dinner with Cat, along with a movie, after which he had taken her home, hoping to be invited in for a drink and some conversation. But she had said she was tired and had to work the next day. So whose fault was that? Not his.

He would take some aspirin and make himself a drink; he

would shower and watch a movie on TV. He would worry about his social life some other time.

As with most advice that he gave himself, it seemed to come too late to do him much good. He was better at advising other people, maybe.

2

*T*he underground sprinkler system was operating this morning, a silvery spray bouncing high into the air. From the road the large sand-colored building rose like a gleaming Oz palace above thick green lawns. Up close it looked less mythical. Housed within its four stories were the various courtrooms, and the offices of the county prosecutors and the other administrative services. He parked his car in the lot at the front of the building. The air felt cooler this morning, the heat saving up for a late-afternoon assault.

Cat was waiting for him in the lobby. Wearing a light-blue dress, high heels, smiling nervously in his direction, one hand smoothing her hair.

"What do you think is going to happen?"

He took her arm and steered her toward the elevators.

"Today, nothing much. It's a preliminary hearing. The court will decide whether or not to take jurisdiction, probably. If they do, they'll set a date for another hearing."

"Another hearing? What for?"

"To listen to the case. This one's to determine whether there is one."

"His parents are here. I saw them in the lobby."

"Did you talk to them?"

She shook her head.

The elevator door opened, and he led her down the hall. Hearing Room 330, he had been told at the Intake office yesterday. A long, narrow chamber without windows, set up like a classroom, with rows of folding chairs arranged before a wooden table; in the center of it a block with a metal nameplate on it: JOHN PELTIER, REFEREE.

At the front of the room a couple sat with their backs to the door. He motioned Cat to take a seat; went up to the table, where a young man was sorting through a pile of manila folders. He introduced himself.

"You got a client here?"

"Gale Murray."

Quickly the young man went through the folders. He withdrew a sheaf of papers and tore off a copy of the petition, handing it to Michael.

"Thanks."

As he turned, the man in front stared directly at him, a long look, meant to slow him down. A thin, angular face with high cheekbones and full lips; light eyes—blue or hazel, he couldn't tell. Beside him, the woman sat with her head down, her hands in her lap. She had soft features, a round, young-looking face. Her hair, tied back with a ribbon, was a rich auburn color. She wore a dark-green suit of some silky material.

The man continued to stare at him. Michael nodded, walked on. Sitting down beside Cat, he began to read:

> . . . that there has been chronic truancy
> . . . that there has been chronic absence from home
> . . . that there has been lying, stealing, and general disobedience
> . . . that there has been a general lack of respect in the home . . .

Halfway down the page the specific charges began: seven separate instances of money having been taken from wallets, purses, dresser drawers, desk drawers. And further down:

> ... that on January 18, said child did willfully violate Public Act #1223, to wit, leaving home without permission ...
> ... that on April 19 he was found to be residing in the home of Catherine Holzman, 712 Arden Avenue in Royal Oak, and that he did willfully refuse to return home ...
> ... that father's efforts to remove him from the premises resulted in threats, abusive language, and violence on the part of said child ...
> ... that Catherine Holzman made no attempt to either contact the parents as to the whereabouts of said child, or to aid them in securing his return ...
> ... that her conduct, when confronted by the father, was threatening and abusive ... that she did also attempt to assault him ...

"I meant to tell you about all that," Cat said.

"Terrific." Michael looked up. "Tell me now. We've got about three minutes."

She made a helpless gesture with her hand. "That wasn't the way it happened."

A door at the back opened; a man dressed in khakis and a white shirt entered. Behind him, Gale stood in the doorway; the man directed him to a chair at the front of the room. Michael went forward.

Pale hair the color of straw; a sulky, pretty mouth. Too pretty for a boy. Maybe that was it. There was something about his looks that Michael found vaguely irritating. He sat now with his hands on his knees, his heels hooked over the front rung of the chair. Sullen and defiant, staring ahead. He would not be impressed by this, would not be taken in.

Michael handed him a copy of the petition.

"What's this for?" He read quickly through it, handed it back. "I didn't do any of this."

"You didn't run away from home?"

"I didn't try to assault him, or whatever he says I did. He assaulted me. You ask her." He jerked his head in Cat's direction.

"What about the money?"

"I didn't take any money from him."

A gray-haired man with glasses entered the room and sat down at the table. The clerk called the session to order.

"Will you read the petition, please?" the referee asked.

When the clerk had finished, Michael rose from his chair.

"Sir, my client and I haven't had a chance to go over this petition, as I only received it this morning. If I could have just a few minutes—"

"Your client should know whether he wishes to contest these charges or not, Mr. Atwood," said the referee. "That is the court's only concern here today."

"I didn't do anything," said Gale.

"Very well." Peltier turned to the couple seated in front of him. "Mr. Murray, the court would like to hear your reasons for requesting a hearing in this matter."

Murray stood. "Sir, I can't see letting him ruin his life. He's been in and out of trouble for years. He ran away from home in January. We've been looking for him—"

"You had no idea where he was staying?"

"No, sir. Not until three weeks ago. When I went to this woman's house"—he turned and pointed a finger in Cat's direction—"she admitted to me that he had been living with her, and she refused to allow him to leave. When I tried to discuss this matter with my son, she interfered—"

"Did your son wish to leave with you, sir?"

Murray was silent. "I don't . . . he doesn't know what he wants, sir. That's the truth."

The referee looked at Cat, then back to Murray. "Do you have some objection to his living with this woman? I mean, apart from the fact that he was absent from home?"

"Yes, sir, I do. There was no supervision there. And no discipline, as far as I could make out. He came and went as he pleased. He did exactly what he wanted. In my opinion, it was not right for him. He can't handle that. He is immature, he's a liar and a thief. It hurts me to have to say these things . . ."

His wife lowered her head. Gale appeared not to have heard it. He sat with his arms folded across his chest, staring in stony concentration at the chair in front of him.

"This is a last resort, your honor," Murray said. "I didn't want it to come to this, but I felt I had no choice."

The referee was consulting the calendar on the table.

"Very well. Court is satisfied that the child understands the charges filed against him and that it will take jurisdiction in this case. Next court date is Thursday, June 11, three weeks from today, if that is acceptable to both parties."

"Yes, sir," Michael said.

Murray echoed him.

"Child to remain in custody at the Center until then. Parents have requested no visitors, and the court will honor that request." He closed the file folder in front of him. "Everything covered, then? Fine."

He called for the next case.

"Wait here," Michael said to Gale, getting up to follow the couple out of the room. The man had his hand on the woman's back and was guiding her toward the elevators. He turned at Michael's approach.

"I don't see any harm in Mrs. Holzman's being able to visit Gale in J Building, do you?"

The man eyed him coldly. "This is a family matter, Mr. Atwood. It is none of your business. Or hers, either." He pressed the button to summon the elevator. Beside him, the woman seemed distracted. "If I didn't see any harm in it, I wouldn't have bothered to make the request."

As he spoke, the elevator doors opened. He took the woman's arm and they stepped inside. She looked at Michael over her shoulder, whispering something into the air. He leaned forward,

trying to catch the words, but they were lost in the swift chan-
neling of the doors.

They were closeted in a small room off the hearing chambers, a
room that looked like the inside of a cardboard box: tan walls and
ceiling, tan tiled floor. There were no pictures on the walls, no
windows. The only furnishings were a wooden table and two
folding chairs. A green metal wastebasket in the corner.

"So, what's the deal?" Gale asked him. "I thought I was getting
out of here."

"What made you think that?"

"Isn't that what you said yesterday?"

"What I said was, it depended on what was in the petition."

"It's all bullshit," he said. "I didn't do any of that. And besides,
there's guys around school who've done lots worse than that, stolen cars and trashed buildings—"

"You want to talk about them?"

He stood with his back against the door, his eyes fixed on a spot
behind Michael's head. He would not come into the room, as if to
do so would be to compromise himself in some irretrievable way.

Up close, the bony shoulders and thin wrists made him look
younger and more vulnerable. If he would ever look up when he
spoke, if he would ever smile. But he was not one to give any part
of himself away. And he would come in and sit down when he
felt like it, not before.

"People do worse things than that all the time," he said. "They
don't get locked up for it."

"They do if their parents are petitioning the court."

He opened the briefcase on the table, taking out the single
sheet of paper. "Here. I need you to sign this."

"What is it?"

"A letter of authorization. Saying you want me to act as your
attorney in this case."

"I don't need any attorney. I haven't done a damn thing."

"Gale, they won't let me help you without it."

"So how have you helped me so far? I'm still in here, right? Cornelius says, 'Go along and do what they tell you, the lawyer will fix it.' Shit, that figures."

"What happened yesterday?" Michael asked. "How come they took you out of school in handcuffs?"

No answer. His eyes narrowed. "This place sucks," he said. "You have to get permission to take a goddamn leak."

Michael sighed. "Listen. We need to get a few things straight. As long as you're in here, you'd better play it smart."

"Meaning?"

"Meaning it won't help to take it out on the people in charge. You've got a lousy attitude—"

"Maybe if you were locked up in some fucking dump for three weeks—"

"You can be locked up for a lot longer than that; now, is that what you want?"

Silence. They stared at each other across the table.

"So, when do I get to see her?" Gale asked.

"You know, I had a feeling you weren't listening in there."

"I've heard it before. Except he left out the part about the lost sheep straying from the fold and Jesus saving everybody."

"What about the part where you stole the money?"

"I didn't steal any money," he said flatly. "I told you that." He moved to the table, picking up the pen. "Where do I have to sign?"

Michael showed him, and he wrote his name in neat, careful script across the bottom of the page.

"There's something else I want you to do," Michael said. "Write a list of the people you know. Anybody you think would be willing to put in a good word for you at the hearing. Starting with your counselor. And Cat, of course."

"That's it," he said. "There isn't anybody else."

"There had better be. What about this guy at the hardware store. What's his name?"

"Wiley," he said. "He won't do it."

"Why not?"

"Because. Why should he? It's a job, that's all."

"Put him down. Put down anybody who comes to your mind. Teachers, neighbors, friends. I'll pick it up from you tomorrow."

He rose and pressed a hand to his cheek. The toothache was worse, demanding all his attention now. He worried that he would not be able to make it to five o'clock, when he had an appointment with the dentist. The pain had moved to a point high in his head.

"You didn't say when I can see her," Gale said.

"You can't," he said patiently. "Your parents asked that there be no visitors."

"You mean he decides I have to stay here, and he says if I can talk to people or not?"

"That's right."

It had been said plainly enough; how could he have missed it?

"What did I sign this stupid paper for?" Gale asked. "You can't do anything for me. This is a joke."

"Friend," Michael said, "it's going to be tough enough without that—"

"And don't call me that. We're not friends," he said.

Michael stood and zipped the briefcase closed. "Don't forget about the list, okay? I'll see you tomorrow."

"They can't keep me in here," Gale said. "They can't lock you up like this when you haven't done anything."

He moved toward the door, thinking to himself: Oh, you dumb kid. Wake up. They're doing it, aren't they?

3

The chair tipped backward and the Morris Louis poster slid by his eyes, liquid shades of blue and brown.

"You grind your teeth, you know that? Got a good-sized muscle developing here. Feel it."

Standing behind him, the dentist pressed firm fingers against his temples. Obediently, Michael raised his hands to his head, felt nothing much—a faint pulsing beneath his sideburns, that was all.

"So, why all the tension?" Pete asked.

"What do you mean?"

"Stress. That's what causes it. You got money problems these days? Work problems?"

"I've got a toothache."

His friend laughed. "Just asking."

He stared up at the ceiling, counting the rows of holes in the cream-colored tiles over his head. *Work problems.* Well, he had wished himself in the past week a Fuller Brush salesman, a professional golfer, a landscape gardener, and a baseball player. Did that qualify as a work problem?

About his own job he knew a couple of things—that he was tired of domestic crisis, tired of lying in bed at night, wide awake and strung out on the minutiae of the day; or worse, being jerked from sleep by the surfacing of some trivial chore (a phone call, a deadline) that had somehow been overlooked. Trivial, but crucial. The two a.m. snaproll, as Bill called it. Another thing he was tired of, having to rise to the challenge of yet one more client who did not believe in lawyers. Screw it, he didn't believe in them much himself these days.

"You've got a crack in that tooth. I'm going to fill it, but there's a chance it may give you more problems. We'll have to see how it goes."

Pete slid the needle into his gum, and almost at once the pain began to ebb. He watched Pete's nurse, a young blonde, assemble the tray of tools at his elbow. His jaw gradually grew numb; his tongue thickened.

They had known each other a long time, he and Pete. Since Daniel was born, when Pete and Camille had bought the house next door to them in Birmingham. He had become their dentist and their friend on the night when eleven-month-old Daniel had fallen out of his high chair, knocking out a front tooth. Pete had taken charge, rescuing the tooth and replanting it in Daniel's mouth, while calming the screaming baby and reassuring his anxious parents.

Now, there was a profession for you. Useful and respectable. You would find no clients in here who did not believe in dentists.

Counting the holes in the ceiling tiles—nine across, nine down—reminded him of a game he had played by the hour as a kid: connect the dots and claim the smaller, inside squares with your initial. Of course, in order to win you had to be able to distract your opponent: get a lot of squares going, so that he wouldn't notice when you were ready to close them in. As in sailing: tacking, to outwit the wind. Another worthy occupation: sailor, world traveler. Cruising the North Atlantic in your yacht with your kids, after having stolen them from under their mother's watchful eye. Hiding out with them in the Azores or the Lesser Antilles for months; years, maybe.

"What are you grinning about?" Pete asked.

He fixed a look of innocence on his face. Had he been grinning? "Nothing."

"What do you hear from Joy and the kids?"

"Not a lot. They're fine, though."

"They like living in Washington?"

"Seem to."

"Camille got a letter from her a few months ago. She said things were going pretty well. That's a big adjustment, don't you think? I mean for the kids. Moving and all. I don't know how mine would handle it. Their social life would be in ruins." He adjusted the light above Michael's head. "How long have they been there now?"

"Nearly a year."

"Jesus, really? Has it been that long? Time flies."

For you, maybe. Aloud, he said, "Well, Natalie was in over Christmas, and Daniel's coming in two weeks for the summer."

"Really? That's great. Hey, let's get together sometime while he's here. Go out to a ball game or something. I know Tommy would like that."

"Sure. Any time."

"As I recall, Joy never did like living here," Pete said. "Detroit wasn't her favorite city."

"No, it wasn't."

As a matter of fact, she had talked of leaving it ever since the day they met. Sometimes he thought the main reason for the divorce had been to make her escape from Detroit. Still, she had stuck around for nearly three years after it.

He thought about the Christmas party where he'd first seen her—the small-boned, pretty brunette in the bright-green jersey dress—and made his way to her side, gaining her attention with his questions. She had beautiful, graceful hands; on her wrist, the thinnest of gold chains was sliding back and forth as she talked to him about her job in the insurance agency, about wanting to eventually move back East, to Boston, where she was born and raised.

He had listened, and not listened, his body under a sudden powerful stir of sexual command, being more concerned with whether she would accept his invitation to dinner that night. She had come to the party alone. She had just broken up with someone, she told him—a long and painful process—and she was emphatically not interested in future involvements; not for a while, at least.

A few days later he got up the nerve to call and ask her out for New Year's Eve. To his surprise, she said yes. They went out with a group of his friends on a wild, drunken evening that ended at Gretchen and Bill's apartment, with Bill passed out on the couch and he and Gretchen and Joy cooking breakfast for everyone.

The following week he asked her to marry him. She refused. One week and two proposals later, she accepted.

The year they were married was the year of the riots. She carried on a pressure campaign to get him to relocate. She hated Detroit. It was dirty; it was dying of crime and pollution and civil neglect. The papers were full of violence and racial hatred. Why not look for a job in another city? Lawyers could relocate the same as other businessmen did.

He listened but did nothing about it. He told her he had an obligation to Bill, and to the firm they were struggling to establish. But the truth was, he loved this city; it was his hometown, and if it had a reputation, if they called it Motown or Murder City, he couldn't care less.

He could remember being a kid in this town, riding the streetcar down Woodward Avenue. He remembered the caramel-colored cane seats, tacky and warm under his hand. Shopping at Hudson's or Crowley's, waiting for his father underneath the Kern's clock. Passing the Institute of Arts and gazing at the hunched figure of *The Thinker* out front. The white balustrade surrounding the marble porches of the main library across the street.

He had grown up in Rosedale Park and lived in the same house that whole time. Just as his parents had done. They had met each other at Northwestern High School, gotten married, and settled down in their hometown. They had lived there and raised a family and died within months of each other while he was in law school at the University of Michigan. To leave Detroit was to lose touch with them forever. So, instead, what had he sacrificed? But no, that wasn't fair. Nor was it the truth. It was not the location of the marriage but the marriage itself that had gone wrong. They were, in the end, off-center with one another. It was nobody's fault. She had told him that often enough.

"Looks as if that crack has been there for a while," Pete said to him. "I'm surprised you haven't had pain before this."

Had he? He couldn't be sure. With his mouth stretched wide and locked open under the tent of gray rubber, he stared up at his friend, thinking of the years of tennis and golf they had played together, the Saturday afternoons of baby-sitting their boys and watching football on TV—ten years of it, nearly. So why was it that Camille and Joy had remained close—having lunch and calling each other, writing letters, keeping in touch—while he and Pete had separated as cleanly and silently as if the connection had never been made? Like strangers who team up on the golf course and play a round together, after which they go on their way— "Thanks, enjoyed it a lot, see you again." Only, of course, they wouldn't. And if they did happen to run into each other, what would they talk about? Their kids. The weather.

Something that women had—a way of communicating emotional truth; men tended to ignore that, either through laziness or fear, he wasn't sure which. There was this women's network that existed, this solid core of support. And men did not possess it. Men could discuss sports and business and politics; they might tell each other some few facts of their individual lives, but only the safe ones, and only if there was no measure of personal pain connected with it. The pain was what you didn't talk about. For all he knew, Pete could be having an affair with this blond hygienist at his elbow. He might even admit to it if asked; but not if it was serious, not if it meant something to him. That was what you made sure you were good and quiet about.

He closed his eyes, thinking again about Cat. A bad time for her. A dangerous time. Bill always referred to it as the Hysteria of the Newly Divorced. Make a million changes in your life. Fill it up with problems. Keep busy. You were vulnerable as hell during that period, he knew, thinking of his own craziness following the breakup of his marriage. He had been out of control with grief, caught up in a cycle of terrible mood swings; one minute euphoric and the next trapped in some dark cave of thought with no knowledge of how to free himself. Cut off from all his former notions of who he was and how to behave.

He remembered the hockey game he had gone to with Pete; sitting at Olympia, with a beer in one hand, a hot dog in the other, cheering as the Wings whipped Toronto. And out of nowhere the tears had come; his face got hot—*No, God, not here!*—and in a panic he had fled to the men's room, standing inside the door with his hands to his face, at one with the drunks in gabardine overcoats who hung out there. Thinking of it made him wince.

He understood about vulnerability; the worst of it was impairment of judgment. He had spent the first six months denying everything—nothing had happened to him, nothing was wrong. This, in the face of his spending every night alone in a two-room apartment across town from his children and their mother; but they were simply on a long vacation from each other, they would soon be back together again.

When he finally saw this as the dream that it was, he resolved to mend his ways. He was finished with sitting hunched in a chair before the TV every night. He would learn all over again how to have fun. He would go out to parties, get drunk, laugh and tell jokes, meet some nice woman and invite her back to his apartment, plow her in his roomy bed, and the next day they would exchange telephone numbers over coffee, promise to keep in touch. He even did this a few times; only, more often than not, what would happen was he'd get too drunk too soon and end up sitting on a couch, filling some poor soul's ear with the mess that his life was in.

For a while he took to hanging around the Friday night hot spots—the Kingsley or the Fox and Hounds—where everybody headed after work to get high and make plans for the weekend. But he could never seem to escape his role of tourist. He was too old to be dating, too old to sit at a bar with a silly grin on his face, waiting for something to happen; he didn't even know what it was that he wanted to happen. Abruptly, one evening, he was through with it. He never went back.

Then he was in hiding again in his apartment, reviewing his life, thinking it over, weighing his own fate in the light of larger, more cosmic truths. He thought of his own specialty, domestic law, and how he would use this experience to understand his clients better in the future. The secret was to view all life as Experience. Capital E. Then you would not spend the rest of your nights sitting on the edge of your bed, staring at the wall, and feeling the weight of IT, like some huge stone in your chest.

Nothing helped. You gained weight; you lost it. You moved out of one apartment and into another. You renewed your library card, became a fiction addict, read as many as four books a week. You bought a new car. You quit smoking. A dozen times a day you told yourself to grow up, all the while realizing that, while you were in terrific pain, your problems were not unique—not even very interesting. To be so full of rage and grief, and to know it didn't matter to anyone, that was what killed you. Looking back, he knew that he had gone insane for a time. He would not want to suffer that period of his life over again. Not for anything.

It occurred to him that all the troubles of the world could be traced to the simple human error of people loving the wrong people—a huge daisy chain, with the one behind loving the one in front, and being loved, hopelessly in turn, by some other.

He had had one rebound love affair, with a friend of a client of his. Her name was Bonnie Miller. No reason why it didn't work

out, except that he had met her too soon. The first time he took
her out they had gone downtown to dinner and a symphony. Afterward he had suggested a walk down by the river. What did he
care if they were mugged behind Ford Auditorium? He wished
somebody would just try it, and he'd grab the man by the throat,
beat his head in, toss the body into the sluggish, oily water—what
release! But nobody did, and on the way home in the car, knowing what he needed from her, how badly he wanted it, wondering
how and if he would be able to ask, he had been so grateful when
she'd suggested that he come up to her place.

They had spent the night together, and it was great to feel
someone's arms around him, the smell of warm, soft skin. She was
generous, flattering him, making him feel for the first time in
months that he wasn't a failure. In the next few weeks he called
her often, saw her nearly every evening.

He had spared her the Sunday outings with the kids, though.
He thought for a time that he was doing it out of kindness. Then
he realized that it was not the real reason. The real reason was
that he liked her and needed her and enjoyed being with her, but
it did not add up to any more than that; it was going nowhere, no
matter how hard he tried to convince himself. He was not in love.

On his birthday she planned a surprise party for him, with all
his friends, and the whole evening he felt guilty as hell, knowing
that something was happening with her that was not happening
with him; knowing, also, that it never would. A few nights later
they talked it out, and even then she was generous, telling him
that it was no one's fault, nothing had been promised, he had
done nothing that he needed to feel sorry for. They parted as
friends, and she wrote him a short, tender note to let him know
that she had no hard feelings about it. Occasionally she would
phone his office; if he was out when she called, he would always
return her call, even though the message read, "Nothing urgent."
But he didn't try to see her again.

A year or so later he heard from Gretchen that she had gotten
married to an old friend, someone she'd known since high school.
She had quit her job and was moving to Hawaii. All that day he'd

wanted to call, just to say hello and to wish her good luck and happiness. He didn't do it. Best to leave things alone. Best, after all, to confine oneself to those love affairs at traffic lights, where you pull up and glance over and she's looking at you—*Yes.* And you lean forward to light a cigarette, wrists balanced lightly against the steering wheel—*Yes and yes.* To all of it—sex, love, and marriage—in the space of thirty seconds while you both wait for the light to change, wait for divorce, moving off slowly. *Goodbye, too bad it didn't work out.* Painless and safe.

"Listen," Pete said, "you might need some adjustment on that occlusion. Or we could be home free with it. We'll know by tonight, in any case." He released him, and walked him to the door. "Give me a call if there's much pain."

"How much?"

"You'll know. Anything that can't be controlled with aspirin, I want to hear about it."

He thought about his mother and the way she used to brag about him. "He has this incredible pain threshold . . . when he had the strep, we didn't even know for days that he was sick . . ." He had seen it as an actual doorway, with transparent skin stretched across it. Once it was torn the pain would come roaring through, though; there was nothing you could do about it. He recalled the agony of it—his throat burned raw and tears of pain rolling down his cheeks. He could barely swallow or even move his jaws for days afterward.

That was the problem with acknowledging pain. You lost control of it. It took over and trapped you; it owned you for a time. He had always been afraid of that.

4

*H*e pulled up in her driveway behind the blue Fiat, got out, and walked under a painter's ladder that was angled against the house. She was doing the outside trim herself on weekends. She had borrowed the ladder a month ago from one of her neighbors. The front lawn needed mowing, he noted, and the area between the sidewalk and the street was thick with dandelions.

Her house was one that had seen too many owners. Too many amateur carpenters had worked on remodeling it; at the same time, too little attention had been paid to the basics. The furnace had died on her only a month after she moved in; the plumbing was bad, probably the wiring, too.

"I got it for practically nothing," she had told him last October, showing him around. Privately he had assessed it as worth exactly that. He had asked her why she did it, why not a nice comfortable apartment nearer to where she worked? Hadn't she told him that she wanted to put all her energy into her art?

"This is art, you dope. It's called *restoration.*"

Eagerly she had led him from room to room, pointing out each separate project as if the work it represented meant nothing to her, as if it would take only minutes of her time. Restored to what? You could put thirty thousand into it, easy, and what would you have when you got through? An $85,000 white elephant in a run-down section of Royal Oak. He didn't say it, though.

She came around the side of the house, brushing her hair back from her face with her hands. She wore bright-yellow shorts and a man's white shirt, tied at the waist. Her feet were bare and her knees were dirt-smudged.

"How did things go at the dentist?"

"All right."

He held the door for her. On the kitchen counter, a small fan was turning slowly on its axis, moving the warm air around. He took off his jacket, tossing it over a chair.

"Want a beer?" she asked.

"Sure."

She pulled two cans out of the refrigerator, opened them on the peach-colored tile counter. Peach with black trim. It was genuine ceramic, she said; you couldn't buy this quality anymore. She had even gotten used to the color scheme; it only needed the right wallpaper to go with it.

"Let's go into the living room. It's cooler."

He followed her to the couch and sat down, stretching his arms along the back of it. She sat at the opposite end, facing him.

Everywhere he looked the tools and materials of her various projects lay scattered—paintbrushes, scrapers, paint pans and rollers, small cans of wood refinisher and varnish. Through the archway that led to the dining room, he could see the old sewing machine that she had picked up at a garage sale; yards of fabric were stacked and folded beside it. Her easel, with a half-finished watercolor, was set up near the window seat to catch the best light.

To all of these activities she was cheerfully and impartially devoted, and the fact that she was surrounded by clutter and incompleteness did not faze her. He thought that it would drive him crazy, never seeing an end to anything. Not if you were an Aries, she had informed him. They were great beginners, lousy finishers. A way of life.

"What did you do all day?" he asked.

"Mostly I gardened. I cleaned out the back beds and replanted some things. I had to do something to take my mind off this whole thing. I talked to Dave Cornelius again. He's upset. He feels responsible."

"What could he have done? They had the papers."

He offered her a cigarette, but she shook her head.

"No, I smoked like a fiend all afternoon."

She was looking down at her hands. The knuckles were faintly gray, her fingernails gray crescents. Gardening without gloves. The white shirt reminded him of his high school days, when the girls wore them with everything.

She had nice legs; a young girl's body, with slim hips and small breasts. Her light hair was cut short and straight, parted on the side. You had to look closely to see that she was forty; faint lines about her eyes and mouth, that was all.

"Tell me what it's like out there," she said.

"You mean at J Building? Cat, you don't need to worry about him. It's not a bad place. It's clean. The help is decent." He described it as well as he could, leaving out what he knew would upset her: the barred and whitewashed windows, the electronic doors that cracked apart with the sound of an ax striking heavy metal. "It's a way station, mostly. The kids are all on their way to other places."

"What other places?"

"Maybe Starr Commonwealth or Boys' Ranch. One of the programs running out of Children's Village."

"Is that what will happen to him?"

"Possibly. Depending on how the judge decides to view the charges."

She sighed, raising a hand to hike her hair. "I don't understand why this is happening. Why they're doing this to him."

"Sometimes parents file petitions because they're scared. They know they're responsible for whatever the kid does—"

"Michael, that man isn't scared. You saw him. Did he look scared to you? And *she* didn't have one word to say through the whole thing." She shook her head. "They're a strange pair. He never did tell me how he knew that Gale was living here. The night he came over, he was so polite, but he didn't explain anything. I thought he might have found out from Gale's boss, but now I'm not so sure."

"If he was so polite," Michael said, "what was this reference to your having assaulted him?"

She looked uncomfortable. "That came later. When he tried to force Gale to leave. It was getting rough, and I guess I threw the telephone receiver at him and hit him with it, I don't know. It was dark. Somehow the lamp got knocked over and broke . . ."

"What happened after that?"

"I told him to get out, and he did. I thought about phoning the police, but Gale asked me not to. I know I probably should have." She looked up. "That was a mistake, wasn't it? Now it's like the whole thing never happened."

"Not exactly. There's his version of it."

"I don't understand why they won't let me see him. What do they think? That I'll corrupt him in some way? Are they afraid that I might smuggle something in to help him escape? They're probably right. I would do that if I could."

For a moment he felt vaguely annoyed, burdened by his affection for her.

"What I want to do," he said, "is have a look around his room. Just to see if there might be something we could use."

Immediately she stood up and moved toward the stairway. He followed her, and they passed her own bedroom, on the left of the hallway—airy and bright, papered in a soft, pale-green floral pattern, with white curtains at the windows. Gale's room, on the right, was done in a tailored gray-and-brown stripe. Bright rag rugs scattered on the floor. The woodwork had been stripped, but not refinished.

"I did everything ass-backward in here," she said. "I should have done the woodwork first, but I was in too much of a hurry. Now who knows if I'll ever get around to it."

He stood at the window and raised the shade. Directly across the street was a brick bungalow, with a lawn of green velvet that looked as if it had been trimmed with manicuring scissors. Spires of tall cedars standing at attention on either side of the front porch. He wondered how the neighbors felt about the dandelions in her yard and the ladder propped against the side of the house. He supposed they were used to it; the former owners had not been model caretakers either.

The room was furnished with a bed, a desk, and a dresser; above the desk was a narrow shelf jammed with paperbacks. Everything neat and orderly. He went to the closet, opened it, glanced inside: two pairs of cords, a navy windbreaker, three short-sleeved shirts, all hanging neatly. On the shelf above, a Kodak Instamatic camera, two rolls of unexposed film, and a half dozen record albums. Nothing more.

He went through the dresser drawers: undershirts, shorts, socks, and handkerchiefs, each in its own place, carefully folded. Two sweaters—one brown, one blue; a gray sweatshirt with a hood, DONDERO HIGH SCHOOL in blue letters across the front.

In the middle drawer he found a bankbook in its plastic sheath. He slipped it out and glanced through it: five entries, all deposits, all at two-week intervals dating from March 15. Total: $217.26. A small spiral notebook beneath it held the record of his weekly expenditures.

He read page 1:

Sat. Mar. 15

Wallet	$9.50
Sweater	$25.00
C.H.	$20.00
Misc.	$5.00

Flipping through the pages, he found the last entry, dated Saturday, May 10.

Grateful Dead album	$8.00
Watch	$16.00
Books	$8.00
C.H.	$20.00
Misc.	$7.00

He marveled at the organization, the tight controlled handwriting. Cat was reading over his shoulder. He looked up at her.

"Well, he's neat. 'C.H.' Is that you?"

"Room and board. It was his idea. I think it made him feel as if he was on his own."

Together they went through the desk drawers. Nothing much there, either: an envelope with his pay stubs from the hardware store, some school notebooks, several folders, each one a different color, labeled for each of his classes: History. English. Geometry. Physical Science. Test papers, compositions, and study sheets, all carefully filed away.

"I think what we should do is try to find his brother," she said.

"What brother?"

"He's older. He left home when Gale was eleven. For a while nobody knew where he was, but it turned out he had joined the Navy. If we could find him, maybe they would let him live there. They do that sometimes, don't they?"

"Sometimes."

She went to the window, looking out at the driveway across the street, where a tall, skinny redhead was bouncing a basketball. It made a hollow, ringing sound against the cement.

"I like that kid," she said. "Bob Schmidt. They're such a nice family. I kept trying to get him to go over and make friends, but he wouldn't do it. Really, he's very shy. He's only got one friend that I know of up at school—a boy named Brian MacKay. At least, it's the only name I've ever heard him mention." She turned to look at him.

"I asked him to write out a list of the people he knows," Michael said. He put a hand to his jaw, rubbed it gently.

"How are you feeling?" she asked.

"Okay, so far." The gum felt tender to his touch. His filled tooth tasted faintly metallic.

"It's all right if you eat, isn't it? I'll fix you something. It's the least I can do . . ." She touched the collar of her shirt, looking back toward the window. "This whole thing is such a mess, isn't it? I guess it was a mistake, letting him move in with me like that. What do you think will happen now?"

"It's hard to tell," he said. "There are a number of options. It's not all that cut-and-dried. A judge might decide to send him away for a while, to one of the six-week or twelve-week or six-month programs. Or they could just have him go home."

"That would never work," she said flatly.

He said nothing, did not bother to tell her it could be worse: they could keep him anywhere they wanted to until he was nineteen, if they chose.

"Are those the only choices?" she asked.

"There's foster care," he said. "But they mostly use that for younger kids. Nobody much wants somebody else's sixteen-year-old problem. It's too risky." He got up and went to the window, stood next to her. "He's pretty tough, Cat. You don't need to worry about him."

"He's not tough," she said. "It's all an act."

Looking down at her, he was struck by the similarities between this boy and Cat—the same fair hair, blue eyes, and delicate features; the same thin, long-waisted frame; she could pass for his mother easily.

"I knew it wasn't the best plan," she murmured. "But you go along thinking any day the right answer will come to you, any day you'll figure out the perfect thing to do. I know how this must look to people, his living here . . ."

"People," Michael said. "Who?"

But he already knew the answer to that one. Alex. The Good Doctor. How it must look to Alex.

The only time he had met him was at the joint meeting to go over the fine points of the settlement. That had been enough. A dazzling smile; even, white teeth; eyes the color of smoked oysters. "Glad you're looking out for her, Counselor," he had said. "Doing a great job." His patients were crazy about him, Cat confided. A man thoroughly convinced of his own superiority, out to romance the world. The type you hate to lose to in tennis; he'd be the guy to call out "Nice *shot!*" as he smashed one into the ground in front of you.

When the meeting was finally over, she had been on the edge of tears, wandering about his office, stopping to pick up the photographs of Natalie and Daniel from his desk.

"He was nice about the house, wasn't he? Letting me have it without a fight."

He said nothing, offering her a cigarette.

"No, thanks, I quit last week."

"Jesus," he said, "you *are* a masochist, aren't you?"

At that she began to cry in earnest, fumbling in her purse for a handkerchief, waving off his apology.

"No, it's not your fault. I do this all the time at home." She blew her nose violently. "It makes me feel better for a minute, but then you can't keep this up indefinitely, can you?"

"It will pass," he said. "Take my word."

But she only shook her head. "Oh, how do you know? I've felt like this for months. I think I have an infinite capacity for feeling like this."

He had offered then to take her to lunch, but she had refused. "I don't want to go out with you and drink, and then get sappy."

"What d'you mean?"

"Sloppy. Dopey. I'd get drunk and then make you listen to the sad story of my life."

"I wouldn't mind."

Again she shook her head. "No, you've had to listen to enough of it already. It's just . . . from holding everything in. My stomach hurts, and my back . . . I wanted to scream at him to just keep his damned house and his lake property in Charlevoix and the stupid municipal bonds. I don't need any of it."

"I'm glad you didn't do that."

She shrugged her shoulders, smiling faintly. "It doesn't matter. Whatever I do, it's exactly what he expects of me."

He wanted to warn her then, and now—but about what? One evening not too long ago they were on their way out the door, and he noticed that she did not lock it. He started to say something to her, then thought better of it. He really did not want to be responsible for all the times she left it unlocked when she was not with him.

5

*H*e stopped in the office on his way to the courthouse. Bill was there, talking on the phone. Fran, his secretary, smiled up at him. "A couple of messages. I put them on your desk."

"Thanks."

He flipped through his mail and checked his telephone pad. Nothing urgent. Good. Sitting down at the desk, he could feel the morning sun on his back as it streamed in through the blinds.

He picked up the file in front of him, leafed through it. *Novak v. Ames.* Christ, what was it with everybody these days? Was it in the air or the water or what? A weird business, this solving of every human problem through legal channels. The New Religion. Complete with ministers, rituals, relics, and holy documents. Lately he felt himself becoming more suspicious and cynical about his profession. It was not just knowing too much about the sleazy, manipulative side of it. But more and more he could not see himself with this mantle of priest about his shoulders. He didn't know enough; worse, didn't care enough. About a handful of people, yes, but not the bleeding multitudes; there were just too damned many of them.

Bill couldn't understand his disillusionment.

"They want reassurance, that's all. Somebody to tell them publicly that they're right."

"Who's to say who's right?"

"Look. People take themselves to doctors every year for checkups. Even if they feel okay, they just want to hear it from somebody who knows. So what's the difference? Mikey, you need something to worry about; do it about radiation impact or whispers in space. Let the job alone."

But it was hard for him to do. He made a note on the file folder: *Call Alan Novak.*

Bill stuck his head in the doorway. "Gretchen says hi."

"Hi to her, too," Michael said.

"She says she hasn't seen you in months, she's feeling deprived."

"Tell her I'm available."

"Tonight?"

He hedged, saying that he had work to do.

"Sometime soon, then. After Daniel gets here."

"That would be good."

"When do you leave for Washington?"

"End of next week."

"You'll be bringing him back with you?"

He nodded.

"Well, maybe things will slow down a little. So you'll have some time for him. We've got calendar call on Tuesday, don't forget."

"I've got it written down."

"How did it go out at Juvenile?"

"It went all right. Nothing much happened. It was just a preliminary hearing."

"You going to represent him?"

"I think so, yes."

"I don't know, Mikey. That sounds like a crazy piece of business to me."

"You think it's crazier than these two guys?" He flicked at the file folder. "Next-door neighbors suing each other over a garage built two inches over onto someone's property?"

Bill shook his head. "Just remember my advice to you about doctors' wives."

"She's an ex-wife."

"Too late. The pattern has been set. You can't be married to one of those guys for twenty years without having it affect you."

"Jesus, you've got a nerve. What about lawyers?"

"No, not even close. Lawyers are realists. They've seen the worst, so they know what to expect. Doctors believe in the gods. They believe in their own mystical powers. It makes them loony, and, by association, all those who come into contact with them. Take care. That's all I'm saying." He sat down on the edge of the desk. "Come over and have dinner tonight. No dishes afterward, no lectures, I swear."

"Like hell, no lectures."

They both laughed.

"All right, but only one or two."

"Next week," he promised, as Bill nodded and left the room.

He thought about the long evenings after the divorce, when Bill and Gretchen had helped him through—listening and advising, soothing him, taking care of him. It was at their house, drinking their Scotch, that he had come up with what he considered his most profound statement concerning marriage—that it was tough to sustain a meaningful relationship with someone over a long period of time. A certain irony there that he was trying to capture, but Gretchen had failed to see the humor in it.

A sweetly serious woman, she was determined to solve his problems. He had learned a lot about her in those months. About their marriage, also. They never seemed to argue about anything, as though they were completely in tune with each other's thoughts. Yet, at the same time, they allowed each other a lot of freedom. They had eloped when Bill was in law school, had had four children in the first six years. Robin, their oldest, born with a hole in her heart, had been the source of much pain and anxiety until, when she was ten, the final repairs had been made. Now she was a healthy eighteen-year-old, into every activity you could name. Bill Jr., while riding his bike to school one day, was hit by a car and ended up in the orthopedic ward at Beaumont Hospital for six months. Gretchen had gone back to work, and her widowed mother had moved in with them to help take care of the kids. Through all of it, they got closer; the marriage grew stronger. Michael noticed that they still held hands at the movies, that they sat near each other at parties and listened to each other's stories as if they were really interested. Maybe that was the secret: a marriage had to have challenge. Maybe when things were too easy, you just got bored.

"It's dull, Michael. Everything's so comfortable. There's nothing new here, nothing more to find out." As if it were a course they had been taking together and Joy had elected to drop it. For a time he had taken a perverse pleasure in blaming himself. He had been stupid, asleep at the switch; hadn't bothered to notice her growing restlessness. Then he began to indulge in all manner of morbid fantasies of deception and betrayal, of deliberate setups designed to make him miss the chance of being a Good Guy. She wanted out; that was that. So she had to see things wrecked in order to justify it. At last he had settled on the fact that eleven years was a respectable length of time, nearly a full-term marriage by today's standards, and you did not have to view the whole thing as a failure because it ended in divorce.

Another bonus: they had parted as friends. No one took sides, and they were each welcomed separately into all the homes that they used to visit together. So it was that relationships folded. If there was no right or wrong to it, there was still the need to survive, and there were no easy roads to peace of mind. All you could do was try not to push any of the suffering off onto others—your kids, or your friends.

When she called last May, asking him to meet her in town for lunch, he had known instantly that there was bad news coming. He had gotten there early; fortified himself with a Scotch-and-water; listened politely through the speech, while making wet circles on the marble top with his glass. He told himself that he should have expected it: Ed's business was such that relocation was almost inevitable. Up to that point the roughest thing had been picking the kids up at the house on weekends, having to be pleasant when all he felt was bruised and diminished. He saw in an instant that things were about to get much rougher.

Looking tanned in her white sleeveless dress, her hair swept up off her neck, she talked to him in that low, measured voice he had always liked: "I'm sorry, Michael, I feel awful about this, but what can I do?"

"You can tell him not to take the promotion," he said. "You can move to Washington and leave the kids with me."

A silence, while he stared at the clock on the wall behind her. Its hands were stopped at ten past five, had been anchored there for years. A favorite restaurant during their courtship days. Why here? Why a public place, for that matter? Did she think it safer, he would be less likely to make a scene? No, not that; she knew him better than that. It was one of the things that had ultimately condemned him: he was a scene avoider, emotionally dull.

"I knew you'd do that," she said quietly. "I knew you would find some way to take it personally."

He laughed. "What the hell does that mean? Is there some other way for me to take it?"

"You're trying to make me out the villain in this, and it's not my fault. I'm the one who's in the middle." Her gray eyes looked hurt. "You know you can have them any time. Give me one day's notice, I'll put them on a plane. For as long as you like, whenever you like."

He had nodded, glancing toward the wide windows set like a blank screen in front of him, the blinding sunlight beyond.

"What do the kids think about it?"

"Well, they're excited about living in a different part of the country." She was picking her words carefully. "Of course, they feel terrible about leaving you."

"And their friends?"

"They'll make new ones."

"What about school? And the neighborhood?"

"They're not upset about that. They're looking forward to something new."

"How long have they known?"

"About the move? Not long—why?"

"Since before Sunday?" Wanting to explore the depths of this betrayal—his kids carrying the knowledge of it on their last visit with him.

"You know," she said, "you might try being happy for them. That they're getting a chance to broaden their experience a little."

"You want it both ways, don't you? You want to do this thing to me, yet, at the same time, you expect me to just smile and bless the whole deal for you."

"No, I don't expect that," she said wearily, and he had read in her face the desire to be finished with it.

My life is falling apart. He had tried it out as he left the restaurant, but even as the words dropped into his mind he rejected them. Too dramatic. The voice she had used was one she usually reserved for reasoning with the kids—all patience and kindness. And she was right. It was nobody's fault, after all. Wasn't Ed just doing his job? Trying to provide as well as possible for this ready-made family of his?

So, in the end, you accepted things. Because what other choice did you have?

Bill's head appeared once again in the doorway. "What did I just get through saying about these medicine men? They are ruthless characters, I tell you. They're bloodthirsty. There is no profession that lives in greater mortal terror of being ripped off. I just had a call from our Dr. McClintock. Remember him? Plastic surgeon. Heavy bucks. Now he wants us to hire a private detective and put a tail on his wife. That's the word he used. *Tail.* My God, I hear these things, but I don't believe them."

"So, what did you tell him?"

"I said we don't do that kind of thing. So of course I am now the certified badass. Old Man River who doesn't give a damn about his problems." He laughed. "You know, sometimes I wonder how I manage to keep my innocence."

"You just said it. You hear things, only you don't believe them."

"Right." He stepped inside. "Look, I don't want to belabor this point about your friend—"

"Then why are you?" Michael grinned at him, stretching, leaning back in the chair.

"I just keep wondering about her. What her angle is. I mean, first she buys this little bungalow over in Royal Oak, and now she's taking kids in off the street."

"One kid, Bill. It's not as though she's opening a home for wayward boys."

"Well, it's suspect. She ought to be hitting these wild weekend parties, telling people it's the first day of the rest of her life."

"Uh uh. Not her style."

"No? And what's yours, then?"

"What does that mean?"

"It means, what are you doing this weekend? For entertainment."

"I'm not sure. Why?"

"You have any idea how long it's been since you've been sure?"

Michael laughed. "You worrying about my love life again?"

"Well, somebody better do it. You act like you're asleep."

"I'm not asleep. Quit worrying."

But after Bill had left he sat staring into space at his desk, wishing he did not feel so much to blame for all the things that had gone wrong in his life. He had sworn he would not end up hating Joy in order to survive the divorce. And he did not, but it wasn't easy. Off-center, she had said about the marriage. Well, he hoped that things were better with Ed. No. What a lie. He hoped just the opposite.

As for Detroit, he could never hate this city, it was his place. But something had gone out of it the day his kids had left. He could not seem to get it back.

6

"What I don't get," Michael said, lighting a cigarette, "is why. I mean, after four months he suddenly decides to go after you. It can't be that he didn't know where you were all this time. He could have found out."

"He knew where I was," Gale said. "Since March, anyway. Maybe before."

"How do you know?"

"Because. My mother . . . she called me at work. In March."

"That's news. Why didn't you tell me? What did she want?"

He shrugged. "Me to come home, I guess."

"What did you say to her?"

"I told her no."

"Does Cat know about this?"

He shook his head.

"You didn't think to tell her? You didn't think she'd be interested, or what?"

No answer. The blue eyes stared coolly back at him. *You figure it out.* Sighing, he pushed his briefcase aside to reach for the ashtray. Gale sat across from him, legs outstretched, ankles crossed, hands shoved into his back pockets. He wore a faded blue T-shirt, stretched out at the neck; blue jeans; white cotton socks; no shoes. None of the kids here wore shoes, he noticed. To discourage the runaways, no doubt. Still, it was hard to imagine anyone escaping from this building, the security was so tight; the guard sat in his glass-enclosed cubicle checking each pass carefully before he pressed the button that activated the heavy metal doors. Even the air inside seemed heavy and hard to breathe, as if the whole place were underwater.

"Did you make a list of names?"

He stood and pulled out a crumpled piece of paper from his back pocket, tossed it on the table. Michael picked it up.

"Who's Mr. Davis?"

"A guy who lives down the street from her. I shoveled his walk a few times."

"Mr. Kearney?"

"My math teacher."

Five names in all, including Cat, Dave Cornelius, and Wiley, from the hardware store. Jesus, this couldn't be it; this was nothing.

"What about your friends?"

"What about them?"

Michael sighed. "Come on, Gale."

"I don't have any friends. I told you that."

"What about this kid Cat mentioned to me? Brian MacKay?"

"Forget him. He's got problems of his own."

"We've all got problems of our own," Michael said dryly. "And what about your brother? Why isn't he on here?"

"My brother." He laughed. "I don't even know where he is."

"That's all right. We'll find him."

"You won't. He joined the Navy. About five years ago. Nobody knows what happened to him. He's probably in New Zealand by now."

Michael took out his pen. "What's his name?"

"Kevin. Don't bother. It's a waste of time, putting him down."

He wrote the name on the paper. "Any other relatives?"

"No. None. There was only my grandmother. But she died."

"When was that?"

"A long time ago."

"How long?"

He shrugged. "Six or seven years."

"Where were you living then? Here?"

"No. In Flint."

It reminded him of the first time they had met, up in his bedroom at Cat's house, months ago. Michael had asked the usual questions, making casual conversation, or so he thought—How did he like Dondero High? What classes was he taking? The message he had gotten was that this was not information you simply gave away to strangers on the street.

"It would help if you talked to me a little bit about this stuff."

"I am talking to you," Gale said.

He got up and went to the window, leaning his back against it with his hands behind him. Like the others, it was heavily screened and whitewashed over. Michael wondered what it was out there that had proved so subversive it had to be painted out. He couldn't understand the purpose of treating these openings like architectural mistakes; this world was narrow enough. By his calculations, the hall they were in ran parallel to the parking lot. Beyond it was a row of flower beds edged with spiky red blooms; some golden foliage rising over the flowers, like wheat. A harmless view.

The boy stood looking at him. The issued clothing did not fit—the jeans too short and too tight in the crotch; the shapeless T-shirt hung from his shoulders.

The bitten-down fingernails made him think of Daniel, and he was reminded of an incident, years ago, when his son had pulled the fire-alarm bell at school. It had touched off a full-scale drill, with the building being evacuated: two hook-and-ladder trucks plus the fire chief showing up to answer the emergency.

Everyone knew that it had been six-year-old Daniel Atwood, on his way back from the boys' lavatory, who had done it. But

Daniel, terrified into silence, was unable to admit it. And so to Michael had fallen the task of breaking him down. Afterward, Joy had told him grimly, "Well, you sure are in the right business."

"What does that mean?"

"He's a curious kid. He saw this big red handle and he pulled it. What's so terrible about that?"

"That isn't the point," he said. "The point is, he needs to learn the value of telling the truth, of owning up to things when he's in the wrong."

"So you grill him like he's a common criminal."

"Would it be better for him to carry the secret around with him for the rest of his life? That's more punishment than he deserves. I think this was best."

"You love knowing what's best for people, don't you?"

As a matter of fact, he had hated it. The confession had been a long time coming, and had turned into a painful, tearful scene at the end. He had often prayed that it was not etched in Daniel's memory as deeply as it was in his own.

No danger of that, here; this kid was not a crier, he could tell.

"Tell me why you ran away all those times," he said.

"I got sick of it," Gale said. "He thinks he's God. He can make you do anything he wants."

"So you just left. And you didn't think to take anything with you. You didn't stop to figure out how you would pay for food, or a bus ticket, or a place to stay."

"That's right. I didn't do any of that stuff he says."

"Why do you think it's in the petition, then? Right down to the dates the money was taken, the amounts of money, and where it was taken from?"

He made no answer, stared at Michael coldly.

"There has to be a reason, doesn't there?"

"There's a reason. He's trying to jack me around, like always. He's a son-of-a-bitch fucking liar, that's the reason."

"And what about your mother? Is she a liar, too?"

"She's afraid of him. She does what he tells her." He looked down at his hands. "Everybody's afraid of him. Except me. Look, I don't know why he lies, but he does. And people always believe him. You believe him, don't you?"

"I want to believe you, Gale."

"But you don't, right? Maybe you ought to be his lawyer then."

Patience, patience. "The thing is, I don't see much use in trying to make him out the bad guy in this. For the simple reason that it isn't going to work."

"You ask me these questions," Gale said, "and I give you the answers. But you don't like the answers. So what am I supposed to do?"

"You'd better do more than just sit there and deny everything," Michael said calmly, "because I think there are some things you're not telling me."

"Okay. I did it. I did everything, just like he said. Is that what you want?"

"What I want," Michael said, "is for you to quit trying to make me mad."

"Get mad, then. Get lost, go to hell! Look, what does it matter, anyway? They'll believe him. And whatever he wants them to do to me, that's what they're going to do."

"They? Who's they? You make it sound like a conspiracy of thousands. How come all these people are out to get you?"

"It doesn't have to be all these people. Just certain ones."

"Like who?"

"Well, it's not exactly going to break your heart if I don't get out of here, now, is it?"

"That doesn't even make sense. Christsake, what do you think I'm doing here, anyway?"

"I don't know what you're doing here. Why don't you leave?"

"Because we're not finished, that's why!"

He reached for the briefcase, and there was a lightning response across the table. The chair flew off to the side suddenly, struck the wall. Gale's fists were raised in front of him, his body tensed. "You don't touch me, man!" he snarled.

Michael stared at him, stunned. His eyes looked wild; there were bright patches of color in his cheeks. How had this happened? Had he caused it? What had he done? He felt confused, his own heart pumping madly inside his chest. They were staring at each other.

"I wasn't going to touch you," he said at last.

"Like hell. I've seen that look before. I know what it means."

"Have you? Maybe it means you ask for it, then."

Abruptly Gale turned away; his arms fell to his sides. Michael reached for his briefcase, zipped it closed. The leather handle felt sticky; the room was suddenly, uncomfortably warm.

"Look, this isn't going to work," Michael said. "I was afraid of that. We'll have to come up with some other plan."

"Forget plans. I don't need a lawyer. I don't need to talk to anybody!"

"Yes, you do. If you want to get out of here, you do. I've got a partner. Maybe you could talk to him."

He said nothing, kept his face turned away. Again Michael got to his feet, slowly this time. He felt weary. "Do it for her, then. She wants to help. Let her think she's helping, okay?"

At that, Gale turned from the window, a closed, fixed expression on his face. "To hell with it. Why should she want to do that?"

"Because she does." He shook his head. "I don't understand you."

"I didn't fuckin' ask you to, man."

CATHERINE

1

She had a martini while she was waiting, sitting on the window seat, with her back against the wall, her feet up. From here she could see the front porch; the paved, curved walk leading up to it; the triangle of flower bed below, filled with red tulips; the driveway.

The front lawn looked dry. She had tried to keep it watered, but you couldn't water enough in weather like this. The grass was thin-bladed, a dark metallic green. She had shoved a garden-fork into the ground, propping the nozzle of the hose through its handle, in lieu of a sprinkler. An old invention of her father's. Not very efficient. But it reminded her of him and of the times she had worked with him in the tiny plot of garden behind the house on Indiana Street. He loved flowers and knew how to care for them. She had been fascinated when she was young; she hoped she would remember all that he had taught her.

Her father. Gone for nearly ten years now; yet something would happen, some pinpoint of memory, and she would know that she never really believed in his death—it was only that he had moved away to some spot too remote for her to visit. All the same, she had seen to the details of the funeral for Rita, her step-mother, who had been crippled with grief and nearly unable to function. Rita had sat on the couch with her hands folded in her lap, shaking her head and saying to everyone who would listen, "Martin didn't mean for this to happen, I know it! He was tough, he meant to lick it!" And didn't she know it, too? For he had out-lived her mother by some seven years, in spite of the sickness that breathed on him and held him down, robbing him of the strength to do the work he wanted to do. A photograph that she had of her mother, her father, and herself showed a young man in shirt-sleeves and vest, laughing and handsome; a serious comely girl beside him, with a baby on her lap. The girl looked wistful, as if already aware of what was ahead; the baby had worried eyes, holding in them the shadow of the person she would someday become.

She dropped her head on her arms, pressing the cool glass to her temple. No good thinking about this. Years ago, at her step-mother's house, she had locked herself in the bathroom, read *Tess of the D'Urbervilles* to keep from thinking and to escape the tear-ful discussions that were a part of the funeral ritual. Here in her own house she didn't have to do that.

She raised her head at the sound of a car turning into the drive-way: Michael, at last. She stood and met him at the door. Step-ping inside, he smiled at her, sniffed the air.

"What's burning?"

"The roast. Never mind. It's already too late. I put it on and went out and forgot about it."

Taking off his jacket, he tossed it on the window seat, looked around the room.

"Where are the bookshelves?"

"I took them down. They were awful, don't you remember?"

"What'd you do with the wood?"

"Stacked it in the basement. I'll do something with it later on."

"Didn't you have enough things going, or what?"

"It helps me to relax. Otherwise, I'd just sit around wringing my hands. How was your day?" she asked.

"Not so great. How about you?"

"I went to see Mr. Wiley, to tell him why Gale was missing work. I told him everything. I asked if he'd help."

"And?"

She shook her head. "He doesn't get involved with his employees, their personal lives, period. There didn't seem to be any point in arguing. He was very firm. Then I went to see Brian MacKay to ask if he would come and be a witness at the hearing." She leaned her head back against the cushions, closing her eyes. "He finally figured out who I must be talking about. There was this kid in his geometry class who sat in the back of the room and never said a word to anyone. He thought maybe his name was Gale."

"It's not important," Michael said. "Witnesses aren't going to be that important."

"God, I can't think straight. It's so hot. I wish it would rain." She pulled the scarf from her hair. "I feel so distracted. People call on the telephone, and while they're talking to me, I forget what the call is about."

"Who's calling?"

"Oh, Gwen. My boss from the gallery. And Dave Cornelius. And Alex. Through it all, I'm cooking this roast. On a day like this. I must be crazy."

"What did he want?"

"Who?"

"Alex. You said he called."

She shook her head. "He just calls to check on me, I think. To see if I'm still here. This time he asked about Chris. Wanting to know if I'd heard from her lately. When she's getting home." She got up and went out to the kitchen. Michael came with her. The remains of the burned roast lay in the sink, where she'd left them. She bundled it up and tossed it into the garbage. "I'll make you a drink. Scotch or gin?"

"I'll have what you're having."

He smiled at her. Such nice eyes, she thought. Dark brown, with thick, heavy brows and long lashes. A nice smile, too. She loved the gentle look he had; she'd noticed it the first time they met. Just his calm voice talking to her in his office about the divorce had given it a sense of legitimacy, had lessened the terror of it. He had talked to her about investments and securities, about money management—the practical aspects. About living alone, and how you eventually got used to it.

She liked the look of his body, too—long legs and broad shoulders—and how he moved. He was graceful for a man who was so tall.

She went to the refrigerator, taking out lettuce, tomatoes, mushrooms, Greek olives, feta cheese. Swiftly she tore the lettuce into a wooden bowl.

"Can I do something?"

"No, that's all right. Well, you could set things up out on the porch."

When she was finished with the salad, she carried it out to the glass-topped table. From the screened-in porch you could look out into the yard and see the lilacs along the fence. They were nearly finished, their lacy white blooms tinged with brown. By next week, only the heart-shaped leaves would remain.

"I need some suggestions," he said. "For a birthday present for a ten-year-old."

"Your daughter?"

He nodded. "I'd like to give her something spectacular this year. Something that will knock her out."

"That shouldn't be too tough. Girls that age aren't hard to please. Anyway, she'll like whatever you give her, I'll bet."

"You think?"

"Sure. It's the thought that counts."

He laughed. "Good. I'll just tell her what I was thinking. Natalie, I thought I'd give you a trip to Europe."

He leaned back in his chair, smiling at her. She glanced into the corner where the cartons of books from the living room were piled for temporary storage. She had pictured in her mind two medical bookcases, one on either side of the mantel, with their glass doors shining in the light from the fire.

"Sometime I want to go up to the Irish Hills and look through some antique stores," she said. "Gale and I were going to do that together. Try to find some bookcases."

"You really are a worker, aren't you? You take on these projects and you never worry about whether you'll ever finish them—"

"What? Of course I'll finish them. Why wouldn't I?" She laughed. "That's what I like about having my own personal lawyer around. Ask his opinion on any topic and he'll give it, whether he has the least idea what he's talking about or not."

She cleared the salad bowls from the table, sat down again across from him. "I wanted to ask you if you've talked to anyone else about my getting into Juvenile. To see him."

"I did." He shook his head. "No deal."

"I wrote him a letter. That's allowed, isn't it? They'll let me do that?"

"Sure."

"Did you talk to him today? How was he?"

"He was all right."

"Did he seem depressed?"

"Not that I noticed."

Going to the desk in the hall, she picked up the note she'd written. She handed it to him, and he slipped it into his shirt pocket. "The more I think about it," she said, "the more I think we have to find his brother. He's twenty-three now. That's old enough to be the responsible party, isn't it? He could be his guardian."

"That depends," Michael said.

"On what?"

"On what he happens to be doing. Say, if he's a ski bum out in Colorado, or if he's dealing on some street corner in Cleveland—"

"No, he won't be. He'll be living in Saginaw or Midland. He'll have a job and his own apartment."

He smiled at her. "How do you know that?"

"It's just a feeling I have. I feel as if it's all settled. They were very close. Gale talked about Kevin a lot this winter, while we were working together. Steaming wallpaper off the bedroom walls. That's a soul-searching operation, you know. Peeling back. Uncovering things."

"Sounds pretty cosmic."

"How do we go about locating him?" she asked.

"I'll call the Naval Recruiting Office and find out where he was last stationed. Get an address. We'll go from there."

"I remember his telling me about a couple of Kevin's friends who might know something. Did you ask him about that?"

"No." Michael set his drink down on the table. "We didn't get that far today. The truth is, I'm having a hell of a lot of trouble talking to him about anything."

She leaned back in her chair. "It's hard for him to trust people, Michael. Even Dave Cornelius told me that. He said that he has to keep proving himself to Gale over and over."

"There's not a lot of time for that," Michael said.

She looked away. "Maybe you come on too strong. Maybe he feels threatened."

"Maybe."

"If you'll just be patient with him, I know he'll calm down."

"He's calm enough. That's not it. The problem is that I don't think he's telling me the truth."

"About what?"

"Mainly about the money. It doesn't make any sense to me that he'd run away without giving any thought to it. He's too smart for that."

"You think he planned it ahead of time? Taking the money and then running away?"

"Oh, hell, it's the third time in a year. What do you think?"

"What does he say about it?"

Michael shrugged. "Not much. He's decided to stonewall it. If I don't believe him, that's tough."

She was silent a moment, staring through the screen into the greenish darkness. It was moving in slowly, pushing the light to the back of the yard.

"He's afraid of men," she said, "so he puts on his act. He's the big, tough guy. Is that so hard to understand?"

He said nothing, leaning forward to put out his cigarette.

"If he won't admit to having done anything wrong, we're going to have trouble when we get to court. These guys see nothing but families in trouble all day long. They see parents trying to teach right and wrong and not having any luck, so they do the only thing they know, which is punish. When it doesn't work, they punish harder. They don't know what the hell else to do."

"That isn't what's happening here, Michael. It's not that simple."

"All right. Say you're right. The problem is, he has this all worked out in his mind. It's a big conspiracy. I'm part of it. I don't see how I can help him when he believes that."

"He doesn't believe that. He just says things. You have to get beyond the things he says sometimes."

"But you also have to go into court with facts. Not with what some kid wishes were true. Or what he thinks he can con people into believing."

"He doesn't con people, Michael."

"No? He conned you pretty well, didn't he? He and Brian MacKay are big buddies, he could move right in, if only the old man wasn't on the sauce. Isn't that what he told you?"

"Don't you think I know exactly why he said that? I don't give a damn about that kind of lying."

"What kind? Lying is lying. If he lies about this . . . Jesus, I don't get it. It's so self-defeating. The judge is going to know it, the same as I do." He stood up. "His whole attitude is self-defeating. I wonder whether he really wants to get out of there at all. He acts as if he's more concerned with getting even."

"Maybe he is," she said. "That doesn't seem so strange to me. I think maybe it's just human."

In the silence, a fluttering scraping sound: some insect frantically beating its wings against the screen, trying to get in.

Michael said, "He doesn't trust me, Cat. There's nothing I can do about it. I asked Bill to take over for me today."

"Michael, you didn't!" She made a move to rise, sat back in her chair.

"It will work out better for everybody this way."

"It won't. Bill doesn't even know him. What does he care about what happens to him?"

He sighed. "I was hoping I could explain it, so that you wouldn't be upset."

No doubt. Well, this was what you got when you picked a lawyer out of the Yellow Pages—someone who told you: Be reasonable, be sensible, don't get upset. An old argument. She would not be moved by it anymore. What had it ever done for her? She got up from the table without a word, began carrying dishes out to the kitchen. Michael followed her.

"I haven't given up on this," he said carefully. "I'm not trying to get out of anything. I'm simply telling you what I think. You don't know much about this kid—"

"I know enough. For some reason you want to see him as this shifty-eyed character who's full of lies and tricks."

"It's got nothing to do with what I want to see." The voice a shade too patient. Fatal mistake.

"Why don't you send me the bill for your time so far?" she asked coldly. "I'll try to find someone else to do the rest."

For a moment he stood there. Then he set his glass down on the counter. Turning, he started down the hall. She shut off the water and dried her hands on a towel, moving automatically, not thinking about anything.

By the time she reached the living room, he was picking up his jacket. She heard the sound of tearing cloth. He had caught the sleeve on the unnailed edge of the window seat. He jerked it free.

"I've had a lousy day," he said. "I think I'll just go on home."

He was looking at her. She said nothing. *Go, then, and be damned.*

He pointed toward the window seat. "You might think about having that thing fixed." The screen door slammed behind him, and she watched from the doorway as his car backed down the drive. She held herself still, fought the urge to go after him. And say what? To hell with him. To hell with his reasonable soul.

What did he know about lying, anyway? Everyone lied—with what they chose to remember and what they let go. You lied every day—with words, gestures: kind lies to keep from hurting people. Lies to let them keep on believing what they would, in any case, believe. Her father was that kind of liar. A dreamer, a wishful thinker. A liar on paper, too, with his gentle and tranquil landscapes; those renderings in pale, soft colors that did not exist except in the eye of the mind.

Oh, Gale, you didn't have to lie to me, though. Not about Brian, or any of it. I would never have held you to it. I would never have kicked you out. It would have been like kicking myself out.

2

*A*fter the divorce the world had suddenly been filled with people she couldn't believe in. Like characters in some pointless play, they performed; each morning she had to read about them in the paper: STREET GANG MURDERS NEWSBOY FOR COLLECTIONS. MAN RAPES TEN-YEAR-OLD DAUGHTER. SNIPER KILLS THREE ON DETROIT FREEWAY. Fanatics, murderers, initiators of crisis; their actions bizarre, stemming from motivations so obscure that you had to doubt their reality; yet they existed. In fact, their numbers were increasing daily, and not just here in the city but all over the world. Everywhere she looked all was hatred, violence, evil.

And what was she, Catherine Elizabeth Holzman, doing about it? Nothing. Nothing at all.

Sitting day after day in her ten-room English Tudor in Bloomfield Hills. Drifting, blotting everything out with Valium and liquor; that was her style. Lucky thing her daughter, Chris, was not around to witness this disintegration. She was in Europe, traveling, taking a year off from school at her father's suggestion.

"There's so much to see, Mother. Taking art courses at school is one thing, but this will mean so much more."

No doubt. Still, she knew the real reason for the trip was not so much that Chris would broaden her education as that her mother would learn to cope. She was becoming too dependent upon her daughter, Alex had told her. She should not rely on Chris to protect her from the world or insulate her from her own thoughts. Of course he was right about that. Yet there was this great black lake of time that had to be crossed. All the while you knew it was hopeless, you would never make it; but what else could you do? You had to keep swimming; you could not drown, either.

Purity of spirit, she decided, was what she was missing. What right had she to this sheltered existence? None whatever. She hadn't earned it, not through physical effort or any personal goodness. In fact, she was a timid, shallow person, living exclusively for herself, suspicious of clubs and causes. She had never joined the Junior League, or NOW, or the League of Women Voters; had never been in on the Mother's March, or canvassed for the United Fund; and years ago, when she had been a Gray Lady at the hospital, she had quit when she was transferred to the Volunteers' Committee. All these things she couldn't do because she couldn't bear to ask people for things—not money or time, not even opinions.

Well, she had laid up precious little treasure in heaven, lived the whole of her life as a freeloader. And you could not expect to take from the world indefinitely, standing by while others did for you. Sooner or later it was bound to catch up with you.

Perhaps this was the punishment: that her life would simply fold in around her, smother her inside this beautiful house with its elegant, expensive furnishings. She felt as hollow and useless as the huge foyer, with its black and white marble floor, its gilt mirror hanging opposite the stairway. All right, then, she would speed up the process. A terrible injustice had been done, but she would suffer it in silence, would not cry out against it, since no doubt it was the consequence of shallow, parasitical living. Now she would let the laundry pile up, let the dishes and the house-work go until it was beyond the doing. That way she would help the disintegration along. And she would not allow anyone in to view the decline.

Her friends, being too polite to intrude, accepted her absence as temporary and necessary. This was the way you handled divorce in suburbia: a brief and private mourning, followed by the awakening of the New You. She let them think that was what was going on. When anyone called, she spoke firmly into the phone about her plans: she would sell the house, she was going back to school, or she might be taking a job, or a trip, or a lover. When? Any day now. This to forestall scolding or advice. Friends love to advise, she already knew, on anything from finance, to travel plans, to a personal philosophy. In spite of her cheerful act, they would insist on saying things like, "You have a whole new life ahead of you," or, "I envy you, Cat, being able to find out who you really are." Embarrassing banalities. They offended her; at the same time, she felt humiliated by them.

It went on like this for months—people trying to reach her over telephone lines, over miles of houses, highways and trees, over death, even; she could hear barely concealed irritation in her mother's voice—"Cat, for heaven's sake, pull yourself together, start acting like an adult. Stop feeling so sorry for yourself."

In fact, she felt nothing. A numbness: smothering and complete. She could stand at the window for hours, staring out, thinking maybe she'd been wrong, maybe she should think about getting her life off dead-center. Looking for a signal of some kind. There. A cardinal at the feeder. That was something, wasn't it? She would consider doing something physical—taking a long walk, or maybe a drive. She would begin some task, carry through with it to the end. But the answering voice was always so much stronger. *What for?* Well, that was it, then; she would not go crazy with this; she would simply go dead.

She had thought, for a while, about relaxing into true madness—the kind where they put you away and did everything for you—except that her cause was not deserving of such release.

People did go mad, and kill themselves, but it would be over much larger issues than this, and they were nobler people—not petty, whining souls like herself. If her friends knew her, knew the truth, they would stop trying; they would have nothing to do with her; they would run the other way. Because who was she, really? A dreamer, a drinker, a timewaster. Not worthy of their concern.

It was as if a poisonous substance had entered her body and was flowing mysteriously through it, carrying a lethal message to her nerves and muscles; soon it would reach her heart. She linked it with the tarry smell of coffee she left simmering on the stove all day.

How did you move from a position of knowing things were bad but would eventually be all right to a state of total paralysis, in which you felt with unshakable certainty that you would not survive, would not get through the next five minutes?

She tried to read. Nearly all her life she had read for escape, everything she could lay her hands on: newspapers, magazines, bad novels, good novels, billboard signs, cereal boxes. She read all her junk mail, putting words, tons of words, between her and the thing that had happened to her; this was how you managed. Only it did not seem to be working anymore. She would find herself staring off into space and realize that she had been sitting with the magazine open on her lap, for hours, seeing nothing. Her head would ache, her back feel stiff; she would put a hand up to her face, find tears on her cheeks. Jesus, this was ridiculous.

How can there be something wrong with you when the person who knows you best doesn't believe in the thing that's wrong with you? "You can't be depressed," Alex would say. "There's nothing to be depressed about. Anyway, it's self-indulgent and sentimental. You're faking it." Not that he ever really said this, not in words; but she knew it was what he was thinking. Alex was not the self-indulgent type. The nature of existence is problematical; coping is what it's about. A doer, he was, a leader of men. Charge ahead, and be cheerful about it. Whoever said that life was easy?

A cold spring. It had rained for weeks, it seemed—sleety stuff that jabbed and pecked at the windows. The sky was always dark, as if it were perpetually late afternoon. She sat on the couch in the living room reading the weekly letter from Chris, written from London. She had been to the Victoria and Albert, to Parliament, to Dr. Johnson's house in Gough Square. She was meeting great people, loving every minute of it.

Each week Cat wrote back, catching the rhythm of the lines, passing on some cheery, impersonal bits of her own—neighborhood gossip, the weather. So her daughter would not think she was in trouble.

Time passed more quickly when she drank; drinking blurred everything to the soft, dreamy tones of a watercolor, and stilled the punishing voices, for a time. She would sit with a Scotch-and-water before the dining room window, looking out, thinking this was the sensible solution, after all. The important thing was not to impose. Avoid public suffering. Who needed it? Everybody had problems.

Yet she knew what she was doing. And she knew if she kept it up that, eventually, she would disappear. It was what had happened to her father—drinking and drinking until he vanished into the bottle. How many years had it gone on before she figured it out? The trips away from home and her mother's tight-lipped edginess during the time he was gone. Sometimes she would be farmed out to her aunt's house, where she would count the days until she would be allowed to return. Her three wild boy cousins tired her out with their noisy roughhousing from morning until night. She was used to the peace and quiet of her own house, and to her own room, having her own things around her. And she hated the way they would grab her around the waist from behind and swing her into the air, or tug at her hair at the table, or poke a knuckle into her ear; affectionate attacks, but they bruised her dignity. By the time she left, she would be ready to cry from nervousness and overexcitement. Although her mother never told her, she learned to estimate the duration of the trips—anywhere from four to seven days—and she would mark the time on the calendar.

When she got older and realized what they meant, she refused to go to her aunt's; stayed instead with her mother, waiting up each night for the telephone to ring or for his key to sound in the lock. They never spoke about it, and after her mother died and her father married Rita, the same ritual prevailed. She marveled at these women, at their capacity for patience and for denial. Including herself. It seemed to her, though, that, sober, her father was the perfect husband: warm and affectionate; a help around the house; cheerful, funny company. When he was drinking he left the house, stayed away from them.

After her mother died, after she had married Alex, she would hear from her father periodically: "Forgive me for calling at this hour, but it's what I do." Late-night calls when he would apologize and explain: "I didn't make her happy, your mother. I should have got her to leave. But I couldn't. I loved her very much. Sweetie, you know that, don't you?"

"Daddy, where are you? Are you all right?"

"Am I all right? I guess not. I guess if I was I wouldn't be calling, would I?"

He would laugh, a gentle chuckle, urging her to see this for what it was: no big thing. Sometimes during a long and rambling speech, he would suddenly stop: "Are you putting up with me, sweetie? You're a good girl to do that." Then he would hang up, and she wouldn't hear from him again for several months.

After her divorce she finally understood the why of it: If, for whatever reason, your life was unbearable, why not ease the suffering any way you could? Since it was your life, what was the sense of listening to outside advice? Advice was simply another person's plan for you. In the end you were the one who had to live through it.

On this cold spring afternoon, when she found herself staring out at the bare trees and bushes, tightly budded, holding out for sunshine and warmth, she thought suddenly that it was time she did something. So she wiped her eyes and got up from the table, turned on the shower in her bathroom. She took off her clothes, scrubbed herself down, washed her hair. Emerging, she dried and brushed her hair carefully, creamed and powdered herself, dressed in her best lacy underwear. Over it she slipped on a gray wool skirt and a white silk blouse, stepped into her gray suede pumps. She put on rouge and eyeshadow and pale-pink lipstick, at each step surveying herself critically in the mirror. Last, she put on perfume, slipped a long gold chain about her neck. Going downstairs, she made herself another drink and watched the six o'clock news as she polished her nails. Afterward she put on her raincoat, slipped her car keys and wallet into her pocket, and left the house.

It was raining hard as she drove down the street. Gray curtains that would not part. Lights were on all over the neighborhood, cars parked in every driveway. All the men home from work.

As she drove down Long Lake Road toward Woodward, without warning a car pulled out of a side street, nearly cutting her off. On the bumper an orange and black sticker: JESUS IS MY SAVIOR. Good for you, she thought.

She needed to be careful along here. Observe all traffic signs. Pay attention. Don't take chances. She knew she was a little high; it would not do to get stopped by the police.

She drove in under the portico of the Fox and Hounds, leaving her car for the attendant to park. It was early, only a little after seven, and she found a seat at the piano bar, ordered a Scotch on the rocks.

She liked this bar; it was quiet and she could barely make out the shadows of couples as they sat at small tables around the room, even after her eyes had adjusted to the darkness. Gradually the place began to fill up, and she sipped her drink slowly, keeping her eyes down, not inviting conversation.

The piano player must be in his early twenties, she thought: blond hair and a mustache. He wore a white shirt with a black bow tie and a bright-red vest. Silly costume, especially when you saw the rest of it as he stood up to take a break: khakis and tennis shoes. But she liked his husky tenor, and he sang all the songs that she loved: "Angel Eyes," "Laura," "Green Dolphin Street."

She sat sipping her Scotch and listening, thinking to herself, *This is nice, this is pleasant.* A pleasant way to spend an evening, in this dark and comfortable cave, with a big bear of a bartender refilling her drink whenever she asked, otherwise leaving her alone. She held her glass with both hands and looked down when the songs troubled her; when he sang one of her particular favorites, she smiled at him.

They began talking between numbers. He told her that he was twenty-three, married, going to law school during the day. His wife was a nurse who worked nights at St. Joseph's, the hospital where her daughter, Chris, had been born.

They talked about music. He asked her if she had any requests. She shook her head.

"It all sounds fine to me."

She was about to order another drink, thinking it was so peaceful here, so relaxing. She would have to do this more often. She noticed that the piano player was gathering his music together, slipping it into a large envelope. The lights had come on over the bar. They were closing. She looked around in surprise. How had it gotten so late?

"I can't help wondering what you're doing here." The piano player stood up. "I mean . . . a good-looking woman like you. It seems like pretty dull stuff to me. You could drink at home."

She smiled. "I do drink at home. That gets dull, too."

Down at the end of the bar a man in a brown suit was staring at her. Time to leave, she thought. As she rose, he moved toward her. She put on her raincoat, feeling in her pocket for her keys. Where were they? Had she left them with the attendant?

The man in the brown suit came forward, nodded to the piano player. "Everything okay?"

They were conferring about her. The man in the suit was the manager. Now all the lights were on and the waiters were standing around, wiping off tables, collecting ashtrays and glasses. Everyone watching her. Suddenly embarrassed, she moved to the door, pushed it open.

Outside, the air was warm, a thick fog rolling in. Her car stood under the portico, waiting for her. The attendant helped her in.

"Take care," he said, smiling.

She did not answer him. Lord, she was drunk, as drunk as she had ever been. She was lucky they hadn't called someone to come and take her home. She had better drive slowly.

The wonderful thing about being drunk was that it simplified your goals. Never mind worrying what direction your life was taking; concentrate on keeping your car on the road. Well, this would be easy. She hadn't far to go, and she would soon be safely back in her own house. She drove cautiously on the narrow, high-crowned road. Steep gullies rose up to bare blank fields on either side. In the dark, nothing looked familiar. Yet she had traveled this stretch thousands of times. She should be coming to the Telegraph intersection soon; then she would be within a mile of home.

The overhead lights threw strange reflections on the windshield—exotic plants and animals; monsters, too—that frightened her.

Don't get lost. The words came at her out of nowhere, out of the growling, gaping faces that looked in on her. She looked to her left and saw a flat expanse of land strewn with rocks and boulders that were half buried in the ground. How could she possibly be lost? She had been paying attention all the way. Yet she had been driving for more than ten minutes now, and nothing looked familiar. She must have taken a wrong turn. How had she managed that?

She pulled over onto the shoulder, felt the car slide to the right. She must not go into the ditch, must not get caught in the mud out here, drunk and helpless.

Silence in the car; the lack of motion terrified her. Her head was aching and she felt dizzy. She could pass out, or go crazy, or die out here, and who would come to her rescue, who would care, for that matter? No one. No one at all.

She gripped the top of the steering wheel and, in despair, laid her head down on her arms.

After a while, she fumbled in the glove compartment for a Kleenex. All right, enough of that. Nobody was going to come along. Get on with things. Be sensible.

She peered at the instrument panel, trying to read the gas gauge. Her vision blurred. She blew her nose and wiped her eyes, tried to think. She had had to make only two turns, but somehow she had gotten confused. The thing to do was to turn around and go back. Or maybe she should just keep driving in the direction she was going. She was bound to hit an intersection; there would be light to read the street signs; she could get her bearings. If she was not too drunk to figure out what she'd done wrong. She was obviously too drunk to stop and ask questions.

She started the car again, pulled out onto the road, anxiously peering through the windshield. It seemed like hours before she reached the next traffic light. Dequindre and Long Lake. Relief then, as she realized what she had done: merely turned the wrong way on Long Lake Road, gone east instead of west. The road was deserted.

She made a careful U-turn, retracing her route, feeling relief as each intersection appeared: John R., Rochester. Livernois. Crooks. She passed the darkened post office on the right just before she came to Woodward Avenue.

Moments later she was pulling into her own driveway, pressing the remote button on her dash, seeing the garage door open. She let herself in through the kitchen, stopping to get a glass from the cupboard. She turned on the cold water tap, let it run. As she drank, the glass slipped from her fingers, fell into the sink, and broke. She managed to pick up the larger pieces and deposit them in the garbage. She wiped up the slivers with a damp paper towel, being careful not to cut herself.

Upstairs she slid into bed, pulling the covers over her shoulders, turning to read the digital clock on the nightstand. Three-fifteen. Wouldn't her friends be proud of her, Finding Out Who She Really Was at last, Living the Whole New Life? Ah, freedom and adventure.

Well, at least she had figured something out. She knew now what was wrong with her. It wasn't that she had proved herself too weak to carry on, or that she needed more time to go by. What she had to face was that she was finally and completely alone in this, that there was no longer anyone to tell her what to do.

What she would do, she decided the next morning, was take her life and give it a good shake until all the crap fell out. But she would need help to do this.

She went to the Yellow Pages, the way she did for everything. *Psychologists—Psychotherapists.* Dr. Robert Anderson had an office in the Washington Square Building; he was a young man, very brisk and businesslike; he wore thick glasses and had a cigarette habit as bad as her own. She trusted him immediately.

"How long have you been feeling like this?" he asked her.

"Ever since the divorce. No. Before that, really. I've had trouble with depression all my life. It's like a kind of virus. You get attacks and then they go away. You learn to live with it."

"When do you think this one will go away?"

"How do I know? It's got nothing to do with what I think."

"No? It's outside you, then? Where? In the cigarettes? The coffee? What?"

"I don't know. It's beyond my control."

"Who controls it, then?"

She wished that he wouldn't dwell on that part of it. She had not come about the depression, which seemed second nature to her, a numbing gray fog that hung like a cruel judgment over everything. That was not her problem. Her problem, as she saw it, was her inability to make decisions. Should she, for instance, put the house up for sale? It was ridiculous for one person to live alone in a place that size—the upkeep was a drain on her finances.

On the other hand, property values were still going up; it could be a good investment. Yet, with all of the new construction in the area, what if things should suddenly turn around in real estate, become a buyer's market; there she would be with this ten-room monstrosity in Bloomfield Hills on her hands. She didn't know what to do. So she did nothing.

"What do you want to do?"

"If I knew that . . . I keep thinking about it, going over the same ground again and again. I get exhausted just trying to make up my mind."

"That's not thinking. That's avoiding thinking."

"Oh, I don't know what the hell I want to do, and that's the truth of it."

"That is not the truth. The truth is, you can sit around picking at things forever. It is a form of self-torture. It is a way of punishing yourself for wanting. So how come you don't think you have a right to want anything?"

For a while she thought she might have made a mistake. This sort of sparring would not do; it would be of no use to her. But she needed direction in her life; she needed to feel that she was working toward something, so she kept going.

She dreamt one night about an endless street; about herself walking down it slowly, stopping every so often to kneel down and scoop some snow off the ground onto a blue-flowered plate—her mother's plate, she thought. She felt very proud as she did it, balancing the plate carefully on one hand, mounding the snow high and patting it into place. She could see that a stream of cars was driving by, felt people's eyes on her, but she gave them no notice, didn't even turn her head. And suddenly she was in front of her own house on Stonehenge Court, and Alex was standing on the porch. He was furious, shouting at her, "What in hell are you doing?" He came off the porch, pounding toward her across the yard, waving his fist in the air. Modestly she stared down at the plate, at the patches of dried grass before her, scraped clean of snow. She felt at peace, and very pleased with herself. He raised a hand as if to hit her, but she knew that he wouldn't; knew also that he was angry at her because she was naked. As she knelt in front of him, she placed her palms flat against the ground, smiling down at the plate of mounded snow.

"What do you think it means?"

"What do you?"

"Jesus, is this what I'm paying you for? What do I know about dreams? I'm not a psychiatrist."

"You don't have to be."

"Well, he's not a monster, you know. He's a fine man. A wonderful doctor. It would be ridiculous to hate him. It would be childish of me." She shifted in the chair. "I thought about leaving him once. A long time ago. It was right after Chris was born. That was the first time . . . well, the first one I'd heard about, anyway. It had happened with one of the nurses at the hospital. I was going to take Chris and leave him, and let him see if he could still manage to be the great lover and the great doctor if he had to cook his own meals and take care of his own house."

"What happened?"

"I didn't do it."

"Why not?"

"I don't know . . . I just didn't. Of course I was drinking, too. I guess I was sort of crazy by then."

"Always good to have one crazy in the family," Dr. Anderson said. "It takes the pressure off everybody else."

In August she decided to go back to school. Not exactly full-time, but a course in career planning was being offered at Dondero, her old high school in Royal Oak. It was taught by a man named Dave Cornelius, a counselor at the high school. He had red-gold hair and a friendly smile; he reminded her of someone she had known in college: Dana Peters. Dana had been in love with her; had been Alex's rival, although Alex never had known it. Dana had not given her up easily. She had heard from him several times after her marriage. He was moving to New York, opening his own photography studio, marrying a model he had met there, but he would never forget her. His words. How would things have turned out if she had married Dana? Hard to tell.

Twenty women in the class: all widows or newly divorced, all over forty. Everyone trying to figure out what to do with the rest of their lives. Dave was thorough and businesslike, helping each one to assess her talents, find her interests. He encouraged them to investigate the job opportunities around, taught them how to prepare a résumé and how to present themselves in an interview.

After several weeks she began to feel much less alone in the world. At least there were plenty of people like her around, single women living by themselves and starting over. The sense of community was a first for her. She grew to like and trust the women in the group. She felt closer to them than to any of her friends or neighbors, even though she never saw any of them outside class. It was amazing how honestly they discussed one another's problems and compared notes without making judgments or denying things, wanting only to help.

She thought it must have a lot to do with Dave, but he told her afterward that he thought the group was unusual in that respect. He had conducted the course a number of times, and he had never seen quite that level of trust before. It made her feel good knowing she was a part of that, seeing that she was capable of it.

One evening on her way to class she took a new route: turned off Main Street onto Arden—a narrow, tree-lined avenue that was connected to Washington, just north of the high school. There was a house for sale: a small brick bungalow. Shabby-looking, but a good design. She liked the way the tall cedars had grown up around the porch, the curved path leading to the sidewalk, the crab-apple tree in the front yard. She liked the size of it—manageable, more suitable for a single person living alone. And she liked the location. The neighborhood had the feel of a small town about it. Nothing ever changed here. The same shops on Main

Street that she remembered from her childhood—Hilzinger's Hardware, Romeyn Pharmacy, Edwards Furniture, Dobie Jewelers.

She went to look at the house the following week. It was shabbier than she had first realized. Too much work. Too many major things wrong with it. Still, when she went back to the place in Bloomfield Hills, it did not feel at all like home anymore. Maybe it never had.

She talked to Dr. Anderson about it.

"Do you think I should put it up for sale?"

"What do you think?"

"I think you make a fetish out of refusing to give advice. It's not natural. You should see someone about it."

"Okay then. I think you should sell the house."

"Thank you."

"If that's what you really want to do."

"Coward."

She put the house on the market, and it sold in two weeks. Of course Alex said that was because she had priced it too low. And where in hell was she going? Not to that abortion over in Royal Oak, for God's sake? Yes, as a matter of fact, she had already put some earnest money down. He couldn't believe that. How could she be so thoughtless? Didn't she care anything for her daughter's feelings? Selling the place right out from under her? Couldn't she have waited until Chris came back from Europe? And what was she trying to prove, anyway, living like a pauper in that run-down section of Royal Oak. Was she trying to make him look bad or what?

"Whatever I do," she said, "is what *I* do. You don't have to be embarrassed about it."

"I'm not embarrassed. I'm in despair. You let a terrific house go for nothing—"

"Two hundred thousand is not nothing."

"—and now you're getting ready to play the starving artist in the garret, and for what?"

"For fun!" she said, and hung up. After which he called her back to scold her again. She accepted it with good humor. Not his fault that she had been unable to do anything without his help for the last twenty years. Old habits die hard.

She became the darling of the group after that—brave Catherine who took the plunge, made a decision, can you beat that?—spurring her on to even greater feats of action. She found a job with a new art gallery in Birmingham—as sort of an all-purpose worker; she did some bookkeeping for them, some hanging, even some selling. She became Dave's example to the group: now here's a life that is Under New Management. Somehow it seemed a little like cheating—all this credit for dubious accomplishments. Who knew how these things would turn out? Alex could be proved right—the house might have been a mistake. As for the job, it would not make her rich. Nor would it train her for any future occupation. *Never confuse Movement with Action.* Hadn't she read that somewhere? Still, she felt better these days, just having a specific place to go in the mornings and some goals confronting her, even if they were only to get the lavatory papered and to take up the linoleum in the kitchen.

In October she moved into the house on Arden, and within the space of one month everything went wrong. The furnace quit one day, belching black smoke throughout the house while she was at work, ruining all the painting and wallpapering she had done up to that point. Less than a week later, her basement flooded. The pine tree in the back yard was the problem: little roots that grew and blocked the pipes. She would probably have the same trouble again two or three years down the road, the sewer man told her.

After that, the water pressure in the shower slowed to a trickle, and the water softener stopped working. She discovered a number of electrical outlets that mysteriously refused to dispense current. A succession of workmen came through to cluck their tongues and sigh over the hopeless condition of the place—electricians, plumbers, furnace men.

Sitting back on her heels one Sunday afternoon, after she had steamed off the wallpaper in the downstairs foyer, she found herself with the scraper in her hand, staring off into space: thinking about a time in the future when she would be feeling content in her mind, without pressure or fear; thinking that any time now she might even start to feel happy. And then she knew. As suddenly and clearly as that. What she had been waiting for all this time was for someone to come along and tell her that she had suffered enough. All these months, thinking how unfair it was that this whole thing had happened to her, that she had been standing on this sturdy dock at the edge of the shore and it had been ripped out from under her for no reason. There had to be retribution, some sort of payment for all this pain. But there wasn't. And there was no one besides herself—fallible and frightened half out of her wits but functioning nevertheless. She was doing as well as she could, and it was best to just get on with it.

She had looked down at herself—at her blue jeans and white wool socks, her tennis shoes and dirty sweatshirt—and thought, I am happy. And again, leaning over to hug her knees: I am happy right now.

A long winter. More snow than Detroit had seen in years. It ground slowly on, through December and January, with subzero temperatures, ice storms, punishing winds.

She went to work in the dark, came home in the dark. Her evenings were busy with plans for the house. She would start one project and then another; plan still another, so that she would never be alone with nothing to do.

Eat right, Dr. Anderson had advised; cut down on the drinking; take long walks; get plenty of rest. She followed his prescription, wanting to keep well, to keep feeling good in her mind. She had stopped her regular visits, thinking she would try again on her own.

"You'll make it," he said. "Just take it easy. And if you feel yourself in trouble, give me a call. We'll talk about what's wrong."

"What if I don't know what's wrong?"

"You don't have to know. Just think of me as your dentist. Plan to come in for your regular checkup."

So far she felt she was doing okay. She sat in front of the brick fireplace, sipping her Scotch-and-water and leafing through some back copies of *Better Homes and Gardens*, looking for window treatments. Something unusual for the living room. The former owners had left her the drapes—heavy brocade, hunter green. She kept them pulled after dark, partly for privacy, partly because of the nightly activity at the end of the street. A gang of boys hung out on the corner, hitching rides on the bumpers of cars as they slowed to make the turn. They would crouch and slide along the snow-packed pavement, sometimes with the driver aware, sometimes not. Such a dangerous game. It would only take someone slamming on the brakes at the wrong moment and they could be thrown under the wheels or into the curb. She tried not to think about that, tried to ignore the honking of horns and occasional angry words from drivers. If anyone called the police, the kids would simply disappear into the darkness and wait. When the patrol car was gone, the game would begin again.

But tonight had been quiet. She glanced at her watch and saw that it was after eleven. The two small windows on either side of the fireplace were flocked with snow. It had been snowing since early evening—big, soft flakes that melted when they hit the glass. But now it was starting to stick. It would be bad driving in the morning, no doubt.

Yawning, she stood and gathered the magazines with their white markers in them, piling them on the end table. The fire in the fireplace was nearly out. She placed the screen in front of it and went to switch out the lamp, when the doorbell summoned her—a sharp, insistent ring that cracked the silence of the house. She went to the window, peering out through the drapes. A slight male figure leaned against the iron railing of the porch. Damn those boys! And damn their parents, too! Didn't they care what went on? Now something had happened, and she would have to handle it!

She went to the door and jerked it open, wincing as the cold air poured in over her. She tried to shield herself from it, standing half behind the door.

The boy looked young—not more than fifteen, she thought. He wore light jeans; a navy pea jacket, buttoned over a dark sweater; no gloves; no hat. Pale, straight hair falling to his eyebrows. His oval face was tilted toward the light. He leaned forward, with his hands in his pockets, an odd, moony smile on his face. She was sure she had never seen him before.

"You're Mrs. Holzman, aren't you? I need help."

Something about the look on his face made her stiffen. Backing away, she kept the door carefully between them. Cold air fastened about her ankles. *He must be on something.*

She didn't know how or why, but she seemed to be the target for the aliens of the world. They sought her out. In a crowd of people on the street, she would be the one that some strange old man would veer into, catching her elbow and holding on while his crazy eyes would stare up into her face. She would stand still for a moment, her heart wrenched with pity, until fear overcame it and she pulled away, hurrying off, hearing the hollow sound of her heels clacking against the cement.

The time in the grocery store when the young woman, dressed all in tan—pants, coat, shoes, and hat—with her tan hair tied back from her face, moved boldly into her path with her hand out, smiled up into her face: "Any spare change?" There were at least ten other people in the aisle; why pick on her? She had shaken her head and looked away, and the woman had rapped her grocery cart smartly with her fist before moving off. Trying to finish her shopping then, with a flush of shame on her cheeks. Why? Someone else would have laughed it off, told the woman to go out and get a job; but all she could think was, Why me? Why have they singled me out? Some sort of strange communion taking place; some sign that she gave, showing that she was open to it. So here it was. Not content with pursuing her in grocery stores or on street corners, they had discovered her hiding place; they knew her by name.

He was mumbling something now, leaning against the door-jamb. His face looked ancient in the light.

"What do you want?" she asked.

"Mr. Cornelius told me to come here."

"You know Mr. Cornelius?"

"He's my counselor. At school. I met you there once, don't you remember?"

He moved forward then, thrusting his hand under her eyes. Something dark and thick, like oil, spread over the surface of the palm. The fingers curved inward as he cradled his left arm against his chest, his head angled downward.

Oh, God. Not oil. Blood. She saw the torn flesh; caught him by the shoulder, pulling him inside. Swiftly she led him down the dim hallway toward the kitchen.

"Sit there," she said. "Take off your jacket. You kids. Somebody could get killed down there, don't you ever think about that? Taking crazy chances. Did anyone else get hurt?"

He shook his head, sitting down and leaning forward in the chair, with his arms crossed over his stomach, rocking back and forth.

She took a mixing bowl down from the cupboard and filled it with cold water from the tap; emptied a tray of ice cubes into it. She brought it to the table and set it in front of him. He let her unbutton the jacket and take it off, and she pushed up the sleeve of his sweater, keeping her eyes averted from the wound. Carefully, she set the bowl of water in his lap.

"Here. Put your hand in here. It's all right. It won't hurt."

But he did not move.

Gently she lifted his arm and slid the wounded hand under the water. She noted then the two long scratches across his throat, beaded with dried blood. An old man's face, the skin stretched tight over the bones. Deep hollows beneath his eyes. He sat very still, with his hand in the water. After a moment he looked up.

"That was weird. Everything stopped."

"For now, anyway. What did Mr. Cornelius say? Does he want me to call someone?"

"No. He said you'd give me something to put on it. For a burn."

"I don't understand. How did you burn it? What happened to the other boys down there? Where are they now?"

"Or if you could give me something to wrap it in." He shifted suddenly in the chair, and the water slid to the lip of the bowl. He righted it, looking up at her. The moony smile was gone. She had been wrong about his being high. His eyes were clear now. He was sweating heavily.

"Where's Mr. Cornelius?" she asked.

For a moment he looked confused. "I think he went home. Yeah, he did. He said you'd take care of it."

"But what does he want me to do? There's nothing more I can do. It will have to be treated. At a hospital, I'm sure."

"No, why? It doesn't hurt that much. It'll be okay."

"It'll hurt the minute you take it out of the water. You're going to have to see a doctor. Tell me your name."

"Gale."

"Gale what?"

Nervously he cleared his throat. "Listen, I haven't done anything. I mean, I'm not in any trouble or anything, so you don't need to worry. You don't need to call anybody, okay? Like the police."

"The police. Why would I do that?"

He shrugged. "I don't know. People do it. Anything goes wrong, they think they have to call. I bet even the cops get sick of it. People always calling them for everything."

"How did you know my name?" she asked. "I don't remember meeting you with Mr. Cornelius."

"Yeah, you did. In his office a couple of months ago. When you were having furnace trouble, don't you remember?"

And then she did: the day, at least, if not the boy. She had needed someone to tell her troubles to, someone to assure her that any normal person would be upset over this—hundreds of dollars in repair work to be done, everything ruined, all of her hard work for nothing. She didn't remember anyone else in the office at the time. Jesus, she must have been in a state, not to have noticed that.

Where was Dave now? Why had he left all this to her? Looking down into the water, she could see the fleshy part of the palm, dark, swollen, with shreds of skin clinging to it. The water in the bowl was pink, settling to a deep rose at the bottom. She took her eyes from the wound, feeling her stomach lift.

"Tell me your last name. I'll call your parents. They'll have to take you to a doctor."

Quickly he stood and set the bowl on the table. "Never mind, it's okay. I'll just go." The tops of his ears were bright red. He started moving slowly, almost lazily across the room. "Could I use your bathroom first?"

She pointed the way, and he headed straight across the room for the doorway; as she watched, he veered and walked solidly into the wall. With a cry she jumped up. He had banged his head smartly against the jamb. He turned toward her, a dazed, vacant look on his face.

"Don't feel so good."

She helped him to the lavatory. Leaning forward with one hand braced against the wall, he vomited milky strings of saliva into the bowl. After a few minutes he straightened up, his face white. He took the washcloth she handed him, wiped his face. She pulled a clean towel from the rack and wrapped it lightly around the wounded hand.

"You'd better lie down for a few minutes."

He let her lead him to the living room. The fire was nearly out now; the logs were hissing in the grate, a pencil line of smoke streaming up the chimney. She helped him to the couch, and he leaned back against the cushions, closing his eyes.

"Don't call anybody, okay? Please."

"I have to call. You need help right away. Let me get your parents, Gale. They're going to have to hear about it. The doctor won't be able to do anything without their permission."

He opened his eyes to stare up at her. A neat white triangle of undershirt was visible beneath the V-neck sweater. Above it the inverted V of his Adam's apple. Across his throat, the scratches appeared deeper than before: red welts raising on his flesh. "They already know," he said. "Who do you think did it to me, anyway?"

Not possible. She looked down at the bulky towel around his hand, the bloodstains on his upper thighs where the hand had rested. The room felt suddenly colder to her, and she wrapped her arms around herself, holding her elbows. Why had he told her that? She didn't want to hear that. Certainly Dave wouldn't have dumped this problem on her if that were true. No, this kid was a liar. She hoped he was a liar; she didn't want him to be anything else.

"I'll get you a blanket," she murmured, moving toward the stairway. He seemed not to have heard her, turned his face toward the back of the couch.

Quickly she went up the stairs and into her bedroom, closing the door after her. She sat down on the edge of the bed, lifting the telephone from the nightstand. She looked up Dave Cornelius on Maple Avenue, dialed the number, waited through ten rings. *Damn, he must be there.* She dialed it again, glancing at her reflection in the dresser mirror. Lord, she looked awful; she hated it when her face got that numb, frightened look. She had walked around for months with just that look on her face; catching sight of herself in a store window, she would flinch; no wonder the strangers of the world were after her!

She went to the closet and pulled on a sweater over her blouse. It felt cold upstairs, too; the wind blowing harder, rattling the windows; snow piling thickly against the lower edges of the glass.

When she spread the quilt over him, he opened his eyes, then closed them again, muttering something under his breath. His brown loafers lay beside the couch; he was still wearing his socks; they were stained with leather dye. He should not be lying there in wet clothes. Probably he should not be lying there at all. She tried to think what she knew about burns; that there were degrees of seriousness. She had no way of knowing how bad this one was, or how to treat it. It had looked very bad to her. Supposing it was worse even than she thought? The pain, the cold, the delay in treatment—all that could send him into shock, and here she would be with him, standing by, doing nothing about it. It would all be her fault. *Think, Catherine. Think what to do about this.*

Putting off the moment, she knelt beside the fireplace to stoke the fire. She put fresh logs on the grate, and after a moment the flame erupted, a faint bluish glow along the logs. She stood before it, warming her hands. Then she turned and went up the stairs, closing the door to her room. She stood before the dresser and ran a comb through her hair, put on fresh lipstick, studying her face again in the glass. There, that was better. She smiled back at herself.

Going to the bed, she sat down, pulled the telephone over onto her lap. She dialed Alex's number quickly, without thinking about it. It was answered on the first ring.

"I'm sorry to call so late, Alex, but there's been an accident."

"Accident? With the car—?"

"No, no. It isn't me, it's . . . everything's all right."

"It isn't Chris, is it?"

"No. Nothing like that. It's just . . . someone from the neighborhood has been hurt. It's a burn. It looks as if it might be serious. I don't know what to do about it."

A pause. His voice came again, wary and alert. "Where are you?"

"I'm at home." She deserved that. After all, she had called him from a bar once, hadn't she? Not drunk but definitely on the way. And all those other times when, sober and despairing, she had called, wanting him to somehow make things right for her. Now she kept her voice low, saying, "It's sort of a freak thing, and I'm not sure . . . I don't know much about burns, but it looks deep and I got scared . . . I was worried about shock . . ."

"Did it happen at the house?"

"No, he just . . . he came here for help, and I've got him lying down on the couch right now."

"Why don't you take him over to Emergency?"

"I thought of that, but . . . listen, I hate to ask . . . do you think you could possibly come over and take a look at it? I know it's late . . ."

"It's after midnight, Cat. I've got surgery in the morning."

She said nothing, looking down at her fist clenched in her lap, blue veins standing out against white skin. His hand was suddenly over the mouthpiece; she could hear muffled voices behind it. She waited, staring across the room at the oak mirror that had belonged to her grandmother. She had refinished it when she took it from her parents' house; grainy golden wood with two carved birds that looked like parrots, their long tails curving about the base. *Shouldn't have called him, it was stupid, what was I thinking of?* Her eyes moved to the red brick chimney between the two side windows. *Apologize and hang up. As simple as that.*

"What's the address, again?"

"712 Arden. It's just off Washington."

From his apartment, not more than a fifteen-minute drive. *You can bring Pam.* She almost said it, too. Well, why not? Since that was what the conversation at the other end of the line was all about. Pam must be wondering why he would do this; why this woman, his ex-wife, had to keep calling him for help. It would not be her style at all. But then she was the twenty-six-year-old woman that he lived with—a much different position. *Bring her along. Let her see that I'm harmless. She doesn't have to be worried about me.* As if she ever was.

"712," Alex repeated. "I'll be right there."

"Thanks."

She hung up and sat with the telephone in her lap. Now that it was over, her mind fastened on a half dozen alternatives at once.

It was as if her sane and sensible self stood behind her, arms folded, shaking her head. *You don't think. You rush around in a state of total confusion, acting on the first idea that comes into your head. Why him, of all people? Is he the only doctor you know? No, but he's the only one that you want to see.*

She had learned this much from Dr. Anderson; that, quick as the knife, her own criticism could do more damage than anything Alex would ever say. *So stop it, now. He didn't have to come. He's got the problem, too, of wanting to keep his hand in; wanting to keep running your life, if remotely.*

Still, before he came, she went down to the living room and retrieved her glass of Scotch, rinsing it out and putting it away in the cupboard.

"You're thin," he said. "Are you eating?"

"What a question. Of course."

He slipped off his jacket; bent to kiss her, with his hands on her shoulders. "Well, I worry about you, you know."

"Don't. I'm fine."

He was looking about the entryway, taking in the patched walls, half-removed wallpaper, the wheat paste and paper-hanging tools stashed underneath the hall table.

"So this is it."

She nodded.

"Well, I guess you like the challenge."

Seeing it through his eyes, she felt embarrassed.

"I'm sorry," she said, "about dragging you out on a night like this. I guess I panicked."

"It's all right. Where is he?"

"There. In the living room."

They spoke softly, but when she got to the couch, the boy's eyes were open. His breathing was faint, his face even more pale than before. She had been right to call. Alex pulled the coffee table over, sat down next to the couch.

"How are you feeling?"

He said nothing, merely stared up at her.

"It's all right," she said. "This is Dr. Holzman. He'll help you."

Alex gently lifted the quilt and folded it back across the boy's knees. The wounded hand lay over his chest; his good hand gripped his belt.

"Pull the lamp closer, will you?"

She slid the floor lamp over so that it was shining directly on the couch. Alex loosened the towel, spreading it out over the boy's chest. He lay motionless, staring upward.

"That's fine. I won't touch it, but I want to have a look. No, just relax, you don't need to sit up."

The hand lay exposed on the towel, the fingers curving inward, more tightly than before. Alex lifted it onto his lap.

"That's a mean burn. How'd you do it?"

"Electric stove." He stared straight ahead at the arm of the couch.

"Can you open your hand for me?"

She looked over Alex's shoulder, saw the bloody palm as the hand slowly opened, dark and pulpy-looking at the center; the edges whitish, with shredded blisters. Again she felt the peculiar lightness at the pit of her stomach.

"Hurts a lot, doesn't it?" Alex leaned in closer. From his bag he took the fluid-filled syringe, fitted a needle into it. "Here. I'm going to give you a shot. Just a few minutes and you won't feel a thing."

This was Alex at his best. Gentle and considerate, respectful of pain. His patients trusted him completely; he would never hurt them unnecessarily, and they knew it. As wary as this boy was, she could see him relax, wanting to give over control.

"Let me know when you're ready," Alex said.

The boy's eyes flicked down at the needle.

"Just do it."

Afterward, he lay with his arm still across Alex's lap. Alex looked up at her.

"Got any coffee?"

"I'll make some."

She went to the kitchen, getting down the glass percolator from the cupboard. Filling the basket, she set it on the stove and waited for the water to boil. When it was ready, she poured two cups, added milk and sugar to his.

When she returned, Gale was lying with his head propped against the pillow, the quilt tucked up around his chest. He looked relaxed and alert. Alex was bandaging the hand, layering gauze into the open palm.

"You have to let it close naturally on itself, but not too tight. Just a good, loose position. That's it." He glanced up at her. "It's not as deep as I thought. He has good movement in the fingers and the thumb." He finished wrapping the hand, taped the gauze at the wrist.

"What have you got in the way of pain pills?"

"Nothing. A little Darvon, that's all."

Reaching into his bag, he handed her a packet. "Try two of these every four hours. That will help." And to Gale: "Think you can sleep, now?"

The boy nodded. Already he had rolled onto his side, with the dressed hand resting on his right shoulder, his face turned, again, to the back of the couch.

She handed Alex his coffee.

"Let's go into the kitchen." He followed her down the narrow hallway, shutting the door behind him. "Okay. What gives?" he asked. "Where did he come from? I thought you said he was some neighbor kid."

"Well, he is. I mean he might be. He came to the door and said that a friend of mine had told him—"

"Who is this friend?"

She told him about Dave Cornelius—that he was a counselor up at the high school, that she had met him through a night-school course she was taking. Don't ask, she prayed; did not want to have to say the name of the course—career planning—out loud. As always, she felt imprisoned by his view of her.

Alex set down his coffee cup. "Is that all you know about him? That he's a friend of a friend of yours? What about his last name? Do you know how old he is?"

She shook her head.

"Cat, do you have any idea what could happen if I got caught even looking at that hand without a release? Where are his parents? Why didn't you call them?"

"He asked me not to."

"Why?"

"Because. He said they were the ones who did it to him."

"Oh, Christ."

"Alex, you don't have to worry. I know he won't tell anyone."

"How do you know that? You don't seem to know any other damned thing about him, and Jesus, you just open your door and let him walk right in, you don't ask any questions, you don't do any checking—"

"I asked," she said. "I checked. Or at least, I tried to. I called Dave at home, but there was no answer—"

"Why didn't you just phone the police? I don't understand you," he said. "You don't make connections. You don't think things through. How do you even know he was telling you the truth?"

"Why would he lie about it?"

"How the hell do I know? The point is, you don't know anything."

"But if he's a friend of Dave's—"

"Why isn't Dave taking care of him?"

She set her coffee cup down, hard. "All right. What do you think I should do, Alex? What do you want me to do?"

"Look, don't get upset—"

"No, tell me," she insisted. "Should I call the police? I'll go and call them right now. Or should I wake him up and throw him out of here?"

Leaning against the counter, he grinned faintly at her. "Okay, I'm sorry. It's just that you act like such a kid sometimes. I think you should be aware that we are on very shaky ground here, that's all."

And at once she felt contrite; it was not just her problem; she had involved him in it, too. He looked tired, she thought. Deep circles under his eyes. So handsome standing there in his gray cashmere slacks and sweater, his soft leather Italian shoes, the silver Rolex watch that she had given him—and then she had to protect herself, harden her heart against him. *Too much fast living, that was what tired him out. Let Pam, the nurse, worry about it now.*

He glanced at his watch. "Jesus, it's late. I've got to get going."

She walked him to the door.

"Don't forget about the pills. When those shots wear off he's not going to feel so hot. Listen, what about one of those Crisis Centers? That's what they're for, isn't it? There's one in Birmingham. You could send him there in the morning."

"All right."

He leaned down to kiss her cheek. "Take care. I'll call you tomorrow."

"You don't need to do that."

"I want to."

The street was dark. There were no lights on in any of the houses. She stood watching the red taillights of his car as they moved slowly down the street, the left one blinking as he turned the corner. Now all was hidden behind a dense curtain of snow. Snow swirled at her feet as she shut the door.

Inside the house it was silent as she went around to the rooms downstairs, turning off lights. She stood for a moment over the couch in the living room, listening to the sound of his light, even breathing. He was sleeping deeply, with his face buried in the pillow.

She thought she would try Dave's number once more. Glancing at her watch, she saw that it was after one o'clock. To hell with it. Tomorrow would be soon enough. And she would be tougher tomorrow; ask better questions and expect some answers.

After all, it was her house. Her couch that he was sleeping on.

She turned off the lamp, moving toward the stairway in the dark. Halfway there she heard him cry out, turned back to see low flames curling over the log. She waited for minutes, it seemed, but there was no other sound.

When she woke up the next morning, she sensed immediately that something was different. The wind was blowing hard, and there was an odd, glaring quality to the light in the room, a brightness that didn't feel like sunlight.

She pulled on her robe and went to look. It was still snowing; it had snowed all night. Snow, drifting in waves, sculpted by the fierce wind, piled high against trees, bushes, and fences. Across the street, stretching from porch to porch, were flat fields of snow. The cars had nearly disappeared; only the roofs and the tops of the windows were visible.

She stood at the window, watching the snow swirl in frenzied patterns along the road. She had never seen anything like this. The sky was white, white smoke rising from chimneys into the body of the storm.

She pulled her robe tightly around her and went downstairs, grateful now that the furnace had gone out on her back in October; it could be worse: it could have quit in this storm. As it was, the house was warm and snug; they had heat and electricity; they had food. They would simply wait this out.

She stopped in the doorway to the living room. The boy was sitting on the edge of the couch with his head down, elbows on his knees. He looked up as she entered.

His left cheek was red and creased, the hair on that one side plastered to his head. He leaned back against the couch, closing his eyes.

"How are you feeling?"

He did not answer her.

She brought him a glass of water and shook two pills from the packet that lay on the table. He swallowed them quickly and lay back, pulling the quilt up over his shoulder.

Kneeling before the grate, she rebuilt the fire. She could hear the wind as it howled about the corner of the house; the windows on the west side were moaning. It must be bitter out there. She thought of Alex driving to the hospital; then realized that no one could be going anywhere this morning.

She went out to the kitchen and heated up the coffee left in the pot while taking a quick survey of the cupboards and refrigerator. She was not the most efficient shopper, preferring quick store trips on the way home from work, but this storm could not last much longer, in any case; soon the plows would be out, and in the meantime, they would get along. She found eggs and bacon and some cheese, a little butter, a little milk. In the freezer, a loaf of rye bread. The cupboards yielded several cans of soup and some canned fruit. Crackers. Mustard pickles. Two tins of smoked oysters. A jar of capers. A jar of martini olives. Jesus, was she having a party? This is what happens when you shop hungry, Catherine.

She made some rye toast; took it, with a glass of milk, out to the living room.

"Those pills are strong," she said. "You shouldn't take them on an empty stomach. They might make you sick."

He sat up and ate the toast, drank the milk, then lay back down again, all without saying a word. He looked exhausted.

Afterward, sitting in the chair by the fireplace, reading and drinking her coffee, she would look up now and then, to see if the fire needed tending, or if he was still asleep, or if, by some miracle, it had suddenly stopped snowing. She thought about how much she loved this kind of a day. It filled her with a great sense of relief. There was nothing going on out there, nobody exploring or accomplishing anything; she was safe; she was as well off as anyone.

It did not stop snowing. The sky gradually grew darker as she replenished the fire and made tomato soup and cheese sandwiches for their lunch. They listened to news and weather bulletins on the radio. Telephone lines were down; in many sections of the city the power was out. Again she felt relief that the telephone was the only thing she had lost. The worst storm in thirteen years, said the reports. Nearly thirty inches of snow in the last twenty hours; more of it on the way.

That night they ate dinner in front of the fire—scrambled eggs, bacon, toast, and coffee. The wind blew the snow in horizontal sheets past the windows.

"What time is it?" he asked, looking up at her.

"A little after six."

"My head feels like I'm in a phone booth. I can't hear right."

"That's the codeine," she said.

"My hand still hurts. It's like it doesn't stop the pain at all, only it makes you not care much about it." He held himself stiffly, as if the wound in his hand had made his whole body vulnerable to pain. "That guy who was here," he said. "Dr. Holzman. Is he your husband?"

"He was. We're divorced."

"You have any kids?"

"A daughter. She's in college. Actually, she's in Europe right now."

He was silent a moment. "You should call yourself Ms.," he said. "Like the teachers at school. You can't tell if they're married or not. They don't wear rings either."

She wondered about herself, what it was that aroused in people this passion to instruct. Even this kid, who was hardly in a position to be giving advice to her, found it irresistible.

"Speaking of teachers," she said, "I tried to get Mr. Cornelius last night at his house. There was no answer when I called."

He looked up at her and shrugged, pushing his plate away with the eggs only half eaten. "Maybe he didn't go straight home."

"You'd better finish that," she said. "We've only got about three meals left before we're in trouble here."

"How come you got divorced?" he asked.

She laughed. "You ask a lot of questions. How about if I ask you some? What do you think will happen when your parents find out about this?"

"Don't worry," he said. "I've done it before. I've been doing it since I was fourteen."

"How old are you now?"

"What do you think?"

"I think about fifteen."

He frowned. "I'm sixteen. I was sixteen last November."

He pulled his plate over in front of him, finished the rest of the eggs.

"Doesn't it seem pointless, then?" she asked. "I mean, if you keep going back?"

"I don't go back. I get taken back."

"By whom?"

"Cops."

That one word silenced her. Why ask about things that she didn't really want to know? The last time she had talked to a policeman was two years ago, when she went to get her driver's license renewed. She didn't even think of them as *cops*.

"Last July," he said, "I got as far as Toledo before I got caught. That won't happen again, though. This time it's different."

"Why is it different?"

But he didn't answer her, merely leaned back against the couch with his eyes closed.

She got up and cleared away the dishes. When she returned to the living room he was lying down again, facing away from her, with the quilt pulled up over his shoulders.

From the bay window she could see light shining on the snow from the houses across the street. She mounted a fresh sheet of watercolor paper on the easel, sketched the corner of her neighbor's house and its low, slanted roofline, the two tall cedars bending beside the porch. Working quickly, she rummaged through the shoebox of paints at her feet, looking for the right shade of red for the bricks.

She painted until she began to feel tired. Standing up to

stretch, she glanced at her watch. It was late: after ten o'clock. She had been painting for nearly three hours.

She switched on the TV in time to hear that Governor Milliken had declared a state of emergency in the northernmost counties of the state. Snow continued to fall: thirty-six inches in thirty-one hours. Not a record, but close to it. Glancing at her painting, she thought that from a distance it looked good. She would call it *Evening Record Snowfall.*

Saturday morning. The air was still and cold. It had stopped snowing during the night, but the sky was overcast; it looked as though it could start up again at any time.

She rummaged in the back of the cupboard and found some dried prunes in a package, set them simmering on the stove. In minutes their sweet-spicy smell filled the kitchen. Behind the crackers was a box of oatmeal, still with its lid taped shut from the move. They would have an old-fashioned breakfast this morning: stewed prunes and hot cereal, with sugar and milk. Climbing up on a chair, she checked to see if she had overlooked anything else on the shelf.

"I like your painting."

She turned. He was standing in the doorway with the quilt draped over his shoulders. He looked healthier this morning; his skin wasn't so pinched-looking, and there was color in his cheeks.

"When did you do it? Last night?"

She nodded, climbing down from the chair. "How are you feeling?"

"Better."

He sat down at the table, with the bandaged hand lying, palm upward, in his lap. His hair hung over his forehead into his eyes. He had good, clear skin. Really, he was quite a handsome kid.

"How did you learn all that?" he asked.

"You mean painting? My father was an artist."

"So he taught you?"

"As much as you can teach it."

What he had taught her was the trick of paying attention, of being conscious of the dailiness of art and of its presence in everything. Yet it seemed that over the years that was the very thing she had lost. And it was essential; without it, there was no need to record. The first thing she noticed last night was that familiar pressure inside, that passion to record.

Sitting day after day in her father's studio, inhaling the smell of oil paint and turpentine and clean, stretched canvas—sometimes it could almost make her dizzy, the odor was so heady. She would wear one of his old shirts over her school dress. She would be working on her own small projects while he made his art. Preparing the canvases; setting out brushes and paints; inventing your own colors and then mixing them to your design. Best of all, waiting for the silence and the white space to tell you how to begin. Later on, of course, she learned about the disadvantages, but at the time she thought it the most romantic and satisfying of all the professions.

"Is that his painting over the fireplace, or yours?"

"It's Andrew Wyeth's. It's not a painting. It's a print."

"I like that one, too."

"Do you like hot cereal?" she asked. "That's what we're having this morning."

After breakfast she carried her coffee into the living room, sat down in the chair near the fire. The book she had been reading all day yesterday, *Great Expectations*, lay on the end table with her glasses on top of it.

"Do you like Dickens?" he asked her.

She nodded.

"Me, too. I've read all of his stuff, I guess. Starting with *David Copperfield*, in sixth grade."

She looked at him. "But he's written so many books."

"Yeah, I know." Again, he smiled. "Well, I might have missed a couple, I guess."

"What else do you like to read?"

"Lots of stuff. Anything. I was looking through your bookcase. I found this." He held up a grayish book with a red binding:

Walden. "We read it in American Lit last semester. It was pretty interesting."

"Was it? I only remember reading the first two chapters about a hundred years ago. How did you get to be such a reader, anyway?"

"It's good for a lot of things," he said. "You can find out things."

She lifted her coffee cup, holding it with both hands. "Tell me something. What would you have done if I hadn't been home the other night?"

"You were, though."

"Just supposing."

"You mean, why didn't I stay with Mr. Cornelius? The thing is, he's got his girlfriend who lives with him. It would be sort of weird for me to be there."

"Oh, and it's not weird for you to be here?"

He only laughed, made no answer.

"What about some of your other friends?" she asked.

"I don't have any other friends."

"Sure you do. People you hang around with and talk to in school—"

"I know what they are," he said dryly. "Okay, I've got this one friend, but his dad drinks. I didn't know if he was on the sauce now or not. I was thinking I'd ask him at school on Monday. Maybe I can stay there for a while. His name's Brian MacKay. You know the Lutheran church on the corner of Main and Thurston? His father's the pastor there."

"You mean he's an alcoholic? I can't believe that."

He shrugged. "They're the worst kind. Freaked out on religion to start with, so it makes it easy to freak out on other stuff."

She set her coffee cup down on the table. "Is your father an alcoholic?" she asked him.

He looked at her. "My father doesn't drink." Leaning back against the couch, he rested his hands in his lap. "He doesn't smoke. And he doesn't swear, either."

"Listen," she said, "you don't think you might have made a mistake?"

"About what?"

"People do terrible things sometimes. They don't always mean to do them. If your father . . . if he was really angry . . ."

"He was angry, all right."

"Then maybe he just didn't know what he was doing."

Again, he was looking at her. His voice matter-of-fact, without expression: "He knew what he was doing."

No call from Alex, even after the phones were fixed. Not that she had been expecting one; he would be busy now at the hospital. There must have been hundreds of emergencies.

When she first lifted the receiver and heard the dial tone, she felt comfort at being back in touch with things; yet she had little desire to contact anyone. It had been such a peaceful time, she almost hated to see it end.

On Sunday morning she awoke to the sound of the plow. All up and down the street her neighbors were shoveling themselves out. The sun was shining on the snow, deep blue shadows falling crisply across the front yard.

She pulled on her jeans and her heavy boots, a white wool turtleneck, and her navy parka; went out to try her hand at cleaning off the porch.

Her neighbor called to her from across the street, "How're you fixed for food?"

"Fine!"

"Sure you don't need anything?"

Her other neighbor offered to plow her driveway as soon as he finished his own. "That's too much for you to shovel," he said. "You won't get out for a week."

Such nice people. She would be friendlier to them all, in the future.

Fine snow misted up around her. Before long she had worked

up a sweat. The sun was so bright it hurt her eyes. Huge puffs of cottony snow clung to the branches of the lilac bushes between the houses. A sparrow flitted across the yard, and she straightened up. Lord, she had forgotten about the birds; they must be starving.

She went around to the back yard and shoveled her way onto the porch, where she kept a bag of birdseed. The snow had drifted here, leaving high dunes next to the garage. She scattered birdseed over the surface, filled the feeder in her maple tree to the brim.

On an impulse she flung herself full length in the snow. Lying on her back, she stared up at the blue sky. She scissored her legs and flailed with her arms. Making angels. Her favorite game when she was a kid. She would do whole chains of them with their wings pointing toward the house, their wide skirts touching. Her father told her that she had imprisoned them inside the house; they couldn't get out without stepping on some angel's head.

Her father. She had been thinking of him a lot. He had never gone to church with her. Neither of her parents went to church, although they both thought that their daughter should have some exposure. In fact, exposure was the word her mother had used, as if religion might be some kind of communicable disease to which she should develop a natural immunity.

What had developed was her belief in the music and in the art. When she was in grade school she had gone to the Lutheran Sunday school on the corner of their street. She loved the stained-glass windows in that stately building and the weekly lesson pamphlets done in four colors on expensive rag paper—scenes of Daniel in the lions' den, of David and Goliath, of Joseph in the Court of the Pharaohs, all perfectly designed and executed. She wished that she had saved them.

When she was in high school she had joined the choir at Northminster Congregational because her friend Carolyn went there. She had loved being in the choir loft, wearing her maroon robe with the gold satin collar. She loved the somber elegance of the service and the huge body of people who spoke only in whispers. She remembered the words of the Easter hymn that they had sung:

> All in the April evening
> April airs were abroad
> The sheep with their little lambs
> Passed me by on the road . . .
> All in the April evening
> I thought on the lamb of God.

All the rest was lost—whatever she was supposed to have learned. Too many churches, that was the problem. She had attended Wednesday evening prayer meetings with another friend who was a Baptist, had gone to Mass on a number of occasions with a high school boyfriend. From time to time she sorted through various scraps of religious knowledge, hoping that the messages would collect themselves into something that she could then label her belief. So far no such magical fusion had occurred.

One of the women in Dave's class had told them of the emotional struggle she had endured after her husband had left her. She had prayed for Jesus to give her the strength to go on, had prayed to be able to accept the fact that this was simply God's will. She knew if she could do that, things would be much easier. Listening, Cat had thought she was all for things getting easier, but she could not count on Jesus to pull her through. She had trouble with Christianity: for all of the things that you had to take on faith, for its sheer conceit. No other religion demanded such exclusive rights to the Salvation/Eternal Life theme. They were not the oldest or the largest; why did they have to be the most pompous?

Embarrassing that at forty years of age she was still shopping around, even though at times it seemed that there was nothing in the store. Or rather, none of it was for sale to her. Or it was on a shelf that was too high and you would have to stand on the soap or kitty litter to reach it.

Well, she was an impulse buyer. You only had to look into her clothes closet to discover that. Her attention could be caught by anything at any time, but the printout continued to read *Insufficient Data.*

That afternoon they watched from the kitchen window as the birds flocked to the feeder. It wasn't only the starlings and sparrows, but cardinals, mourning doves, blue jays, even a couple of grosbeaks.

"We should only be that well off," she said. "Maybe I should try hiking down to the store."

"What makes you think it would be open? Or that they would have anything to sell you, if it was?"

"Smart kid."

Her next-door neighbor came over to plow her driveway, and she went out on the porch to thank him.

"My wife says to tell you if you need anything to just holler. We were a little worried about you. Over here all alone."

She said that she had rather enjoyed the holiday from work.

He grinned. "Well, I'd rather pick my times off. Hunting season would suit me a little better."

She thanked him again, closed the door to see Gale standing just inside the doorway to the living room.

"Would it be okay if I took a shower?"

"We'll have to rig up something," she said. "Wait. I know." She found a plastic bag in one of her kitchen drawers, drew it snugly over the bandaged hand and taped it at the wrist. She went through her closet and pulled out an old pair of her jeans, a plaid flannel shirt that had belonged to Alex, a pair of clean wool socks. She dropped them outside the bathroom door.

"Just leave your clothes out here when you're through. I'll wash them," she said.

"You don't need to do that."

"It's all right. I'm going to do a load of my own, anyway. I've left some others for you to put on."

It was no trouble for her. And tomorrow he would be gone. The first thing she would do when she saw Dave was make it plain: no more referrals, please. This was not some halfway house she was running.

By Monday morning she was ready to pick up with her life. The two had a skimpy breakfast together—rye toast without butter and the last of the oatmeal—before Gale left for school. He thanked her for letting him stay. She watched him as he walked down the middle of the street, with the bandaged hand tucked carefully beneath his navy pea jacket.

The snow had already developed a heavy crust. Things must have melted some during the night. The valleys and dunes were no longer moved by the wind. The main streets had all been plowed, the radio said. Schools were open. It was business as usual. She dressed warmly in slacks, her wool sweater, and her parka, went out to start her car. Lucky for her she had thought to park it in the garage; so often she didn't bother with that.

As she drove past the high school, she looked idly toward the groups of kids gathered on the wide sidewalk in front. She did not see Gale among them.

"Ah, you survived! Wonderful!"

Gwen, her boss, looked up as she entered the gallery.

"Harlan and I were going to try to make a snowmobile run over to your place, only we couldn't get out of our own neighborhood. In fact, we barely got out this morning. I tried to call you on Friday, so I knew your phone was out."

She took off her parka, hung it up in the back room. Gwen had the water on for tea. She made herself a cup, looking out the window at the bare branches of the oak tree in the back yard. The gallery was in an old house in the downtown section of Birmingham, surrounded by other old houses: some of them had been made over into businesses, some not. A pretty neighborhood; pleasant working conditions. She liked what she did here, liked Gwen and Harlan Fisher, too. But she was not making any money to speak of. Soon she would have to think about getting a job. A real job, as Alex would say.

Gwen came into the kitchen. "So, how was your weekend? Anybody get snowed in with you?"

She laughed. "As a matter of fact, yes."

"Good. Then it was a worthwhile experience? You were supposed to make the most of it, you know. Everyone else did. Read the paper this morning."

"Well, I blew it, then," she said. "How did you and Harlan do?"

"Oh, great. We ate peanut-butter-and-banana sandwiches and drank lots of Scotch. One night we had a Blizzard Party with our neighbors and talked about God and the Red Wings. Which was having the best season. Typical middle-class suburbia stuff."

"Sounds like fun."

"It was."

The gallery was quiet all that day, which didn't surprise her. People didn't think about art when they had grocery shopping to do, errands to run, all of life's details to attend to. They closed up early, a little after four o'clock, and she drove to the A & P on Adams Road, parking in the lot next to a huge mountain of snow. The store was filled with people; she'd never seen it so busy. She found that she was hungry for everything; picked out a steak and fresh mushrooms, ice cream, potato salad, apple pie. Whole-wheat English muffins. She would have one, with butter and honey, as soon as she got home. Just this one time she indulged herself, buying whatever caught her eye. It wouldn't be wasted, she thought. She could freeze whatever was left.

Turning off Washington Street, she was relieved not to see any of the boys hanging around on the corner. The snow was piled so high that there was no place to stand except in the middle of the street.

She turned into the driveway, and the headlights of her car caught something at the side of the porch: a dark blur framed against the white cedars. Light hair. A navy pea jacket. The white of the bandaged hand. She parked in the driveway; got out slowly, gathering her purse and the two bags of groceries in her arms. He was waiting for her on the front steps as she came up the walk.

"Hi."

"What are you doing here?"

He looked down at the wrought-iron railing, then back up at her again. His arms were crossed over his chest. His nose and cheeks and the tips of his ears were bright red.

She shifted the bags of groceries in her arms, and he took one of them from her, held it against his hip as she fumbled in her purse for her key.

"What happened at the school?"

"Nothing much."

"Did you see your friend Brian?"

He nodded. "His dad's not in very good shape right now. It's not a good time, that's the problem."

"What about Mr. Cornelius? What did he say about it?"

"He wasn't in school today. Someone said he was sick."

"What is it with you?" she asked. "Don't you ever have any good luck?"

He looked down again, not saying anything.

"How does your hand feel?"

"It feels okay."

"How long have you been sitting out here?"

"Since school let out."

"You're kidding. You've been here on my front porch since three o'clock this afternoon? What do you suppose my neighbors think? Have you eaten anything?"

"Lunch. Up at school."

She unlocked the front door, and it gave smoothly, opening into the warmth and darkness of the house.

He followed her inside, setting the bag of groceries on the table in the hall. She switched on the overhead light, went to the closet to hang up her coat. The mail box was just inside the door. She pulled out a handful of envelopes, flipped through them quickly. An airmail letter from her daughter, postmarked *Gt. Britain.*

"I really just wanted to use your phone," he said.

"There aren't any pay phones at school?"

She looked at him standing there, staring at nothing, brushing snow from the arm of his jacket.

"All right, I bought too much food, anyway. You may as well stay for dinner. But that's it. Really. This is crazy, Gale. I mean it."

He nodded, unbuttoning his jacket and hanging it on the handle of the door. Then, stepping aside for her, he picked up the bag of groceries and followed her out to the kitchen.

The note from Chris was short: she was in Oxford this week. She was traveling with several students she had met at the American Express office in London. It wasn't clear whether they were American or foreign students. They were going on to the Cotswolds as soon as they arranged for a car. Stratford had been a disappointment—very commercial and dirty, but she had picked up some beautiful postcards. They would make terrific watercolors.

"Is that from your daughter?"

She nodded without looking up.

"Where should I put this stuff?"

"What stuff?"

"We're not going to eat all this, are we?"

She saw that he had emptied the bags onto the table and was standing, smiling at her. Enough food for a week.

She laughed. "I was hungry, I guess."

After dinner they sat at the kitchen table while Cat changed the dressing on his hand. The wound looked better today. The palm was swollen, but the angry red color had begun to fade and the edges were acquiring a glossy hardness, turning dark. She layered fresh gauze into the palm, rewrapped the hand, taped it carefully as Alex had done.

"So what will you do now?" she asked.

"I've got a couple of ideas."

"Do you have money?"

"Some."

"Dr. Holzman thought you should go to one of those Crisis Centers."

He shook his head. "They make you sign stuff there. I'm not signing anything."

Did they? She really had no idea. What would he be expected to sign?

"I'll talk to Brian again tomorrow. Maybe I can work something out with him."

"Brian doesn't sound like much of a bet to me. I'd ask someone else if I were you."

"If I was eighteen I could join the Navy. That would probably be the best thing. Maybe I could lie about my age."

"I don't think so. Why don't we try calling Mr. Cornelius again? He might have an idea."

She stood up, and he said quickly, "No, don't do that. Don't call him."

"Why not?"

He gave her a long look. Slowly she sat down. "Gale. Mr. Cornelius doesn't know anything about this, does he?"

"No."

"How did you get here, then?"

"I remembered your name and address. From when you were in his office that day."

"Why didn't you go to him for help?"

"I did. Only he wasn't at home. So I came here."

"Well," she said after a moment, "you're quite the planner, aren't you?"

He said nothing, looking away from her, toward the window.

"So what's the plan now?"

He shrugged.

"You must have something in mind. Why don't you just tell me?"

He looked at her calmly. "I need a couple of days. To find someplace. I need to talk to some more people."

"Yes," she said. "You do. Because you can't stay here indefinitely. It's out of the question."

He nodded.

"Two days?"

"Two or three," he said.

"All right. But that's it. I'll make up the bed in the spare room."

"No, that's all right. I don't mind sleeping on the couch."

"Well, I do. It reminds me of tenement housing. The bedroom is empty. You may as well use it."

Afterward she thought that, in a peculiar way, catching him in the lie had been the thing that made her heart go out to him. He had made no move to cover himself; merely sat, waiting for her to decide what to do about it.

Her move. She was in control. She knew what Alex would think. *Jesus, can't you see how this kid is using you?* True. And she was using him, also. The truth was, she was lonely. And so was he. What was so wrong with giving him a few more days?

Looking out the window at the crusted snow, she thought about her absolute aloneness in this world—mother dead, father dead, husband gone; daughter, too, for all practical purposes. Here was someone who needed her. She liked the feel of it.

She looked in on him on her way up to bed. He was buried under the blankets, with the pillow over his head, as if he were in a bunker or a cave. His clothes were neatly folded over the back of the chair, his loafers under it.

3

The clock on the bureau read six-thirty. Already it was hot. Last night when she opened the windows she had imagined the faintest stirrings of a breeze, but now the air was still; the shades hung motionless above the line of white sunlight painted along the window ledge.

She lay listening to the birds. Amazing how noisy they were at this hour. During the day you hardly noticed them. She wondered if they had their quiet times, or if it was the sound of traffic and human activity that drowned them out.

She sat on the bed, looking at herself in the mirror. A tired old crone today: wrinkles around her eyes and mouth, strands of damp hair clinging to her neck. Careful. Nothing to be gained by this. Clearly, her mood was not a charitable one this morning.

She felt better after she had showered, washed her hair. Standing on the rag rug in front of the closet, she toweled herself dry, just as the alarm rang. She reached across the bed to shut it off. Last night, she thought, had been handled all wrong. Something more she should have said. But what?

Downstairs in the kitchen she made coffee in the small percolator and squeezed a glass of fresh orange juice for herself. Going to the front door, she bent to retrieve the *Free Press* from the porch. The beauty of the day was oppressive; an absolutely dazzling morning. How could anything be wrong in the world on a day like this? She stood, feeling a wave of anxiety sweep over her. She should have called Michael last night and apologized, asked him to reconsider. Why hadn't she been able to convince him? She tried to reconstruct the conversation, could only recall that he'd left abruptly. He said he was tired, but it was more than that.

Damnit. Here she was doing it again. Why assume it was her fault? After all, he was the one who gave her the bad news; she had done nothing but react to it. Well, there were plenty of other lawyers around. She would simply have to find one, that was all.

While she was occupied with that thought, she heard a low, hissing sound coming from the kitchen, spun around, and raced back inside to find the coffee boiling over on the stove. By the time she had finished cleaning up the liquid and grounds from the burner and the oven door, she was perspiring in the heat.

She carried her cup out to the porch. Hot here, also, in spite of the shade from the maple tree. Her sandals felt damp and sticky; the top of her yellow cotton dress was clinging to her back. Staring through the glass tabletop, she studied the rush matting beneath her feet. What the hell, she was a person for whom coffee always boiled over, parking meters ran out of time, and cars mysteriously stalled in the middle of traffic. Face it, another lawyer in this same situation would probably be doing less than Michael.

A pair of mourning doves pecked lazily at the birdseed scattered below the feeder. So many times she had sat here watching the bird activity until it was time for Gale to leave for school. She had watched him read the paper at this table, sitting with his shoulders hunched, the pages spread flat beneath his folded arms.

And their evening ritual, begun after that first night he had come upon the raccoon out by the garage, prying the lid from the garbage can: spreading bits of stale bread with peanut butter, setting them out, and waiting in the shadows of the darkened porch for the animal's return. And every night after that, he prepared a tin plate with vegetable peelings and table scraps, carrying it out to the garage. He never once forgot to do it.

The telephone rang, making her jump. Relief flooded through her. She hadn't realized how tightly she had been holding herself in, waiting for his call.

"Hello, Cat. Gillian Brooks. Sorry to call so early, but I thought you might leave for work and I wanted to catch you. I'm going to be in town today. Could we meet for lunch?"

Gillian. Her old neighbor and friend. She tried to keep the disappointment out of her voice.

"Gee, I don't know about today."

"Please. I'd love to see you. It's been months. You're still working at the art gallery, aren't you? The one over on Yosemite? I could stop by early. We could zip over to Machus and beat the crowd. That is, unless you've already got a date."

"No, it's not that."

"Oh, great. Say around eleven-thirty?"

"All right," she said. "Sure."

"Terrific. See you then."

She hung up and sat with the receiver down, her hand upon it, for several minutes. She could call and catch him before he left for the office. Then she remembered the look on his face last night, just before he left. What right did he have to give her that look? As if he had something on her. *Damn him.* She'd had enough of people thinking they knew her better than she knew herself. That was the way it had been in the old neighborhood, too. The last time she had seen Gillian was at a Christmas luncheon. All the women with whom she had been in driving pools and played bridge and discussed books, all watching her and being so careful with her feelings—nobody even mentioned Alex's name. It was as if he had mysteriously died; more like she was the one who had died, since they all knew for a fact that he was alive and well. Just that week a surgical technique that he had developed had been written up in the paper; they had all read about it. "How's that for fair?" she had asked cheerfully. "The bastard rejects me and the AMA gives him a damned award for it!" Pained, embarrassed smiles all around. And no wonder. She'd had a few that day. Well, maybe Gillian needed a more up-to-the-minute report on the state of her mental health to take back to the girls. No, Gillian was not like that.

Again, the telephone rang. She picked it up on the first ring. Again, it was not Michael. Dave, calling from school.

"Hi. Thought I'd give you the latest. Got a few minutes? I can get him at least one advocacy letter. From his math teacher. I'm hoping to pick up a couple more today. Also, I'll stop around and talk with Brian MacKay—"

"I talked to Brian yesterday," she said. "He doesn't know Gale."

A pause. The counselor gave a long sigh. "You know, I was afraid of that. I just had a feeling. I've never seen the two of them together up here. *Damn*. Well, what about this guy Wiley, up at the hardware store?"

"I talked to him, too. He won't come."

"Why not? Geez, what is it with these people, anyway? The way they just stand there and watch." He cleared his throat. "All right, tell your lawyer friend to give me a call. I've got everything together here—health records, attendance records, test scores—whatever he thinks he can use, I'll sign over to him."

"I'll tell him."

"Just once," he said, "I'd like to see a kid not get chewed up by the system. Those damned gears start grinding, and I get this creepy feeling in my stomach. I don't know, I think I've been in this business too long. I talked to his English teacher yesterday. He thinks maybe it would be a good thing for Gale to get sent away. Says he's got a lot of negative attitudes and maybe this will help straighten him out. What the hell kind of place does he think it is?"

She felt her heart start to pound inside her chest. *That won't happen. It mustn't. Somehow this will work out.*

"Dave," she said, "Michael's not on the case anymore. And I don't know where else to go. He told me that he gave it to someone else, but what good will that do when they don't even know him?"

"Jesus," Dave said. "Lawyers. They don't trust anybody, do they? Maybe it's because they do so damn much hustling themselves. Why should they care about some sixteen-year-old's problems? It's not as if they're going to make a dime from it, like they would from some honcho in the car business who's on his third divorce."

Already she wished she hadn't started this: it was making it real for her, in a way that it had not been before.

"What happened?" Dave asked. "Why doesn't he want to handle it?"

"He says Gale isn't telling the truth."

Dave was silent for a moment. "The problem is," he said, "that for some people, it's not always the best option. Sometimes you tell the truth and you end up getting your head shoved through a wall. Listen, let me check around. Maybe I can get the name of another lawyer. I'll call you back."

Her first impulse was to tell him not to do that, but she checked it. *Don't be dumb. Michael is not going to call.*

"If you could see my list of referrals," Dave said. "This one won't do his homework, that one sleeps through class or cheats on tests or swears at the teacher. So I pull the records and call them in. And if I can get anywhere, if I can get him or her to talk to me, most of the time what I end up thinking is that it's a goddamn miracle the kid functions at all. I could show you stuff in my files, I swear you wouldn't believe it."

"I don't understand," she said. "People like that—what do they want from their children? Why do they want to keep them? I know it isn't love. It must be pride. Something."

"I've got my theory," Dave said. "I think it's ownership."

She sat by the telephone after she hung up. She would give Michael a few more minutes. Remembering the afternoon in his office when she had cried and he had been so good with her, not in the least embarrassed by her tears, assuring her that life would go on, that she would get over this. The pragmatic approach, and it had helped. Yet now it crossed her mind that maybe Michael was a little too practical. He was smart, he had a good sense of humor, he was fun to be with. They had had some good talks together. What had he told her about his wife? That their marriage had been a "solid working relationship," that the divorce had been "friendly."

Face it. Michael was cold. And he was a sloppy dresser; his hair too wild, his mouth too wide. She liked graceful, fine-featured men who knew how to wear clothes and when to get their hair cut, who were not always reading the sports page or bumping into things because they were too big for the rooms they inhabited. *Be glad you didn't sleep with him.* There. Out at last. The way things were headed, it might have happened, and she would have had to defend that piece of bad judgment forever.

The restaurant was busy at noon, a popular cafeteria in the middle of the crowded shopping center. Gillian set down her tray.

"You look just terrific, you know that?"

"Thanks."

"I mean it, you really do. I'll bet you've lost fifteen pounds since I saw you."

She laughed. "There must be easier ways to take off weight."

"Oh, I don't know. I've missed you, Cat."

"I've missed you." Finding, as she said it, that it was true. She was glad now that her friend had pressed her; it was her own fault, their having drifted apart. Some people you borrowed milk from, and you waved to them on the street when you passed; then you moved away and wrote notes on Christmas cards for a few years, until you got to the one with just the names printed on it, after which you managed to lose the address. That was not the kind of friendship she and Gillian had. She didn't want that to happen here.

Gillian's dark hair was pulled back from her face, a simple, elegant style that absolutely became her clear-skinned English beauty. She wore a collarless silk dress of a dark print, similar to the one Cat had copied from a newspaper ad, sketching it for her portfolio. Her long slim hands were poised on the edge of the table.

"I have to say that divorce has done something for you," she said. "I mean, something good. Or am I being simple? I know I'm being nosy, but that's nothing new."

They both laughed. Cat sipped her iced tea, letting the cool liquid slide over the roof of her mouth. "I don't know how to answer that."

"Well, let's be blunt. How's your love life?"

She shook her head, and Gillian smiled. "I was hoping you'd tell me about all these painters and poets you've been hanging around with."

"No. Where do you find them?"

"Okay. No big romance to report. What have you been doing with yourself?"

She told about her house and her decorating projects and about the job at the gallery. She said that she had been working on a fashion portfolio for several months.

Gillian leaned forward. "You wouldn't believe," she said, "how much I've been thinking about you lately."

"Why is that?"

"Oh, I don't know. Marriage is really the craziest institution, isn't it? I mean, think about the ceremony itself—in ours, we each took lighted candles and went to the altar to light one together. Two people becoming one. It's ridiculous. Now I think each person should carry at least two candles down the aisle, and on the way they should light just as many as they can. That's the only kind of symbolism that makes sense." She sighed, leaning back in her chair. "You and Alex splitting made me realize something. Part of the power of the institution is all the damn *history* behind it. You feel as if you have to justify all that time you've put in."

"Tell me," Cat said. "How are things with you and Drew?"

Gillian smiled at her. "Funny you should ask. You mean what's happening with us? Nothing. That's it. Absolutely nothing has been happening with us for years."

"Gillian . . ."

"Oh, never mind, it's all right. That's not the problem. I don't even know what the problem is. You see? He's this very nice man. I'm a very nice woman. We have these three very nice kids, and we live in a nice house in Bloomfield Hills. What more could anyone want?"

She made no answer.

Gillian lit a cigarette, said quietly, "If I'm hurting you, please just tell me to shut up."

"You're not hurting me."

"Yes. Well. It's just that it's so damned *boring*. Years and years of the same conversations, the same body lying next to you in bed, doing the same boring things with your body . . . and I started thinking, Christ, this isn't enough, I'll go nuts if something doesn't happen pretty soon. And so, of course, it did."

"Meaning, you do know what the problem is."

"Yes."

"Does Drew know about it?"

"No. I doubt he would believe it, even if someone told him. We're still the perfect couple. The way we've always been."

"You don't think he suspects?"

"No. Oh, for a while things got rough. I started picking our whole life apart, focusing on all the petty little things that annoyed the hell out of me over the years—like the way he hacks and coughs every morning when he gets up. And when he hums these old songs like 'Tea for Two' and 'I Found a Million Dollar Baby' as if they're right up there on the charts. And how he refuses to sort out which of Phoebe's friends is which. I mean, these girls practically live at our house, and it's still, 'Now, which one is that? Is that Barbara or Joanne?' But I saw pretty quickly what that was all about. If he's impossible to live with, it certainly helps to justify what I'm doing, doesn't it? So I decided to just stop making excuses for myself. Go ahead and do it and be damned." She looked up, smiling lightly. "You look shocked. Say it. You always liked Drew. Everybody does."

"I do. But I'm not shocked. People do what they have to do. Anyway, why would you think I'd be making judgments?"

"I don't know. Because I am. I feel as if I'm not a very nice woman anymore. You give up a lot when you get into something like this: your picture of yourself as the woman of integrity who wouldn't stoop to playing around with another woman's husband."

"He's married, then?"

"Oh, yes. With three children. The same ages as ours."

"Well, that's messy."

"Isn't it?" She looked down at her hands. "Sometimes I feel as if I've just gone right off the hairy edge. I have this vague memory of what I used to be like—sensible, stable, down-to-earth . . ."

"Which Gillian is that? I don't think I know her."

They both laughed.

Cat asked, "Are you happy?"

"I've never been so happy in my entire life. At the same time, I'm a wreck."

"Well, you don't look it."

"Of course not! What do you expect? I wash my hair three times a week, I've been on a diet for six months, I've probably spent a million dollars on underwear!"

"What happens now?"

"I don't know. We're in a holding pattern, I guess. Trying to figure things out. Jesus, what's to figure out? The timing on this is terrible, with Phoebe going into high school and the other two still in junior high. Probably in six months what we'll have figured out is how it was just sex talking, and we had better both grow up and get back in line, get on with the job of being married, forget the romance business."

"That sounds so cynical."

"I feel cynical," Gillian said. "I feel as if I've only got this one life, damn it. I don't want to spend it sleepwalking. But I also don't want to spend it on hold for six days of the week while I wait to see him for four hours in the afternoon at some motel. Life's too short." She sipped her tea. "So you see? You make your own hell."

"Tell me about him," Cat said. "What is he like?"

"He's tall and dark, and he has blue eyes and wears glasses. He's got everything, you know—arms and legs and the rest. He looks cute in his underwear."

Again they laughed. Gillian sat back, lit another cigarette. "The thing is," she said, "I really don't know if I can do this. As much as I believe that I want to do it."

"Do what?"

"Get a divorce."

They looked at each other. Cat scratched her fingernail along the tablecloth. "There isn't much to it," she said, "once it's in motion."

"But what does it feel like?"

"When? You mean now? Now it feels inevitable. A year ago I don't know what I would have said to that. Probably not much of anything: I was still in shock. Gillian . . ." She hesitated, looking down at the table in front of her.

"Say it. I can take it."

"Just . . . well . . . your situation isn't exactly like mine."

"No, it's not," Gillian said. "Everyone knew you were in the right." She waved a hand in the air. "Alex was impossible. You were a saint to have put up with it."

She felt her heart contract; did not want to hear this, even from a friend. "I wasn't a saint."

"Forgive me," Gillian said. "I'm always doing that. I didn't mean anything by it. But everybody liked you so much. And he could be such an ass at times. Why did he always have to be so goddamned honest about everything?"

It was true. He never lied about the "situations"—his term—or tried to cover up. "This situation has gotten out of hand," he would say. "She shouldn't have called you. It's nothing for you to be concerned about. She won't call again."

"Should I be concerned about whether the sheets are clean on my bed? Does she come over here and wait for you to get off work, while Chris and I are up at the lake?"

"Don't be melodramatic."

"I feel melodramatic, goddamn you! My husband is screwing some twenty-two-year-old scrub nurse and I'm not supposed to give a damn."

"It was a sex thing. Period. I saw her three times. I won't be seeing her anymore."

"So what am I supposed to do about it? Go to Florida for the winter? Cut up your clothes and leave them in a pile in the middle of the living room? Kill myself? Kill you?"

"Why don't you just relax and stop making more of it than there is? I tell you, it doesn't mean anything. Why can't you believe that? And lower your voice, please. You'll wake up Chris."

She could read in the set of his shoulders when he was through talking about it. He would never admit that she had any reason to be hurt or angry. Yet these abrupt road turnings, these sickening jolts, would cause her to live on the edge of hysteria for weeks at a time. They were, in the end, what had broken her. She knew the truth: he was not going to stop, and she was not going to leave him over it. That decision had been made long ago. What else was there to talk about? Still, she persisted in fighting this cold war with him in her head. And the worst part of it—the fact that he was still exciting to her, a good lover—how could she blame those women? She really couldn't, not at all.

"I gave up sainthood," she said to Gillian. "It was too much work."

Gillian drove her back to the gallery. They promised each other to get together again soon. Watching as she drove away, Cat thought about the separate and distinct lives of Men and Women. It seemed to her that men took such scant interest in those areas of life that absolutely consumed women. How could Drew not be aware of what was happening in his marriage? Yet she was sure that Gillian was telling the truth about that. Maybe he didn't want to know. Men seemed preoccupied with the practicalities, pausing only to check in now and then, making sure they were represented. Was that world too ambiguous for them? Too soft. A lot of whispering in a foreign language.

Or else they were afraid of it. This was, after all, a world without absolutes. It could be dangerous. She remembered once when she had frightened Alex with it, but good: on the way home from a party one night, staring out at the dark blades of trees sliding by the car window, the gin singing in her head. He had taken the long way home in order to deliver a lecture.

"You have the emotional maturity of a sixteen-year-old. What in hell were you thinking, asking Liz Gardner a question like that? What was she supposed to do with it?"

"Oh, that," she said. "She didn't have to do anything. Just answer it."

"Why didn't you ask me? I would have told you."

"All right. Did you ever sleep with her?"

"No, goddamnit."

"Why not? She's pretty enough, don't you think? Prettier than Norah Williams or that nurse in Pediatrics—what was her name? Ginny something—"

"You're drunk. I'm goddamn sick and tired of going to parties and dragging you home drunk!"

"Good. Let's not go to any more of them, then. I hate them anyway, and I hate all those people—"

"What is wrong with you? Christ, I do not understand you—"

"Divorce me, then!"

She had hit her wrist against the door handle, hard, flinging herself against it. Alex slammed on the brakes as the door swung open. Dark movement below her as she jumped out of the car, landing on her knees in the soft earth. Kicking off her shoes, she had staggered to her feet and plunged off into the bushes below the shoulder of the road, lifting the skirt of her brown linen dress high above her knees. Behind her Alex called, "Cat! What the hell are you doing? Where are you?"

She ignored him, made her way through cattails and tall grass as she went deeper and deeper into the marsh. She knew where she was, had been coming here for years to hunt for wild-flowers—Indian paintbrush and blue vervain. She knew how easily she could be hidden, and she moved steadily away from him as the moon slid behind a cloud. Brambles pulled at her dress and her hair. Darkness as thick as mud. She heard him crashing through brush behind her, but she would not be found. Not unless she wanted to be. At last she sat down on a dry hump of grass, resting, with her head on her knees. He had gone off in the wrong direction, had given up finally, left without her.

She came home just before dawn, when the birds started their shrilling. She had found the road, traveled it, sober and subdued, until she came to the subdivision. Her linen dress was torn, her arms were covered with scratches. She had lost her good brown leather pumps. When she entered the house, Alex, who had been asleep in a chair in the living room, got up and went to her, took her in his arms without a word. Passion and remorse. Her life had swung between those two compass points for as long as she could remember.

Gillian was right: it was absurd to think of marriage as two people becoming one. What it amounted to, in truth, was one of the two being submerged, lost within the other, the dominant soul prevailing, always.

Everyone knew you were in the right. She wasn't sure that, given the alternatives—in the right and helpless versus in the wrong and in control—she wouldn't prefer to opt for the domi-nant position. Submergence was a form of dying. And resurrec-tion was painful. It took a long time to happen, too.

But Gillian was into the romance of divorce. A dream of free-dom. Understandable, if you hadn't been through it. You didn't *know.* The trouble was, not knowing, you weighed the wrong choices. It was not bondage versus freedom but bondage versus aloneness, the total absence of personal ties. A much different choice.

A letter from Chris in her mailbox when she arrived home, post-marked FIRENZE.

Dear Mother,

So glad to hear from you and to know you're happy with the house. You sound so *organized!* I'll be anxious to see it.

I'm in love with Florence. I know I could live here. Art every-where—in churches, museums, buildings, shops, on the streets, even the people. How could you not have gotten hooked on this place when you were here? I've bought more postcards. You'll be busy this winter.

Made my reservations today—arriving Kennedy Airport on June 24th. I may stay for a while in New York, but I'll phone you as soon as I get in.

Missing you,

Love,
Chris

She carried the single sheet upstairs, ran water in the tub while reading it over. How could she not have gotten hooked? Of course she had. The ego of the young: nothing was ever real for them until they had personally encountered it. She had talked about Europe, about Florence in particular, with Chris; had given her her art books to look through, had told her about all of the things she absolutely must not miss. Well, good, she hadn't missed them. That was a comfort.

Stripping quickly, she settled herself beneath the water, closed her eyes. That way she could ignore the stained and peeling wall-paper, the curls of creamy paint hanging from the ceiling, the cracked tiles around the faucets. This room was next on her list. Bad bathrooms were a sign of acute moral decay; people who tol-erated them were the sort who would leave dirty dishes in the sink and sleep overnight in their clothes.

She smiled to herself, sliding deeper into the water. Her mother's opinions—often acutely mournful observations of human behavior—were in there all right, lodged so firmly and deeply that she had difficulty figuring out where they left off and her own ideas began. *Pink and red together look foreign. Bangs and pierced ears are for gypsies. Girls who call boys are looking for trouble.* Was that the reason she hadn't gotten around to phoning Michael today?

She turned crosswise in the tub, in order to dangle her legs over the side, resting her shoulders against the smoothly rounded side. The telephone rang and she closed her eyes, tried to close her ears as well. At this hour it would not be anyone she wanted to talk to. The dinner hour was the favorite time of telephone salesmen—helpful souls who wanted to send her to Arizona to look at retirement property or to hand her a raft of magazines or a ticket to the Firemen's Field Day—"No need to attend, ma'am, we'll simply give your ticket to some needy child, and through your generosity someone will gain real pleasure."

But don't you know—the denial of pleasure is character-building? This she wanted to say and never did. Lots of things she wanted to say and never, ever did. On occasion, one ought to be able to let a ringing telephone go unanswered.

Cursing her dutiful nature, she climbed out of the tub, wrapping a towel around herself, and walked on tiptoe to her bedroom.

"I got you from somewhere." Michael's voice, smooth and polite.

"The bathtub," she said. She sat on the edge of the bed and wrapped the towel tightly around her. Several beats of silence; she resisted the urge to fill them with words. *He* had called *her*, hadn't he?

"I did some checking today," he said. "Naval Recruiting is going through the files. They'll get back to me tomorrow."

"You mean the office here?"

"No, Washington. I called. I also got the names of two high school buddies of his brother."

"From where?"

"I stopped in to see him this morning. Bill was busy. I thought we ought to get moving on this right away."

A pause while she studied the golden bars of light that lay along the floor beneath the window. The maple leaves turning in a sudden gust of wind.

"Thanks. That was nice of you."

"I'll just give you these names. If either of them knows how to get in touch with him, they might be more willing to talk to you. Some people don't like talking to lawyers."

"I'll get a pencil," she said.

"I thought I'd just drop them by," he said casually. "That is, if you're not doing anything."

"Tonight?"

"Yes."

Silence again. She sat, staring at the floor.

"You still there?"

"Yes."

"Look," he said, "I acted like a jerk last night. I'm sorry."

Confused, she sat, her hand smoothing the quilt. It felt warm under her touch. Her turn to do something now? She drew in her breath. *This is ridiculous. I am getting ready to apologize and I don't even know what for.*

Aloud she said, "You weren't such a jerk, Michael."

He laughed. "No? Well, thanks. Is it all right if I stop by, then?"

He said that he was at work, that he would be there in twenty minutes. She hung up the phone, went to stand beside the window, raising the shade. His voice sounded so young. She lifted her hair from her neck, felt cool drops of water on her bare shoulders. Glancing at herself in the mirror, she thought that she really didn't look all that bad in this soft, tea-colored light of late afternoon. From now on, she would only look at herself around this time of day.

"Exactly how did this happen?" Michael asked. "Do you know?"

She lifted her head from the pillow. "First you walked into the house. Then you said, 'Let's go upstairs.' "

They had moved to the middle of the bed, and he had his arms around her, his face buried in her hair. From this angle, looking up, she could see spears of coral and amber and emerald caught in the beveled edges of the mirror.

"About last night," he said. "I was in a lousy mood before I got here."

"I didn't help any. Fixing us those huge martinis."

"Listen. I think you worry too much about your drinking."

"Who says I'm worried about *my* drinking?"

He laughed. Tracing a finger along her thigh, he asked, "What did you do last night after I left?"

"Nothing. Went to bed and thought about things. The world situation. Crime in the streets. How I behave badly with my friends."

"You didn't behave badly. I did. I came and dumped the whole thing in your lap and then expected you to feel sorry for me. It was dumb."

"Anyway," she said, "I'm glad you called."

"Me, too."

"I really didn't think you would."

"When? Tonight, you mean?"

"Any night."

"What did you think? That we were never going to see each other again?"

"I didn't know."

"Well, did you care?"

"Of course I cared!"

"I didn't think about much else all day," he said.

"Oh, Michael . . ."

"What do you mean, 'Oh, Michael'?"

"I mean, if you weren't thinking of anything else, why did it take you until six o'clock to call?"

He grinned. "Because. I'm chicken. I hate taking medicine. Even over the phone."

"Well, if it makes you feel any better, I ate like a crazy person all day. I always do. When I get upset, I eat. That makes me more upset, so I eat some more. I ate all day until I was frantic."

He laughed. "I don't suppose you'll let me take you out to dinner, then?"

"Oh, no. Tonight I starve. Just little sips of water, it's all I deserve." She sat up. "I want to tell you something. This was the first time for me. Since the divorce."

"What were you waiting for?"

"Nothing . . . I don't know. I wasn't waiting. I wasn't even thinking about it."

"Well, I've been thinking about it. A lot."

They sat for a moment, relaxed in the silence.

"What did you do last night?" she asked.

"Went home. Took off my tie and threw it in the corner. Swore at my jacket."

"I'm sorry, I felt awful about that—"

"My goddamn best suit," he said, grinning at her. He lay back against the pillows. "So tell me, how did you manage to consume all this food? Did they truck it in to the gallery?"

She shook her head. "I had lunch out."

"Who with? Anyone I know?"

"No. A friend from the old neighborhood called. She wanted to get together. We talked about all sorts of things."

"Like what?"

"I guess mostly about the affair she's been having. She's met someone and they're madly in love."

"Good for them."

She made a face. "Well. They're both married to other people."

"Not so good, huh? What was that look about? The marriages? Or the mad love?"

She shrugged. "I don't know . . . I guess I don't trust passion. When I was a kid, there was this family who lived next door. They had four kids under seven. He was the night manager at a gas station. She looked like a Manet—all this beautiful long black hair. About twice a year she would go off with some encyclopedia salesman or the Jewel Tea man. Drop the kids at her mother's. Then in a week she'd be back, and they would have a terrific battle, pots and pans flying. He would lock her out, and she would scream until one of the neighbors called the police. Then the next day you would see them, arm in arm, walking down the street, with the kids trailing behind like guests at a wedding. That's passion for you."

"Four kids under seven," Michael murmured. "That's enough to make you crazy."

"They were beautiful kids, too," she said.

"Anyway, I don't believe it. That's not why."

"Why what?"

"You don't trust passion."

"Maybe not," she said. "Maybe because it makes you call somebody in the middle of the night and beg him to take you back, be your friend, even though you know it's over."

"Don't," he said.

"What?"

"Talk like that about yourself."

She looked up in surprise, hadn't meant for it to sound mocking or cynical. Those were the facts; he knew them as well as she did.

"You always take on the burden of that whole thing."

"Do I?"

"Sure. And he lets you, too. You don't have to put up with that crap anymore, you know."

"What crap?"

"His damned hovering and worrying. As if you were some kind of invalid."

"It's how he sees me."

"Is that how you see yourself?"

She pushed herself up on her elbows. "What a nerve. With all that privileged information. Using it to lecture me. I ought to throw you right out of here."

He laughed. "Sorry. I take it all back."

"What do any of your clients know about your divorce? Nothing. Not one single thing. Is that fair?"

"Go ahead. Ask me anything."

"Never mind."

"No, I want to confess. I'll feel better. I was a mean, fucking Bluebeard. I wouldn't take her to Las Vegas. I slept on my back and drove her nuts with my snoring."

"Lawyers," she said. "They pump you and pick your brain, and what you get in return are jokes and bad opinions."

"Hey. When did I ever give you a bad opinion?"

They lay for a time in a pleasant, half-drowsing silence, Michael's hand on her back, near the end of her spine, hers on his upper arm, with her face turned toward the window. She looked out into the darkness, into the crooked V of the maple that rose above the roof.

"Was it your idea, or hers?" she asked idly. "The divorce."

"Hers," he said.

She turned her head. "I don't think I'm quite used to the whole idea of it yet. Of being divorced."

"It's nothing to get used to. It's lonely, that's all."

She rose up on her elbow, glancing over her shoulder at his profile, sharp against the pillow. He had slender legs and heavily muscled thighs. She reached out to touch the curve of his hip.

"I was thinking," she said, "that you're very good in bed."

"Thanks. You make that sound like less than a compliment, though."

"No. I just meant ... people who are good at it are usually good for a reason. Not that I'm against that. But I just like to know."

"Know what?"

She didn't answer.

"How many? Is that what you're asking?" He sat up, reaching around her to the nightstand for his cigarettes. "The answer is not many."

"You don't have to say that."

"Okay, I'm lying. Actually, I teach a course in it. Continuing Education. I could have been chairman of the department, but it's all politics."

"Do you grade on the curve?"

"I do. But you don't need to worry about that—Ow!"

She pinched him on the inside of his thigh, and he grabbed her wrists, pulling her down on top of him. "Listen, that hurt. You start hurting people in bed, it reveals your latent hostility toward the opposite sex. I'll have to lower your grade."

"Not so latent," she said, wriggling free of his grasp. She stood up, put on her shorts and shirt.

"Where are you going?"

"I'm thirsty. I need something to drink. What would you like?"

"What I'd like is for you to answer me something."

"What?"

"How do you feel about me?"

She stood at the foot of the bed, looking down at him.

"Seriously?"

"Seriously."

"We're friends. I owe you a lot. I'm very grateful to you for everything you've done . . ."

"Okay, forget it. Forget I asked."

"Michael . . ."

"No, it was bad timing. Never mind. We'll wait on it."

He got up then and took her in his arms, kissed her.

"I think you are the best lawyer in the whole city," she whispered against his chest.

He laughed. "Are you dazzled, then, by my reputation? That's good."

"You always act as if it's nothing—"

"Ah, but that's my conceit, you see. I'm so damned modest."

GALE

1

The door to the conference room was open. He stood outside, watching Atwood light a cigarette, shake out the match, and toss it into the wastebasket. The glow from the whitewashed window made a fuzzy halo around his head.

"You coming in?"

"I thought I was supposed to be seeing somebody else today."

"He couldn't make it. Had to be in court all day. There were some things I wanted to bring over."

The briefcase lay open in front of him. Reaching in, he took out a handful of paperbacks, set them on the table. *Cat's Cradle, The Old Man and the Sea, Catch-22.*

"Thought you might like something to read."

"I've read them."

"I know. They're yours. I got them from your room." The man smiled. "Don't you ever read books twice?"

"I've read them twice." He looked away. "Anyway, there's no place to keep them. They'll just get ripped off here."

"What about your schoolbooks? Should I pick those up? You can study here for your finals. I already checked."

Jesus, how could he ever think you'd be able to study in this place? Looking like the jerk of all time, walking around with your algebra, your *American Government* book under your arm. This morning, during the first hour, one of the supervisors had handed out sets of mimeo sheets: "Today, we're going to talk about sentences, okay? What do we know about them?" The sheets were labeled RULES OF GRAMMAR. From the back of the room, somebody else said, "They start with a capital." "Good. What else?" The black kid sitting next to him announced, "They ends with a period." Making a loud, snapping noise with his tongue. *Tock!* The class snickered. Khakis, and a red T-shirt; an orange comb stuck up, high, in his Afro. Funny man. It had taken the group twenty minutes to figure out that a sentence contains a noun and a verb, expresses a complete thought. After that the supervisor went around the room; everybody had to give an example. When it was his turn, the black kid looked him up and down: "Who you? Mus' be new here. Never seen you before." More snickering.

The same kid—Streeter was his name—was in his mathematics class. Another work sheet handed out. Columns of problems. The top two on the list were:

$$24 \times 3 = \underline{\quad ?} \qquad\qquad 5\overline{)25}^{\,?}$$

He tried to remember when it was that he had first learned this stuff. He couldn't: it seemed as though he had always known it. Fewer whites in that class, and fewer girls. Everybody looked about his age. Nobody looked scared, or angry, or upset. Nobody looked any particular way, except bored maybe. He wondered how he would look to somebody who was watching.

After class, when everybody lined up at the desk with their green class cards in their hands, he saw that he was the only one who had done the problems. Streeter, glancing over at him, had drawled, "Man, you sure mus' be smart, you know all them answers." Laughing at him. Now Atwood. Telling him this place was no different from Dondero High School in Royal Oak; just study and do your homework, get ready to take your finals. What bullshit; there would be no finals. They had taken his wallet, his watch, all of his clothes. "Relax, you'll get it all back." Shoving it into a drawer where it would stay for all time; he would never see it again. He hated it when people told you to relax. It always meant they were getting ready to pimp you.

Atwood said, "I've been thinking. There ought to be a better way for us to handle this."

"Handle what?"

"Everything we need to know. Whatever made you decide to leave home."

"I told you all that."

But Atwood was taking a spiral notebook from his briefcase—tan colored: PENRITE printed across the top in red letters. *Wide-ruled. 80 sheets.* The same kind that they sold in the supply office at school.

"This way, you can get it all down. Organize it, so you'll have it straight in your own mind."

"I've got it straight in my own mind."

"Fine. No problem, then. It'll be easy for you."

The lawyer slid the notebook across the table. He let it lie there, feeling new anger at him, at everybody in this who thought they had it all figured out—Odgers, his American Lit teacher, who must have been in on it, too; Cornelius, who screwed him; Martinson, the social worker, spending an hour with him yesterday, telling him how stupid he was to have gotten himself sent here in the first place. "You get yourself sent here, you give all kinds of people permission to treat you like a little kid, run your life for you, tell you what to do." The fact that he hadn't done this to himself was of no interest to anyone; not even Atwood, who *knew.* Right now, he was tapping the edge of the table with his pen.

"Look, would you rather stand up in front of a judge in three weeks and have nothing to say for yourself?"

As if it made any damned difference! He did not know how to behave with this man, the way his eyes were always fixed so intently upon his face. He looked to the side, checked again on the long crack in the wall, running below and parallel to the window ledge, spilling white plaster dust out onto the floor.

Atwood leaned forward in the chair. "I forgot to give this to you. It's from Cat."

He reached out and took the folded sheet of paper from him, shoving it quickly into his back pocket. He would read it later.

Atwood said, "She went to see Brian MacKay the other day."

A sinking in the pit of his stomach; he felt his face get hot. No, why? What had she done that for? He had nearly forgotten about that. He looked down at the table. "I didn't want her to think she was . . . that it was all up to her. That's all."

"She's worried about you. She's afraid you're not eating." Atwood was pushing the notebook at him again. "It doesn't have to be anything fancy. Just write whatever comes to your mind."

"Nothing comes to my mind," he said. "Not about that. I never think about it."

"You think about it all the time."

"How do you know what I think about?"

"Look, you won't get graded on it. No big thing. I just thought it might help." He put out his cigarette in the ashtray. "I was looking at your bankbook the other day. That's quite a bit of money you've got saved."

She had let him do that. Enter his room and go through his drawers, handle all his things.

"It's my money. I earned it."

"I know that."

Silence. Atwood was looking at his watch. "Look, just do this thing, will you? It's for you. I know you don't trust me, and that's a problem, but think about it. How can it hurt?"

He said nothing, thinking, at once, of one way it could hurt a lot: the words taken and twisted, used against him. And how were you supposed to write your life, as if it was an English theme, an autobiography? He had read only one of those in school; it hadn't made him feel as if he knew Ben Franklin any better.

"I don't know what you want," he said at last, looking down.

"The truth," Atwood said. "Just tell the truth."

2

*I*f he could get the breathing thing settled, that would help; take one deep breath and push aside this mountain of dead air in front of him. It was hard to think with his chest so tight; it felt as if there were steel ropes about his rib cage, locking all the good air out.

The examining room had no windows. Stripped to his shorts and socks, he sat on the high table with his back to the door. The walls of the room were a dull gray, the color of pavement. Next to him on the chair were the jeans and T-shirt that he had taken off. Across from him, a small metal table; next to that, a sink. That was it in the way of furnishings. Not much to look at.

Outside in the hall he heard voices and low laughter, and the sound of rubber-soled shoes squeaking over the tiled floor. He had been breathing all right out there when the nurse had taken his blood pressure, his height and weight. She had made him blow air into a plastic tube attached to a machine, watching as the results came up on the small television screen. No comment, so he must have passed. But now his chest ached; the room felt cold.

Behind him the door opened suddenly. The man who entered

had longish hair and a mustache. He was wearing gray cords and tennis shoes, a long white coat. He had a clipboard in his hand.

"Gale Thomas Murray," he said, glancing down at it. "Sounds Irish. Okay, Gale, let's have a look at you. Lie down on the table."

He checked him over quickly—eyes, ears, nose, throat. He tapped his chest, his stomach. Lifting the band of his shorts to feel him up down there.

"You look pretty healthy to me. Stay that way, okay? Got a full house over here. Have to put you in the closet if you get sick."

He helped him to sit up, then bent his head over the clipboard, writing. Gale stared at the wall in front of him.

"Any health problems you can think of?"

"I can't breathe."

"Like when?"

"Like now."

The man looked up. "You're nervous, that's all. It's normal."

"I'm not nervous," he said. "I can't fucking breathe."

"Relax," the man said calmly. "You're breathing fine. Stand up, will you? Turn around. Drop your shorts."

He stood and did what he was told, hooking his thumbs inside the waistband of his shorts, sliding them down. His arms felt cold against his sides. He listened to the pen scratching away on the clipboard.

"Those scars from cuts or from burns?"

"Both."

"Anybody ever take a look at them before? A doctor, I mean?"

"No."

The blood pounded inside his head. The man continued to write for several minutes while he stood, without breathing, facing the wall.

"Okay, you can get dressed. The supervisor will take you back."

The man walked to the door. "Take it easy, Gary," he said as he left.

He sat in Martinson's office. Barely enough space for a desk and two chairs, while outside, people kept walking by, poking their heads into the room. He was having trouble concentrating. He studied Martinson's silver belt buckle with the turquoise eagle mounted on it.

"This place works on a point system," Martinson was saying. "You do things right, you get the points. Then you're allowed to spend them, just like money."

The man was shuffling through a pile of papers on his desk. He fished out a card labeled SPENDING OPPORTUNITIES. There was a store inside the building, he explained, that was open each evening after dinner. You could buy things like soda pop, candy, potato chips, combs, toothbrushes, whatever.

"You have to earn your quota, though. Ninety points a week and you can use them any way you like."

How many would it take to buy your way out, he wondered.

Martinson opened the metal file box on his desk. "These are your earning cards," he said, handing him two thin strips of cardboard, pink and green. "Don't forget to have them marked by the supervisor at the end of the period. That's your job. You don't do it, you lose the points."

The ring that he wore had the same design on it as the belt buckle—a turquoise eagle with the wings outstretched.

"We start fresh every week. That way, if you don't do so hot one time, it won't hurt you for the next. Anything you can't handle, you come to me before it gets to be a problem. Got that?"

Sure. Come to me. I'll explain how it's not really a problem. He had one problem already. It was Time. How much of it was passing, and how little he could do about it. He pocketed the cards in silence.

"Do your best in here," Martinson said. "Don't screw around. Just remember, everything goes on your daily record. Good or bad. Don't lose those cards, either. They're just like money to you. When is your hearing?"

Gale told him.

"Okay." He nodded and stood up to signal that the interview was over. His shirtsleeves were rolled above his elbows. The hair on his forearms was thick and dark; it curled tightly against his skin.

"What if you don't?" Gale asked.

"Don't what?"

"Do your best. Then what happens?"

Martinson frowned. He leaned forward to rest his hands on the corners of his desk.

"We don't hit kids in here," he said. "If that's what you mean."

In the shower line, the black kid was in front of him, laughing with another, taller black that he hadn't seen before. Both had high, narrow Afros; both wore khakis and red T-shirts and stood with knees straight, arms crossed over their chests.

He stayed away from the blacks at school; something about the way they used their bodies made him nervous. Too much shoving and reaching; their leathery hands with pale-pink palms always in motion. He would walk close to the lockers during changing of classes, keeping out of range. He did not want to risk being touched.

"Hey, what you lookin' at?" Streeter asked. Both boys were staring at him. Heads turning all down the line.

"I seen you come in here the other day," the taller one said. "They bring you in handcuffs. What for? You shoot somebody or what?"

"He don't shoot nobody, fool," Streeter drawled. "Hey, what you name, anyway? Ein Stein, I bet. He do the work sheet today in math. Tough stuff. Two times three. He smart as shit!"

They both laughed. Streeter asked his name again.

"Girl, you say? Kinda name is that? Hey, Girl, what you in here for, huh? What you do?"

He didn't answer. The tall black said, "He in here for nothin', I guess. Oh, boo hoo!"

The night supervisor came down the line. "Okay, that's enough, you two. Mills and Ramsay, you guys separate. C'mon, hustle up now, let's keep the line moving."

When he was gone, Streeter whispered to Gale, "Watch you ass. That guy mean as shit. Got a belt. Keep it in the closet. Whomp you with it, you mess with him."

So Martinson was a liar; it did not surprise him.

The line moved through the wide double doors as the supervisor stood watching. Everybody stripped, threw their clothing into the hamper inside the door, and entered the shower area. He did the same, ducking into the first empty space, gasping as the water hit him—a warm, sharp spray of needles against his back. It felt good, and he scrubbed himself, using the sliver of soap he had found on the ledge above his head.

Next to him was a tall boy: dark-haired, with powerful legs and shoulders—a man's build. A faint trace of beard on his cheeks, wiry hair thick at his crotch. He had a deep, two-inch, sickle-shaped scar on his right shoulder. The boy glanced briefly in his direction, looked away.

The supervisor stopped beside him. "Murray, where's your soap?"

He opened his hand.

"You need more soap, ask for it." The man handed him a new bar. "Wash your hair, too."

Gradually the water grew cooler, and one by one, the boys stepped out, dried off, using the towels folded on the chair next to the door. He watched the routine carefully. *You do things right, you get the points.* Afterward, they stood in the clothing line for the next day's shorts, socks, T-shirt, and jeans. From there to the rooms. They were smaller, even, than Martinson's office, each the same as the one next to it. None had windows, only a small, rectangular viewing hole in the upper-left-hand corner of the door. A raised platform in one corner with a mattress on it; sheets, pillow, a green-and-white-striped blanket. The rooms were numbered; his was 10.

He lay in the dark, listening to the sound of cool air being pumped in through a ventilator near the ceiling. He thought of an article he had read about a prison down South where a fire had started in the kitchen and the smoke had gone all through the ductwork, smothering the prisoners in their beds. Something sitting on his chest coiled like a snake, keeping him from breathing.

After they turned the lights out, the rooms were locked for the night. He hated that sound of the bolt being slid into place. The first few nights he had tried to think himself still at her house, upstairs in his room, in his bed next to the window. It had made things worse, so he stopped; thought now of the picture over the fireplace: a wall of rock with an abandoned boat oar lying on it, the ocean shoreline behind. He could go to sleep to that if it stayed in his mind long enough.

3

Dear Gale,

This morning in the back yard—a warbler. Cape May, I think.
Pretty exciting.

I wish you were here. Everything is missing parts and otherwise
not working right.

I'm sorry about Brian. He's a nice kid, and I think you could
have trusted him.

Be kind to yourself.

Love,
Cat

He sat at a table in the library reading her note. He had read it
at least a hundred times. Slipping it into the back of the notebook,
he glanced up at the clock: just after eight-thirty. The longest
hours of the day—after dinner and before bed. Seconds, minutes,
hours spun out to a thread of excruciating boredom. Next door in
the lounge people were watching TV—those with enough points,
that is. Everything cost you; everything was points, from TV to
checkers to an extra helping of dessert. All so stupid. At the same

time, there was no room to move or think, even to breathe, unless you had someone's permission.

He leaned back in the chair, pushing the front legs up off the floor and balancing himself against the wall. The library was a small room containing several tables, a few chairs, along with two small bookcases filled with tattered paperbacks and magazines. On a lower shelf were some textbooks: *How to Write a Letter. Poems in English. History of the World,* Volume II. Volume I was missing. He should have taken the books Atwood had brought for him. He could have hidden them somewhere. No one would have bothered them.

The lighting was bad in here; it hurt your eyes. Always so dim, as if they were not operating on full power. He stared at the floor—dark-green tiles streaked with white, like foam on a dark river. He could not think what to write. Every time he tried, his mind filled up with garbage. The tiles on the floor reminded him of the stuff they had ripped up from her kitchen in March; under it they had found the original tongue-and-groove maple floor. They had gotten to work with the sander, and after the tarpaper and glue had been scraped away, they varnished it until the boards glowed. In the sunlight of early morning the room turned the color of honey.

His favorite room. Every day after school he would wait in there for her to come home from work. He would make a pot of coffee and study at the kitchen table; afterward he would help her with dinner—peeling potatoes or cutting up vegetables for the salad. Or she would hand him a box from the cupboard: "Here. Be a useful kid, make us some gingerbread."

He took the note out and read it again. The last line worried him: *Be kind to yourself.* What did that mean? He suspected it meant she was finished with him. He wouldn't blame her, not after the thing with Brian MacKay. But then, why was Atwood still around? It didn't make sense.

None of it made sense. How could he tell the truth? He didn't know what that was. Could not think at all why he was here. Could only think what it would be like *not* to be here: to be in the front hallway of the house on Arden, standing by the old desk with its deep-grained wood banded with sunlight from the front door, the day's mail on it. None of it for him, but that didn't matter.

He leaned forward to put his head down on his arms. He wanted to be free, with the light pouring in. But that was nothing to write. Just words. Words had not gotten him in here. They would not get him out.

4

*I*n January, on the way to her house, he had used every trick he
knew to hold the pain back: counting his steps, willing it into
things outside himself—trees and bushes and street signs, headlights of cars as they rolled toward him in the dark. The streets
were packed hard with snow; it was snowing again lightly. He
ran along, hiding the pain beneath his jacket, against his side,
watching where he planted his feet: he couldn't afford to trip
and fall. Thinking that he was merely running, not running
away.

Pain: worse than he could ever remember. The moon a white
fingernail-cutting in the sky; think about that: think about floating down a bright river with the water rushing over your face.
Don't think about the pain; that way, you don't have to care
about it.

Later he dreamt of running, but stupidly, as if he were drunk,
staggering and falling over himself; running toward a huge black
hole in the ground with flames all around it, and the heat drawing
him forward, always; it would not let go.

He would wake up in a sweat, lying on her couch, with the hand, bandaged and on fire, against his shoulder. Even in sleep the muscles would tense. A flood of pain would follow, wake him with its hot, harsh burning. He would lie there, waiting for it to loosen its hold and spread itself through his body. He felt like crying, not so much from that as from his own helplessness. He would thrash and swear and whimper under the blanket. Each time he fell asleep, he hoped it would mean the end of it, that he would sleep it off.

The pills did nothing. She would bring them with a glass of water or juice, and then lay her hand against his forehead: "No fever, yet." She would straighten the blanket about his shoulders, go back to her chair by the fireplace, and read. She wore long white socks beneath the blue robe; sat with her legs tucked up under her, her glasses pulled down on her nose.

For a while he lost track of time; knew only that the windows had been dark and were light, then dark again. The room was warm, even when the fire burned low; outside, the wind blew hard enough to rattle the windows.

As he began to feel better, he became aware of other, minor things—a rusty soreness in his shoulder, a needle of pain when he moved his left wrist. But these didn't threaten him as the wound in his hand had done. He lay on his back staring up at the bookcases lining the walls. On either side of the mantel were windows of leaded glass that winked, red and yellow, in the firelight.

"You ought to see this," she said, standing by the window, looking out. He got up to stand beside her and couldn't believe his eyes. Stretched out before him was an ocean of snow. Drifted and soft, it would cut like butter if you walked through it. But you couldn't: it was too deep; you would sink below the surface, flounder and drown.

He couldn't believe his luck, either; it was as if he had pulled the whole thing off himself. No one would think to look for him here. No one could, in any case.

They sat in the living room, drinking cocoa and eating rye toast. They talked about books, and he told her about the one he had read that described a climbing expedition on the south face of Annapurna. A bad job; several of the climbers had died. She thought that mountain climbing was a pointless task—too much time and energy and money, and for what?

"You could say that about a lot of things," he said. "Gene research. Space exploration. The pyramids."

She laughed. "Okay. You win this time."

From the window he watched while she shoveled snow, working to clear a path from the porch to the street. She wore heavy boots laced up over her jeans, her hair hidden beneath the hood of the navy-blue parka. When she came inside, her face was bright pink, and she stamped her feet and brushed the snow from her clothes.

"Whew! Hard work! The stuff's heavy."

She put on some music—Beethoven's Fifth Symphony—and sat before the fireplace, cross-legged, gripping her toes with her fingers. The music pounded loudly, filling the small living room.

Later, after he had been there for a while, he began to notice certain things about her: how swiftly and efficiently she did things, whether it was clearing the table after dinner or doing a fashion sketch for her portfolio. There was never any wasted motion. In the spring when they started working in the yard, she would have a whole row of seedlings planted before he even had his out of the flat.

She was a good teacher. She went around the yard with him, reciting the names of the flowers and plants: peony, hydrangea, mock orange, forsythia. One day, when he came in from school, he found a book on the kitchen table: *Field Identification: Plants of North America*. She had hunted it up for him when he had told her out in the yard that he wanted to learn more about them.

She liked people, and was always coming in from work telling him about someone who had come into the gallery, or some story about one of her neighbors. She had tried a few times to get him to go across the street and make friends with the kid who lived there. Bob Schmidt. He'd seen him around school.

"He's all alone in the driveway, playing basketball. He looks lonesome."

"He's not, though."

"How do you know?"

"Because I know him. He's a jock."

"So?"

"He's got his jock friends. They tell jock jokes in the bathroom. If he's by himself, he wants to be."

"Maybe not. I'll bet you're wrong. I'll bet he'd like some company."

"Why don't you go hoop a few with him, then?"

She laughed. "I'm not the one who needs company."

"Neither am I."

He wasn't, either. All the talk he heard up at school in the halls and at lunch—talk about football games, pep rallies, dances, and who went to them and who wouldn't be caught dead.

"How'd you do on the chem exam?"

"Flunked it."

"I aced it."

"That's decent."

"Think the Wings'll win the Stanley Cup this year?"

"God, if they don't, I'll die."

In study hall one day two girls were whispering over some guy at the next table who couldn't have cared less about them; when his buddy showed up, they spent the rest of the hour talking about tennis racquets.

"You think steel or aluminum?"

"Aluminum. You got more control."

"Yeah, but how much do you have to pay?"

"Hundred and a half. My dad got a deal on it."

They thought they knew so much, but they were babies; they didn't know a damn thing. Sometimes, listening to them, he would feel a sudden charge of power come over him; what would they think if he should cut himself loose from them, if they were to look up and see him soaring, weightless, over their heads? He knew he could do it, too. What was gravity? You could master that in the same way that you secured the secrets of the universe and learned all the words in all the books in the library—a matter of time, only. A matter of space in determining the meaning of the different patterns of light filtering in through the slatted blinds. But nobody here understood about time and space; nobody cared, either. They cared about what brand of gym shoes the jocks wore and who sat next to whose girl at the Ferndale basketball game. So fuck them.

Somewhere she had read an article on the virtues of eliminating meat from the diet—how you got better digestion and better circulation, how you lost unwanted pounds and your disposition automatically became sunny and optimistic. She thought that they should become vegetarians.

She began checking books out of the library and poring over them at night, planning their menus for the next month. They would eat rice dishes, bean dishes, soups and curries, eggs, all kinds of cheese; they would even make their own yogurt and bake bread from whole-wheat flour. Each morning at breakfast she asked how he felt.

"Never better."

"Me, too."

They never once cheated with chicken or fish; they were purists to the end. This lasted for nearly a month. One morning at the table, she handed him some money.

"On your way home tonight, stop at the meat market and pick up a pound of ground beef and some hamburger buns."

"You're kidding."

"No. Get some bacon, too. For breakfast, tomorrow."

"Listen, maybe we should have started slower. Maybe we should just take a day off from it . . ."

"No, I've fallen, I'm totally corrupt. But you do what you want."

That afternoon he stopped at Bernard's Market on Farnum

Street, the oldest store in the neighborhood. It had a wooden floor that creaked under your feet, and its narrow aisles were crammed with canned goods that overflowed the shelves. The whole place smelled of oranges, and of the spicy homemade sausages that hung behind the meat counter.

The butcher was waiting on a woman in a fur coat. She had blue hair and wore her glasses the way Cat did—pushed down on her nose.

". . . died on the spot," she was saying. "Fell right over. Aorta burst. So now she's all alone in that big house . . ."

"Too bad," the butcher said, slapping red curls of meat onto a cardboard dish.

". . . got central air and Andersen windows, nine thousand dollars in the living room alone . . ."

"What a shame." He looked up. "Hi there, be right with you, son."

"Well, they never did pay full price for anything . . ."

The butcher nodded as he wrapped the meat into a tight white bundle.

"Haven't seen you in here before," he said. "You go to Dondero?"

He said that he did.

"Maybe you know my son. Bill Fisher? Plays guard on the basketball team."

"I know who he is."

"Thanks much," said the woman.

"Welcome. Take care of those azaleas now."

"Azaleas." She sniffed. "Never worry about 'em. Azaleas are pushy, you have to curb 'em if anything, they'll take right over on you. See you tomorrow."

She left and the butcher smiled at him. "What'll it be?"

He gave his order, watched while the man made it up.

"What's your name, son?"

"Bob."

"You live around here?"

He nodded. The butcher handed him his package.

"Okay, Bob, you tell your mom that's prime beef, the best you can buy. Come again now."

He told him that he would.

5

"Anybody want to play some basketball?"

They filed silently into the small gym—eight boys and four girls. A slow Sunday afternoon. A lot of kids gone on weekend passes.

LaVack, the day supervisor, unlocked the equipment closet and threw out a couple of balls. He dragged the box of gym shoes into the light.

"Streeter and TeBe, you two guys be captains."

Gale found a pair of black hightops in the box. Leaning against the tiled wall, he put them on.

Near the door the girls stood whispering together. He had noticed one of them before: a stocky girl with full breasts, loose under the striped T-shirt. She had fair skin, dark curly hair cut short like a boy's. The others were black; he didn't know them. The white girl's name was Penny. As he glanced up, he saw that she was looking at him, one hand resting on her hip. Above her wrist was a tattoo—a red heart with an arrow through it.

LaVack said, "Come on, guys, choose up, let's play."

Streeter picked first: Oliver, a Puerto Rican kid; Anson, the one who had stood next to Gale in the showers. TeBe took Malcolm and Lewis.

"Give me Girl, then," Streeter said. "You take Kelvin."

TeBe picked Penny and Ramona, the tallest of the black girls. That left Streeter with Ivy and Grace.

It took a lot of time, with much arguing back and forth over what would be fair teams. Then, a last-minute conference, with Streeter issuing orders.

"Anybody get the ball, they feeds it to me!"

They broke and scattered over the floor. Gale's body felt tense. He wanted to play loose and fast, the way he had seen it done at school; wanted also not to make a fool of himself in front of all of them. He knew they had played more than he had and were better.

Oliver took the jump and passed off to Streeter, who dribbled wildly down the floor and shot from the foul line; the ball hit the rim and bounced away. Ramona caught it and passed to TeBe. He went the length of the court for a lay-up.

"You guys is done for!" he jeered.

"To *me!*" Streeter yelled at them all. "Pass it to *me!*"

Gale got a rebound, saw that Anson was open. He threw the ball hard and high. Anson took it, shot and missed, and suddenly TeBe had the ball again. He passed to Lewis, and the ball angled off the backboard and went in. TeBe danced down the floor, laughing. In minutes the score was 10–0.

"Press! We got to press!" Streeter screamed.

"Next time we play by the Ramsay Mercy Rule," TeBe called out. "Any time we up by twenty, you guys gets to quit!"

Streeter took another long shot and missed; Penny got the rebound, passing off to Malcolm, who scored easily. 12–0. Under the boards, Lewis shoved into Anson, hard. "Fuckhead! You don't know nothin' about this game!"

"I know as much as you do!"

"Better know more," Streeter advised. "That guy dumb as shit."

LaVack blew his whistle. "Okay, okay, let's play."

Oliver brought the ball up the court, circling, motioning to Gale under the basket. He snapped the ball and Gale caught it stiffly, on the ends of his fingers. He went for the lay-up, missed.

"Nice shot, Girl!"

It came from behind. He turned and saw Penny laughing at him.

"Murray no good either!" Streeter was frantic. "Shit, I got nobody, this team sucks!"

"Want to give?" TeBe drawled, as Malcolm passed the ball to Penny, then danced away to take a position under the basket. She started dribbling toward him. Gale approached her; saw dark hair curled damply at her temples, sweat on her forehead. He slammed into her, hard, catching her on the hip, and she went down. Her elbow cracked against the floor.

LaVack called time and helped her to her feet. She was biting her lip. There were tears in her eyes.

Ramona swung up next to Gale, aiming a long finger at his chest. "Bang," she said. "You dead."

Afterward, LaVack came and stood beside him.

"Murray, I don't like to see that kind of rough stuff. It's a game, man."

"I didn't do it on purpose."

"I didn't hear you saying you were sorry."

He dropped his gym shoes into the box, walking away. Outside in the hall he could hear TeBe crooning: "Oh, we is number one, oh yeah!"

"Nigger, you is number-one pussy," Streeter said. "That is how I defines it."

He started after them and the next instant was flying through the doorway. Hit from behind, square and low, he landed on his hands and knees in the hall. For a moment he knelt there, not moving. When he turned, the girls were inside the gym. They were taking off their shoes; their backs were to the door. Penny glanced at him over her shoulder.

"Better be careful," she drawled.

6

Alone in the library, he took out the notebook and wrote:

I had this job at a hardware store in Royal Oak. I got it in March. Stock boy. They have a repair shop in back where the guy who owns it and his son fix power mowers. How I got it was there was a sign in the window so I went in and asked, and first he said you had to be sixteen, so I showed him my school ID, but then he said he didn't think so, it was mostly manual labor and you don't look like you can handle it. I told him I could, I was good at lifting heavy things and also at adding up figures, in case there was more to it. He said he just put the sign in the window a little while ago and I should come back later in the week. So I left and walked around the block a couple of times. Then I went back and told him I could do the job, he should just try me out, I'd work the first day for him for nothing, he didn't have to take the sign out of the window. That way, if it didn't work out, he wouldn't lose anything. He said he couldn't pass up a deal like that, so I started that afternoon. I worked every day after school and all day Saturdays. The stuff that was delivered during the week had to be uncrated and priced and stocked, and after the first week I mostly did that all myself, although sometimes he helped me.

It's a real hardware store—not like the ones where they sell all kinds of other stuff like oil paintings and wristwatches and little statues you put on tables. I learned a lot about the different kinds of fertilizers and weed killers, also about the sizes of nails and which kinds are used for what jobs. I was going to start on the floor next week, meaning I would get to sell some things whenever it was busy, at least that was the plan before all this happened.

I got paid on Saturdays. He let me go early for lunch so I could get to the bank before it closed. He always told me to put my money in the bank, not blow it on junk that I'd be sorry about the next day. He had two favorite expressions—"Money's tight" and "When I was a kid, they made this stuff out of wood."

The first time I went to the bank, it felt weird to be standing in line with guys in suits and ties and all the other people, talking to this teller about my account, did I want checking or savings, etc. It still seems pretty cheap to me that the government takes so much of it, but anyway, I did get paid for my first day on the job, which I sort of thought I would. I kept out forty dollars because I needed a lot of things. I went across the street then, to the bakery on the corner, and bought two coffee cakes, a dozen glazed doughnuts, cookies, and four chocolate eclairs. I also went to the fruit market and got tangerines, strawberries, pears, and a melon. Split in half and the center filled with vanilla ice cream makes a good dessert. We used to have that a lot at her house. From her house I would walk to work on Saturdays. It took exactly twenty minutes. Down Washington to Eleven Mile and over to Main. I went that way because it felt like you were inside this long green tunnel with all the trees curving over your head. Main Street is not as nice since the trees have been cut down.

On my way there one day, I ran into these two kids trying to fly *their kite in this vacant lot. There was no wind, and what there was kept taking it up a couple of feet and wheeling it around back into the ground. They were about crying they were so ticked, yelling at each other over whose fault it was. I was going over to help, but they saw me coming and said, "Take a picture, why don't you?" so I stopped, and then the other one said, "Ah, go pee!" Tough guys. About four years old. They followed me to the corner, only they couldn't cross Eleven Mile, so when the light changed they had to go back.*

I like days like that where you sort of duff along. Sundays, when we read the Free Press *in the morning and then maybe worked for a while in the yard, trimming bushes or planting a rock garden in the back. At night we'd watch TV, and usually there'd be a movie on, or else we would work on some project around the house. We were starting to paint the outside of it before all this happened.*

He stopped and stared, hard, at the wall. What was this? Not what Atwood had asked for. This was garbage; it was horseshit. He slid his eyes away from the page.

He had spent the morning on his knees, scrubbing the red-tiled floor of the dining room, while the others were at chapel. LaVack had lined them all up, saying attendance was optional. He had asked to be excused. Someone shoved an elbow in his ribs: "It's free time, jerk!" It had not looked so free to him. He had seen the room with its row of straight-backed chairs before a long white table, white candles at each end, in the middle an open Bible on a stand. The room was dark, wood-paneled, with no windows. Just to look inside made his chest feel tight.

In the dining room the windows had not been whitewashed over. It was quiet. The water in the scrub bucket was hot, smelling of medicine, but he didn't mind the work. He was alone; he could stop whenever he felt like it and sit back, stare out of the window. The sky was low, shelved with clouds; smooth green lawn stretching all the way to Telegraph Road, and from there to Canada, or even Alaska. You could hitch a ride and be on your way. You would not be sitting here trying to fill up time by writing about your life in some dumb notebook. You would be free.

7

"He dead," Streeter said. "Professor Plum gone for good. The lead pipe in the ballroom."

"Play right, or don't play," Lewis snapped.

Streeter stood up, signaling to TeBe. "Let's go, man, I'm tired."

They were playing at a small table in the lounge. Behind them on the wall was a sign:

RULES OF THE LOUNGE

no TV after 10 p.m.
no sitting on floor
no wrestling
no fighting
no cursing

Lewis, a tall redhead with freckles the size of grape seeds, had the room at the end of the hall, number 15. At mealtimes he would sit at the table in the dining room and mutter to himself. The ends of his fingers were purple, the nails bitten down.

"Asshole nigger," he said, "you fuck up every game."

"Hey, Lewis, you gots a fart like burnt onions, you know that?" TeBe stood, stretching his arms over his head.

"Least I never beat up no old person," Streeter said. "Least I never hid in no bushes for some old lady to come out so's I could roll her."

Lewis spun the board off the table, threw down his cards, and stalked away.

TeBe tapped the side of his head. "Coked out, man. Nothin' but air up there."

At the other end of the room a mountain was erupting over the islands of the mid-Atlantic drift. A TV special on volcanos, the sound turned down so that only those who paid could hear, but you could see what was happening: sparks shot high into the air, red-hot lava pumping out the top and pouring down the side of the mountain.

He felt restless and keyed up, watching as the two blacks moved lazily toward the door. On the screen now, tiny, antlike creatures scurried back to the town to search through the smoking ruins.

Streeter turned his head. "Girl. C'mon."

He got up and followed them out into the hall.

"I seen this special on TV once," TeBe was saying, "all about killer bees. They was goin' around stingin' people to death. Doctors was tryin' to cure 'em, only everything they done made 'em worser. Might happen to Lewis someday." He grinned.

"That guy drives me sickly," Streeter drawled. "I gets a heart attack jus' lookin' at him." He glanced down the hallway, then at Gale: "You smoke?"

He shook his head.

"I mean, smoke," Streeter said softly. "This is the real stuff, it's good. You cop a super rush right off. Anyway, we got some."

"In here, you mean?"

"No, in heaven, man, what you think?"

"Where'd you get it?"

"We be the milkmen. Home delivery as you needs it. Listen, you want it or not?"

"I'll think about it."

"Never mind that. Yes or no."

He hesitated. "Yeah. Sure."

"It'll cost you."

"Cost me what? I don't have any money."

TeBe grinned again. "We think of somethin'."

Martinson opened the file box, handed him a fresh set of earning cards. He recorded the marks onto a separate sheet of paper and tossed the old ones into the wastebasket.

"I see you made status this week. Got all your points, that's good. So how's it going? You finding any problem with the routines?"

"No." Looking at the date on the cards he held in his hand; Thursday, May 28. The day of his English final at school. He had been in here eight days already. He fought the sudden feeling of panic that swept over him.

"Heard you played some B-ball last week," Martinson was saying. "LaVack told me you were a little wired. You want to be careful about that. How're you getting along with the other kids? You making some friends in here?"

Was that on the daily schedule? He shrugged, sensing movement across the desk. Martinson leaned forward, resting his elbows on the arms of his chair.

"How do you think your parents are taking all of this?"

"My parents?"

"Yes. How do you think they like the idea of you being in here? All the mess that goes with it? Having to go to court and to worry about you all the time. Don't you think this is pretty rough for them?"

Jesus. What did these guys know about anything? He made no answer to that one, simply sat with his head down, saying nothing.

"Look," Martinson said. "I know what this can be like. People telling you what to do all the time, how to behave, it's degrading as hell. But you're here. That's a fact. And what you do about it is important. You understand?"

He didn't, but again he said nothing, slipping the cards into his back pocket. Was it time to leave? He stood up.

Martinson said, "You're a smart kid, Gale. Remember. Some of the kids in here are in a lot worse shape than you are."

"What does that mean?"

"I think you know. Take care, that's all."

They stood outside the dining room after breakfast, while La-Vack read off the morning work assignments.

"Mills and Lewis, garbage detail. Ramsay and Cole, kitchen. Bradford and Tekel, West Hall. Murray and Lonto, East Hall. Hustle up, you got thirty minutes."

They took the buckets, heading toward the cleaning closet. While he filled them at the sink, Anson collected soap, brushes, and rags. Together they walked back to the long hallway of rooms at the far end of the building.

He knelt and dipped the brush into the water as Anson went down the hall.

Slowly they worked their way toward each other. He preferred the scrub assignments: the slow, rhythmic motion, the water soapy and hot. It was better than emptying garbage cans or scraping dishes.

They had work detail each morning. He found himself looking forward to that time; he could do the task he was given without having to think about anything.

He glanced up and saw that Anson was watching him.

"Where you from? You from Pontiac?"

"Royal Oak," Gale said.

"What grade you in?"

"Eleventh."

"Me, too."

They continued to work toward each other. Anson's sweep was wider, and he finished his section early; sat with his knees up, leaning back on his arms.

"You don't look old enough for eleventh," he said. "I guess maybe you might be, though."

LaVack appeared at the end of the hall. "You guys finished yet?"

They rose and started back.

"What day is it?" Anson asked.

"Friday."

"I mean the date."

"May 29."

He was silent a moment. "I been here five weeks tomorrow."

They turned the corner, heading back to the cleaning closet. At the end of the hall Streeter and Lewis wrestled the last of the garbage cans through the doorway. The metal door clanged shut behind them.

Anson asked, "How come you don't go to chapel?"

"Why?"

He shrugged. "You ought to. Makes you feel better."

"Better than what?"

They dumped their buckets into the sink, rinsed them, and stacked them in the corner of the closet. Gale shook out the rags, hanging them over the towel bar.

"Five weeks," he said. "I didn't think they kept you here that long."

"How long you been here?" Anson asked.

"Nine days."

"They have to see which court can take you, that's what the lawyer said. But I should be getting out pretty soon." He glanced over his shoulder. "I hate this place. Too many niggers."

TeBe and Malcolm came around the corner.

"So we stole this Dodge Charger, man, an' drove it for a fuckin' week. Never did get caught . . ."

"Man, who give a damn about a fuckin' Dodge Charger? Steal a fuckin' car, why don'tcha?"

Anson lounged against the wall with his head to one side. He spoke softly. "Always gotta let you know they're around. Think they're something. I stay away from 'em. They're all pimps and whores."

They sat across from each other at the table in the conference room. Atwood took out his handkerchief to blow his nose.

"Damn spring colds," he said. "I hate them."

"There's this theory," Gale said, "that there's only twenty-six varieties in the whole world. You get each one once, you're immune for life."

"Who told you that?"

"I read it."

"Well, don't believe everything you read. This is the same cold I get every year."

Gale looked at him. "Thirteen, six, and two are a lot alike," he said. "Maybe you just can't tell the difference."

Atwood laughed, leaning back in the chair, tucking the handkerchief into his pocket. He didn't have his briefcase with him today. Just a quick trip; he was on his way to an appointment.

"How's it going with the notebook?" he asked.

"It's not. You can't just sit down and do it."

"Why not?"

"Because. Nothing comes. Or else just a lot of garbage comes."

"What kind of garbage?"

But he shook his head, would not be lured into exposing himself that way.

Atwood said, "Maybe you have to write some garbage to get to the other stuff." He lit a cigarette, coughing behind his hand.

"You smoke a lot."

"Does it bother you? I'll put it out."

"I just meant . . . it's not good for people."

"You're right. I'm thinking of giving it up." He smiled. "I give it up every couple of months."

They sat in silence for a moment. Atwood stretched his legs out under the table, crossed his ankles.

"So what's with this other guy?" Gale asked. "How come he never shows?"

"He will. He's been busy. Look, Cat told me something the other day. I wanted to check it out. About the time you were in the hospital in Flint."

"What about it?"

"I'd like you just to tell me what happened."

He shrugged. "He pushed me down the stairs, and I broke my leg. That's all."

"How old were you?"

"Eleven."

"How long were you in the hospital?"

"Six weeks. I was in traction. They put a pin in my knee."

"Did they ask you how it happened?"

"Sure. Yeah."

"What did you tell them?"

"I said I fell."

"Why?"

"Why do you think?"

"I don't know. I'm asking."

"He would have killed me if I told."

"You were in the hospital, weren't you? You were safe. It seems like the perfect time to ask for help."

Silence. He stared down at his hands.

"I mean, you're telling me now, aren't you? And you told her."

"Look, you don't have to believe it. I don't give a damn if you believe it or not—"

"Because I ask you questions about it doesn't necessarily mean I don't believe you."

"I wasn't going to be in there forever, was I? Anyway, why should they buy it any more than you do?"

"Gale," Atwood said, "I buy it."

Abruptly he rose and went to the window. The thick mesh covering was bolted to the frame. He touched the metal with his hand; it felt damp.

"This is what I meant," Atwood said. "The things you have trouble talking about. That's what ought to go in the notebook."

He said nothing, stayed with his back to the room.

"You're going to have to talk about these things when you get to court. You think you can do it without getting upset? Look at me, will you?"

He turned, saw Atwood leaning with an elbow on the edge of the table. He wore the familiar brown suit with the pale-blue pinstripe. Didn't he own any others?

"I'm not upset," he said. "I don't get upset."

They looked at each other; then he lowered his gaze to the edge of the table. Mistakes happened when you started depending on people. He would not do that, ever again.

Caught by a sudden memory—his mother's voice, tearful and pleading: "You have to come home, now. It will be better if you come on your own. Gale, don't make him come after you." A hollow, frozen feeling inside his chest; seeing the house on Vinsetta Boulevard with its dark brick and dark shutters, the shades drawn tightly against the sun. What hurt most was that she would talk only of obedience, of doing what was right; as if it were a matter of one commanding and the other refusing; as if it had anything at all to do with behavior.

"He loves you. He only wants what's best for you. And you can't live apart from us like this, it's wrong."

"It's not wrong for me."

"I know that's what you think now, but what about the future?"

And she did not mean tomorrow or the next week or even next year, but Eternity. What of Eternity? What if you glimpse the Rapture, the Ecstasy, through the Window of the Spirit, and then you turn your back on it? You mustn't, because then there will be nothing, nothing at all for you but Everlasting Pain and Punishment, the Lake of Fire.

All that she knows about life is in the tracts and in the gold-bordered tissue-paper pages of the book that she reads every day, prays over every night.

Standing at the telephone in the hardware store, he listened, staring ahead while his hand moved slowly up and down the smooth, wooden door frame.

"You know what I'm saying, don't you? You know it's the truth."

The trigger that finally released him; he could hang up then. The truth is not available to her; he has known that for years. "When they ask, you must tell them the truth, that you slipped and fell, because that's what happened, you know that."

In the back seat of the car, on the way to the hospital, with his head in her lap. "Oh, if only you wouldn't do these things. If you would just try to be a good boy . . ."

Himself, listening for clues, because it was all that he wanted, too: to be good, to be *safe*, and why couldn't he ever seem to find the right way to it? What he was being punished for was the sin of ignorance.

The doctor's hands, cool and gentle, in the emergency room; lifting him, turning him carefully, swish of scissors cutting away cloth. "Okay, take it easy, we'll have you fixed up. You tell me when it hurts." Milky clouds of pain released from his knee as he raised an arm to shield his eyes. It hurt all the time, but he would not cry; instead, trapping the pain within, he kept it there, feeling his face get hot, everything hot and dark and still.

Lying with his leg in a cast held in the air by pulleys and ropes; across the room on the dresser a white plastic Christmas tree with red and green lights winking at the ends of the branches. Down the halls of the hospital carolers came, singing, ". . . love of Jesus, love of Jesus, down in my heart . . ." Two doctors came into the room together, standing on either side of the bed. "We can help you, son . . . Just tell us the truth . . ." Which truth was it they wanted? No, he would not trust them; didn't know them at all; safer to depend upon yourself. *The truth.* Whatever it was, it didn't matter anyway; what mattered was the absence of pain.

Sauntering, hands in their back pockets, TeBe and Streeter entered the library.

"What you doin', Girl?"

"Nothing."

"Nothin', huh? Let's see . . ."

Streeter made a grab for the notebook. Gale snatched it back. "Fuck off."

They laughed, backing up to a safe distance. TeBe ran a comb through his hair. "Penny say to tell you something."

"What?"

"She say to tell you she like you."

"Bull."

"Jesus truth," Streeter said. "She say she give you a good time, you want it."

"She like the sun," TeBe drawled. "She go down on you, you ask her." He waited a moment. "So you want it?"

"Nah, he don't want it," Streeter said. "He too busy bein' Mister Cool, writin' his book in here. Hey, I'm writin' a book. Called *Diary of a Fart.* Part One. I was blowed into this big gold room with velvet chairs an' thickass curtains on the wall—what you laughin', man? This ain't no comedy—" And he reached again for the notebook.

"Cut it out!" Gale knocked his hand away.

"Why you got that fairy name?" TeBe asked. "*Girl.* How come you mama name you that?"

"How come yours named you a disease?"

"Lissen, you gots a bad attitude, you know that? Ten points, gimme yer card."

"What he gots," Streeter said, "is no willpower." Gotta smart off. You watch it, Girl. Smart off here, you get the belt. They stick you ass in Control. Know what that is? Lock you up in the dark. Hey, I'm writin' another book. Called *Controllin' the Fart with Willpower.*"

He zipped one off; they all laughed.

"No kiddin', she tell me that," TeBe said. "Think about it. We fix you up."

"That guy who come to see you," Streeter said, "he your old man?"

TeBe snickered. "He a real dude. Wears a vest."

"He's not my old man," Gale said.

"No? You gots one?"

"Yeah. Do you?"

"Nope, never did."

"Me neither," TeBe said.

"You haven't missed much."

"Anson neither," Streeter said. "Know why?"

TeBe wandered to the bookcase, riffling through the magazines, yawning. "Let's go, man, let's find us somethin' to do."

"Killed him is why," Streeter said.

"Killed who?"

"Anson. Killed his old man."

Gale stared.

"Jesus truth." Streeter snapped his fingers. "Blam. One shot. Blew him away."

"How do you know that?"

"Everybody know. Ask him, he'll tell you."

They drifted out then, leaving him alone with his heart drumming painfully; a dry, metallic taste in his mouth. He heard their laughter slipping, high and hard, along the hallway.

When he was in sixth grade, a boy from Montana had told them all how he helped his father shoot a bear that had been prowling around outside their cabin; he had thrown the door wide open, ducking out of the way as his father pulled the trigger and fired into the darkness. Afterward they had had to sit for hours, listening to the bear's dying groans. Had it been like that for Anson? How had he done it? With a rifle? It must have been a rifle. *Blam. One shot. Blew him away.*

No need to ask; he knew it was the truth. He remembered reading about it in the paper. BOY KILLS FATHER IN ARGUMENT OVER CHORES. A long article. He had read it more than once.

Aware of the tight feeling inside his chest—he was used to it by now. It had started years ago, whenever he heard the sound of thunder. He would rush outside to stare anxiously at the clouds. Were they moving too fast? Or not fast enough? If their undersides were dark gray and thick and rolling, he would run back inside to hide his head under his pillow.

"What're you so scared for?" Kevin would ask. "It's only rain. Nobody dies from rain."

"It might be the Judgment."

"What judgment? What did we do?"

How to explain? The terror he felt was real and personal; it did not matter that, if the clouds crashed around him, others would be lost; it was his own fate that concerned him; the horror of Not Being.

Down the street in a vacant lot he had dug himself a deep hole, covered it with a roof of plywood, weighted it down with stones. He had stocked it carefully with milk cartons filled with water, envelopes of sugar from the drugstore lunch counter, candy bars and oranges and packages of cheese that he had stolen from the A & P. When the Judgment came, he would be ready; he would be safely hidden away in the secret darkness.

"What judgment? What did we do?" The questions were pointless. From time to time punishment was visited upon them without regard to reason or purpose. Why, then, should God's Judgment be any different?

Walking down a street in downtown Flint one day, they saw an old man rolling along on a wooden platform with wheels, a man with no legs. *"You see? He is a sinner. God's laws must be obeyed. No exceptions. Transgression brings loss."*

The reason was, simply, that he thought they were guilty. But it has been a long time since he, Gale, believed in any of it. Now when it rained he thought, Good. Wash us all down into the river of eternal hell. Only, there was no hell, he knew. And judgment was settled here on earth. Nowhere else. *Blam. One shot. Blew him away.*

The diagram of the power assembly lay on the table beside him. He stared at it, but his mind refused to focus; his hands fumbled with the tiny screws. He tried to insert them. They would not catch.

Next to him, on a high stool, Anson was bent over the silver skeleton of a gearbox. Bits of wire and hollow tubing along with flat pieces of metal lay in a neat semicircle in front of him.

The Voc Ed teacher sat facing them, with the long table between them. Streeter had told him why. Two years ago someone had picked up the armature of a motor and beaten the instructor over the head with it. The kid who did it was hustled off to Green Oaks—no hearing, no nothing. How had Streeter heard about it? The boy laughed.

"Didn't hear about it. Saw it."

"You been here two years?"

"Off and on. Not steady."

"Why are you in here now?"

Streeter laughed. "Just all 'round bad livin', man."

He had eaten little lunch today; still, his stomach was full. His hands were icy. Anson, leaning toward him, took the assembly from his hands.

"Don't know much about this stuff, do you?"

He fitted the screws in place, locking them with several quick turns of the screwdriver.

"Don't force it. Here. Hitch that wire over there to that stem. You'll be all set."

His hand grazed Gale's wrist as he handed the assembly back. A transfer of heat; a strange, restless energy entering his body. He clamped his jaw tight, kept his eyes on the table in front of him.

Outside the lounge they sat on the tile floor, side by side. Anson's dark eyes swept the length of the hall. Above the shadow of beard, he had wide cheekbones, a broad nose, like an Indian's. While he talked he played with a rubber band, winding it over and under his fingers.

Gale shifted position against the wall, resting his elbows on his raised knees. Across from them the green of the wall looked shiny in the dim light.

"How'd you get caught?" he asked.

"My mother. She called the cops. She was crying and everything, saying I must of not meant to do it."

Inside the lounge it was noisy. Carey, the night supervisor, would be along any minute.

"I thought she'd be glad about it," Anson said. "Only she wasn't. I don't know why. He used to beat on her, too. Not just when he was drunk, either."

"Does she come to see you?"

"Oh, yeah. And my sisters, they come, too. They were glad, anyway. I done them a favor." His eyes narrowed. "He was mean, you know? You'd look at him wrong and he'd throw you across the room."

"Where'd you get the gun?"

"He had it. It was in the upstairs closet. He was always figuring somebody would break in." He snapped the rubber band. It flew across the hall. "Right afterward he stood up and came at me. He was talking the whole time. 'I'm shot,' he says. 'Goddamnit. Call an ambulance.' Just like he was still the boss, still telling me what to do."

Carey came down the hall, hurrying toward the lounge.

"There's too much evil in the world," Anson said. "Too many bad people, you know?"

He made no reply, could think of none at the moment. Anson was looking at him.

"You ever pray?"

"What for? No."

"Just if you need to feel some peace. You don't have to be

in chapel to do it. You can just talk to Him right where you are. Sometimes He gives you answers. He helps you figure stuff out."

Gale was silent for a moment. "I like to figure stuff out for my-self," he said.

8

*W*hen I was eight we lived with my grandmother for a while. That was when my father wasn't working, I don't know why. My mother was born in that house, but my father really hated it, he complained how it was drafty and smelled like onions. Once my grandmother said if he didn't like it he could leave any time, nobody would stop him. My mother used to cry and say Why couldn't everybody just try to get along with each other and live in peace, but my grandmother told her you could only live in peace with a man like that when you were dead. While my grandmother was around things went okay but as soon as she left it would get bad again around there. One day we were working outside and he got mad at me for something. I forget exactly what it was. Anyway he hit me and I fell against the wheelbarrow and it tipped over and dirt got spilled all over the driveway. He was really mad then. He grabbed me by the shirt and threw me up against the garage. I saw my grandmother come running out of the house and that's all I remember until I woke up in my bedroom and she was sitting beside the bed. He was standing there and she kept telling him to get out, she didn't *want to see his face, he made her sick. It's not my doing, he said, it's his doing. But she wouldn't let him in the room. She stayed there all night and left the light on beside the bed.*

We lived with her about six months until my father took the job with AC Spark Plug. Afterward we moved into our own place and my mother said we wouldn't be seeing my grandmother anymore, she and my father didn't get along. A couple years later she told us that she had gotten cancer. I wish I knew why people like her are the ones who get cancer and die.

9

*B*ehind him Ivy scratched at his shirt, slipping a folded piece of paper into his hand. "Pass it on," she whispered.

He handed the paper to the kid in front of him, who opened it, read it, and threw it into the middle of the hall.

"Fucker!"

They were standing in the lunch line. The girl for whom the note was intended turned and gave the boy the finger. From the end of the line Streeter called out to Gale: "Hey! Girl! What you tell me about Penny? Oh, yeah, I remember. You say she pretty cute for a ugly person. Right?"

Ivy leaned toward him, giggling. "Penny say you look like somebody she know. Named Larry or Jimmy, somethin' like that. She say you got nice hair."

"Liar, Ivy, I never did!"

Standing near him in the line, wearing the striped T-shirt, her hands in the back pockets of her jeans.

He felt his face redden; looked straight at the wall, then down at his feet.

"Slop chewy for lunch," Streeter announced lazily. "Fucksgetti tonight. Tomorrow, sea poop and rotpost."

Waves of laughter rippled down the line.

She was waiting for him in the hall that night after dinner. He had been expecting something; Streeter, stopping by his table, had asked, "What you doin' tonight?"

"Why?"

He had shrugged, taking the orange comb out, dragging it through his hair. "Nothin'. Jus' keep open, man."

He thought it had to do with the grass; wondered how Streeter would manage to pull it off, everything seemed so controlled in here. People watching you all the time.

She stood against the wall with her hands behind her back, a red ribbon in her hair. The striped T-shirt was sleeveless; again he noticed the red heart with the arrow through it.

"You coming?" she asked.

"Where?"

She gave him an impatient toss of her head, turning away, moving down the hall. He glanced back through the doorway of the dining room. Only a few stragglers remained; Streeter was nowhere in sight. A queer little lift of excitement in his stomach. He followed her down the hall.

At the door to the cleaning closet she paused, glanced back over her shoulder, then tried the handle. The door opened easily, and she took his arm, pulling him inside.

He saw the low sink at the far end of the small room glowing eerily in the light. Scrub clothes hanging, like bits of moss, on the wall. Mops, buckets, brooms stacked in the corners.

"What's in here?"

She grinned at him. "You scared?"

Leaning close, she lifted her arms up around his neck. He felt her breasts and thighs, warm against him through layers of clothing.

"I like you, Jimmy," she whispered.

"What?"

"I only don't like your name, but everything else I like."

He put his arms around her, feeling a lightness at the pit of his stomach; her body pressed all down the length of his. For seconds they stood together, not moving; then he bent to kiss her. She turned her head away.

"No, I don't like that. Here. Touch me here."

She lifted her T-shirt, guiding his hand to her breast; soft mound of flesh. He pressed his palm against her nipple, buried his face in her hair; it smelled clean and sweet.

She slipped her arms from around his neck to his waist, pulled his shirt loose from his pants. The floor fell away, the lightness moving between his legs; his knees, liquid.

Suddenly she reached out and pushed the door closed, plunging them into darkness. His shoulders were against the wall. Everything slid out from under him; blackness all around.

"What'd you do that for?"

"Ssshhh!"

Reaching for his fly, she pulled the zipper down. Her nails grazed his skin, sending a charge of electricity through his body.

"Cut it out!"

He grabbed her wrists and threw her off, turning to find the door, but he could not, everything was blackness.

But it was all right it was all right he was not tied he could move could get away from the hands at his belt cold hands forcing him to his knees forcing the powerful rhythm upon him never a way out only submit to darkness pain pray for it to be over and all the while I don't like to hurt you like this but you make me hurt you when you are bad Jesus stand by me with strength this is a holy act!

A mistake to go there; he did not think about these things, ever.

Reaching out, he found the handle at last and flung the door open. Cold bright air against his face. Walking quickly away, he tucked his shirt inside his pants, zipped his fly. He did not look back.

At the doorway of the lounge, Carey, the night supervisor, stopped him: "Murray, where you been?"

"Nowhere."

"What?"

"Bathroom," he said.

"You okay?"

He did not answer. His mouth felt dry; there was a fierce pain behind his eyes. He went to sit by himself in the lounge, waiting for the shower bell to ring.

10

Rolling to his side in the bed, he drew his knees up and locked his arms around them. He kept his eyes closed, listening as LaVack went down the corridor: "Okay, guys, move it, hustle it up."

He pressed his face into the pillow. A bomb was ticking away in his stomach. He pushed his fist into it, forced it back under his ribs. His door was opened, and LaVack said, "What're you waiting for, Murray? Let's go."

He pulled on his jeans and T-shirt, knelt to make the bed. A smell of stale grease in the hallway. He did not feel like eating this morning.

LaVack walked them down the hall to the dining room. Outside, he stopped to talk to another supervisor, waving them into the line. The girls were already there; Penny stood with her back to him, whispering with Ivy and Ramona. He kept his eyes carefully away from them, feeling the back of his neck get hot.

Pushing his tray along, he took juice and milk, a plate of scrambled eggs, two slices of toast. He knew he would not be able to eat half of it. *Eat what you take.* One of the rules of the dining room.

He hadn't slept, and his head ached. The light coming in through the windows hurt his eyes. LaVack passed his table, walking slowly, with his arms folded over his chest. Gale bent his head, turning his face away.

"You want that toast?"

The boy sitting next to him had his hand poised. Against the rules to eat someone else's food; you lost points if you were caught.

"Take it," he said.

When LaVack was at the other end of the room, Penny stood and walked by the table. He could not look at her. She went to talk to Streeter in the line, hands on her hips, laughing up into his face.

"Penny, settle down," LaVack called to her, and she turned, went back to her seat. She passed his table again and dropped a folded piece of paper next to his plate. He thrust it into his pocket without looking at it.

LaVack was reading off the names: "Ramsay and Oliver, you guys sweep up that mess in the lounge. That should've been taken care of last night. Lewis and Anson take West Hall . . ."

"I ain't workin' with that jerkoff," Lewis said under his breath.

"What's that?"

"He said he ain't workin' with that jerkoff," Streeter said.

"Look, it's hot. Let's not have any trouble, okay? Murray, you and Malcolm take kitchen duty. Mills, East Hall . . ."

The whole time in the kitchen, Malcolm talked. His voice was high and shrill. He liked to tell the plots of the TV shows he watched. "There were these giant tarantulas . . . an' they was sittin' right there when she opens up this drawer an' sticks her hand in . . ."

He could smell fresh air. Somewhere, someone had opened a

door to the outside. He washed the pots and pans while Malcolm stacked the dirty dishes in the machine. The cook, a large, white-haired woman in a blue uniform, instructed them the whole time they worked. "Now you be sure and get all that egg off of those dishes . . ." And to Gale, "You know where those pots go, don't you? Put 'em away, soon as you finish."

"Why I gotta scrape 'em so good, if I put 'em in the machine ennaway?" Malcolm asked her.

Both their voices seemed keyed to a pitch that hurt his ears. He was having trouble keeping things in focus this morning; his head would not clear.

They finished up in the kitchen and headed, together, down the hall toward the lounge. A current of fresh air was blowing through the corridor, drying the floor in streaks. Ahead of them, carrying buckets and brushes, Anson and Lewis were walking back to the cleaning closet.

"Takes brains," Lewis was saying.

Anson shifted the bucket to his other hand, paying no attention as Lewis leaned toward him. "Y'know, you're crazy as shit, man, they going to put you away out in Eloise with the rest of the crazies. It'll be for good, too. Not no six-week program."

He saw Anson turn his head to stare, saw Malcolm's back retreating down the hall; all of it in slow motion, as from a great distance.

"You hear me?" Lewis said. "Oh, yeah, I forgot, you too busy listenin' to Jesus, waitin' on him to tell you what to do."

"Shut up," Gale said.

Lewis glanced over his shoulder.

"Piss off, Murray, I ain't talkin' to you."

Everything noisy and hot, a roaring in his ears like the inside of a volcano. And then he was moving through darkness, through space; a light exploding at the end of a long tunnel—a moment of waking or dreaming—he couldn't tell. An arc of bright water spilled over them.

"Now, you . . . Gale! You stop it!"

His arm was caught and held behind his back; he was shoved, hard, against the wall. The grip on his wrist was like iron; his hand went instantly numb.

"You hear me? Cut it out!"

His knees banged into the wall as LaVack shouted in his ear. All other voices blurred, stilled, sinking into that hole of darkness behind him.

"You're gonna get hurt, now stop it!"

Stop what? Inside his head there was pain, as if from a blow; then all was suddenly calm. He felt LaVack hurrying him down the hall, holding his arm in such a way that he could not pull free. They reached the end of the corridor.

"Damnit, let go," he said.

And then they were in his room at the end of the hall, and La-Vack had released him; he sprang away to the opposite wall, his body tight.

"This is what happens," LaVack said, "when you move before you think. You get in trouble."

The door closed, and he was left alone in the room. *Fuck that, you move or don't move, you're in trouble all the same.* He worked to settle his breathing, putting out a trembling hand to steady himself against the wall.

They brought lunch in on a tray. He left it beside the door, didn't touch it. Vegetable soup, a cheese sandwich, a blood-red square of gelatin. Looking at it, he felt sick to his stomach. His head ached, and his throat felt raw. Maybe he was sick. Coming down with the flu or something worse. Good. They would have to take him to the infirmary.

Sitting with his back against the wall, he stared at the door. He was exhausted, yet he could not relax, his nerves at the mercy of every sound—footsteps, someone coughing out in the hall, a door being slammed. He froze and lifted his head, waiting. Part of the punishment. Waiting.

Because, often it happened at the dinner table. Sitting and waiting, staring down at his plate, and knowing—that being ig-nored meant being in danger it meant he was in the man's thoughts Do you know why you are being punished? Never knew, knew only that staying calm pulling himself inward he could keep some of his own I asked you a question! as the thing would stir and uncoil itself in ugliness waiting Because you are evil sinful and don't think Jesus doesn't see this don't think he isn't taking your measure from it.

He shifted position against the wall and dropped his head on his arms. Above him the fan kicked on. They could keep him locked up like this for a long time; forever, if they wanted to. So all right, he would lie down on the bed, wrap up in the blanket, and go to sleep. Only he couldn't sleep, he knew that. He lifted his head to look at his arms. The red mark had disappeared, but his wrist still hurt. He rubbed it with his hand. Would it be La-Vack who would come? Probably not; probably it would be Martinson; he was the one who did all the talking; he would be the one to handle it.

He reached into his pocket and took out the note Penny had passed to him that morning.

> Gale the queer,
>
> Just so you know it was Streeter's idea, he was the one said you was for it. Someone around here's a big baby so why don't you just go fuck your mother?

He tore the note across, then tore it again, stuffing the pieces into his pocket. Underneath his shirt, his skin felt itchy and hot. He stared at the floor in front of him, at the white edge of blanket pulled loose from the mattress.

"You want to give me your version of what happened out there?"

Martinson closed the door behind him, leaned against it. Khakis and blue sneakers; a white dress shirt, the sleeves rolled above the elbows. Hairy arms and thick wrists.

"Lewis was hassling Anson," he said. "Calling him crazy."

"And you don't have enough problems, you have to take on Anson's too?"

Did he want an answer to that? There were no right answers, he knew. Better to say nothing.

"What were you trying to prove?"

He cleared his throat. "He wouldn't shut up . . . I was just telling him to shut up."

"What about LaVack?"

"What about him?"

"Punching Lewis is one thing. Punching out the supervisor is something else."

A silence while he took this in. Some kind of trick; someone trying to get at him. He raised his eyes.

"I didn't hit anybody."

"Gale, I saw you."

Pressure at the back of his throat. He saw the silver belt buckle with the turquoise eagle mounted on it; would not be tricked again; it did not matter what you said or did, either it was coming or it was not.

A breaking and circling inside his head: *You see how God punishes? He punished liars he punished thieves and himself tied to the bed can't think can't breathe no help for it none is available*

Martinson said from miles away, "What's the matter with you, are you sick?"

He got to his feet, wiping his hands on his pants. It was hot in here, the air heavy.

"I don't want to fucking talk," he said. "Just get this over with."

Martinson moved slowly, walking to the bed, lowering himself.

"You know, you're the kind of kid who wears me down. I told you that first day. We don't hit kids here."

"Streeter told me different."

"Streeter's full of it. And you're too bright a kid to be still buying his crap, so why are you? It seems to me you want to believe the worst."

"I believe what I see!" he burst out. "I saw what happened to Anson, and he didn't do a damn thing!"

"What did happen to Anson? You tell me."

"Somebody's on your ass, bugging you, and when you try to do something about it, you get locked up—"

"Anson's not locked up," Martinson said. "Neither is Lewis. You're the one who's locked up. Just you. Now, does that tell you anything?"

Silence. He stood, staring in fury at the wall, feeling the man's eyes on him.

"What did you think?" Martinson said. "That I was going to come in here and knock your brains around the room? I'm on your side, Gale. What the hell, it's my job. Let me do my job."

"Whatever you say." He looked at the floor.

"What does that mean?"

"It means you're the guy with the keys."

Martinson looked at him. Reaching into his back pocket, he pulled out his key ring, tossed the bright tags of metal in his palm. He threw them underhand, lightly. They landed at Gale's feet.

"Big deal," he said, "I can walk out of this room. Can I walk out of the building?"

He bent to pick them up, tossed them back.

Martinson pocketed them in silence. "All your life," he said, "you'll be having to decide who wants to hurt you and who wants to help. It's important you learn to do it right. Otherwise you'll be making a lot of mistakes. Anson and Lewis are the reason you're in here today. It's going on your record, not theirs."

"Fuck the record!"

"That's like saying, 'Fuck Gale Murray.' Now, is that what you want?"

Again he looked down, as Martinson leaned toward him.

"I want to tell you something," Martinson said. "Anson is a very sick kid—"

"He's not so sick. He's right about a lot of things. And other people shouldn't be making judgments when they don't know a damn thing about it!"

"All right," the man said quietly. "Maybe that's what we should be talking about."

But he had said too much already. Lowering his head, he dug his wrists into the wall at his back, a distracting pain. After a moment, Martinson got to his feet, unlocked the metal door.

"Come on. We'll get you something to eat."

He did not want anything. The sight of the untouched tray made him feel queasy—the dried-out sandwich, the soup with its skin of yellow fat congealed on the surface. They walked down the hall together, Martinson carrying the tray. At the supervisor's desk he stopped, unlocked one of the drawers, and took out the notebook.

"Somebody found this in the hall. Streeter says it's yours."

"Throw it away," he said. "I don't want it."

Again Martinson's eyes were on him, but he turned his head, did not want to be talked to anymore: about anything.

MICHAEL

1

*H*e stopped to pick up a card for Natalie in the airport. In the greeting-card business birthdays meant booze and breasts and being twenty-nine; he had to settle for *Happy Birthday Ten-year-old* chirped by a little tyke in pink and blue bonnet and pinafore. Not exactly her style, but it would do.

All of the aisle seats were taken when he checked in at the gate. He inched his way toward the back of the plane, noting a number of bearded, scruffy types along the way. The flight seemed to have more than its share. A useless task, trying to identify the hijacker or bomb carrier. It would never be one of those guys, anyway, but some poor soul in a three-piece suit who had suddenly had it with air travel and a boring job; somebody in need of some servicing under his hood. He didn't worry much anymore about crazy people taking to the air; there was enough happening on the ground these days.

The woman on the aisle looked up at his approach and offered to move over.

"You wouldn't mind?" he asked.

Gratefully, he settled himself, slid his overnight bag under the seat in front of him. Next to the window an old man sat, holding matches and cigarettes in one hand, waiting for takeoff. The ends of his fingers were stained with nicotine; his fingernails ridged, yellowish. A dirty habit, he thought. He ought to give it up, would give it up. After this weekend.

Leaning back in the seat, he went over the list of birthday presents in his suitcase. He had been pleased with his choices at the time, but now he wondered, were they too impersonal? Or too old for her? Too young? He had not bought the riding boots, thinking it would be hard to carry them on the plane. Plus, he wasn't sure about the size. And what style did she like? What color? Still, he wished now that he had taken the chance. A flashy gift. But what was he doing? This was Natalie, after all. The easiest kid in the world to please; it was her nature. Thinking about seeing her again after the long winter made him smile.

The woman next to him offered him the sports section. Folding it over, he sat with his eyes on the page, his mind on the evening to come. Nearly a year since they had all been together. Last summer at the cottage he had rented on Lake Huron. Walking the beach to gather wood for a fire; sitting around it as it grew dark, to watch the moon rise up out of the lake. A perfect week. They had been lucky with the weather. June was not a month to rely on, but it had been balmy and warm the whole time; the kids had gone swimming every day.

The stewardess stopped beside him. "Something to drink?"

"Nothing for me, thanks."

He felt for Daniel's ticket inside his coat pocket. What should they do, then, the two of them, on that first night back home? Go to a Tiger game? He had already checked to see, and they were in town. Or it might be better to just let him unpack, settle in, make a few phone calls. He suggested to Cat that maybe they could have dinner together. He wanted the two of them to meet as soon as possible. So many options; it made him feel oddly nervous. In any case, he didn't have to decide this minute.

He glanced over at the woman. "You from Detroit?"

"No. Washington," she said. "You?"

He started to tell her, but even as the thought formed he was sobered by it. The truth was, he didn't like telling people that he didn't live with his kids; it shamed him. Let her think he was just another husband on his way home from a business trip, the wife waiting in the station wagon at the airport; it had been true once.

"I'm from Detroit," he said.

"Off to a wild weekend in D.C.?"

"Right."

Smiling, he turned his attention to the paper: read through the sports, read his horoscope:

> You may want to sacrifice leisure time in favor of work, reflection tonight.

Not likely. What he wanted was not to think about work for at least two days. He turned his head to look out the window, seeing nothing but smooth blue space before him, the whole summer rolling out in front of his eyes.

2

*H*e drove along a winding boulevard planted with large trees. Joy had offered to pick him up when he called for directions, but he declined; he had already rented a car.

"That's a shame. You could have used mine. Listen, I made reservations for you for dinner, I hope you don't mind. Sometimes they're hard to get on a Friday night."

He thanked her, said he appreciated it. Now, turning into the subdivision, he was at once struck by the monotony of it—all large frame houses on small lots; all done in pastel colors, trimmed with dark brick; all looking brand-new. The trees on the median looked newly planted.

He found the house on Elder Lane at the edge of the cul-de-sac. As he parked, the screen door burst open and Natalie came running down the walk. He caught her to him. Straightening, he saw Ed on the front porch; they waved to each other.

"How you doing?"

"Fine."

Joy appeared in the doorway. He walked up to the porch as the screen door opened again. Daniel came and stood beside her. He was a full head taller than she, nearly as tall as Michael now; dark curly hair, a faint shadow of beard on his face. No, not possible; it had only been a year.

Shyly he stuck out his hand. "Hi, Dad."

A sudden feeling of loss overwhelmed him. He shook the hand, forcing himself to smile.

Ed said, "Quite a shock, huh? Would you have known him?"

"Barely."

"Yeah, he's changed. Grew up all of a sudden."

They stood on the porch, smiling awkwardly at one another. Michael could feel the strain.

"Daddy, you're late," Natalie said.

"No, I'm not. Am I?"

"She's just impatient." Joy ruffled Natalie's hair. "She's been dressed and holding her breath since this morning."

"How about a drink?" Ed asked. "You've got time before dinner. Gin-and-tonic? Scotch . . . ?"

"Scotch is fine. A little water."

They entered the house. Joy turned Michael toward the living room.

"How was your flight?"

"Fine."

"You like flying, Daddy?" Natalie asked.

"Yeah, I do. Do you?"

Natalie shrugged her shoulders. "I haven't done that much. I liked the flight at Christmas. I wish I was going back with you this time."

"You do? I thought you were all hot to go to that riding camp."

"Well, I am, but . . ."

"She wants to do both," Joy said. "Actually, she wants to do everything at once. You know how she is."

The room was cool. He had an impression of softness, of elegance: pale-blue carpeting that looked silvery in the light; cream-colored curtains, letting in the late-afternoon sun. On the table in front of the window was a pitcher of blue glass filled with tall white flowers.

"Nice place," he said.

"Thanks."

She led him through to the dining room beyond, and then to a sliding glass door that opened onto a redwood deck.

"It's cooled off out here finally. Sit down. Natalie, take your father's coat for him."

It didn't feel cool to him. The air was muggy and still; the sky cloudless, turning a deep rose pink. Natalie took his coat, disappearing with it inside the house. Daniel leaned with his elbows on the railing, looking down into the yard, where two dogs were running around, chasing each other.

"Knock it off!" he yelled at them. "Get lost!"

"Ed's done a lot of work here," Joy said, sitting down across from him. "He and Daniel built this deck last fall."

"I'm impressed." Michael turned to look at his son. "I didn't know you were a carpenter."

"I'm not. I'm just the slave labor."

"Watch it, your dad will get the wrong idea."

Ed had come through the doorway to hand Michael his drink. "How is it out here? Anybody getting bitten? I rigged up the insect lights. I can turn them on."

"No, it's fine."

"It's been hotter than hell here these last few weeks. Bugs are terrible. How's the weather in Detroit, Mike?"

"Like this," he said. "A heat wave."

"Seems like it's all over the country."

Natalie came out and took the seat next to Michael. She held on to his arm. "We're going to my favorite place for dinner," she announced. "It's called The White House, only it's not the real White House, Daddy."

"No kidding," said Daniel.

She stuck out her tongue.

Joy leaned back in her chair. "God, I'm so *bushed.* I've been running all day."

"How is the real estate business?"

"Busy. You could work all night if you wanted to. I think I made a mistake. All I wanted was a change of pace. This is *work*, you know what I mean?"

Inside the house the telephone rang. Daniel went to answer it.

"Don't kid yourself," Ed said. "Anything less, and you'd be bored to death."

"Better bored than burnt out," she said, yawning. "So how's the law business these days?"

"It's fine. Bill said to say hi. Also, Pete and Camille."

"Yes, I had a nice letter from her the other day. They're building a house out on Wing Lake."

"Is Bill the one with the sailboat?" Natalie asked.

"You know who Bill is, honey. He's your dad's partner. Robin and Billy's daddy."

"Oh, yeah."

Daniel appeared in the doorway. "It's Craig on the phone. He wants to know if I can go swimming tomorrow night."

Joy looked at him. "I don't see how."

"It's a party, Mom."

She shook her head.

"Why not?"

"Because, for one thing, your room's a mess, and for another, you haven't finished packing yet."

"I'll get it done."

"Daniel, we've already discussed this—"

"I don't see why I can't, when I'm going to be gone the whole summer, anyway."

"Your mother said no," Ed said.

A brief, uncomfortable silence. Without another word, Daniel turned, went inside.

Joy sighed, looking straight at Ed. "That kid," she said, "will someday drive me to it."

Michael, lowering his eyes, said nothing, struck again by a curious sense of loss. Through the rest of the conversation he felt unable to concentrate, felt Ed looking at him in a way that made him want to take the glass and heave it out over the redwood deck into the rosy, heat-pressed air.

"Turn here," Daniel directed him.

He pulled into a large, busy parking lot next to the white brick house.

"It looks like an old mansion."

"It is," Natalie said. "They have great food, Daddy, you'll love it."

"It's not that great," Daniel said.

They got out of the car, a dark-blue Mustang with wire wheels. He had picked it because of its snappy look, and it had paid off; Daniel had walked all around it, admiring. Now he climbed out of the back, saying, "It rides nice."

Michael agreed. He went to the trunk, opened it, took out his bag to get at the small stack of wrapped presents inside. Turning, he handed them to Natalie. "Here. Take these in with you."

"Geez, do we have to do that in there?" Daniel asked.

Remembering, too late, his son's strict sense of privacy. You never call attention to yourself, no matter what the circumstances. But Natalie was smiling up at him: "Oh, goody!"

The sky was thick with stars, the air smelling sweetly of honeysuckle. Inside the restaurant it was crowded; he was glad Joy had thought to call ahead. Their table stood next to a window looking out onto a back garden where rows of flowering trees gleamed white in the darkness.

Natalie opened each package swiftly, crying out, "It's beautiful, I love it!" as she snatched the pink sweater from the box. The record of *Swan Lake* and the jar of Sanders Hot Fudge each earned him a hug, but her favorite was the silver charm bracelet with the ballerina.

"I've been wanting one like this forever, Daddy."

"Good, I'm glad."

"I love you." And she was out of her chair, giving him a kiss and a hug. Daniel sat in stoic silence, watching them.

They ordered dinner: steak for Daniel and himself, chicken for Natalie. The waitress brought a loaf of warm whole-wheat bread to the table, along with a dish of sweet butter.

"This friend of mine, Margaret, eats here a lot," Natalie confided.

"Who's Margaret?"

"She lives down the street. She's my best friend, really."

"Your best friend, huh? I'd like to meet her."

"She lives with her brother and her mom. Her dad lives in Washington. They're divorced. You probably can't meet her this time, because she usually goes on weekends to her dad's apartment."

"Pass the bread," Daniel said.

Michael handed it across the table.

"Her dad has a girlfriend. Her name's Marian. When Margaret goes to visit him, they do stuff together, like shop and go to museums. I went with them once. It was fun."

The waitress brought their salads. Natalie looked up. "I don't care for any, thanks," she said politely.

"No? How about some Jell-O or cottage cheese?"

"No, thanks, I really don't like any kind of salad."

"Tell her your life history, why don't you?" Daniel said.

"Shut up, why don't you?"

"Hey, you guys," Michael said, but he was laughing.

The meal arrived, and Natalie was right. Everything was delicious: the steaks cooked perfectly; the chicken in a delicate sauce; the vegetables—broccoli and potatoes and beets—served family style. The waitress brought more bread and butter. When he finished eating, Michael felt nearly relaxed, at home.

The waitress cleared the dishes, returned to the table bearing a chocolate cake on a glass plate. The other waitresses gathered about the table. They sang "Happy Birthday" while Natalie sat, beaming.

"Was this your idea, Daddy?"

He shook his head. "I wish it was."

"It must have been Mom and Ed's, then."

Afterward, as they were leaving, she thanked everybody she saw. Michael thought of another birthday—Daniel's seventh, when they had taken him to an ice cream parlor in Southfield that specialized in such occasions. The waiters, dressed in red-and-white-striped shirts, with bright suspenders and derby hats, reciting loud birthday greetings over the ice cream and cake; everybody in the place joining in the chorus. Daniel had sat through the entire ordeal with head bowed, afterward raising stricken eyes to Michael's: *Can we leave now?*

He started to remind his son of this, thought better of it. Maybe later, after things had loosened up a little.

Natalie sighed as she snuggled next to him in the car.

"That was so fun. I wish you came here more often, Daddy." Her hand was on his leg; he covered it with his own. "Do you think you can make it in October? For the ballet?"

"I think so."

She was looking up at him, her eyes liquid in the darkness. "You know, Margaret's dad might get married. Margaret says she hopes he does. She likes Marian a whole lot."

From the back seat, Daniel said, "Why do you always talk in that dippy voice when you talk about Margaret? She must be a real dip."

"Do you have a girlfriend, Daddy?"

"Yeah, I guess I do."

"What's her name? Does she live in your building?"

"In my building? No. Why?"

"I just wondered," she said, "why I didn't meet her when I was there."

"I guess I didn't have her then. We were just friends."

"What's her name? Does she have any kids?"

"Her name's Catherine. And, yes—she's got a daughter."

"The same age as me?"

"Jesus," Daniel said.

"No," Michael said. "She's older."

"Are you going to get married to her?"

"Don't act so dumb, you talk like you're talking to your dolls."

"You *shut up!*" She turned on him. "You don't know everything!"

Incredibly, she was near tears; his golden daughter just turned
ten, wearing her new sweater and bracelet, burying her face
against his chest. Bewildered, Michael put his arm around her.

"Dad," Daniel said, "you missed the turn."

3

*H*e unpacked his bag when he got to the motel room, hanging his shirts in the closet and setting his toothbrush and shaving gear on the shelf in the bathroom. He sat on the edge of the bed, stripped off his tie, unbuttoned the top button of his shirt. He felt very tired, although it was not late, only just after ten. It was probably the flight.

Lying back on the bed, he stared up at the ceiling. Natalie had wanted him to come in when he had taken them back, but he hadn't really wanted to do that. He was picking them up at eight-thirty. Natalie had a ballet lesson, and he and Daniel were dropping her off and going out to breakfast. Afterward they would all spend the day together. *Doing what?* The talk about it in the car had been unproductive. Daniel put down all of Natalie's suggestions, came up with none of his own. Finally they had tabled it; they would decide in the morning. *Why am I depressed? Nothing went wrong.* The dinner had been pleasant enough. As for the rest of it—what had he expected? To pick up exactly where they had left off, as if no interruption had occurred? Not very realistic.

Besides, when he thought about it, nothing much had changed. Natalie was still the one who smiled on everything. Daniel sat back and waited for things to happen; any minute now and he would begin having a terrific time.

Nuts, they were just kids, after all; they grew up, no matter what you did. What had Cat said to him about her daughter? "Once, there was this little redhead who had to be put to bed a hundred times a night. Then about a week later, she went away to college." And look at Bill—how he brooded over and complained about those kids of his, and he was living with them twenty-four hours a day.

Still, he had sensed a distancing. Was it his fault? He hardly knew enough anymore to ask the right questions, felt as if he were being Uncle Michael at the table—"How's school? What courses are you taking this year?" Jesus, he hated that. With Natalie he could always seem to find his way. Maybe things would be better when he and Daniel were off on their own again, away from this town and really living together.

He had a sudden memory of the hospital nursery fourteen years ago, peering through the glass at the crib labeled ATWOOD, BOY, 8 lbs. 13 oz.—a flat red face framed with spiky black hair; puffy slits for eyes; those tiny, starfish hands folding and unfolding in the air. The nurses, so fiercely protective, would shoo the visitors out at feeding time—"The babies are coming, the babies are on the floor!" He had heard that they no longer did this; men were allowed to be present, to watch this sacred stuff, now; were even encouraged to think themselves a part of it all. He couldn't help comparing that sterile environment with the scene when they first arrived with him at the apartment in Royal Oak: their friends all there; the case of beer on the kitchen table; the box of cigars—blue bands proclaiming, *It's a Boy!* The apartment reeked of smoke and booze, and Daniel had slept placidly through the party. Always such a good baby.

He glanced at his watch, saw that it was after eleven o'clock. Too late to call now; no, hell, he wanted to talk to her; he dialed her number and waited through ten rings. No answer. Odd, since she had mentioned that she would be home all weekend. *Don't panic. She hadn't said she wouldn't leave the house.*

Again he lay back, hands behind his head, staring upward, wishing now that things had gone better with Gale. Maybe then he would feel more confidence about Daniel. But that didn't really make any sense; they were nothing alike.

Bill had stopped by his office early in the afternoon to talk about the hearing. "You got everything together on it?"

"Yeah, I think so. Just about."

"Okay, let's go over it together on Monday. Any drugs involved?"

"Not that I know of."

"Great. A change of pace from my regular clientele."

They had both laughed.

Lying on the bed, listening to the night sounds—a whisper of air through the elevator shaft, a rhythmic clanging in the distance as a train signaled its approach to a crossing—he wondered how it had happened that suddenly he had gotten old.

Let things go right this summer. If he could only count on that, everything else would fall into place.

4

*J*oy answered the door. "You're prompt. I haven't heard any action up there yet. Let me check."

She went lightly up the stairs, and he stood in the hall, staring at the ship's clock hanging on the wall in front of him, the hands set at five-thirty. The couch and chairs in the living room he now recognized as their old furniture. It had looked different to him yesterday in the unfamiliar setting. The only piece that he had taken with him was the chrome-and-glass coffee table, one of his own purchases early in the marriage. He saw now why she had never liked it—not her style at all; it was unlike anything else they had owned together.

"They'll be ready in a few minutes," she said, coming down the stairs. "How about some coffee?"

He followed her out to the kitchen. Last night he had noticed the rows of corn and tomatoes, the cucumbers and pale-green leaf lettuce growing at the back of the yard. She was a great gardener; it relaxed her to work out in the sun.

"You still find time for all that," he said, indicating the potted plants arranged on glass shelves in the sunny window.

"It's what I like to do. Next year I'm thinking that I'll plant some grapevines along the fence."

She poured their coffee, sat down opposite him.

"So," she said, "how are things with you, really?"

"What do you mean, really?"

"You seeing anyone?"

"I see lots of people, sure."

She smiled. "A non-answer if I ever heard one."

"I figured you already had the answer."

"From Natalie, you mean? Yes, she said something last night. I was just curious—is it someone I know?"

She was wearing red shorts this morning, leather sandals. Already her skin was deeply tanned. A white frilly blouse, her dark hair done up in a loose knot on top of her head; it gave her a gentle, old-fashioned look.

"It's no one you know," he said.

"Mom, where did you put my purple tights?" Natalie called down.

"They're in the dirty-clothes basket. Where you left them."

"Aren't they clean *yet?*"

"No, they're not. Wear the green ones. And hurry up, or you'll be late."

She got up to put some bread into the toaster.

"Natalie told me about your new apartment. It sounds very nice."

"Yeah, I like it."

"She said you picked out everything yourself. You never used to like doing that."

"I didn't?"

"No. I used to have to drag you along—don't you remember?"

She refilled his cup. On a rack above the stove hung a row of shiny copper-bottomed pans, neatly positioned smallest to largest. The wallpaper was a yellow-and-white check, white ruffled curtains at the windows. He lit a cigarette, sat back in the chair.

"How about coming to dinner tonight?" she asked. "I've got

some steaks in the freezer. We can grill out. Nothing fancy, but it might be nicer than a restaurant. After a tough day of sightseeing."

"That would be great." Caught by surprise, unable to think of a polite way to refuse. The last thing he wanted was to spend time in this house with Ed the handyman, the provider, mixing his drinks for him, trying to make him feel at home. Just one happy family they were; Ed raising his children for him, too, doing a damn fine job of it. No. He would think of some excuse later, put her off.

Daniel appeared in the doorway, eyes puffy from sleep. Yawning, he rubbed his bare arms as he squinted into the sun.

"Morning."

"Hi."

"Geez, I overslept, I guess."

His mother was looking at him. "You're going to wear something besides that T-shirt into town, I hope."

"What would you like me to wear, Mom? Tell me."

"Oh, please."

"No, really. I'll wear whatever you say."

"Fine. Your blue plaid, then. It's hanging up in the laundry room."

He gave her a smart salute, leaving the room as Natalie came in. Dressed all in green—shorts, tights, and a short-sleeved jersey. Her hair was tied back with a green ribbon. She gave Michael a quick kiss and a hug, accepted the toast that her mother held out to her.

"How about a glass of juice?"

"Do I have time?"

"If you're late, they'll wait," Daniel said, coming up the stairs. "You're the star, aren't you?"

"Shut up."

"Dinner will be around six," Joy said to Michael. "We'll have drinks any time after four-thirty. You ought to be ready for them by then."

"Oh, is he eating here tonight?" Natalie asked. "Goody."

"Goody," Daniel mimicked.

"You two," Joy said firmly. "Don't fight today. *Please.*"

They dropped Natalie off at ballet class. Michael watched her run up the steps of the red brick Victorian house.

"Where shall we go now?"

"There's a restaurant down near the water. I think it's open on Saturdays."

Daniel directed him. Soon they arrived at the modest gray frame building in the downtown section of Alexandria. A beautiful day, he thought, as he got out of the car. Perfect weather: warm, but without the stifling humidity of yesterday. They ate outside on the terrace, with the sun shining down through a thick awning of leaves.

"What would you like to do today?"

Daniel shrugged. "Whatever you want. Mom said you might like to see the Space Museum."

"I'm not much for hanging around museums on a day like this."

Daniel's face brightened. "Me either. Anyway, I've seen it about ten times."

"I haven't been to this town since high school. I wouldn't mind just walking around, seeing the Lincoln Memorial and the Washington Monument."

"Have you ever been down M Street, where all the embassies are?"

"Not since my senior-class trip."

Afterward they left the restaurant to walk down the hill toward the water. The narrow row houses with their shallow lawns and tall, curtained windows tempted him to peer inside.

"All of these places used to be owned by the ships' captains," Daniel explained. "They'd just dock their boats and walk home at night."

They reached the pier in a few moments, stood at the railing, looking out at the dozens of sailboats anchored offshore, rocking gently in the greenish water. Michael leaned his arms on the railing, staring out at the distant shoreline of Maryland across the bay. The wind was picking up. In the distance he could see several kids wind-surfing. The brightly colored sails skimmed over the water.

"You ever tried that?"

"A couple of times. A friend of mine has one. He said he'd teach me. It's hard, though. He said it took him a year to learn."

"We'll do some sailing this summer," Michael said. "Bill's got his boat down at Bayview. He'd like to take you on it."

Daniel shoved his hands into his pockets, squinting into the sun.

"What else do you do around here?" Michael asked.

"Do?"

"With your time, I mean."

"The usual stuff. School. Studying. This spring I took some tennis lessons."

"How did you like that?"

"I liked it. The guys I hang around with all play tennis."

Michael looked at him. "I was worried at first that this might be tough on you, having to move away and leave all your old buddies."

Daniel shrugged. "It wasn't that tough."

They started back up the hill, passing a small enclosed area that he had missed on the way down. It was filled with low, flowering shrubs, surrounded by an iron fence; inside was a statue of a man on a horse.

"There's a lot of history here," Daniel said. "You can't help getting into it. Before, I was never very interested, but here, there's statues and monuments everywhere you look. Seems like everybody who ever lived here ended up being famous. They were all generals or inventors or politicians or something."

Michael nodded. "Let's see, Detroit's got its share of famous guys. Father Marquette. Chief Pontiac. Henry Ford. Ty Cobb, even though he wasn't born there."

Daniel found a stone at the edge of the sidewalk. He kicked it with his shoe. "Dad. Just because I say something good about this place doesn't mean I'm putting Detroit down."

"I know that."

An awkward silence. Something was wrong. Daniel was not good at hiding things; not for long, at least.

"What's the matter?" Michael asked.

"Nothing."

"Come on."

"No. It isn't fair to bother you."

"Never mind that. Just tell me."

"It really isn't anything. It's just that I've met these guys here and I'm having a pretty good time with them. And everybody's making all these plans for the summer . . ." His son shot him a look, stopped walking, stared off into the distance. Michael stopped also.

And you would rather be here for it. You would rather not be going to Detroit. He was aware, suddenly, of the faintly fishy odor of the bay, mixed with the smell of boxwood and honey-suckle.

"I'm gonna be in trouble over this," Daniel mumbled.

"Who says so?"

"Mom. She acts like it's all been written in blood."

"Nothing is written in blood," Michael said. "And I'm glad you like it here. I'd feel worse if you didn't."

He winced at the look of relief that came over Daniel's face. They resumed walking: arrived in a few minutes at the car. Michael leaned against the fender, feeling the heat of the metal through his slacks. Daniel turned to face him.

"It's not that I don't want to come with you. I do. And I want to see my old friends and do stuff with them. But whenever I try to talk to her about it, she keeps saying how I promised and I can't go back on my word, like it's some big crime or something . . ." Again he looked away.

"What are you trying to talk to her about?"

"Just that maybe you had some other things you wanted to do, too. And you'd probably be busy with work a lot of the time, so it wouldn't make that much difference if I was there for the whole summer or not."

Lesson number one: Count on nothing. All situations are temporary. He thought of the day that he had moved out of the house—that place where they had all been scheduled to live happily ever after—carrying out boxes of his belongings, trying to get things loaded into the car before the kids came home from school. Daniel had shown up early; stood by, solemn and silent, as he wrestled a heavy suitcase into the back seat, talking over his shoulder: "You kids will have to come over this weekend and see my new place. It's up on the third floor of the building. You can look out and see half the city." And then Daniel was gone. He had hunted all over the house, found him hiding in the front closet sobbing into the coats. Even as he tried to explain in his best adult-to-child manner how nothing had changed, they would all make it through this, those tears had killed him.

"I wish you had told me," he said, "before I got here."

"How could I, Dad? I couldn't tell you over the phone, could I?"

"Maybe not."

He turned to unlock the door on the passenger side.

"Geez, and then she says I can't go to this swimming party tonight, when she knows it'll be my last chance to see these guys ..." He turned to stare out the window on the passenger side. After a moment, he glanced over at Michael.

"You mad at me?"

"No. But the thing is, I won't be happy dragging you to Detroit. Not if you don't really want to go."

"You're not dragging me. Let's forget it. I do want to go. And don't tell her I said anything, okay? She'll just be mad."

"It's got nothing to do with your mother," he said. "It's between you and me. Anyway, I think we should talk more about it. Plans can be changed, you know."

"No. I don't want to change them. I've decided."

"You're sure?"

He nodded. "It was nothing ... it was ... we'll have a good time, I know." He leaned back against the seat with his hands behind his head. After a moment Michael pushed the lighter on the dashboard, shook a cigarette from the pack on the seat. They drove in silence to the ballet school.

5

"Need any help?" Ed called through the sliding glass door. "Everything under control," Joy called back. "Check on the steaks, will you? I'm ready to serve."

Ed went down the steps into the back yard, returned in a moment to the deck. "Another drink, Mike?"

"No, thanks." He glanced at his watch. Nearly seven-thirty. He had been here since a little after five o'clock, was not used to eating this late. He had a pretty good buzz on now; if he wasn't careful . . . That is what comes of living alone: routine becomes all, you lose flexibility. He smiled at Ed over his glass.

". . . anyway, I figure I'll have all the ductwork finished by the middle of August or so, and we'll have air conditioning all hooked up and ready to go by the first of October." Ed laughed. "Story of my life. Bad timing."

"It's great you can do all this stuff," Michael said. "I'm not much of a do-it-yourselfer."

"It's not everybody's thing, that's for sure. But it relaxes me. By the way, Daniel has turned into quite the mechanic. You ought to have him tell you about the project he submitted to the Science Fair."

Natalie appeared in the doorway. "Dinner's on."

They rose and went inside. Joy, in white slacks and a pale-pink blouse, was bringing a platter of vegetables to the table—potatoes, carrots, onions.

"Ed, the *steaks.*"

"Oh, yeah." He laughed and disappeared out the door.

"Where's Daniel? Natalie, go tell your brother dinner's ready."

They sat with Ed at the head, Joy at the foot, and Michael across the table from Daniel and Natalie. He helped himself to salad from the wooden bowl.

"I assume all this stuff is home-grown."

"Oh, sure," Daniel said. "Mom's thinking of buying a cow, so she can grow her own milk and churn her own butter."

"Just a little farm girl at heart," Ed said. He patted Natalie's hand. "How did the lesson go today, Toots?"

"You won't believe it. You know Denise Phillips? She got picked for the Lilac Fairy."

"No kidding? That's nice."

"It's not. That was the part Margaret wanted. I thought for sure she'd get it."

"Politics," Daniel said, but his tone was kind. He seemed more relaxed tonight, gentler. They were just one happy family after all; they could pull this off.

"Coffee, Michael?"

"Please."

Joy rose to pour it just as a horn sounded in the driveway. Daniel dropped his napkin on the table. "That's for me."

"What?"

"I finished my packing. My room is clean. So is it okay if I go out for a while? I talked to Dad about it. He doesn't mind, do you, Dad?"

They were all looking at Michael. He cleared his throat. "It's all right with me."

"Well, it's not all right with me." Joy stared across the table at

Ed, who shrugged his shoulders. "I don't like this, Daniel."

"Does that mean no? They're waiting out there."

A silence. The adults avoided looking at one another. After a moment Ed said, "I guess it will be okay. But no later than eleven, buddy, is that understood?"

"Right. Okay."

And he was gone. They heard the car pull out of the driveway. Joy set the coffeepot down on the table.

"That was all settled yesterday."

"Well," Ed said, "it *is* his last night home."

"He always gets his way," Natalie said, her tone matter-of-fact. The objective observer. And suddenly the evening had taken a wrong turn; he felt off balance, wishing he hadn't had quite so much to drink before dinner. Joy was looking at him, and he braced himself, but she only smiled. "Who's ready for dessert?"

They sat in the living room after dinner, drinking their coffee and talking casually, while Michael waited out the interval that would allow him to politely take his leave.

"I've been reading about these money markets," Ed was saying. "What do you think? The interest rates look good. Any tax advantages?"

"I'm afraid I don't know much about them. My partner's the tax man in our outfit."

Don't know much about much, do you? He heard the words in his own head. He could not do this, could not sit here discussing investments with this man, as if they were old friends; they were not friends, and never would be; he desired no such connection.

He glanced at his watch. A little after nine. Natalie had already gone up to bed. He had promised that he would see her in the morning, when he came to pick up Daniel.

He wanted to get back to the hotel, try Cat again. He wanted to hear her voice, hear her laugh. He was missing her, wishing he was back there with her now.

"... supposed to be the beginning of tough times, eh?"

He shrugged. "I don't know that the climate's much worse than it was a few months ago."

"I meant Daniel," Ed said. "You know, the teenage years and all."

"Oh. I guess so. Yes."

Joy was sitting across from him, studying her fingernails, the backs of her hands. "Daniel's been giving us a little bit of a hard time," she said. "How did it go with him today?"

"It went fine."

"No problems?"

"Were you expecting some?"

Joy looked at Ed, then at the arm of her chair. She smoothed it with her hand.

"If you mean his feelings about going to Detroit, yes. I heard about that."

"I thought you would. He's being very manipulative lately. That scene at dinner, for example. The way he maneuvered you into doing his dirty work for him."

"I didn't think about it that way. I didn't see any harm in his going out tonight."

"That's not the point. The point is, I told him no earlier, so he put you on the spot. All of us, really." She shook her head. "He moped around here something fierce for months, wouldn't talk about it, wouldn't even admit that he was unhappy. Then he started to make friends and things got better. Before that, all he could talk about was going home and spending the summer with you. Now he says he really doesn't have any friends back there, he'll lose all the ones he's made here if he goes, et cetera, et cetera. The truth is, I'm tired of being made the heavy in all of this. We're always expected to feel sorry for him."

"It might have helped," he said, "if you had clued me in about all this before I got here."

"Why? What good would that have done? He changes his mind every other day. What was the point in passing all of that on to you?"

"Well, for one thing, I wouldn't have felt so out of it when I was going on about the terrific time we were going to have and everybody else was looking at me as if I were simpleminded."

Joy gave a sigh. "Nobody was looking at you, Michael. Don't be paranoid. This hasn't been easy for any of us." A special truth that she had been saving, worrying over like an anxious mother. *This hurts me more than it does you.*

Ed stood. "I need some more coffee. Anyone else?"

"Don't leave, Ed," Joy said. "You're as much a part of this discussion as anyone."

He sat down again.

"I don't think I'm being paranoid when I say I feel out of it," Michael said. "I am out of it, let's face it."

"Mike, I hope you don't think I'm trying to take over for you in this thing. That was never my intention."

"You have taken over for me," Michael said. "Screw the intention."

In the silence they looked at the floor.

After a moment Joy said, "It bothers me that he went and told you all that. It was selfish of him. And he puts me in the wrong, when all I'm trying to do is make things work out as fairly as possible."

"What's fair? Nothing about this is fair, so forget that."

"You know," Ed said, "Danny's a good kid, really. He just needs a kick in the butt now and then to remind him he isn't the center of the universe."

"Ed, I'd appreciate it if you wouldn't keep trying to explain my own kid to me."

"Oh, don't be so pompous," Joy snapped. "Can't you see he's trying to help? It also bothers me the way you come here and right away start finding fault—"

"I'm not finding fault. I expressed an opinion."

"Words. You haven't changed much. You've seen him once this past year. It doesn't qualify you for Father of the Year. You don't have all the answers, Michael!"

"Once a year wasn't my doing," he said. "It wasn't my idea, your moving to Washington."

They stared at each other. Ed stood and began quietly clearing away the coffee cups. Michael bent to pick up his cigarettes.

"Thanks for dinner," he said.

"I'm sorry," Joy said. "I didn't mean that. Damnit, you make me say those things."

"Look, it's nobody's fault. I don't mean to sound as if I'm blaming you. I get these shitty feelings sometimes, that's all. They pass."

Ed walked him out to the car. "I know how you feel, Mike. I'd feel the same way if I were you."

It did not comfort him. He had known these same feelings before, during that period after the divorce, when he had shown up at the house unexpectedly a few times to find Ed there, playing basketball with Daniel in the driveway or sitting out front with Natalie on the porch. Ed, the widower, with no children of his own, cheerfully taking on this burden of parenthood without question or complaint. Still, you couldn't fault someone for doing a job that had to be done, could you?

"I'll see you tomorrow," he said.

Under cover of darkness, the two men shook hands.

6

The same two dogs were chasing each other in front of the house when he drove up the next morning. They rolled in the grass, barking joyfully as he pulled into the driveway. He got out and opened the trunk of the Mustang, moving his bag to make room for Daniel's gear.

His son stood on the porch. He was wearing the same blue plaid shirt and navy-blue cords he had had on yesterday. Sunlight filtered down through the leaves, making bright patches on the walk. Daniel started toward him.

"Dad. I changed my mind."

"What?"

"I thought it over. I'd rather come later in the summer. Like in August. That would still give us a month, and Natalie could come too, after she gets home from camp. We could do what we did last year. Rent a cottage on Lake Huron. What do you think?"

He said nothing; couldn't think of anything to say. Daniel was moving toward him, leaving dark footprints across the lawn. He straightened up to stare at the house, at the narrow windows that looked blankly back at him.

"I was gonna call you at the motel, but I thought it would be better if I told you in person." His son shot him a frightened glance. "You told me the plans could be changed. That I should do whatever I wanted."

He closed the trunk, stood for a moment with his hand resting on it. "I don't get it," he said. "What did your mother say?"

Daniel hung his head. "You told me it was just between us."

"You haven't said anything to her?"

"No."

"Where is everybody?"

"They're all out back. On the deck."

Slowly he walked around the car to the driver's side. His muscles felt stiff, no smoothness in the movement.

"It's not too late, is it?" Daniel asked. "You can still get your money back on the ticket."

He made no answer. After a moment, the boy said, "You're mad, aren't you?"

No answer to that one, either. He searched his mind, waiting for some signal to let him know. He slid in behind the wheel of the car, cracked his knee against the steering column. An arrow of pain shooting up into his leg. He ignored it, fitted the key into the ignition. He turned the key and the car started up, idling smoothly.

"You want me to tell them?" Daniel asked.

"You'd better." Hearing the cool, grim tone. So he was mad, after all. So be it. He glanced at his watch. "I'll miss the flight. I've got to get going."

"What do you think about August? Will it be okay?"

"I'll call you."

He backed slowly out of the driveway. When the car started forward he did not look around, did not check to see if Daniel was still standing there by the side of the porch.

He got rid of the car at the airport, rode the shuttle to the terminal. Heading for the gate after cashing in Daniel's ticket, he glanced again at his watch, saw that he still had time to spare. An hour, in fact, before his flight was taking off. He sat in the waiting area, drinking coffee and smoking, while, across the way, the silver bank of telephones reproached him.

Act like an adult, why don't you? Act like a parent for Christsake. Kids want rules; they want limits. To be told where they stand. "Look, Dan, you're being a shit. Shape up and get your bag, let's have no more of this." Why hadn't he done that? Back there all would be turmoil and confusion. Both Joy and Ed would be upset. He should have gone out back and discussed it with them, everything out in the open, a good scene to clear the air. Instead of driving off that way, the victim and the villain, for surely he had punished Natalie by handling it like this, his anger pushed off onto her also. *Forgive me. I'm sorry.*

But someone else was in control now. His pride was taking over. Staring at the telephones. Unable to move. Amazing how, out of a long series of disasters, the mind selects one as the absolute worst—this is the one that will surely kill you—and somehow, horribly, that is the one that materializes, the one for which you will be put to the test. *Let's see if you can survive this.* Only a matter of time before Natalie grows up too, and grows apart from you. In the same way. *I am losing them. I have lost them both.*

The thought dropped a curtain of despair so powerful and smothering he couldn't breathe; had to stand up and walk out to the wide hallway, pacing and staring out of the window at the huge whitish-gray clouds foaming upward. A vow he had made four years ago—to not be hurt again; to never let on how much it had hurt—*No, Jesus, this is terrible. Stop it.* Things were not that bad. They couldn't be. He would think good thoughts, healthy thoughts. *But I cannot imagine my life without them.*

You went to cross a street, and from around the corner, a vehicle came hurtling out of control; you tried to jump out of the way, but it was already too late; the thing ran you down; no chance. In this way a memory could trap him. Daniel as a little boy; the two of them shopping together; a store with long aisles, long tubes of light overhead. Crowds of people, but Daniel would not be carried. Each time he tried to pick him up, the child would wave him off, screaming, "I walk! I walk!" *So, all right, walk. Get lost once. See how it feels.* Turning down an aisle and going on without him, not looking back. Until he realized that Daniel was no longer following. Vainly backtracking down aisle after aisle, asking people, trying to describe what he was wearing, feeling his mind go blank. Hearing the name Daniel Atwood called again and again over the loudspeaker. Imagining that he was no longer in the store at all, or anywhere else. *Get lost once. See how it feels.* He was into lessons back then, not anymore.

Finishing his cigarette, he went back inside the gate area, sat down. With his head lowered, his hands clasped between his knees, he willed himself to relax, willed the feelings to pass.

The plane was half full; there was open seating on board. He found an aisle seat halfway back, stowed his bag. The woman sitting next to the window smiled at him. She asked about the flight—did he know how long it was? She hadn't flown much. She was on her way to Detroit to take care of her new granddaughter. While they waited for takeoff, she pulled a packet of snapshots from her bag—pictures that her son-in-law had taken at the hospital of the first grandchild in both families.

Michael admired the baby, handed the pictures back. Reaching under the seat, he pulled some papers out of the suitcase. He had better plan to occupy himself with something during the flight or else he would end up talking. About everything. And to a perfect stranger. He didn't want that.

He had Gale's notebook in his hand, along with the school files that Cornelius had sent over to his office. The notebook Martinson had given him the other day in the hall. Gale's name was lettered carefully in the lower right-hand corner.

After takeoff he opened it and began to read:

About people who might want to help, there aren't that many.
My teachers don't know me very well. The ones who do aren't
that thrilled. For instance, Mr. Odgers, my English teacher, I've
had him now for two semesters, English Comp and American
Lit. I wrote a lot of papers in his class. One was supposed to be
about your "Personal Philosophy." So I wrote on how I didn't
believe in God. In the paper I said belief in a Supreme Power
meant that you had to believe in the power of evil, or why else
were there famines and wars and people always hurting and kill-
ing each other? Odgers is a guy who tells you all the time how
teaching is more than a job with him, it's a Life Work. He likes
to ask for your opinion so he can tell you how wrong it is. I had
to come in after school and discuss my paper with him. He hands
it back to me with a D on it and says, You don't really believe this
nonsense, do you? I ask, What nonsense? and he says, This stuff
about not believing in God, and then he starts in on how you
have to let these evil thoughts flow out of you, let goodness rush
in and take its place, make your peace through Jesus Christ.
Open yourself to him. Jesus is Lord. That means everything's
great and you can take any shit that gets dished out after that.
This kind of thinking can make you crazy. I know. So I told him
I would take the D and skip the lecture, and he said, Some people
will walk away from a helping hand every time, now why is that?
I said, Maybe it's because you're telling them what to think, I
don't need anybody doing that, I've had that up to here all my life.
He says, Gale, I'm not telling you what to think, but how to
think, and this paper is false thinking, it's dishonest. I said, Give
me the D then, for Dishonest, and tore up the paper and threw it
in the wastebasket. So now he leaves me pretty much alone. Fine
with me, I never want to be anybody's Life Work.

Teaching and social work, he thought. A couple of burn-out
professions. How long could you be expected to stay with it
when so often your best efforts went for nothing?

"Some of these kids are walking dynamite factories," Martinson had told him. "We just try to keep them from lighting the fuses."

One thing was certain: you kept your expectations low; otherwise you did not prosper. It would be like baking the best cookies you knew how to make and having to shove them down some kid's throat.

He turned the page to the next entry, dated June 1, written in pencil:

You think I'm in here because of my bad attitude. This is bullshit. I'm in here because someone wants me to be here and it doesn't make any difference what my attitude is or if I change it. You said I should write how it happened. I was in English class when they said over the PA that I had to go to the office, and when I got there Mr. Cornelius, my counselor, and the principal, Mr. Hammon, were waiting with two other guys. They were both in suits and ties, but I knew they were cops, and Hammon says, These are juvenile officers from Pontiac, they're here to take you in. So I said, What for? and the one cop says, How about if we talk about that in the car? and I said, How about if we talk about it right now, because I don't think you can just do this without telling me why. So he pulls a paper out of his pocket and reads it—home truancy and school truancy—and I said, I'm not truant, I'm here every day, I'm here today, aren't I? Cornelius says the papers were filed in court, so I have to go, and the one cop says, Come on, buddy, let's not make a big deal out of this. I asked if I could make a phone call, and the cop says, Make it from Pontiac.

We start to walk out, and we pass the john and before they can do anything I duck inside. Once I'm in there I climb up on the windowsill, but the damn thing is painted shut, so when they come charging in after me, there I am like some dumbass bird sitting on the ledge and the one cop says, Any way you want it, buddy, you want us to carry you out kicking and screaming, it's up to you, only you ought to have more respect for yourself. I said I had respect for myself, what the hell did he think I was doing on the fucking windowsill? while I was pulling at the handles and then the window flew up and when I looked out I saw the cement driveway that went into the basement about twenty feet down. Cornelius comes into the john and the cop says, Okay, let's get on with it, jump or don't jump, and Cornelius says I should just come down and everything will be fine. As if there was a choice. I knew if I jumped I'd break my leg, and anyway, the cop would shoot me from the window—home truancy and school truancy, the guy's a maniac and dangerous—so I got down. They weren't taking any chances this time, the one cop walking ahead of me and the other behind holding on to my belt. Once we got outside, they pushed me up against the car with my hands behind my back and put the handcuffs on. I said, Wow, you're sure a big tough cop, and he says, Tell you what I'm not, buddy, I'm not your high school counselor, so don't waste your shit on me. In the car I asked whose idea it was that somebody come and pick me up. No answer. So I asked if somebody had to sign something for it to happen. Still no answer. Then I said, I thought we were going to talk about this in the car, and the one cop says, The way I see it, buddy, you gave up that option back there in the bif. Tell you what I'm not, I said, I'm not your buddy, so fuck it. They both told me I'd better start taking the whole thing seriously pretty soon. They haul you out of class and make you go with them no matter what you say, and they won't even let you make a god-damn phone call and then they tell you to have respect for yourself. You say they never bring people in here in handcuffs, as if that means something. What it means is, they can do whatever they want to and you'd better not get caught having a bad attitude about it.

He sat back, looking out the window at the tundra landscape, grayish, windswept, with bumpy clouds that looked like snow. The woman turned toward him.

"Were you in Washington on business?"

"No," he said. "Pleasure."

"Well, you had a beautiful weekend. I hope you enjoyed it."

He said that he had. Off in the distance, a strange metallic glow that lit up the edges of the clouds. He would not think of Daniel now, no use in it. He would wait until he was at home, until he felt calm, able to think more clearly.

Setting the notebook aside, he picked up the manila folder. Copies of standardized tests, evaluation reports, grade transcripts. Two sheets of light-blue paper headed STUDENT ACCIDENT AND INJURY REPORT.

On the first sheet, someone had written: *Right eye discolored, swollen. Caused by car door being opened while student was walking through parking lot.*

And on the second: *Contusions, lacerations forehead and below right eye, no information as to cause of injury.*

He picked up the notebook again, paging through it until he found the next entry.

There's not much chance of you finding my brother. Wherever he is, he won't want to come here. When he was eighteen he joined the Navy, didn't tell anybody about it, just left. We talked a lot about running away together. We had this puzzle map of the United States and we would pick out the places to go, like Florida or California, because they were far away and warm. We planned to do it once, but when the time came Kevin said it was too risky and he had changed his mind, so we decided to wait. We were just sitting outside on the porch talking about it and I saw up in the tree a red and white plastic bobber hanging by a piece of fishing line. You could squint your eyes and make it look just like a giant hot-air balloon that was floating up in the sky

The writing stopped. Michael turned the page. Nothing on the back. He leafed through the notebook.

Even if you do things wrong there are some things I wouldn't do to a person, like locking them up in a closet. This is common, but if people knew what it felt like. A darkness where you can't see or hear anything and it presses down on you and fills every hole with blackness until you are choking, you can't breathe or think and you don't know how much time goes by. It feels like years. You are sick and dying in this closet. Maybe you are already dead. Just let me write this however it comes out it will be the truth not what he says because he is the liar, not me

The rest of the page was blank. Again he leafed through the notebook, turning page after page until he found the last entry. It was undated.

I wish he was dead. I wish someday this huge machine would come down on him and crush him and he would scream and die in agony.

Michael looked up, saw at the end of the aisle the stewardess pulling the curtain closed across the galley. The plane was descending, gliding through a bluish haze. No sound but the smooth rolling of the engines. The man across the aisle was asleep. The woman next to him was looking toward the window. He could just make out the buildings, roads and trees—a map of Detroit—far below them. He closed the notebook, holding it in both hands on his lap.

The seat-belt light was flashing, the stewardesses making everything ready; they would be landing in minutes. Eyes unfocused, he stared ahead for a long moment; then, looking again toward the window, he watched as the scenery tilted slowly, sliding beneath the solid gray angle of the wing.

CATHERINE

1

She saw the gray Porsche turn into the driveway, and she watched him get out of the car, carefully locking the door behind him. A strange neighborhood; you never knew. It made her smile.

She was downstairs with her hand on the doorknob when he rang the bell.

"Just on my way home," he said. "Thought I'd stop."

"From the hospital?"

"Where else?"

She pushed open the screen, and he followed her to the living room. He had to step over a box of books to get to the couch.

Through the archway the sewing machine was visible on the dining room table, piles of fabric next to it. The ironing board was set up in one corner of the room.

"God, nothing changes, does it?"

"Sure it does. This isn't the same mess from January. It's a completely different mess."

In his dark slacks, his fawn-colored silk shirt, he looked tanned and handsome. Wearing his hair a little longer than usual. "You look healthy," she said. "Have you been somewhere?"

"Aruba. Just got back."

"Would you care for a drink?"

"Sure. Got any Scotch?"

She went out to the kitchen, poured them each a short Scotch over ice. When she came back, he was sitting, relaxed, with his arms along the back of the couch.

"You know, you have very good taste," he said. "I always did like these chairs."

"No trades. You had your chance."

She handed him his glass; took the chair across from him, next to the fireplace. "So. How was Aruba?"

"Dull. A lot of water, sand, and bars. Here," he said, reaching into his shirt pocket. "I brought you something."

"What for?"

"For nothing. For the hell of it."

She took the small tissue-paper package from him, opened it. Inside was a necklace of delicate seashells, each one tied separately to a woven length of lavender string.

"It's beautiful," she said. "Thanks."

"My pleasure."

"Aruba. I always get that place mixed up with the stuff that grew in the yard, under the trees, remember?"

"Ajuga." He grinned. "Very funny."

"How is the weather there?"

"Terrific. Still, it's a lot to pay for weather."

"Did Pam like it?"

"Yes," he said. "She did. So what have you been up to? Still working at the gallery?"

She nodded.

"When do you plan on getting a real job?"

"Don't nag."

"I'm not. But you could do better, you know."

"I suppose."

"You like being overqualified, is that it?"

"I love it." She smiled at him over the rim of her glass.

He asked, "Heard from our daughter lately?"

"Yes. I had a letter last week. She'll be home sometime next month."

"So I gathered. Did she tell you about her artist friend? The one she met in Florence?"

"No."

"He's French. It seems that he may be coming back with her. He's interested in doing some studying over here in the States for a while."

"She said in her letter that she thought she could live there. I wondered about that. Does it sound . . . ?"

"It sounds involved," Alex said. "Well, we'll see about it when she gets here, I guess."

She caught him glancing at his watch when he thought she wasn't looking, felt an immediate surge of irritation. He was the one who dropped in on her and interrupted her evening, wasn't he?

She asked, "Was there something special you wanted to talk about? I'm going out of town tomorrow, I have a lot of things to do tonight."

"Where are you going?"

"Chicago."

"Flying?"

"No. Driving."

He picked up his glass, turning it idly in his hands. "Your lawyer going with you?"

She looked at him. "You know, I wouldn't have believed this town was that small."

"It isn't. I just happen to know someone who knows someone."

"Who's that?"

"A friend of his partner's. I swear, I wasn't checking up. It just happened to come out in the conversation. Are you serious about him?"

"Why not ask this someone who knows someone?"

"Come on. Be nice. I'm interested, that's all. Is that a crime?"

"I like him," she said.

"I did, too. Although he wasn't too fond of me, as I recall."

She laughed. "Well, what did you expect? You were so patronizing. You were insufferable."

"Was I?" He leaned back in the chair, grinning. "I was surprised to hear he's still practicing law. He told me it was a constant embarrassment to him how he made his living. I figured he'd be off somewhere in the wilderness by now, canoeing and catching fish."

"He was kidding."

"I wonder. How does a guy like that keep on doing something after he discovers he really doesn't believe in it anymore?"

"Spoken like a true saver of lives. Would that all of us had jobs so full of goodness and meaning."

"Jesus, you're hard on me. So what's the deal? You and he taking off for the weekend?"

"Michael isn't going with me," she said. "This is business."

"What kind of business? Artistic or otherwise?"

She hesitated. Absurd, this endless debt of information she felt she owed him. What was the source of her obligation, anyway? "You remember the boy you took care of last winter? His name was Gale Murray. His brother lives in Chicago. I'm going to see him. Gale's in some trouble. I'm hoping he'll be able to help him out of it."

"You're still in contact with this kid?"

"He's been living here."

"You're kidding. I thought you were getting rid of him the next day."

"Well, I didn't."

"You mean he just moved in here permanently? Cat, you really do amaze me sometimes."

"I know. But it's all right. He's not here anymore," she said. "He's in jail."

She couldn't help herself; there was something so irresistible about it; she felt this constant perverse desire to feed his dismay.

Alex sat back. "That's great," he said. "Just great. You know, you're too damned easy with people. You let them use you. I'll never understand it."

"Me either," she said.

"I mean it. You let them move into your life and then you're stuck. What the hell are you doing? What does your lawyer friend think?"

"He thinks it's my business," she said. "And would you mind not using that tone with me?"

"What tone?"

"That teacher tone. I've always hated it. You can relax. This isn't any reflection on you."

"That's not fair. That's not why I'm concerned." He leaned forward. "What do you think Chris is going to think about all of this?"

"Are you worried? I have an idea. Why doesn't she just move in with you and Pam? That wouldn't offend her sensibilities, would it? Living with her father and his twenty-six-year-old receptionist?"

"All right. I feel it coming. You're getting ready to tell me off. Go ahead."

She laughed. "Men are so dense," she said. "I already have."

"You're absolutely right about me. I ought to mind my own business. I will from now on, I promise."

"Oh, sure. Now that you've poked your finger into every corner of mine. Tell me, how is it with you? Are you and Pam planning on getting married?"

"No. What for?"

"I thought that was true love."

"It is," he said. "We get along." He gave her a look. "You know, I miss you. Your politics and your jokes. I miss the screwy way you think."

She laughed. "If you could hear yourself! Tell the truth. You miss having somebody to boss around."

"All right. You're not afraid of me. You don't have to kick me out of here just to prove it. Anyway, I do miss you."

It was as if her mind stepped back from it, slipping free; at the same time amazed at the volume of pain it released. How could she still care about this? It was incredible. She stood up. "Alex, really, I do have a lot to do."

He rose gracefully, smiling at her, satisfied with whatever it was that he had worked out in his mind. At the door he turned. "You meant that, didn't you? About my teacher tone?"

"Yes. Of course."

"You should have told me. A long time ago."

She had never known what it was he was thinking, not then or now. Maybe it was why she was always so willing to answer his questions. She would complete the equation, gather clues from it; eventually she would discover what went on in his head. Only it had never happened. She watched his car back out of the driveway with a sense of relief, as if she had escaped from some part of herself that still wanted to be held prisoner, the part that was dumb about men, about their sexy eyes and hands and the backs of their necks and how they looked in their pants. Because he still looked good to her, as good as he had looked that first summer when they met at an art show in Ann Arbor. He had touched her with the fire, standing there in his black crew-neck, his khaki pants and brown loafers, his clean blond hair and brown eyes with the lush dark lashes. He had been with a girl that day—a slim brunette, sorority-type, who was obviously bored by the activity—her eyes had moved impatiently from the car back to Alex as he stood studying the watercolors that Catherine Bryant had entered in the show. She should have known back then; he was with another girl and flirting with her, Catherine, the whole time.

For twenty years no one had known her better. He was the expert at knowing, and at *judging*. Near the end the criticism had taken the form of an eyebrow being raised at just the precise moment—no need for words, even. He always seemed to know everything there was to know about her. Through his eyes she could see this new life of hers—her life!—neatly dissected, laid out upon the grid and found wanting. *Under New Management—Worse Than Before.*

"You let him push you around, Ma," Chris had said to her

once. "I wouldn't put up with it. Next time he does it, just hit him with that vase."

But after a number of years relationships are set in stone. She did not know how to change things with him anymore; they were the way they were.

2

She drove through the city of Chicago and got a room at a motel in Evanston, where Kevin was living. She was proud of herself, how swiftly she had managed to track him down. Michael had given her the two names—Bob Sullivan and Dave Brown—and she had taken them that next day to the main library. Checking the Flint telephone directory, she had found columns of Sullivans, pages of Browns. She consulted a city map, noted the streets nearest Flint Central High School; then back to the lists of names, to copy out the most likely ones.

That afternoon she began making her calls. Down the list of Sullivans (it was shorter), trying not to think how futile it might be. Suppose the number she needed was unlisted or the family had moved away? Suppose she found someone who knew something about Kevin and refused to tell her? She hated to think about the rest of it—finishing with the Sullivans and having to start on the Browns, or getting through both lists without having any luck.

She didn't have to think about it. On the eighth call she got lucky. The woman who answered had a son named Bob, who had graduated from Flint Central.

"But he hasn't seen Kevin in years, I'm sure."

Cat asked for her son's telephone number. Without hesitating the woman gave it to her.

She had a harder time with the next call; had to explain several times to Bob Sullivan who she was and why she had to find Kevin Murray.

"I can save you the trouble," he said. "Kevin won't come to Detroit, I'm sure of it."

She went over it all again: how important this was to Gale, how she knew she could convince Kevin to help if Bob would only trust her. There was a long silence, during which she willed him to understand. At last he said, "Wait a minute," and left the line. When he returned: "I'll catch hell for this, I know." But he gave her the number.

The call to Kevin took only a few minutes. Her goal had been to persuade him to see her, nothing more.

"I live in Chicago," he said.

"That doesn't matter. I'll come there."

"When?"

"Any time you say."

At first he had tried to put her off, but she had insisted. His brother was in trouble, and she needed to talk with him about it; she would not take up much of his time. At last he had agreed, given her the address, and she had thanked him and quickly gotten off before he could change his mind.

She liked the look of this smaller city north of Chicago. Driving down Chicago Road, she saw sidewalk cafés, pottery and jewelry shops, yarn boutiques, and an old-fashioned movie house, its marquee announcing in red letters: BOGART BONANZA***CASABLANCA***THE BIG SLEEP.

Along the thoroughfare, tanned young men and women were jogging; mothers were walking toddlers and pushing babies in strollers and buggies.

She found Lee Street, a shady avenue lined with tall, vase-shaped elms. Brick apartment buildings alternating with large single-family dwellings. Lots of light-colored stucco. The apartment house where Kevin lived was on a corner. The entrance to the parking lot faced the other street. She parked in back, as Kevin had told her to.

In the doorway of the building an old man stood smoking a cigarette. He wore walking shorts, a bright-orange shirt, and leather sandals; his shoulder-length white hair was thin, wispy-looking. He waved to her as she entered.

In the lobby she made her way around several scooters and tricycles to the bank of nameplates against the far wall. She pressed the buzzer opposite K. MURRAY, 220.

"Who is it?"

A sharp voice, unmistakably female. Cat spoke her name carefully into the speaker.

"Just a minute."

The connection went dead. She stood for what seemed a long time in the lobby, wondering if she should ring the buzzer again. Suddenly a young woman appeared at the head of the stairs. Small and blond, dressed in cutoffs and a blue work shirt. She carried a baby in her arms.

"Mrs. Holzman? Come on up."

Cat climbed the stairs toward the woman, holding out her hand.

"I'm Lisa," the woman said. "I'm Kevin's wife. This is Jamie."

The baby eyed her solemnly, his thumb in his mouth, fingers curving over his nose. He swung his foot in its white high-topped shoe against his mother's leg.

"I didn't know Kevin was married," Cat said.

Lisa, walking ahead of her, said nothing as she shifted the baby to her other side. They had reached the second floor. Turning right, Lisa led her down the carpeted hallway to an open door. Beyond it, Cat saw immaculate white walls; a polished floor of dark wood, strewn with rag rugs. Across the room was a couch, slipcovered in tan corduroy, a Miro print tacked to the wall. A small wicker table and two wicker chairs were arranged in front of the large window facing onto Lee Street. Sun streamed in through the narrow blinds.

Lisa set the baby on the floor. Immediately he began to cry and held up his arms to her. She bent to pick him up again. Over her shoulder, she smiled. "He thinks you're the baby-sitter."

She went to the small L-shaped kitchen at the end of the room. "Sit down, Kevin's in the shower. He just got home. Can I get you some coffee?"

"That would be nice. Thanks."

Lisa lifted Jamie into his high chair, fastened a bib around his neck. She went to the cupboard, took down a box of graham crackers, and handed one to him. He was light-haired, fair-skinned, with round blue eyes, like his mother's. He began to gnaw on the cracker, still keeping his eyes on Cat. Lisa turned on the fire under the coffeepot.

"He's teething," she said.

"How old is he?"

"Eight months."

"I like your apartment," Cat said, looking around.

"Thanks. It's convenient. We're within five minutes of anything you need. We can walk to work."

"You're both working, then? That must be hard."

"It's not bad. It'll be better as soon as school gets out. Kevin has a pretty heavy schedule right now. He goes full time, and he's working nights." She smoothed Jamie's hair back from his forehead. "Kevin doesn't talk much about his family. I didn't even know they were living in Detroit."

She poured coffee for them both.

"Have you lived here long?"

"Since we were married. About two years. The rent's fairly cheap, and the people who own the building are nice."

"How did you two meet?"

"At the hospital where I work. Kevin works there, too. As an orderly."

Standing in the pleasant, airy living room, she felt a surge of confidence; everything would be all right. Here was someone she could talk to, someone who would understand the situation and know what had to be done. There was room for Gale here. She could see him pushing Jamie in his stroller or doing the grocery shopping for Lisa; helping with the housework, the meals. He could be useful. It would not be a one-way street.

A slight sound behind her, and she turned. Kevin was standing in the doorway in cutoffs and a dark striped shirt, freshly pressed, looking so much like his brother that it shocked her. The same light hair and blue eyes, the same thin, angular build. He had Gale's high cheekbones and long, straight nose. The baby caught sight of him and raised his arms to be picked up. Kevin went to him, ruffling his hair.

Cat introduced herself.

"I meant to ask," Kevin said, "how did you get my number? Did my father give it to you?"

"Your father doesn't know where you are, Kevin. I won't tell him. You don't need to worry about that."

He shrugged. "I'm not worried." Going to the stove, he poured himself a cup of coffee, reached into the cupboard for the sugar bowl. "What's for lunch?" he asked.

Lisa went to the refrigerator, busying herself, with her back to them.

"Was it Sully who gave you my number?" he asked.

Cat nodded.

"What's this all about? What kind of trouble is Gale in?"

"Your father filed a petition in court. He wants them to send Gale away somewhere. To a training school. Or someplace worse."

"What did he do?"

"Nothing."

He stirred sugar into his coffee. "I don't really see how I can be much help. I haven't seen any of those people in five years."

"I know that. Gale told me." She leaned toward him. "He doesn't have anyone to speak for him, Kevin. To be on his side."

"Well, I don't know anything about it. I was in Pensacola. Then I was in Texas." His tone distant and polite.

"You know what went on there."

"No, I don't." He was half turned away from her, holding the coffee cup in both hands. "Look. I'm sorry he's in trouble, but they don't send you away for doing nothing. Anyway, it's none of my business."

"He's your brother."

"So what? It doesn't mean anything. It doesn't mean we have any connection with each other." Again his voice was remote. He would not look at her.

"He told me how you talked about running away together. There are a lot of things you could tell, Kevin. If you would come."

Lisa turned around. "When is this hearing?" she asked.

"Next week. Thursday."

"Kevin couldn't come if he wanted to. He's got finals all next week. It would be an all-day deal just getting to Detroit and back."

"The hearing shouldn't take more than an hour, Kevin. You could fly. I'd pay for it."

"Who are you, anyway? Are you a social worker? How does he know you?"

"He's been living with me since he ran away in January."

She looked at them both: Kevin standing near Jamie's high chair, with his hand on the back of it; Lisa next to him.

"I don't think this would be a good thing for Kevin to do," Lisa said quietly. "Not right now at least."

Cat looked away toward the window; a red brick tower was framed in the center of it against a background of bright sky. "Something happened," she said, "after you left to join the Navy. Your father threw him down the basement stairs and broke his leg—"

"No, you don't," Kevin said. "You're not doing that to me, I won't let you pin that on me—"

"I didn't mean to."

"The hell you didn't! Listen, I don't know those people any-more, they're dead to me! I never think about them!"

"You keep saying 'them,' " she said. "I'm talking about him. I can't believe you don't care about him."

"Believe it!"

In the silence that followed, he leaned over, tossing the remains of his coffee into the sink. When he spoke again his voice was calm. "Look, I'm sorry, I can't help you. They're not my family anymore. This is my family, right here. My wife and my son."

She wrote out her name and the name of the motel on a piece of paper, handed it to him. "In case you change your mind. I'll be here until tomorrow."

He took it without a word, without so much as glancing at it. At the door she turned and blurted, "You know, you look just like him, Kevin."

"I can't help that."

She came out of the apartment building, made a right turn, and kept walking past the corner and across the street. She had no de-sire to get back into the car. There was nowhere to go other than the motel. It was only three-thirty.

A group of girls wearing bathing suits, carrying beach towels over their arms, passed her; seconds later she saw the water up ahead. She hadn't known the lake was this close. Another two blocks and she was outside a small well-kept area called Elliott Park. She walked through to the worn footpath, where, on her right, gray rocks formed a breakwater. Beyond it, Lake Michigan. Rough ribbons of light; the horizon was spiked with white sails.

She shoved her hands deep into the pockets of her skirt, walk-ing with her head down. What had gone wrong? Why hadn't she been able to convince him? Not enough time. Yet she would have stayed if there had been anything more to say. A mistake, trusting to luck instead of planning it out. Her one chance and she had blown it. What would Michael have done? If he had been here, he would have known how to apply pressure in the right way, without putting him on the defensive. *Damn.* She shouldn't have rushed off on this errand alone, should have waited for Michael. She should have tried harder with Lisa.

She sat down on a bench facing the lake. Nearby, in a sandy area, children were playing on slides and swings. On top of the jungle gym a sturdy little black boy, dressed in short pants, cowboy boots, and a straw hat, shouted orders to his troops on the ground. From the swings, a pink-cheeked girl called out, "Lamar, you come push me. Lamar, you push me, and I'll push you, then! Come on!"

He ignored her cries. After a while she fell silent, watching the boys as they ducked and charged around the jungle gym. She was sucking on a worn paper cup. When Cat looked at her, she looked away.

The park was large; there were no other adults around. Would she have let Chris play this close to the lake without supervision? Maybe when you lived by a natural hazard, you learned to respect it; still, these kids looked so young, none of them more than four or five years old. And it wasn't just the lake, either, it was all the strange people of the world; how could you bear to let someone out of your sight for even a second? She looked around at the houses that bordered the park. Perhaps, behind the curtained windows, the mothers were watching, checking her out as she sat on this bench, making sure all was well. She hoped that was true.

Rummaging in her purse, she searched among grocery tapes, movie ticket stubs, matchbooks, loose change, wallet, and keys for her cigarettes, remembering she had left them on the front seat of the car. She pulled out the folded sheet of paper where she had scribbled Kevin's address. On the back of a receipt: *from Catherine Holzman, $67.50 pd. by ck.* She had no idea what it was for. Typical.

She had been so sure this would be the answer. So many things she had wanted to say to him. She wondered if he ever had bad dreams. She knew that Gale did. A restless sleeper, tossing and muttering in the room next to hers, sometimes crying out in the night. Several times she had gone in to awaken him from a wild nightmare.

You can trust me, Kevin. I know about it. But he had turned from her, a hard, blank look on his face, as if he no longer remembered anything.

3

She had thought at first it was a neighbor at the door; the man's face looked familiar as she turned on the porch light. He smiled pleasantly at her. It had turned warm suddenly in mid-April: a damp, earthy smell in the air, the smell of spring. In the driveway next door, the neighbor boys were playing kick-the-can, shouting at one another over the tangle of bikes on the lawn. The man looked calmly at her through the screen.

"Mrs. Holzman? I'm Thomas Murray. Gale's father."

She stared at him, not knowing what to say, her heart responding at once; a quick, uneven rhythm. "He's not here."

"I know. He's at work, isn't he? I came to see you. May I come in?"

Definitely not the man she had pictured in her mind; that one was heavy-set and rough-looking, with hard eyes and a cruel mouth. The man standing here was real; he existed. Yet it had not crossed her mind that someday she would have to deal with him. She could feel her cheeks getting hot, the warmth spreading downward to her neck and shoulders. Behind him, the street noises seemed suddenly very loud.

The man cleared his throat. "I know this is awkward. I'm not here to make trouble. I would just like to talk to you."

She pushed open the screen, stood back to let him enter. Thin and tall, dressed in a dark suit, white shirt, and tie, he looked like a businessman on his way to some important meeting. He was smiling at her in a warm, friendly way. She led him into the living room.

"This is nice," Murray said. "Have you lived here long?"

"Since last October."

"And you're here alone? You and Gale?"

"Yes."

"You're not married, I take it."

"I'm divorced."

"What about children?" he asked. "Forgive the questions. I hope you don't mind."

"I don't mind. I have a daughter. She doesn't live at home."

He nodded. "His mother . . . I'm sure you understand . . . she's very upset about this. We've been looking for him since January. She was sure that something had happened to him. He's done this before, but I guess you always worry." He leaned forward. "I hope you don't think that I blame you for any of this. I know you thought you were doing the right thing."

The pounding moved up into her throat; she would have to get hold of herself or she would not be able to think straight, ask her own questions. The light in the room was dim; it was hard to see his face.

"I was hoping all along that he would be able to figure things out for himself. There's always that chance. That he'll make a right move on his own." He was looking at her. "What has he told you, anyway? About us?"

She tried to think of something to say that would not sound completely damning, that would not make things worse. If she could be sure of her own voice, that it would stay under control, not go trembling off in that schoolgirl way. "He said that you haven't . . . that you don't get along very well together . . ."

"Did he have any ideas about that? Why it was."

She shook her head. Had they ever discussed it? The man pulled back his sleeve to look at his watch. Heavy and expensive, with a dark, square face, a gold band.

"He's been in trouble off and on over the years. I don't know what you've heard. Probably not much. Did he tell you about the money he stole?"

"No."

"Have you missed any, since he's been here?"

Had she? She kept such poor track. How would she know?

"That's the worst of it," Murray said. "The trust that gets broken. You assume that people are honest. You expect them to be. It's a shock when it happens. You don't want to believe these things, so you start to juggle facts in your mind. I did it long enough, I should know."

"He hasn't been any trouble to me," she said.

"Well, I'm grateful for that. But then you don't really know him, do you?" He stood and went to the window. "The hardest thing is feeling responsible. I ask myself what I did wrong. Lots of things, I guess. He doesn't learn. He's always been different. From the beginning." Again he glanced at his watch. "He gets off work at nine, is that right? How does he get home? Does he walk?"

She nodded.

"I'll wait for him, then. If you don't mind."

Wait for what, she started to ask, as he turned away from the window. "You're being very understanding. I appreciate this. I really didn't know what to expect. I must say I feel better, now that I've met you."

A car turned the corner on Washington, went by the house with its radio blaring. The sound stayed in her head for a long time.

"Could I get you something to drink?"

"Thanks," he said. "I don't drink."

"I meant . . . there's lemonade. Or I have some iced tea."

He shook his head. Before her, on the coffee table, her Scotch-and-water reproached her. She felt awkward, as though she were the stranger here.

She heard footsteps on the front porch, heard the screen door open and close.

"Hi, I'm home."

His shadow fell across the slate floor. Murray rose from the couch.

"Hello, Gale."

Silence. For a moment he stood frozen in the doorway. Then he came slowly into the room, taking off his jacket, hanging it over the back of the chair. A look on his face that she could not identify.

"How are you?" Murray asked.

No answer. Gale put a hand to his shirtfront, brushing something away. His sleeves were rolled to the elbows; the tan cords were wrinkled, stained with grease.

"How did you find me?" He looked at Cat. "Did you tell him where I was?"

"It doesn't matter," Murray said. "I'm here now. So if you'll just go and get your things—"

"What for?"

"You know what for. You don't belong here. This isn't your home."

He stood motionless, his arms at his sides. His face was gray in the light. "Why did you come?" he asked. "Why now?"

"Are you serious? Because you're my son. Because you're my *problem*, that's why. How long were you planning to stay away this time?"

But he was shaking his head. "No, man, I've had it with you. You think you can make me do anything."

"I can make you do this. Or I can call the police and they'll make you."

"Do it, then. Call them. Send me to jail. I'd rather go to jail."

"Then you will."

Silence. He was looking down at the floor. When he spoke again, his voice was low: "Look, I've got some money saved—"

"I didn't come here for money."

"Why can't you leave me alone? I'm not hurting you, am I? I'm not doing anything wrong!"

"You are living with a woman who is divorced—"

"So what?"

"Do you think I'm not aware of what goes on here? You are living without discipline, without rules of any kind. Do you honestly think I can't see why she wants to keep you here?"

"She doesn't . . . why do you think these things? Why do you always think the worst?"

"You have been living here for nearly four months without our permission. In all that time she has made no attempt to contact us—"

Cat said, "Mr. Murray, I don't know what it is that you think has been going on here—"

"Please. Don't bother. I am not a stupid man. And I am certainly not putting all the blame for this whole thing on you. I know my son well enough. But this is not your concern any longer and you must not interfere." He turned to Gale. "You are asleep. I've waited long enough for you to wake up."

"I'm not going with you."

"You're going," Murray said, "one way or another."

"No."

But Murray was moving forward slowly, backing Gale into the hall. "You go and get your things."

The air between them suddenly flat, dead. Gale stared at him. "You go and get fucked," he said.

For a moment nothing moved. And then Murray's hand cracked, hard, across Gale's mouth. The blow sent him stumbling across the room. She heard his head strike the side of the desk. The lamp flew into the air and hit the wall in an explosion of light, making the room swing crazily.

She saw Gale on his knees, with his hands out, Murray holding on to the front of his shirt, hitting him with his fist—sharp, downward punches. For a time that she could not measure, she stood there; then she ran forward, grabbing at the man's arm.

"Stop it! Stop it!"

He shook her off. "Stay out of this!"

She ran to the telephone, snatching it up, dragging it across the desk as she dialed. Her knees were watery; her breath jammed in the back of her throat. "Get me the police! I want the police!"

Murray's head jerked up. He turned to look at her. "What are you doing?"

He was moving toward her, and she backed away, banging her hip against the corner of the desk. Keeping her eyes on him, she gave her name and address into the receiver.

He bent to catch Gale's shirt in his hand.

"Get away from him!" she said. "Don't you touch him!"

Shards of glass shining over the slate floor. The desk looked oddly slanted in the light. Again he started toward her, and she threw the receiver at him; it struck him in the chest.

"Get out of my house!" she said.

She held her side, pulling breath into her burning lungs. Gale was on the floor, his shirt torn, his face bloody. Blood on the front of his pants.

Murray stood looking at her. "You don't know what you're doing," he said.

"Get out." With an effort she kept her voice steady.

He stared at her for a long moment. Then, stepping over the glass and metal, he moved to the door. She followed him, holding back a sob of relief as he went out. She slammed the heavy door behind him, leaning against it and locking it, all in one motion.

Blackness and silence outside. Her knees trembled as she stood there. Then she turned to the boy crouched on the floor.

"Are you all right? Let me see."

Getting to his feet, he pushed her hand away. Without a word he went down the hall to the lavatory. She heard him turn on the water.

She went to stand outside the door. He was leaning against the sink, splashing water up into his face. Blood was streaming from his nose. A deep cut over his right eye; the eye was already closing.

She took a towel from the rack. "Here. Let me do it."

She led him out to the kitchen; made him sit at the table while she gently sponged his face. He could not sit still. His body jerked, and he mumbled behind the towel, "I gotta go."

She touched the back of his head. "You have a lump back here the size of my fist. Are you all right? Look at me."

"I'm all right. I need to go. They're coming . . ."

"Relax. No one's coming. I didn't call the police. There wasn't time." She looked down at his face. "Why did you say that to him? He's a crazy man. You must have known what he would do."

He said nothing, leaning back in the chair as she wiped up the blood. The gash on his forehead had a hard white center, the skin round it already turning dark. His nose was bleeding.

"He'll be back," he said.

"No, he won't. Not tonight. He wouldn't take the chance. He thinks I've called them. You're safe here. Tomorrow I'll call Michael and tell him—"

"No, Jesus, don't do that, don't tell anyone!"

"Why not?"

"Because! I don't want anybody knowing about this!"

"Don't get so upset, it's all right. We'll talk about it in the morning. You need to get some sleep."

"I knew he was coming," he said. "I felt funny all day. His car . . . it wasn't anywhere on the street. I looked. He drives this gray Olds with a white top. I always look, but he must have parked somewhere else . . ." His head jerked suddenly. "Did you hear that?"

"It was nothing. Don't worry."

"He must have called the police."

"He wouldn't do that. Anyway, they can't just walk in anywhere, not without a warrant. This isn't Russia." Drawing on her vast knowledge of the law; all that she had gleaned from watching TV. It made her want to laugh. He was silent, looking up at her. She got him to go upstairs, and minutes later, as she was cleaning up blood and broken glass from the hall floor, she heard him turn on the shower.

Despite her exhaustion, she swept and scrubbed and went over everything; she did not want to come down in the morning to any reminders. Once in bed, she found that she couldn't sleep. Her mind was racing and her whole body ached. She could not seem to relax. At last, turning on her bed lamp, she reached over to the night table for her book. She read until the tight knot at the base of her spine began to loosen, until she was no longer listening for sounds in the night.

In the morning, she found that his bed had been made; his schoolbooks were on the desk; everything was neat as usual. Piles of clothing on the bed, carefully folded. His records, his camera and film, a stack of paperbacks. He had been packing.

She went downstairs and found him in the kitchen, drinking a glass of orange juice. His right eye was closed; his mouth swollen, with the upper lip rolled back.

She put on a pot of coffee, scrambled some eggs, made some toast. When she set the plate in front of him, he kept his head down, facing away from her. He wore a light-blue shirt, one of the new ones he had bought for himself. The collar of his corduroy jacket was turned up.

"Do you feel like eating?"

"I feel okay."

Outside, the sky was overcast and dull; another warm day, the air perfectly still. He ate slowly, his jaws hardly moving. She could tell that he was in pain.

She sat down across from him with her coffee.

"What's the plan?"

"I've got some money saved. I'll go to the bus station this morning. Get a ticket."

"Where to?"

He shrugged. "Away from here. I don't know."

"Do you think that's necessary? Couldn't you just be more careful? Watch for his car when you leave school, and after work at night?"

"What do you think I've been doing? Listen, he's not just going to forget about this. You don't know him."

"He made a mistake last night. He won't be back," she said. "He knows I'd call the police."

"Get it straight about the police," he said harshly. "They're not on my side. They're on his side. Jesus, don't you think I know that by now?"

"You're wrong. This is different. A person can't just come into a private home like that and assault someone. It's against the law, Gale."

"He's my father! He can do any damn thing he feels like and nobody will say a word about it! That's the law!" He pushed his plate away, his hand trembling.

"At least talk to Mr. Cornelius before you go."

He shook his head. "I don't want to talk to anybody. Talking just takes time."

She stood up then and went to her purse on the counter. Taking out her wallet, she pulled out the bills she had and handed them to him. Sixty dollars.

"I've got money," he said.

"You'll need more. And there's a duffel bag in the basement. You can have that if you like."

"Thanks."

"You'll write and let me know where you are?"

He promised that he would. All that day she worried about him, about all the kids who took off alone, drifting in a current that was moving too fast with too many possible wrong turns. Take one by accident, it could be over for you in seconds. She saw him getting off the bus in a strange town, trying to find a place to stay in some sleazy section that he could afford—and then what? It seemed to her that there was nothing but danger out there: a world charged with confusion, the wrong people winning in it all the time.

She let herself in the side door that night thinking how much she missed the music. The times when he would be at the kitchen table doing his homework, with the stereo playing loudly from the living room. Now the house seemed dead.

He had cleaned up the kitchen before he left, done the break-fast dishes and stacked them in the drainer. Even scoured the sink. Her gray sweater was folded neatly on the kitchen counter.

She turned the fire on under the kettle to make herself some tea. Then she caught sight of the bills—two twenties and two tens—lying on the table. She stared at them for a moment. Taking the stairs quickly, she went up to his room. The door was open, and he lay asleep on his back in the narrow studio bed. The duffel, open and packed, was on the floor beside him.

The shades were drawn, the room washed in chilly light. She stood for a moment in the doorway, then, going to the bed, she touched his shoulder.

He woke up instantly, covering his mouth with his hand.

"Is it late?"

"Five o'clock."

Sitting up, he swung his legs over the side of the bed.

"I didn't feel so good. I was going to lie down for a minute. I guess I fell asleep."

The room was cool; she went to close the window.

"I thought maybe you had changed your mind."

He was silent, looking down at the floor.

"You probably wouldn't want me to stay here now. After all this."

"Gale, I want you to stay."

His voice was low. "The thing is, I don't know where to go. I don't have any place to go."

So he had remained with her. And now the problem was that she could not shake the feeling that it was she who had, somehow, brought the danger to him.

4

They walked side by side on two paths that ran parallel to the lake, separated from each other by a narrow strip of grass. Kevin seemed preoccupied, his gaze fixed far in the distance. They passed the row of swings, empty at this early hour.

She indicated a bench near the shore.

"We could sit here."

"Let's walk for a while."

The sun glowed in the sky; another beautiful day.

"I'm glad you called," she said. "I was going to call you anyway, before I left."

"Nothing's changed. It's just that I didn't explain myself very well yesterday. I wanted to clear up a few things. Lisa thought I should. Anyway, I wanted you to understand the situation."

She nodded, not believing him; after all, he was here, wasn't he? He had called her; he wanted to be won; she would win him this time.

"You were right," she said. "I was trying to pin that whole thing on you."

"It doesn't matter. I had to do it. I had to leave, and there was no way I could have taken him with me."

"He knows that."

"Does he? I want to ask you something. You said you were his friend. What's your involvement here? How well do you know him?"

"Well enough. Why?"

"Because. I was thinking that maybe a training school might not be so bad. Like the Navy. The Navy saved my life." He was looking at her. "Do you know my father?"

"I met him once."

"That house," he said. "From the outside you couldn't even tell anyone lived there. It was always locked up, with the curtains drawn. I couldn't breathe anymore. I had to get out. He was killing me."

"But a training school. It wouldn't be like the Navy, Kevin. It's a prison. He could be there for two years. Longer even."

"That house was a prison," he said. "At least this way he'd be with other people. There'd be an endpoint in sight. Something he could look forward to." He shoved his hands into his pockets, shaking his head. "He has to get out of this on his own. The same way I did."

"He's sixteen years old. He did the only thing he could do. That's what they'll send him away for—running."

He stopped then to lean against the wall of gray stone, looked out at the lake. "He made a mistake. He didn't run far enough. The whole time I kept thinking my father would figure it out. Find out where I was and keep me from going, somehow. For the first six months, all I did was look out windows. I knew I'd see him out there any minute, banging on doors, demanding that they send me home. I saw them doing it, too! That's how damned powerful I thought he was! I didn't feel safe from him until I was on a ship halfway across the ocean." He gave a dry laugh. "He thinks he's God, you know."

"How did you get away without his finding out where you were?"

"Sully helped. He's a good friend. I stayed at his house for a couple of days, until my orders came through. His parents weren't too happy about it. They hated being involved. But they did it. That's all I cared about."

"What I can't figure out," she said, "is your mother's part in all of this. How can she just let him do these things?"

"She believes in him completely. He never does anything wrong. That's how it is."

They stood together in silence, watching the water lapping against the shore. "Let's sit down," she said, turning toward a bench behind her. He followed, reaching into his shirt pocket for his cigarettes, offering her one.

"Thanks." She bent her head over his cupped hands.

"I tried telling a teacher once," he said. "Back in fourth grade. She didn't want anything to do with it. Told me to go and talk it over with my minister." He laughed. *"My minister.* Jesus." His eyes searched the shoreline. "He scared the hell out of me, every day of my life. I remember one time he marked a line on the kitchen floor with tape. Down the center of the room. He told us we weren't supposed to cross it. Not until he said it was all right. He was always doing that. Making rules just for the hell of it. Today you couldn't use this door, tomorrow this room was off limits. Or that chair. Anyway, I forgot about the line and I walked across it, and he picked me up and threw me across the room. Just slammed me up against the wall as hard as he could, like I was a stick of wood, a *thing.* I thought I was going deaf. My ears rang for a week. That night she came upstairs and told me how lucky I was to have a father like that, somebody who really cared about me, cared enough to teach these hard lessons."

She looked up. "Kevin, if you would just come to the hearing and say these things in court—"

"I can't," he said. "I can't do that. Listen, you've got the wrong idea, you see me as some kind of rescuer. I'm not."

"I see you as a good person—"

"Really? I'd ask Gale about that, if I were you."

"He told me you helped him. That you were his friend. He said you took care of him when he got hurt."

"He was a lot tougher than me," he said. "It took him forever to cry. I remember he wouldn't do it, just wouldn't give in, no matter what." He took a drag off his cigarette, ground it under his heel. "Most of the time I was just damned glad he was the one getting it instead of me."

"I think you're being too hard on yourself."

She stared out at the lake, seeing in its calm reflection a child's painting—white puffs of clouds anchored in the sky, gulls skimming low over the water.

"Kevin," she said, "he needs more than just you coming to talk for him. He needs a place to go. Someone to take responsibility. Someone with a job and a family. He needs you. If he could come here and move in with you—"

But he was shaking his head. "You just won't get it, will you? You're making all these assumptions about my life, and you don't even know me. You don't know anything about me. Do you know how I met my wife? Did she tell you that?"

"You work at the hospital together."

"I was a patient there. I was in treatment. For alcoholism. I've been in three times. This last time I've been dry eight months. Since Jamie was born. I wouldn't exactly say I was home free." He stood up and went to lean against the wall of rock, resting his folded arms on top of it.

"Lots of people are alcoholics," she said. "There are worse things you can be."

"No kidding." He gave a sharp laugh.

"You're right," she said, "he is strong, but that doesn't mean he can do this all alone. He needs your help. Kevin, there is no one else."

"Then he's screwed. I don't have room in my life for him right now. I've got all I can do just taking care of myself. I'm hanging on by my fingernails, can't you see that?"

"I see that you both have problems. If you could just come and talk to him—"

"No. I can't ever see those people again. I'm sorry." He turned around. "Look, you're his friend. Why don't you help him?"

"I am," she said. "I'm trying to."

"Well, you're wrong about me. It is not in me. I don't have it to give."

"And you're a liar, Kevin Murray," she said evenly. "I saw your face yesterday when I told you about the fall."

He shook his head. "If he had any brains at all he'd hate me. I fucked him over good. I'd do it again if I had to. It was a matter of survival."

"And what about his survival?"

"That's his problem."

5

She let herself into the house, and a gust of warm, stale air greeted her. No relief from the radiant heat outside. Her blouse was sticking to her back. She smoothed the wrinkles in her skirt. A long drive for nothing. All the way home the sky had been overcast and dark. It looked as though a storm was coming.

She unpacked her overnight bag, putting things away. It was after four o'clock. She needed to relax for a few minutes. Slipping out of her clothes, she went into the bathroom and filled the tub. She lay in the warm water with her eyes closed, listening to the faint roll of thunder in the distance.

After her bath, she wrapped herself in a towel, sat on the bed to call Michael. When had he said that he would be home? Early afternoon, she thought, but now she wasn't sure.

She sat listening to the telephone ring. No answer at his apartment. They might have gone to the baseball game. Or maybe they took a later flight. She would try him again in an hour or so. Glancing at her clock, she started to replace the receiver, caught the click at the other end of the line.

"Oh! You *are* home."

"Yeah." His voice sounded muffled, as though he had been sleeping.

"Did I wake you?"

A pause. "Yeah. Hang on a second." He left the phone. In a moment he was back. "Couldn't hear. The television was on."

"When did you get home?"

"I guess around one-thirty or so. What time is it now?"

"Almost five," she said. "How was Washington?"

"All right. Well, it could have been better. I tried to call you from there."

"Michael, I found Kevin. He's in Chicago. I went to see him over the weekend."

"You did? How did it go? Did you have any luck?"

"Yes and no. I need to talk to you about it. Could you come over for dinner?"

"Tonight?"

"Yes. Or do you already have plans?"

A pause. "No," he said. "No plans."

"Good. Bring Daniel and we'll talk afterward."

"Daniel's not here."

"He's not? What happened?"

"A change of plan." His voice was curt. "I'll tell you about it. I'll take a shower and be over."

He hung up, and she sat with the phone in her hand. Outside, the birds were fluttering nervously from branch to branch, anticipating the coming storm. She raised the window and the curtains billowed toward her.

She stood a moment looking down at the street; then, moving slowly, she dressed, and went from room to room, opening the windows to let in the cooler air.

He sat with his legs stretched out in front of him, his ankles crossed, hands in his pockets. His head was back against the seat of the couch, his eyes closed.

"You didn't go in and talk it over with them?"

"What for? No. I didn't feel like talking. I'll phone them later. Tomorrow, maybe."

"I'm sorry," she said. "You were so looking forward to it."

He shrugged. "I thought about it on the way home. You do divorce your kids. There's no way around it."

"Michael, that's not true."

"It is. What do they need me for? Nothing, really. Ed's a nice guy. Ed's doing the job. He's there. All the time. That's what counts."

"No, it's not. Kids can be so dumb sometimes. So selfish. They're used to taking—whether it's time or love or money—and they don't stop to think that other people might have needs, that maybe they could give something—"

"I don't want that," he said flatly. "I don't want him coming here to please me. So I can get what I need."

"Why? What's so terrible about that?"

He opened his eyes to look at her. "No. Let him do what he wants."

"Don't say it like that."

"Like what?"

"Like it doesn't matter to you what he does," she said. "You know it matters."

"What's the use? I make a big deal of this, I screw myself. I don't make a big deal, I screw myself, anyway."

"I'm sorry."

She reached for his hand, linking her fingers through his. Then she leaned toward him, kissed him. His skin smelled fresh and clean, like soap. His mouth covered hers, and she stroked the back of his neck, smoothing his hair. She slipped her arms around him and felt at once the quick stir inside her body; yet it was as if she were watching both of them from a great distance.

They shifted position on the couch, Michael leaning back to pull her over against him. His hand was at her waist; his leg between her thighs, pressing, hard, up into her.

"I missed you," she whispered.

He lifted her to her feet, still with his arms around her, moving them toward the stairs. She kept her open palm against his chest, felt his heart beating under her hand. On the stairway he stopped, held her tightly against him, lowering his head to her. His tongue was in her mouth. She let him kiss her; let him guide them both upward, with his hand at her back.

They lay on the bed as the storm broke: sheets of rain slamming against the windows; lightning flickering, blue-white, eerie. She had her head on her arm, looking down the length of his body.

"You've got some dangerous moves," she said. "We could end up on the floor."

"Never. I'm in perfect control at all times. Except for the end."

"I should get up and close the windows."

"I'll help."

They did not move; after a moment he rolled to his stomach, burying his face in the pillow.

She trailed a hand across his back, thinking that she would like to paint him like this, using that rush of pure energy that came after sex. Only he would never allow it, she knew; just as she knew by the careful way he held himself that he didn't think his body was beautiful or graceful. She wondered why some men, Alex for example, could be so confident and sure of themselves when naked—but then Alex was so absolutely sure of himself, period—while this man, sexy in bed, eager to please and be pleased, had about him at times an air of hesitancy, a certain lack of smoothness that she found appealing.

"I didn't mean to go off so fast. I wanted to hole up here for a few days and love the hell out of you. I thought about it a lot when I was in Washington." He reached over her for his cigarettes; nice wrists, narrow and strong-looking.

"I liked it," she said.

"You might have liked it better with more time to think about it." He traced his finger lightly over her shoulders. "Tell me about Chicago. How did it go?"

"Kevin won't help," she said. "Not even just to come to the

hearing. I think he's afraid." Surprising herself with that observation; yet she knew it was the truth.

She recounted the search and the telephone calls, the talk she had had with Bob Sullivan.

"You were right on the money, weren't you? There he was, settled in some city, with a job and a family."

"I wish I could have been right about the rest of it. I wish I had waited and gone with you."

"That wouldn't have worked. I told you, people don't like talking to lawyers."

He pulled her back against him, his arms across her breasts. "Anyway, you don't seem too upset about it."

"That's because I've thought of another plan."

"What is it?"

"You might not approve."

He laughed. "That's a great beginning. Why not just tell me?"

"Do you remember when we were talking about alternatives? About Boys' Ranch and Starr Commonwealth, and those other places? You said something about foster care."

"What I said was, they usually do it for kids who are a lot younger."

"But there's no rule against it, is there?"

"No."

"Well, then, that's what I want. I want to ask the court if he can come and live with me. What do I have to do?"

"You have to file a petition with Juvenile Court. Then you wait to see if it's approved."

"And how long does that take?"

"Longer than we've got."

"You mean it's too late?"

"Not necessarily. A lot depends upon which judge we get. Some of them are more flexible. Others won't do anything unless it's right out of the book."

"When will you know about that?"

"Not until we get there. It's a blind draw with Juvenile. Listen, have you really thought this through?"

"I thought about it all the way from Chicago, Michael. I don't know why it took me this long."

"But do you realize you would be responsible for him? For everything he does? It would be a legal commitment. Not like before. You couldn't just ask him to leave if things didn't work out."

"Things were working out just fine before all of this happened. That doesn't bother me."

"Why do you want to do this?" he asked. "It seems to me you're just getting ready to start on some projects of your own—"

"There's nothing I need to do that I can't do with him around." She sat up, looking over at him. "Someone has to help him, Michael."

"Uh uh. Not a good enough reason."

"Why isn't it? I can do this with one hand tied behind my back. I've done it before. I'm good at it."

"I know that. You've proved it already. You've been a good mother once. Why do it again? Cat, I'm afraid for this kid. He's got big problems. Worse than you think."

"I know that."

"There's a lot going on there. One of these days it's all going to come out in a flood."

"Michael, I know there's risk. Look at me. Am I a daring person? I'm forty-one years old, still living off my ex-husband, working part-time in an art gallery. I'm not the type to live dangerously. But if you don't take a chance once in a while, you may as well be dead."

He pulled her back against him, stroking her hair.

"I know what's wrong," he said. "I'm jealous."

"Of what?"

"You're so damned committed to him. I want that for myself. I want someone to commit to me like that."

"Like what? You mean you want someone to be your mother?"

"No. Not exactly."

They lay like that for a time, listening to the storm as it gradually moved off.

"I'm starting to get used to this place," he said. "I'm getting hooked on rolls of wallpaper underneath tables and buckets of paste in the bathroom."

"Meaning . . ."

"Meaning maybe we should think about being roommates. Three-fifty each per month, plus half of the electric. How does that sound to you?"

"It sounds scary," she said. His hand was on her shoulder; in front of her eyes, the dark line of his wrist as he kissed her.

"Like you said. About taking risks."

GALE

1

A couple of things we need to get straight," Atwood said.
"First, pay attention in there. Try not to let your mind wander. You'll have paper and pencil, so you can write down anything you have a question on. Okay?"

He nodded, glancing down at the yellow pad; it lay on the table. Atwood's pen was on top of it.

"Second. Look at the judge when he's talking to you. Let him know you're there. Just be present, in a polite way. You think you can do that?"

"Sure. Yeah."

"Do it now, then. With me."

"I am."

"No, you're not. You're a million miles away. You have been ever since I got here. What's the matter?"

"Nothing."

"You sure? How did the weekend go?"

"It went okay."

Pulling his briefcase over in front of him, Atwood opened it and lifted out the tan notebook. "I was in Washington this weekend," he said. "I read this on the plane coming back."

He merely looked at it.

"Why did you stop writing?"

"Because. It was shit. I didn't like doing it. How it made me feel."

"How was that?"

"Weird. I don't know."

"I didn't think it was shit. It helped a lot. Only I wanted more." He pushed the notebook across the table.

Gale shook his head. "I can't. I don't even remember what I said."

"Do you want me to read it to you?"

"No."

He felt suddenly uneasy. Inside his chest was a lump the size of a fist; it hurt to breathe. What could he have written that would be of interest to anyone? Nothing. Six or seven entries to fill up some pages, having to do with nothing.

"Tell me about this rule he had," Atwood said, "about being late."

"What about it? You had to be in when he told you to. That's all."

"What about the business of the chart on the wall?"

"When you came in from school you had to write down the time. You got twenty minutes. That was how long it took to walk home. He checked it out himself."

"What if you wanted to stay after some night, for a basketball game or whatever?"

"He didn't believe in that."

"Were you ever late?"

"Once in a while."

"What would happen?"

Silence. He looked away, feeling a warning signal in his lower back, a peculiar ripple of tension. There was danger here. "You had to face the wall with your hands behind your head. You couldn't move until he told you to."

"For how long? Are we talking minutes? Hours?"

"Hours."

At least it felt like hours; sometimes it could feel like whole days and nights, standing at attention with his legs tensed in pain, arms and hands gone numb. The dead weight of fear as it pressed against his back. Abruptly he pulled away from the thought. No good fooling with it; he knew what would come after: the feeling of hot, helpless rage burning out of control.

"When did he stop keeping this chart?" Atwood asked.

"He didn't."

"You mean he was still doing it last January, when you left?"

He nodded. Atwood made some notes on the pad, looked up at him again.

"What about the times he locked you in the closet?"

"Look, why are we talking about this? It's a waste," he said. "Stuff happens to you, it's happening to people all the time, that doesn't mean you have to pay attention to it. Just because I wrote something—it was dumb to write it down, I shouldn't have."

"Why? Isn't it the truth?"

"You start thinking about this stuff, and it makes it too important."

"And you don't think it's important?"

"No. Not to me."

"Oh, Gale, bullshit," Atwood said. He shook a cigarette from the pack at his elbow and lit it. "Tell me something. When are you going to stop letting this guy run your life?"

"He doesn't run my life."

"No? Look around. I don't see him in here, do you? So who made these rules? Who says you have to keep on being this hard guy who doesn't feel anything?" Atwood pulled the notebook toward himself, flipped through several pages and read aloud: " '... sometimes it hurt so much I felt like crying, only I wouldn't give him the satisfaction.' " He looked up. "So what else can't you do?"

"What do you mean?"

"Well, you can't cry. And you can't talk about these things. It was a mistake to write them down. Now you say you can't even think about them."

"I didn't say that. I didn't say I couldn't."

"How is a judge supposed to figure out what's really going on here? Unless he can read your mind."

He rose and went to the window, slipping his fingers through the wire mesh. So what did that mean? That it was all his fault? He closed his eyes, feeling a sudden smothering rush of fear, *Swear on the cross of Jesus that you are telling the truth!* He had sworn to so many things—lies, half-truths, anything that would satisfy—and he was a good liar. Lies were weapons; they protected him from punishment. Looking down at the window ledge, he saw that the crack below it had widened; the metal frame felt cold against his hand.

"Whatever happened to this other guy?" he asked. "The one who was supposed to be taking over for you?"

Behind him, Atwood cleared his throat. "What I'd like to do is forget about that. We were both pretty tense. It was a bad day."

Silence. He stared at the blank window, dimming into darkness at the foot of the stairs. *Do you know why you are being punished?* He never knew; knew only what it felt like to live within the shadow of another's plan, his own needs counting for nothing, his own reasoning useless in the face of it. He was in his father's thoughts, caught and trapped there, no escape possible.

He turned from the window, could not look at Atwood. *To admit is to invite punishment.* So what was he doing? No, this was a mistake, a wrong step; it would bring the furies down upon his head.

"I have to tell you something," he said.

"Tell me what?"

"You don't know everything."

Atwood smiled. "No kidding."

"I mean about me." He spoke carefully, keeping his head down. "You aren't going to like this."

"Never mind. Just tell me."

"Okay. I took the money."

A pause. "How much?"

"All of it. Whatever he says."

"What did you do with it?"

"It's in my locker at school. In an envelope taped inside my math book." He took a breath. "It was escape money. Just like you said."

"All right," Atwood said. His voice was calm, no sign of anger, but that might not mean anything. "It's good you didn't spend it. That will help. I'll call Mr. Cornelius and tell him to pick it up. We'll get it on record that you turned it over to me before the hearing." He sat back in the chair, again making notes on the yellow pad. At last he looked up. "You haven't said yet how you feel about my handling this for you."

"Do you still want to?"

"Sure. Of course. Didn't I tell you that?"

He turned back to the window; for a moment he thought he glimpsed something beyond that opaque wall of white, but when he tried to focus in on it, there was nothing to see.

"Something else you should know," Atwood said. "Cat wants you to come and live with her. She's filed an application for foster care with the court."

He shook his head. "They won't let me do that."

At least he knew enough not to waste his hope on anything as unlikely as that. Some things were as certain as punishment, as unavoidable as a blow. The shadow behind him, the voice in his head saying: *Uh uh, you want that too much.* You did not need anything more than that to convince you that you would not be getting it.

"I wish you could believe this," Atwood said. "Nothing has been decided yet. That's not the way it works."

Again he turned from the window. "Who's going to be there?" he asked.

"You mean at the hearing? The judge. Martinson, from Juvenile. Your parents. Cat and me. Why?"

"I just wondered." He had sworn that he would not ask this, yet he could not help himself. "I guess you never found him, huh? My brother?"

A split second before Atwood's hesitation gave it away.

"We found him."

He forced himself to smile. "And he's not coming, right?"

"Gale, it's not what you think—"

"Listen, I was the one who told you, remember? I said he wouldn't come. Anyway, it's no big deal, I could care less. He can go screw himself, it's nothing to me."

The most important thing that he had learned: what mattered was to see the blow coming and not to flinch. That way you could not be broken by it; you could not be made to care.

"I was going to wait on this," Atwood said, "until you were out of here."

"Look, you can quit trying to bullshit me on that. I'm not getting out of here. We both know that."

Atwood leaned forward. "Don't talk like that, don't be dumb—"

"I'm not dumb! I'm not just . . . some dumb kid!"

"I didn't mean that."

"You meant it. Just like you meant it when you said I asked for it. Well, I never asked for it. Not ever. Not once."

They stared at each other. At last Atwood said quietly, "I'd like you to try to forgive me for that. It was a stupid thing to say. I'm sorry."

Silence. He stood there feeling surprised, obscurely embarrassed. Not what he had expected at all. He thought of that first time that he had run away and had been picked up while hitchhiking on I-75 going south. The cops had found him. Driving back in the state police car, no handles on the inside of the back doors, the one cop leaning across the seat: *My advice is to go back home and take your medicine.* He had tried, then, to explain, but they did not seem to hear him. Or they did not want to.

"You think because he's won all those other times he can't lose," Atwood said. "He can lose, Gale."

He did not believe that, but he did not argue. The sins of pride, of self-interest, were perhaps the greatest sins of all, and for those you would surely be punished. For who were you, after all, to desire anything?

2

*T*hat long and dangerous week after Kevin had disappeared, he had hung around the high school waiting for Sully. Kevin's best friend would surely know where he was and what had happened. Sully would help. Sully would tell Gale what to do. The air was smoky and thick, gathering itself for another winter storm. He stood on the school steps, hands in his jacket pockets, trying to ignore the numb feeling around his heart. He looked for Sully's red hair and the blue denim jacket; spotted him coming out of the main door with a small dark-haired girl at his side. She wore a dark fur coat; her arm was linked through his. They did not see him at first.

"Sully, I need to talk to you."

"Hey, Gale, how're you doing?"

They stopped, and the girl threw him a curious glance. He had planned his speech carefully, had planned to be so calm and matter-of-fact, but at the look on Sully's face, all of the words were wiped out of his memory, and he made an awkward, pleading gesture with his hand, saying, half under his breath, "I need to see Kevin right away."

Sully shook his head. "Man, I don't know where he is."

"I promise I won't tell anybody about it. I just have to talk to him."

"I can't help you. Sorry."

He started off down the street, with the girl still holding on to his arm. Gale watched him go, and he absolutely knew—both heart-knew and stomach-knew—that it was a lie, that the reason Sully would not look at him was that he did not trust himself to do so; and he called after him, "What if I write a letter and give it to you?"

Sully turned. "Man, I don't know anything, believe me."

He wrote the letter anyway, delivering it by hand to Sully's door, dropping it in the mail slot; afterward waiting for the return message that was certain to come, the message that would summon him to wherever it was that Kevin had gone. He would leave the moment he got word. All through the rest of that terrible month he waited. Only the word never came.

What came was the fight with his father and the fall down the stairs. And then the certainty of that pale, quiet morning when he woke up in the hospital bed and discovered what he had known all along: that he was alone. It brought no alarm or fear, in fact very little feeling, since by that time the worst was over and he had accepted it, as he had accepted their bedroom being flooded with light and a sermon delivered in the middle of the night. They were never told who the guilty one was until it was time for the punishment. And he would lie there, listening for clues, praying silently, with his heart in his throat. A prayer that he knew was in Kevin's mind as well: *God please let it be him this time let it be him and not me.*

If it was his turn to be lucky, then he would close himself off, pressing the insides of his wrists against his eyes, holding his breath to get to that dark, hard core within himself where he could shut down all feeling, where it was safe and he could drift, loosened from the scene. It was not real, not happening, the light did not reach him there. It was only afterward that his throat would ache when he heard the sound of his father's voice: *You see this is what happens I don't like to be angry with you but you make me do this you don't listen you don't obey and now you have hurt yourself again.*

3

For too long he has been living on hate, wired up to some great internal scream. Memories twisted back and forth, changing themselves into dreams until somewhere he has lost the power to distinguish between them and to keep them separate.

There were too many rules. You could not learn them all. You could not sort out the ones that must be obeyed from the ones that would be forgotten tomorrow. It was too easy to make a mistake. Something would be accidentally spilled on the floor: *You are like an animal, a careless, brainless animal! Well, get down, animal, and clean it up!* No, he hadn't dreamt that; nor did he dream himself crouched, trembling, on his knees, his head a hollow, echoing cave. Raising his shoulder to ward off the blow and seeing his mother's face across the room: that blank, stiff look of hers; it was the look she wore just before she would turn her back.

Branded and exiled, do you hear? Cain didn't die! He was branded and exiled! And himself, seated on the kitchen stool, fists clenched on his lap. He will not look, will not watch as the clots of hair are sheared from his head. They drop onto his thighs and slide off onto the floor, while that voice, like a million knives in his head again: *This is what they do to criminals! Brand them and shave their heads!* And all of it mixed up with the smell of lilac outside the window. He is ten years old then, and he does not cry. He has learned that lesson long ago.

Are you crying? I told you never to do that! The blow that knocks him across the room the flash of pain inside his head the blood burning in his nostrils. He has bitten his tongue. *Now I am going to teach you a lesson you won't forget. I am going to hit you until you stop crying.*

Years ago he had discovered a way to win, by taking himself out of the game completely. The trick was to sleep. He had taught himself to do this whenever things got bad. He could do it for days at a time. He would get up in the morning and go to school, answer questions in class, walk around with his eyes open, asleep.

There he would be, asleep, and something would trigger it—a bell ringing or a spin of bright color on the stairway exploding in front of his eyes, and suddenly he would be awake, in touch, staring down at his scuffed loafers and gray cords, the dark-green crew-neck he wore over a white shirt. He would have no memory of dressing himself or of getting to school, or of going to his locker, or to homeroom.

Once, in geometry, he woke up that way, and he raised his eyes to the blackboard at the front of the room:

> Two non-vertical lines are parallel
> if and only if their slopes are equal

"What did you have for number six?"

His desk partner, Tim Johnson, turned toward him, one leg sprawled in the aisle, his arm hooked around the back of the seat. He glanced down at his paper; read the date: *October 10.* The rest was a blur, and he passed the paper across the desk. While Tim was studying it the bell rang. Quickly Tim handed it back, got up, and moved toward the door. He was behind Tim and Mike Sayers, his books balanced under his wrist, listening to them as they talked football. *If they knew.*

The thought came and went before he could grasp it. Walking alone down the hall toward fourth-hour class, he felt pain in his lower back, felt his legs trembling under him, saw the black lettering on the door: BOYS LAVATORY. He went inside to sit in the narrow cubicle, with his head on his knees. *If they knew they would despise him for it.*

The windows were open and the room was chilly. In the stall next to him someone was smoking. Blue haze rose above the walls. He heard the bell ring for the start of fourth hour, and the smoker coughed and flushed the toilet; a moment later he left. Gale sat staring down at the tops of his thighs, bare and bloodless, covered with gooseflesh. Above his left knee was a large purple bruise. He moved to cover it with his hand; the skin was hot to the touch. Black and blue marks on his wrists; raw, swollen flesh.

Abruptly he stood. Across the bridge of his nose was a band of hot iron; he thought that he would faint; bent his head, taking long, slow breaths. His lungs hurt, and he leaned against the wall, pressing his cheek against the smooth surface. After a few minutes he began to feel better. He tucked his shirt inside his pants and fastened his belt, pulling his sweater down. He picked up his books and left the lavatory.

Across the hall Cornelius, his counselor, was waiting in the empty hallway. "Let's take a walk over to my office."

"I'm late for class," he said.

"I'll write you a pass. Come on."

He followed him into the office complex, back to the counselor's room, a glassed-in area hung with red curtains. Cornelius motioned him to a chair, closing the curtains and sitting opposite him on the edge of the desk.

"What's up? You don't look as if you feel any too well today."

"I feel okay."

The calendar on the wall was a scene of a mountain lake, with tall pine trees surrounding it. He stared at it, then lowered his eyes to his books, balanced on his lap.

"You want to tell me where you got the black eye?" Cornelius asked.

Silence. He looked up, felt his heart knocking against his ribs. Cornelius had his arms folded across his chest. In the filtered, uneven light it was hard to read the expression on his face.

"I got in a fight."

"With who?"

He shrugged his shoulders.

"Somebody blacks your eye, but you don't know who, is that it?"

A mistake. He should not have come here. He felt the walls pressing around him. The counselor's voice was loud in his ears.

"Maybe you'd like to go home."

"No." The back of his neck felt suddenly hot, his stomach loose and watery. Jesus, was he going to be sick? He couldn't be sick right here in the guy's office. He stood up, clearing his throat.

"Gale," Cornelius said, "I'd like to help you if I can."

Help him what? There was nothing to be done. He needed to get some breathing space, some fresh air. Just to feel better, to have this moment pass, to wait it out.

"I'm late. I've got to go," he mumbled.

Cornelius got up and went behind the desk. "Where are you this hour?"

"History."

"Mrs. Hedburg?"

For a moment he couldn't think. Then he nodded, waiting while the counselor wrote out the hall pass and gave it to him.

"Listen, if you want to talk, I'm here, okay?"

He made no answer to that, could not think what to say. *Ye shall know the truth, and the truth shall make you free.* Well, he knew the truth all right, but he didn't feel so goddamned free. He was on a short chain with the collar tight around his neck, and if he moved too suddenly or went too far—you just didn't do it, that's all. The truth was that to be alive was to be in danger. All the time. And you didn't talk about that.

4

*A*nson was gone. One morning he was at breakfast, and the next he was not. Nothing was said about it; no one mentioned his absence.

He asked Streeter if he knew what had happened.

"How it goes, man." Streeter shrugged. "You in, you out."

But he knew it was not that simple. Was it what Martinson had hinted at? That he was sick, and they had taken him away to a hospital of some kind? He doubted it. More likely that they had sent him off to prison. This was murder, and they would have to punish you; it was the law.

"What you so worried for?" Streeter asked.

"I'm not worried."

The boy laughed. They were standing next to each other in the shower, and he pointed a slender brown finger at him. "Hell, even you weenie look worried, all shrunk up like that. Oh, I know. You gots a hearin' this week, right? Ain't you never had one before?"

He shook his head.

"No big thing. The dude say, You do dis? You do dat? You

say, Yah. Then he say, Don't do it no more. You say, Okay. All
they is to it. Anyways, you gots a lawyer, don't you? Tell him
what you wants."

"It doesn't work that way."

"No? What he for, then? Wouldn't have no lawyer, he didn't
do like I told him." Leaning against the shower wall, Streeter
spread his hands flat in front of him. "No sweat. You be lucky.
They send you to Boys' Ranch eight weeks. Then they send you
home."

He said that he didn't think that would be so lucky.

Streeter turned away, eyeing him coolly over his shoulder.
"Whatever happens," he said, "you be lucky. Shit, you white,
ain't you?"

That night, lying on his back in the narrow room, he tried to
keep his thoughts away from Anson, tried not to let his mind
stray to anything that would cause the furies to rise up and attack.
He needed to stay calm and relaxed, as Atwood had said.

Still, how did these things come about? Anson had said, once,
"I didn't want to kill him. I just wanted him to leave me alone."
He believed that was true. Yet it had happened. And now who
was the guilty one? What would they do to him? How would he
be punished?

Face down on the bed wrists and ankles bound with wire cut-
ting into flesh a towel jammed deep in his throat Do you know
why you are being punished? It is to make you clean again! Fall-
ing through space through the terrible rhythm that will not stop
through pain and searing heat while shadows move in and out of
his head the hands at his back are cold against his skin breaking
him lifting him to darkness and release but there is no help not
yet and the voice in his ear goes on forever To make you clean!

He would not think of these things, would not touch them with
his mind. If you did not choose to believe something, you could
blank it out, separate yourself from it. Even if it was the truth, it
was what came after you in the dark and held you down; you
could drown in it.

A night of wild dreams. He is in a car first, hurtling downhill and around curves, going at a tremendous rate of speed. He cannot stop himself. He is not the driver; there is no driver.

And then he is in a house, not his own house, but it is familiar to him all the same. Outside in the darkness a wild beast is roaming the streets. The rumbling sound of heavy machinery as it moves over the roads. People are screaming. Inside the house he struggles with the lock on the door, but it is broken; he is frantic, trying to fix it, knowing that, even if he can do it in time, it is only a flimsy screen and it will not make him safe from the thing wandering there in the streets. He is furious at whoever it is that has left him in this predicament, helpless and unprotected. The world is ending, and everyone knows it. No help, no help.

And then he is suddenly on a dark street alone, seeing, huddled in a doorway, the naked figure of an old man. He goes forward to stare into the shadows, and without a word, the man stretches out his hand to him. He strikes it away, strikes the old man to the ground with his fist. He cowers against the building, sobbing, shielding his head with his hands, trying to save himself. *Tell me to stop! Tell me to stop!* It is his own voice that he hears crying out to the old man, even while he is hitting him again and again. At last the old man topples into the street, lying still, with his bloody head propped against the curb. Dead. He has killed him. *A heart full of evil and the burden will not be lifted cast out into the void damned to hell for all eternity*

He came awake in a sweat, black air jammed into the back of his throat. The room was hot and dark and still. He stumbled to the door, pounding on it with both fists. In seconds the door was opened, and Carey, the night supervisor, stood there with a paperback book in his hand, his finger marking the place.

"What's the matter?"

"I need to go to the bathroom." Blinking in the light, feeling the cool air from the hallway across his naked shoulders. Behind him in the corner, the thing from his dream crouched, naked, its bloody head against the floor. He could smell it in the darkness. He shivered.

"You just went, Murray. It's only eleven o'clock."

"I need to go again."

Carey sighed. Turning, he set the book on the table behind him. "Okay. Come on."

They walked together down the hall to the lavatory. The floor tile felt warm and damp under his bare feet. He walked slowly, managing just to keep up with Carey's pace. At the doorway the supervisor motioned him to go inside.

"Make it fast."

He stood in front of the urinal. The room was warm, brightly lit; it smelled of cooked eggs and disinfectant. He stalled for as long as he could, washing his hands at the circular basin afterward, letting the cool water run over his wrists and arms, drying his hands on a paper towel, until Carey stuck his head inside.

"Murray, what's the problem?"

He dropped the towel into the wastebasket and left the room. They walked back, and at the door, Carey stepped aside. His mouth felt dry, and he braced himself in the doorway, hands flat against the jamb. He could not do it; the thing was still there in the corner, waiting for him. He looked at Carey, who stood waiting also.

"I can't," he muttered, looking down at the floor.

"Can't what?"

"Go in there. I can't breathe with the door closed."

"Murray, there's nothing I can do about that. Those are the rules."

So be it. He would disappear, then; swallowed up in the darkness. Still, he stood without moving until Carey touched his arm.

"Listen to me. I want you to go in there and lie down. No trouble, understand? If I hear you move off of that bed or make a sound, you've had it."

He took a breath and entered, as if he were going underwater; found his way to the bed; lay down on it, the blanket pulled up high. Squeezing his eyes shut, he clamped his hands over his ears so that he would not hear the sound of the door closing, the click of the lock. He lay on his side with his face to the wall, counting slowly to one hundred, two hundred, three hundred, would not think, would not feel, would simply count off the seconds, minutes, hours until the time had passed and it was morning. He did not know how long it was before he opened his eyes and saw bright light streaming in through the doorway. Not daylight. Behind his back the hall was silent, except for the sound of pages being turned. He moved his head until he could see Carey's leg and the leg of the table, one white tennis shoe with black stripes.

Shifting cautiously to his back, he slid his hands beneath his head. He was safe, could breathe again. The room was empty. He lay like that for a long time, with his eyes open, his face turned toward the light.

5

"I don't have to worry about you, do I?" Martinson asked. "You're not going to jump out of the car on me or grab the wheel. Nah, you wouldn't do that."

Kidding with him, smiling. He couldn't respond; the day felt too strange. He was wearing his own clothes, after three weeks: LaVack had brought them down from Intake this morning. The navy cords were wrinkled. The white knit shirt had a smear of grease across the front. His tennis shoes felt tight after all this time.

Beside him on the front seat was a manila folder with his name on it, written in pencil: *Gale Thomas Murray.* He kept looking at it, wondering what the social worker would think if he were to pick it up and start reading it. Was that against the rules?

Martinson drove from J Building across Telegraph Road to the courthouse. It was raining. The car was dusty, and the falling drops made marks the size of quarters on the hood.

The granite and brick building loomed ahead of them out of the mist. A huge structure, the color of sand. They drove into the parking lot, where a Coca-Cola truck was idling. Two men were loading orange plastic crates onto a small handcart. Their voices on the other side of the rolled-up window were diminished, blurred.

"We're late. We'd better make a run for it."

Martinson zipped his jacket, opened the car door. It was raining harder now as they sprinted for the entrance.

Once inside, they climbed the stairs to the second floor, where Martinson opened the fire door and motioned him down the hall. The light was dim. Together they walked down the long corridor to a set of double doors. Behind these doors was a large open room lined with chairs along all four walls. The chairs were filled mostly with kids, a few adults. Martinson continued on through the room to a door opposite that opened onto an inner hallway, carpeted and narrow. There were rows of offices on both sides. As they passed by, he read the names on all the doors, but they did not stay in his mind.

"In here."

Martinson had come to a door marked PRIVATE. He opened this one, stepped inside. The large rectangular room had paneled walls and wooden benches that looked like church pews. Opposite the door was a long row of windows covered in heavy white draperies. The social worker pointed to the front of the room, where two wooden tables were set, side by side, in front of a low railing.

"Sit there. On the right."

His mother and father were seated at the left-hand table, close together. They did not turn around as he entered. Atwood, leaning across the first row of benches, also seemed not to have noticed him. He was talking with Cat.

He felt a warning tug inside his chest. If they would keep the air moving in here, if the breathing thing did not start up again, he would get through this all right.

He sat down in the chair Martinson had indicated. His body felt stiff, and he turned his head to the left, where his mother sat, not six feet away from him. She had on a rose-colored dress of some soft material that fell in folds about her knees. Her hair was lifted off her neck, tied back from her face with a dark ribbon. Her hands, resting lightly on the arms of the chair, were still. Long, oval nails, unpolished. She never wore polish. Or perfume. Or jewelry. Those things were sinful.

He stared at her, willing her to look at him, but she would not; she continued to face the front of the room without so much as a glance in his direction. She did not know him, and that was that.

His father leaned toward her, putting his arm on the back of her chair. As he did so, his eyes rested for an instant on Gale's face. No sign of recognition. Then what are you doing here? he thought, pulling his gaze away to the front of the room, where he stared at the wooden railing, the bench beyond it. A plaque was mounted on the bench: EUGENE B. FOX, PROBATE JUDGE. At the right, a flag of the United States; at the left, the flag of Michigan. Two large rectangles of gray marble were mounted on the wall. Atwood had moved away from Cat and was standing now with Martinson and another man who looked as if he had some official duty in the courtroom. The lawyer was looking through the manila folder that Martinson had handed him. They were talking quietly, and as he watched, Martinson said something and Atwood nodded and grinned. They looked completely relaxed. Nothing to this.

He clenched his fists on his thighs, swept at once by a sudden, fierce wave of emotion. *Get this thing over with!*

"All rise, please."

The door at the back of the platform had opened, and a man wearing a black robe, carrying a sheaf of papers, entered the room, followed by a gray-haired woman who seated herself at his left. The man standing with Atwood and Martinson was the one who had spoken. Atwood came to the table.

"How are you doing? You okay?"

He nodded.

The judge sat down, and the other man began to read from a

paper in his hand: "Your Honor, concerning Gale Thomas Murray, D33619, this is a contested hearing involving a home incorrigibility petition that was filed on May 21 by parents, Thomas and Yvonne Murray. Present in the courtroom are Gale, his parents, his attorney Michael Atwood, caseworker Timothy Martinson, and witness Catherine Holzman. Parents have requested the court have jurisdiction in this matter."

Atwood stood. "Your Honor, we waive the reading of the petition. Gale admits to being absent from home during the periods stated and also to having stolen the money."

"I see that there is a receipt for eighty dollars here in the file," said the judge. "That is the full amount of the thefts?"

"Yes, sir. The money was turned over to Juvenile on Tuesday."

Silence. The judge turned over some papers on his desk. "Well, Gale," he said, "why don't you tell us how you think you got here?"

He lowered his eyes to the wooden railing. This was not how he had imagined it—that he would be expected to talk first. On his right, Atwood was sitting with the briefcase opened in front of him. The yellow pad lay on the table. Atwood's pen was on top of it. He took a breath. "They picked me up at school. I'm not sure why."

"How old are you, son?"

"Sixteen."

"Have you ever been in court before?"

He hesitated. "Three weeks ago . . ."

"Before that?"

"No."

Atwood wrote something on the pad, slid it under his eyes: *SIR*. The word was underlined.

"This is a contested hearing, isn't it? I'm assuming you intend to argue some of the charges in it. Now you have already admitted to the truancies. And you say you also took the money, is that correct?"

"Yes. Sir."

"Well, that doesn't leave much in dispute, does it?"

The kind of question he understood. No answer was expected; in fact, any answer would only serve to get him in deeper; it was better to say nothing. He lowered his head, looking down at his hands, at the network of pale scars across the left palm, the blue vein in the hollow of his wrist.

"You have run away three times in the past year, I see. Can you tell me the reason for these truancies?"

He looked up, his mind a blank. Starting off stupid. Exactly what Atwood had warned him about. Again he slid his eyes to the right, where the lawyer was doodling on his yellow pad: loose, flowing lines that looked like waves or flames, he couldn't tell which.

"I guess . . . I just didn't like it there," he said faintly.

"This is what you do when you don't like things, then. You run away from them?"

He said nothing, and after a moment the judge turned his attention to the papers on his desk. "Mr. Murray," he said, "tell me what kind of work you do."

His father stood up. "Sir, I'm an accountant. I work for General Motors, Pontiac Division."

"How long have you been employed there?"

"Four years, sir."

"And before that?"

"Before that I was with AC Spark Plug in Flint."

The gray suit was freshly pressed, not a wrinkle in it. A red-and-gray-striped tie. A half inch of white shirt collar showing. The voice was firm, full of confidence. He knew what he was doing, all right.

"Do you have other children?" the judge asked.

"I have another son. He's older. He doesn't live at home anymore."

"Is your wife employed outside the home?"

"No, sir."

He shifted position in the chair, feeling a tightness at the base of his spine. The judge was asking now about Kevin; had there been similar trouble with him? No. No trouble, his father was saying. Kevin was a good boy. Obedient and trustworthy. An easy child to handle.

"Tell me something about the problems you have had with your younger son," said the judge.

"Well, there were a number of things that I thought I should include in the petition, but I was told not to put them down because they went back beyond six months' time. But since he hasn't lived at home for the last four of those months . . ."

The room seemed uncomfortably warm. His mouth was suddenly very dry. He sat staring ahead while his father talked on about lack of respect, about general disobedience, lying, stealing.

". . . I could never relax with him. If I allowed one mistake he would only make another. He never thought about consequences. There is a complete lack of self-discipline," he said. "Everything had to come from outside."

Again he looked down at the smear of dirt across the front of his shirt, remembering the scene in the boys' lavatory: himself on the window ledge, and the cops below him; Cornelius telling him to get down, everything would be all right. But, no, it was too late. At that very moment it was already too late, and he should have known it. This whole thing was pointless. He should not have allowed himself to think otherwise.

The judge leaned forward. "Mr. Martinson, what about this incident in J Building?"

Martinson stood, began to describe what had happened with Lewis and Anson and himself in the hallway. He tried to pay attention, but he saw it all taking on that same unreal quality of his dreams, exactly as the arrest had done. He tried to think back to the circumstances surrounding it, to the mood of the day. Nothing would come clear.

"Fighting with staff, it says here."

"Yes, sir. Staff had to break it up. Gale took a swing at one of the supervisors."

The judge was looking at him. "What about this, Gale?"

He answered without looking up. "I did it. Is that what you mean?"

"I meant that I would like some explanation of your behavior."

Silence. His palms were wet, and he wiped them slowly on his pants, thinking again about Atwood's instructions. Keep focused. Answer the questions. How could he answer this when he had no explanation for himself?

"I take it you knew that your actions were being watched, and that they would have some importance in this hearing?"

"Yes, sir."

"Well, that doesn't seem to say much for your judgment, then. Or your self-control."

Beside him Atwood rose from his chair and began to talk about restrictive environments, about emotional pressure and depression; he could not seem to hear the words as clearly as before. A dull drumming sound coming from inside his head. He looked toward the curtained windows; they were glowing with a peculiar lead-colored light.

Raising his eyes to the platform, he realized that the sound was coming from a small boxlike machine. The gray-haired woman sat before it, typing. She was recording everything that was being said. A million words had to be fed into the box, arranged, and examined before this was over. The trick was, simply, to hold himself at dead center long enough. He did not know whether he would be able to do it.

Now his mother was speaking. The soft, sad voice explaining how money was taken from her purse, from her dresser and the desk drawer. "I worry about what will happen to him," she said, "out there in the world . . . He won't do things right. He takes things . . . He is always in some kind of trouble . . ."

He turned his head toward her, sat absolutely still so as not to miss a single word.

"Thomas is a good father," she said. "My husband is a man who loves his children very much. He has tried to teach them to be good citizens . . . to bring them up in Jesus, but it's very hard. In this world, it is so hard . . ."

Sweat was running down his sides underneath his shirt. He could feel the judge's eyes on him, and he willed himself to relax. Something was wrong: a pain behind his eyes, a crushing weight inside his chest.

His father stood. "He's easily led. That is part of the problem. He will get in with the wrong people someday. He will end up in far worse trouble than this. I'm sure of it. He was gone for four months, without giving a thought to us."

"I'd like to talk about that," said the judge. "Do you have any ideas about that?"

"I'm sure it had something to do with the fact that I'm strict with him, that I'm not a person who believes in rewarding people for bad behavior. I have rules, and I expect them to be followed. A person can't get along in this world without rules, without certain principles . . ."

Above the door was a sign: EMERGENCY EXIT. Red letters on a white background. He stared at it until the letters began to blur; the pain behind his eyes was fierce.

"Fuck your principles," he said; instantly he felt Atwood's hand on his arm. He shook it off. "You only had one principle. That was to make me eat shit my whole life. All this about the love of Jesus is bullshit! You never talk about anything but sins and evil and the bad things people do. Well, what about you? What kind of a person do you think you are, anyway?"

"Gale, I want you to sit down," said the judge.

He looked around, hadn't realized that he was standing. He saw Martinson on his feet, heading for the doorway. Atwood, too, with his hand on the back of his chair.

"Sir, if I could have a minute with him—"

"That shouldn't be necessary, Mr. Atwood," the judge said. "Gale, did you hear me?"

"I heard. I heard everything. I heard him say that stuff about my brother. How he doesn't live at home. Do you know why he doesn't? Because he beat the hell out of him, the same as me. So he ran away and joined the Navy. I don't care what you do to me.

Send me any place you want, only not back there; I won't go back there."

"Gale, do you understand the issue here?"

"Every time he opens his mouth, nothing comes out but lies! Lies and religious shit! I've been listening to it all my life—"

"That is not the issue. The issue is whether or not you are in sufficient control to allow me to continue with this hearing. In other words, are you able to sit down?"

Out of the corner of his eye, he saw Cat leaning forward, with her hands on the bench rail in front of her. He could not read her expression. His knees suddenly felt stiff.

"I'm able," he said. "But . . ."

"Good," said the judge. "Prove it, then. Do it."

Atwood was holding the chair for him. He sat with his fists clenched on his thighs, his gaze fixed on the edge of the table. Now he had done it, shamed himself in front of them. His face felt hot. Behind him he could hear movement, the rustle of cloth. They were bringing her into it, asking her about the incident in January, when he had come to her house; the burning. Now she was telling about the night in April, and his father was on his feet at once.

"Sir, I assaulted no one. She saw what she chose to see. She had been drinking. She continued to drink while I was there, and offered me liquor as well. I informed her that I did not drink—"

"When you say that she saw what she chose to see, do you mean that you did not hit your son in her presence?"

His father cleared his throat. "I'm saying that I did not assault him. Not the way she claims. I believe in discipline. I'm not afraid to do my duty. He is a stubborn boy who refuses to learn. Everything has to be taught the hard way. You can't allow some-one to get away with lying and stealing and taking the Lord's name in vain. 'Chasten thy son while there is hope and let not thy soul spare for his crying.' It's all there in the Bible. I had to pun-ish him, isn't that obvious? Whoever he is, whatever he does, it reflects on me. I am the one who's responsible. I don't expect him to love me for it, that's not the point."

Silence. The judge leaned forward. "Tell me, Gale," he said, "why you went on doing these things if you knew you were going to be punished?"

"Which things?"

"Well, let's start with the money. Why did you take it?"

He gripped the chair seat, keeping his head down. "It was to live on. For when I left again."

"How did you know you would be leaving?"

He took a breath. "I just knew. You go along for a long time thinking things will get better and that there's a reason for all of it . . . and then one day you just know: This is the way things are. They won't ever be any different. It's stupid to hope for that anymore."

"When did you decide that?"

He hesitated. "I guess maybe when my brother left. My father was real mad about that, raving all one night about how the Navy shouldn't have taken him without the family being told. And then all of a sudden I had something to do with it. I don't know what made him think that, but he pushed me down a flight of stairs, and I broke my leg—"

"That is a lie," said his father, in his firm, calm voice. "That is a lie, and you know it. I didn't push you. You fell. When I tried to grab your shirt and keep you from falling—"

"You're right," he said. "You didn't push me, you *threw* me—down the basement steps, and then you walked away! You left me there, and I couldn't even move—"

"I left you there to show you that God punishes those who are disobedient, just as he punishes liars and thieves. He punishes all sinners. It was your own doing; you brought it on yourself. And it amazes me how you can sit here and lie about it, when your mother saw the whole thing—"

"What difference does it make? She believes what you tell her. She sees what you want her to see."

At that his mother raised her head to look at him. "I don't understand . . . why are you doing this? How can you do this to us?"

Again his face felt hot; he turned his head away from her. A silence, while the judge shuffled through the papers on his desk, making notes. At last he looked up.

"Mr. Martinson, maybe you can explain to me why there's been no social history taken here?"

"Sir, application has been made, but they're backed up in that department, as usual. There was a home study scheduled for next week."

"Well, that doesn't help us much today, I'm afraid." Again the judge was looking at him. "Tell me some of the other things you were punished for, Gale."

He tried to order his thoughts. "Sometimes he'd read about something in the paper—some kid who robbed a gas station or stole a car—and he'd get mad. He'd say no kid of his had better ever do a thing like that, he'd make sure of it. And then I knew I'd be getting it."

"I never denied that I punished him. I did it to make him think."

"Did you burn his hand on the top of the stove, Mr. Murray?"

"Yes. I caught him stealing from me. It was to teach him a lesson. Those examples in the newspaper, they were proof of what can happen in a house where children are allowed to run wild. Things can get out of control before you realize it. When I was a young boy I was taught those same lessons by my own father. And he was a hard man. You learned to do right, or else. And now there isn't a day that goes by in my life that I don't get down on my knees and thank that man for all that he taught me."

The room was suddenly very quiet. Beside him Atwood was drawing dark rectangles on the pad of paper.

"Mr. Murray," the judge said, "did you think your son would thank you for punishing him for a crime that someone else had committed?"

No answer. He kept his head down, pressing his hands together between his knees. He heard the judge move some papers around on his desk.

"Gale, can you tell me what you think you learned from those beatings?" he asked.

The question made no sense. He didn't know how to answer it.

"How often did the beatings occur?"

"I'm not . . . I didn't keep track."

"Well, a rough estimate, then. Once a month?"

"It was more often than that."

"Twice a month? . . . Once a week?"

"Maybe between those two," he said; did not look up; could not if he had wanted to. A queer pressure on the back of his neck, as if something had forced it to this angle.

"During these beatings, were you tied?" the judge asked.

"Sometimes."

"With your clothes on or off?"

"Off," he said. "Usually."

Another silence. "I know this is hard for you," said the judge, "but you'll have to speak up. The secretary can't hear you."

He repeated the answer without listening to it. Words only, without the power to hurt or to help him. He heard the judge say something about the home study that was pending, about setting another date for disposition. What did that mean? That he would be going back to J Building? Well, it was what he had expected, wasn't it?

"I see here that application has been made by Mrs. Holzman for a license for foster care—"

"Your Honor, that would not be an acceptable alternative, in my opinion," said his father. "I feel that the moral climate of that home is entirely unsuitable."

"I'm curious," said the judge, "as to why it's taken you so long to act on this feeling. You did know where he was, didn't you, for most of that time?"

"I knew and I didn't know."

"How is that possible, sir?"

"Well, I knew he was going to school. I was watching for him. I'd seen him leaving the building a number of times. But, then, I would never go to the school authorities for help."

"Why not?"

"Because they can't be trusted. I know that from past experience. So it wasn't until he started working at the hardware store that I actually found out where he was living." His father was shaking his head. "I have to say that I disapprove of the situation. She's a divorced woman, living alone. There is liquor on the premises; there are men who visit her all hours of the day and night—"

"How do you know that?" Atwood asked.

"Because I've seen them. I've seen you, Mr. Atwood. Your car has been in her driveway late at night and again the next morning."

"Is there some law against that?"

"I'm not accusing her of breaking any laws. I'm simply saying that I do not approve of her standards of behavior and I object to those standards being imposed upon my son."

"What standards would you favor, sir?" the judge asked.

"I think he should be confined and be under strict supervision. He needs to learn the rules of proper conduct."

"You're talking about institutional confinement, I assume."

"Yes."

"And you are aware that you would be expected to share with the county the expense of such a confinement?"

"I'm not concerned about money," said his father. "I'm concerned about his getting help."

"Of course, this is only a temporary solution, you realize," said the judge. "If I were to send him to Starr Commonwealth or Boys' Ranch, at the end of such a program he would be returning home."

He made a move, and Atwood's hand shot out, gripped his arm firmly. "Stay loose," he said.

"After which there would be periodic home checkups and a program of family therapy instituted. That is, if you were agreeable to that."

"I don't know that I see the point of it."

"The point is, Mr. Murray, that this isn't just Gale's problem."

Another silence. "If you mean that I am not aware there has been failure on both sides, you're wrong. I am certainly aware of that. I haven't been able to provide the proper discipline, for one thing."

"I wouldn't presume to tell you how you have failed, sir, but I doubt if it's through a lack of discipline." The judge lifted a sheet of paper from his desk. "This is a portion of the medical report that was filed with the court after your son's physical examination. I want to read the last paragraph. '. . . scar through right eyebrow . . . scar on point of chin . . . multiple burn scars on palm of left hand . . . five-inch scar across left knee . . . multiple permanent scars on lower back, buttocks, backs of thighs . . .' Are these the lessons you were speaking of earlier?"

"The body," said his father, "is the vessel of the spirit. As the spirit is scarred, so shall the body be, also."

"I'm not sure I understand . . . are you saying these scars appeared on your son's body independently of you?"

"I am saying that he is a person with anarchy in his heart. I am saying that no one is perfect, that a child may appear to be the most innocent, most harmless of souls, and still harbor within himself a vileness of spirit that will take over at any moment if it is allowed the least opportunity to do so. And to withhold the rod of correction in such a situation would be, perhaps, the greatest sin of all."

"Yes. Well." The judge was nodding, as though in agreement.

Gale sat without moving, hands in his lap. *Then settle it. Make it quick.*

"I would like to know," said the judge, "how you would like to see this thing resolved, Gale."

He was looking straight at him. *Concentrate. Think about this.* Could it be a trick? A way to make him admit to something that could then be used against him? Atwood wrote something on the yellow pad, slid it under his eyes: *Tell him.*

He swallowed. "I want to live with her."

"With Mrs. Holzman, you mean."

He nodded.

It seemed to him then that an endless amount of time went by. He glanced toward the windows. Behind the broad expanse of white, he could suddenly smell the rain, could hear it being caught in a gutter somewhere.

"I've read through the school reports," the judge said. "Also, your employment record is good." He was gathering the papers together in front of him. "You seem to have a number of people who are concerned about your welfare. Do you realize that?"

Under the table Atwood nudged his leg.

"Yes," he said. "Sir."

"I don't want to give you the impression that I condone home truancy. I don't. Nearly every family situation has its problems. If you were to live with Mrs. Holzman, I'm sure there would be times when the two of you would disagree. I hope you don't think the only answer is to run away when things get rough."

Across the aisle his mother gave him a long, searching look. He bent his head.

"Your parents have petitioned this court for judgment. In my opinion, there is no evidence to support the idea that you are a danger either to yourself or to the community. Further, I fail to see that you have suffered morally or any other way from living with Mrs. Holzman. Therefore, I will release you into her custody. I'm assuming the foster-care license will be approved. If it is, you will be expected to reside at her home in Royal Oak until the date of your eighteenth birthday, or until such time as the court decides otherwise."

His father rose from his chair. "Your Honor, I have to say that I don't understand this—"

"If you and your wife will come into my office, sir, I'll be happy to explain it. There are some papers that need to be signed, in any case." He stood up then. The gray-haired woman rose also, exiting through the doorway. Martinson came from between the rows of benches to stand beside Atwood.

"Come on. We'll pick up the rest of your things."

"That's it? I can just go?"

"That's it."

Atwood was smiling, zipping the briefcase closed, lifting it from the table. Gale heard the door open behind them, turned around in time to see it closing on his father's back. Cat bent over him to touch his shoulder; he saw the handkerchief in her hand. Had she been crying? He felt nothing: felt numb, as though he were drifting through darkness, through space. He rubbed a hand over his eyes to clear his vision.

No resolution here, no sense of finality. It was as though he were suspended, waiting for something more to happen. Yet he had no awareness of what it could be.

MICHAEL

1

A message on his desk to call Daniel. The second one this week. He looked at it, put it down. He would do it later. They had talked for a long time on Monday. An emotional conversation, ending with apologies on both sides.

"I didn't think it mattered that much to you if I came or not," Daniel had said.

"What can I say? It matters to me."

And then they had both pulled back. He could not issue another invitation, and Daniel did not ask. Maybe more time had to pass.

Bill stuck his head in the doorway. "How did it go today?"

"It went fine."

"Good. Terrific. Glad to hear it. We need a few days like that around here." He sat down on the edge of the desk. "On this Frazer-Tufts thing," he said. "They're going to settle."

"You're kidding."

"Nope. They called this morning. Wanted me to give you the message. Said they'd be over in the morning to discuss it."

"Did you tell them what we thought about the offer?"

"Oh, sure. But they think it's safer."

"Too bad, they deserve more. We'd get more in court, Bill. You know that."

"I know it, yeah. But look at it this way. Now you won't be gagging on your toothbrush next Monday morning. You can even take some time off."

"And do what with it?"

Bill grinned. "What have I been telling you? Go out and meet some new people, start taking an interest in things. Ask that blonde if she likes beer and pizza. Maybe she'd like to go sailing this weekend."

"What blonde?"

"Come on, Mikey. Don't be dumb. I'm not. The one who looks so good in shorts. The one who wants to give away all her money."

He laughed. "I haven't heard any more about that."

"That doesn't mean she's forgotten." Bill picked up the glass ashtray on his desk, turned it over in his hands. "I don't mean to bring up painful subjects," he said, "but how are things with Daniel?"

"They're okay."

"You get it all straightened out?"

"No. Not really."

"Kids," Bill said, "can be a real pain sometimes."

"Tell me about it."

"You know, I was talking with Gretchen the other night. That Robin breaks my heart about three times a week. She'll do about the dumbest thing you can imagine. And when you call her on it, she makes you feel like a rotten guy for noticing. If it weren't for these demanding, critical people she has to live with, she could be really happy, her life would be perfecto. And the dumb thing is, I buy right into it, because that's exactly what I want for her. I want her life to just be worry-free and easy and happy. Mostly I want her not to screw up and get hurt."

"Yeah."

"Yeah, what?"

"Yeah, they can break your heart."

"Don't let him do it, Mikey. You got to be tough. You got to be hard as nails when they try to slip something by."

He laughed. "Like who? Like you?"

"No, Jesus, not like me. Do like I *say*."

"In this case, I don't think it would help much."

"What does Joy think?"

"She's upset about it. Mostly she's upset with me. She thinks I acted like a jerk, not coming in to talk about it."

"Do you?"

He shrugged. "What difference? I did it. It's done."

He stood up, taking off his jacket, hanging it up in his closet. It was damp from the rain.

"It'll work out," Bill said.

"I guess."

"Anyway, you did the job today, huh? Got him out?"

"Better than that. Got him back into her place."

"How did the parents take that?"

"The old man was not amused. I let him think a little on the possibility of a lawsuit charging gross abuse. He loosened up somewhat after that."

"That bad, huh?"

"Pretty bad." He leaned back in the chair. "Jesus, here I am, all dressed up and no place to go next week. The Settlement Blues, I feel them coming on me already."

Bill grinned. "Ask the lady if she'd like to play some tennis."

"I don't think she plays."

"Ask her if she'd like to learn."

It was still raining late that afternoon as he headed for Cat's house. The sky was dense, the color of lead, reflected in the pools of dark water on the streets. He parked in her driveway, between the two houses, and let himself in through the side door.

She was standing with her back to him in the kitchen, looking small and trim in her jeans, a short-sleeved pink shirt. Her feet were bare. He grabbed her from behind, planted a kiss against her neck.

"Hey, nice," she said, "you're right on time."

"I'm always on time. I'm what is known as reliable. It's my biggest fault."

"That's not a fault."

"No? Listen, I've got an idea. Let's play house. I'll be the dad, you be the mom. Where's the kid?"

"The kid is upstairs."

"So how's it going? How are you feeling?"

She gave him a too-bright smile. "Scared, I guess. It's been such a strange day. In court this morning I thought if anybody even looked at me wrong I'd start blubbering."

"It's the setting," he said. "People do it all the time."

"I think it's the mystery." She turned back to the stove, stirring the spaghetti sauce.

"Like a drink?" he asked.

"No, thanks."

He took off his coat and sat down at the kitchen table, his legs stretched out in front of him, his hands behind his head.

"He got a letter today from Kevin," she said.

"Oh? What did it say?"

"He wouldn't read it. Told me to burn it."

"Dramatic."

"Do you think so?"

"Well, he could have told you to throw it away."

She put the spoon down, turned from the stove. "Michael, I wish you'd go up and talk to him."

"And say what?"

"I don't know. Something to make him feel better about all of this."

"What makes you think he's not feeling good?"

"He's been in his room with the door closed all afternoon."

"Maybe he's sleeping."

"He's not. He's pacing."

More drama. He thought about the silent walk to the car this morning, with Gale between them both, stepping carefully over the puddles in the parking lot, moving through the lanes without speaking a single word. Hard to imagine what, or if, he was feeling. He was vaguely hurt and bewildered by it; later on, when he remembered it, merely annoyed. *To hell with him, then.*

"He trusts you," she said. "You were good with him today. He kept looking to you the whole time."

"Did he? I didn't notice it."

"He's trying so hard to find someone that he can depend on."

"He depends on you."

"Yes, but in a different way."

She came and stood before him, and he pulled her onto his lap. "Maybe he just needs to mourn a little over this."

She nodded, but she did not seem convinced.

"Don't worry about it. He'll be okay." He kissed her shoulder through the pink shirt, and she wrapped her arms around his neck.

"I want to thank you again. For everything you did."

"Good. I like that. How were you planning on doing it?"

She laughed. "You never think about anything but sex, do you?"

"Not so. Sometimes I think about eating."

"Well, dinner's ready." She stood up and went to the refrigerator, taking out greens for the salad. "I'll just set the table."

"You know, I just noticed something," he said. "Every clock in this house is set for a different time."

"That's not even my worst fault," she said.

"It's not? Why don't we make a list and then exchange and see what we think? I'll tell you my worst one right now. I hate like hell to ask directions. I'd rather be lost for a week than admit I can't find my way around."

"Now, that is a fault," she said. "Remind me never to go on vacation with you."

"Depends on where we go." He caught her as she went by his chair, sat her back on his lap again. "Have you thought about it any more?"

"Thought about what?"

"What we talked about the other night."

"No."

"Why not?"

She looked away. "You know, it's not that I don't care about you, Michael."

"Good. That's a start."

"But, sooner or later, it all gets reduced to domestics. The grocery shopping and the laundry and picking up the newspapers. I've had that."

"So have I." She made a move to rise, and he released her. "I wish I could make you see," he said, "that just because we're good together in bed doesn't mean I don't love you."

She laughed. "Now you're trying to confuse me."

"You're already confused. I'm trying to straighten you out. Say in fifteen years we both get sick of it, and I decide to move to Alaska and open a bait shop and you join the circus. So what? Or maybe we'll just stay together until we're old and cranky and write letters to *Newsweek* and baby-sit the grandchildren—"

"The grandchildren! Oh, Michael . . ."

"You want to think it all away before it's happened. Why do that?" He stood up. "All right. Enough for tonight. There's plenty of time, anyway. My next worst fault. I'm always in a hurry."

He went upstairs. The bedroom door was open, and Gale stood at the window, looking down into the street. He had changed clothes since this morning. The tan cords looked neatly pressed; he had on a light-blue dress shirt, with the sleeves rolled to the elbow, the shirttail out. His hair was still wet from the shower.

"Dinner's ready."

He did not turn around. Standing with his hands on top of his head, the fingers interlaced, he looked thinner to Michael than he had this morning, his build less solid. The watch on his wrist with its bulky leather strap seemed too large.

Michael came into the room and moved toward the desk, where

Gale's books were piled carefully in one corner. A notebook lay open, with his pen on top of it.

"Doing some studying?"

"Just thinking about it."

"I talked to Cornelius today. It's all set for you to take your finals. He said when you thought you were ready to give him a call."

A pause. "Thanks."

"Also, I stopped in at the hardware store. Wiley wants you to work this weekend. He needs you for inventory. That is, if you still want the job."

"Did you tell him? About me, I mean?"

"What was I supposed to tell him? He knows you were in Juvenile. He knows you're out now."

He reached into his pocket for his cigarettes. He had left them downstairs in his coat. The room lay half in shadow. Across from the doorway, a line of light was drawn sharply down the wall.

"I was thinking," Gale said, "about how I could pay you for this. I know it must have cost a lot."

"Forget it. It's not important."

"Why isn't it? You don't do jobs for nothing, do you?"

He smiled. "Not usually. No."

"I've got about two hundred dollars saved."

"Look, I don't want your money. You keep it."

"Is she going to pay you, then? I don't want her doing that. It's too much." He dropped his hands to his sides. The blond hair, grown long these past weeks, was feathered over the collar of his shirt.

"Why don't we talk about it some other time?" Michael asked. "Anyway, I think you've got something else on your mind."

No answer. He was reminded of that first session in J Building; the feeling of having to dig for everything. Glancing toward the window, he noted a silvery stillness in the air. The rain had stopped; the leaves hung motionless.

"It's nothing you'd want to hear," Gale said in a voice so low that Michael almost missed it.

"Yes, I would."

A silence. He continued to stand with his back to the room, his legs slightly apart, his back rigid. "Just once I'd like to talk about this, or even think about it, without feeling so shitty afterward. It's like this crummy movie that keeps playing inside your head. You can't shut it off."

"Does it make it harder now? Because we know?"

He shook his head. "I just wish I didn't. I wish I could hit myself over the head and forget all about it."

"I wish you could, too."

He made a sound then, at the back of his throat.

"I hate the guy so much it makes me feel sick. I start to think about some of the stuff . . . and I just get sick. All those times he hurt me and I just let him do it!"

"What were you supposed to do?"

"I don't know." His voice grew fainter, and all at once it broke. "God, I don't want to feel like this anymore . . . just . . . so damned fucked . . . !"

Michael rose and went to him; at his touch, Gale's shoulder jerked.

"Don't . . . I just . . . really don't like it when people do that!"

"All right, I won't touch you. Come and sit down over here."

He let himself be led to the bed; once there pulling away to lie on his side, with his arm shielding his face. He was weeping uncontrollably. Watching him, Michael felt his own throat ache. He sat for a time in silence, reached again for his cigarettes, smoothing the empty shirt pocket with his hand.

"I thought this one time she'd be able to see it," he said, "but now I know she never will. It doesn't matter a *damn* to her! I hate her, too!" He rolled to his stomach, with his face in his hands. The blue shirt was pulled up, exposing bare skin at his waist. "There were other things," he said, "that I'd never talk about in a courtroom . . . or anyplace else! There's stuff you should just forget about. Pretend it never happened . . ."

"All right," Michael said gently. "All right."

But he did not believe this, believed instead that whatever it was, was not worth this pain of keeping it a secret, but he said nothing more, shifted his gaze to the low shelf of books that was mounted over the desk. He kept his hands flat on his knees.

After a while the tears stopped and Gale lay quietly beside him. He gave a long sigh, his voice muffled against his arm. "That was dumb."

"No, it wasn't."

He reached into his back pocket, pulling out his handkerchief, handing it over. Propped on his elbows, Gale blew his nose loudly. His eyes were bright; his cheeks looked sunburned.

"I don't get why I'm feeling like this."

"That was a rough thing you had to go through," Michael said. "It hurts. It's like a divorce."

"But nothing's changed. I was alone before. So now I'm alone again. Why do I feel like I'm dying or something?" He rolled to his back, with a hand over his eyes. Pale strands of hair clung to the blanket. Michael saw the white scar on the underside of his chin.

"Did you get any sleep last night?"

"Some, yeah."

"That's part of it, don't you think? You'll feel better tomorrow. After you've had some rest."

"Maybe," he said. "I don't know."

"Anyway, you're not alone. You've got friends. You've got Cat. And me."

"How can you say that? When I've been such a jerk to you?"

"Come on. I was a jerk to you, too. I thought we settled that. We got past that, didn't we?"

Again he turned his head away. Michael looked toward the window. It was beginning to get dark. There would be no sunset this evening: just deepening gray, spilling over into black.

"Did you ever think," he said, "that what you might be doing is trying to turn this whole thing into a defeat?"

Silence. At last, Gale turned to look at him. "Is that what you think?"

"Could be. Maybe."

He raised himself on his elbows. "What happened this morning—I didn't expect it. I never thought you'd be able to pull it off."

"I didn't pull anything off. That was you."

"No. I almost blew it, I made a fool of myself—"

"I don't think so. You scared me plenty. But it sure as hell loosened things up. And it worked, didn't it? Listen, lots of people are afraid to win. Or they're afraid to recognize it when they do. As if it's bad luck. But you know better than that."

"I don't know what I know anymore," he said wearily. "I never figured out anything. Why he did things, or why he hates me so much . . ."

"He hates himself, Gale. It's not you."

"Why? Why does he?"

"How much do you know about the Bible?"

He gave a brief laugh. "More than I want to."

"Do you know about the sins of the fathers? How they're visited upon the sons? Just don't let him do that to you."

"How do you stop it?"

"You've already stopped it."

He said nothing, closing his eyes. Then, a moment later: "Afterward, when it was over, I wanted to thank you, only I couldn't even think what to say. I feel so . . . I can't seem to think right anymore."

"Thinking is deciding," Michael said, "what it is you want. What you have to do to get it. You know how to think, don't worry about that."

More tears. He covered his eyes, and Michael reached out to lay a hand gently on his chest. He did not move this time. Did not pull away.

CATHERINE

*H*e sat, facing backward on the kitchen chair with his arms along the back of it, the sheet pinned up high around his neck. Fine hair, like cornsilk, falling straight and thick from his crown.

"I used to do this in college," she said. "For cigarettes. I don't think I ever bought a pack in the four years I was there."

"I'll buy you some tomorrow."

"No, don't. I'm quitting." She handed him the mirror. "There. How's that?"

"Great."

A warm breeze coming in through the windows. She picked up her coffee cup, sipped slowly, as he unpinned the sheet from around his neck, gathering it in so as not to spill clippings onto the floor. He looked tired this morning, his eyes swollen from sleep.

"Sorry I spoiled the party last night," he said.

"You didn't spoil it. You went to bed early. That's all right."

"Mike went home, huh?"

"Michael doesn't live here," she said. "He has his own apartment, you know."

"I know."

He went to the closet, taking out the broom and dustpan to sweep up the floor. "I was wondering," he said, "what your daughter will think when she gets home from Europe. About me being here, I mean."

"I wouldn't worry about Chris. You and she will get along fine. She'll like you."

"How do you know that?"

"Why shouldn't she? You're a likable kid. I'll just tell her how you fed the raccoon all last winter. She's an animal lover, too. She'll be impressed."

"Also, I was wondering about the money," he said.

"What money?"

"Aren't you paying him to do this?"

"We haven't talked about it. Don't worry so. There's plenty of time."

He bent to sweep up the clippings from the floor into the dustpan, deposited them into the wastebasket. Glancing toward the window, he called softly to her, "Hey. Nuthatch at the feeder."

She came to stand beside him. Together they watched the small black and white bird, his tail flashing, hanging nearly upside down as he pecked away at the suet.

She said, "You would think he'd fall on his head."

"Nah. He's smarter than that."

"You wouldn't believe the warblers I spotted during the last storm. The maple tree was a hotel. They were coming and going faster than you could look them up in the book."

He leaned his back against the counter. "One other thing," he said carefully. "About Mike. Will he be moving in here, do you think?"

"Up to your old tricks, I see." She grinned. "Are you asking me how I feel about Michael?"

"Not really. I just figured there was probably a reason why he went to all that trouble."

"All what trouble? You mean you? Of course there is. He cares about you. Don't you know that yet?"

For a moment, he seemed not to have heard her. Then, to her dismay, he turned to the counter and, lowering his head on his arms, began to cry. She went to him at once, felt his body stiffen at her touch.

"I don't know why I'm doing this," he said. "I don't do this. All last night I kept waking up and thinking about stuff."

"What stuff?"

"I don't know! Dumb stuff . . . like what would happen if you changed your mind!"

"Gale, I wouldn't do that. Why would I do that?"

". . . and Mike . . . I don't know . . ."

"Michael wouldn't either. He wants to help you."

He pulled free of her then, going to stand by the window. "Jesus, I never cried this much in my whole life."

"Don't worry about that."

He made a sound: laughing or crying, she couldn't tell. "Everybody keeps saying, 'Don't worry.' "

"Everybody's right."

"Yeah, I guess."

He wiped his eyes with his hands, going to the table and picking up the sheet. Folding it over his arm, he carried it to the door. A moment later, he was outside the house, in the back yard.

She thought about the letter from Kevin, knew she was right to have kept it. If anything was ever to happen between those two, Gale would have to be the one. Kevin was right; he was the stronger.

Looking out, she saw him fold the sheet carefully, set it beside the tree, and go to stand next to the fence, his T-shirt tucked neatly into his jeans, his hands in his back pockets. He would remember all the names of the flowers and plants that she had taught him. He had a photographic memory—reels of film stored away with notes on every subject from astronomy to carpentry to mythology to jazz. A nudge only, and it was stirred up and into the projector. He would figure everything out for himself. He wanted to know things, to get the answers.

He turned toward the window, and she saw that she had cut his hair crooked in front; she would have to fix it.

Even at this early hour of the morning, the sun was white-hot and burning. A waterfall of light spilling down over his head. As for love—that most passionate of religions—what did anyone ever really know about it? You did what you had to do; that was all.

Rising, she picked up her coffee cup to go outside and warm herself in the heat of the day.